Praise for Stephen R. Lawhead

"Lawhead brilliantly creates an authentic and
vivid Arthurian Britain [and] never forsakes
a sense of wonder."

—*Publishers Weekly* on *Pendragon*

"Lawhead demonstrates a genuine love for and
understanding of Anglo-Celtic mythology."

—*Library Journal* on *The Paradise War*

"Lawhead treats his Celtic lore with respect."

—*Kirkus Reviews* on *The Paradise War*

"In the sweeping style of George R. R. Martin and
J. R. R. Tolkien, Lawhead has created a diverse
universe and rich cast of characters."

—*Library Journal* on the Bright Empires series

TOR BOOKS BY STEPHEN R. LAWHEAD

In the Region of the Summer Stars
In the Land of the Everliving

EIRLANDIA ✦ Book One

* * *
*   *

IN THE REGION OF THE SUMMER STARS

Stephen R. Lawhead

TOR®
fantasy

A Tom Doherty Associates Book
NEW YORK

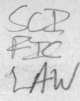

SCP
FIC
LAW

This is a work of fiction. All of the characters, organizations, and events portrayed in this novel are either products of the author's imagination or are used fictitiously.

IN THE REGION OF THE SUMMER STARS

Map by Jon Landsberg

A Tor Book
Published by Tom Doherty Associates
175 Fifth Avenue
New York, NY 10010

www.tor-forge.com

Tor® is a registered trademark of Macmillan Publishing Group, LLC.

ISBN 978-0-7653-8345-7

Our books may be purchased in bulk for promotional, educational, or business use. Please contact your local bookseller or the Macmillan Corporate and Premium Sales Department at 1-800-221-7945, extension 5442, or by email at MacmillanSpecialMarkets@macmillan.com.

First Edition: May 2018
First Mass Market Edition: February 2019

Printed in the United States of America

0 9 8 7 6 5 4 3 2 1

In Memory of My Favourite Mother-in-Law
Margaret Erickson Slaikeu Holm

GREAT SEA
NARROW SEA
Robogdi
Venceni
Eridani
Dúnaird
Darini
Concani
Volunti
Nagnati
Vlaid
Cauci
Hill of Tara
Coriondi
Auteini
Brigantes
Laigini
Dead Lands
Cruithne
Bréifne
Lands the Scálda Stole

In the Region of the Summer Stars

Conor

I was ten summers old when the world changed. Twelve more have passed since then, yet I recall the details of that day as if it had happened yesterday and I was still that bare-legged boy.

Along with the other boys of the ráth, my younger brothers and I were playing at hare and hounds when a rider appeared on the coast path. Visitors were a rare enough diversion that we dropped our game and ran to see who it might be.

We followed him for a closer look. The stranger was tall and gaunt, with a face burned brown by the sun and burnished by the wind. His eyes were sunk deep in his skull and looked out upon the world with the keen and haughty stare of a hunting hawk. His clothing and appearance marked him at once as something strange and mysterious to our young eyes. Instead of the ordinary breecs and brócs, siarc and belt we knew, the stranger wore a knee-length robe of rough grey cloth and high-laced brócs of soft leather; a blue-and-yellow-checked cloak, folded neatly, lay across the rump of his mount. Instead of a leather belt, he wore a wide band of horsehair and wool dyed blue and green and woven into peculiar patterns; on a wide strap across his chest hung a large sparán of the same stuff, bearing the same odd symbols and, around his neck, a silver torc as thick as a ram's horn.

If his manner and dress seemed bizarre to us, his horse was

even more extraordinary. A fine and spirited animal it was, with a glossy coat the colour of new-peeled chestnuts. Lean, well-muscled, and elegant in every line and sinew, it was surely a very prince of its breed. Its mane and tail were plaited with threads of gold, and a collar of golden sun disks hung around its sleek and graceful neck. The heavy horsecloth on his back was worked in the colours of the rainbow, and finer and more costly than any garment ever worn by anyone we knew. No one in our tribe had ever seen, much less owned, such a mount—not even our king, whose last horse was an old flea-bitten mare that died some while before I was born.

But this! This animal—oh, it was a handsome creature and its value well beyond our poor ability to reckon. That alone should have given our lord fair warning. It did not.

With the other lads, I stood in flat-footed awe and admiration of the magnificent beast, and received a sharp elbow in the ribs. 'Oi!' I glanced around to see who had jabbed me and saw Fergal, my best friend, pointing at the stranger.

'Look . . . ,' he whispered in a half-swallowed voice.

'I see him,' I hissed. 'Why did you poke me?'

'His *hair* . . .'

'What so?'

'He's a *druid*!' said Fergal, scarcely breathing the last word.

I tore my gaze from the horse and again regarded our visitor; he did possess a curious cut: close shaven from ear to ear over the top of his head, yet falling long everywhere else, save two short braids—one at either temple. We boys had never seen one of the druid kind, but Fergal seemed to know all about them. Even so, the fact that the stranger travelled alone on a mount the worth of an entire herd of lesser steeds gave us all to know that we were gazing upon a person of high rank and importance.

Still, it did not take a druid skilled in the arts of augury to foresee the future that day. Even a gang of muddy, skinny-shanked boys knew and understood that a thing of great significance was about to take place.

Looking neither right nor left, the druid proceeded directly through the gates of the stronghold and into the common yard, reining up outside the king's hall. There he sat on his splendid horse, upright as a hickory rod, his hooded eyes sharp, all-seeing, taking in the measure of the place while he waited to be received in a manner befitting his exalted status.

When our king sent Barga, his hearth master, in his stead the muttering began.

'Great of Wisdom, may you prosper in all things as you so richly deserve,' declared Barga grandly. Clearly embarrassed, he tried to disguise his discomfort with high-sounding flattery. 'As the sun honours the earth with light, so you honour us with your radiant presence. My lord and king waits with intense eagerness within.' He put out a hand to the open door of the hall. 'Will you join him and share the welcome cúach?'

The druid frowned, but slid down from his horse and tossed the reins to one of the men standing near. The two entered the hall and, as we boys were not allowed inside, we all huddled around the door and peeped around the edges of the speckled ox-hide covering, hoping to catch any glimpse of what might happen within. The hall was dark; there was no fire in the hearth, no meat roasting or bread baking. Darkness suited our king's mood most days. Besides, meal and meat is costly and our lord knew well the value of such things.

Jostling around the doorposts, we saw little and heard less. But our elders clucked their tongues and shook their heads and wore their worried faces. Then, Barga appeared at the door and shooed us away. We scattered and ran off to further examine the druid's horse instead. One of the men, Aideen's father as I recall, had led the animal to the stone trough where it now stood with its broad muzzle sunk deep in the water. The creature's legs were straight and sturdy, its shoulders and haunches strong; the ruddy coat seemed to glow in the sunlight with a fire all its own. I know I had never seen such a beautiful animal in my life, and I believed then that I never would see another like it.

'Someday, I will own a horse like this,' I announced grandly, and was disappointed to see that none of my friends took me seriously.

'Ach, and where would *you* be getting a horse like *this*?' demanded Fergal.

'From the faéry folk, maybe?' laughed Donal.

By way of reply, I gave him a punch on the arm. 'I will, you know. I'll get one—wait and see if I don't.'

Our appraisal of the animal was interrupted just then as one of the king's handmaids emerged from the hall, leading the strange druid to a house on the common—the little house used as a guest lodge. So few visitors troubled our king's hospitality that the building was less lodging for guests and more storeroom; its furniture was old stuff, and there were grain sacks stacked along the walls and casks of ale and mead and wine in the corners. Women sometimes used the hearth for drying fish and cloth, and on rainy days we were often allowed to play there.

We saw the maid lead our visitor into the house, linger a little at the door, and then walk slowly back to the hall as if to a funeral, perhaps her own. But she had not yet reached the hall before the druid appeared again in the yard. And, oh, his face was black with rage. The quick among us realised at once what was wrong. Thanks to our niggardly king, our guest had been snubbed and his position held small: not the promised drink in the silver cúach, nor bread on the board or meat on the platter—not even so much as a smear of honey on a barley cake or humble pinch of salt and sip of wine to welcome him and ease the pangs of his journey. That alone would have been enough to anger him, but the shabby lodgings taxed his forbearance beyond reason. Who could blame him?

By now, some few of the warriors had come out of the hall and others had abandoned their chores and weapons practice. Most of the clan had gathered to get the measure of the visitor, and everyone witnessed his humiliation at the hands of our king. The muttering grew louder and more anxious.

Glaring poison at us, the great man marched to the centre of the common yard and squatted down in the dirt. Placing the palm of his hands one on either cheek, he closed his eyes and in a moment began swaying back and forth on his haunches. Then, rousing himself, he reached down and drew a circle in the dust. Into this circle, he inscribed three lines and covered the lines with his hand, pressing down upon them; he then drew the outline of that hand in the dust with the thumb of his free hand.

This last I remember most clearly, for next he stuck that dirty thumb in his mouth, closed his eyes, and chewed. He chewed hard on that thumb as if on a marrowbone. After a time, he stood and raised his right arm to the sky as if he would drag down the sun. Stretching out his left arm, he pointed straight at the king's hall. Then, with his arms so extended, he turned slowly around taking in the entire fortress with the wide sweep of his outstretched hand.

We watched enthralled by these curious actions as he made one turn, then two more. On completing the third circle, the great man brushed the dirt from his hands and, stalking to where the men stood holding his horse, he snatched away the reins, mounted his steed, and rode to the centre of the yard. Drawing himself upright in the saddle, the druid lowered his brow and, in voice loud and terrible enough to wake the dead, he called, 'Woe to you, Eochaid Tight-Fist, and woe to the people who must live beneath the grudging meanness of your wicked gold-lust.'

The elders among us groaned at this, but worse was to come. 'Woe to you, little king! This day a reckoning is required of you. This is the day of your undoing,' he proclaimed. 'Know you, the disaster soon to devour this land might have been blunted if only you had shown a proper respect. Instead, suffering shall fill your cup and the cups of all who call you lord. Tribulations without number will rain down upon Eirlandia and its people until they are ground to dust and scattered to the four winds.'

Then, turning his face to the sky, he intoned a long incantation in the Dark Tongue. I heard the strange, unsettling words and my young heart seized in my chest.

When he finished, the druid looked down from his horse and said, 'The curse has been sealed to the fifth generation. It cannot be broken.'

Picking up the reins, he wheeled his mount and rode from the ráth. We all gaped in horror at his judgement. No one lifted a hand to prevent his leaving until, as he passed through the gate and out onto the track beyond the walls, one of the warriors broke ranks and ran after him. I looked and was startled to see that it was my own da. I did not know my father could move so fast. Since there was no one to restrain me, I ran after him.

Father caught up with the horse and rider out on the coast track a short distance from the fortress walls. 'Wait!' he called. 'A word, Learned One, for mercy's sake.'

The druid halted and turned around. My father dropped to his knees and went down on all fours in the middle of the trail. 'You have condemned our king and his punishment is not a day too soon. The world knows our people have suffered enough under his rule. But I beg you, sir, wise prince—I beg you on my life and honour as a warrior of rank and skill—please, lift your curse for the sake of our tribe.'

The druid, his face like flint, sat silent as an oak and gazed upon my father, grovelling on hands and knees in the dust—a thing no warrior would ever do, even in the face of death. And yet my father did just that. My gut squirmed with embarrassment for him; I glanced around, fearful that the whole world should be watching and see him so, and me with him. The blood-red birthmark that stains the right side of my face tingled and burned with shame; I lowered my gaze and looked away.

Even so, I was close enough now to hear what passed, and when the druid spoke again, his voice had lost much of its righteous anger. He spoke more like an ordinary man. 'Sooner call back a spear in flight,' he replied with a bitter laugh. 'Sooner call back the stone hurled from the sling.'

Though it broke my young heart to see my father so debased before this haughty man, and though that proud warrior must have known the eyes of his son—and those of the greater part of our clansmen—were witness to his disgrace, still my father did not relent. 'I know you are wise in the ways of all things under heaven,' he said. 'If such a thing can be done, you are the very man to do it. That is why your servant begs you, please, for the sake of my innocent sons and the sons of our clan, and those of our daughters yet to be born, take back your curse.'

The druid sat long and stared at the man pleading before him. 'You say you have sons,' he replied at last, gazing down from his high horse. 'How many?'

'I have three.'

'What are they to you?'

My father paused to consider his answer.

'I ask you, warrior, and demand an answer. What are your sons to you?'

'They are the light in my eyes, the breath in my lungs, and the sweet honey mead on my tongue.' My father's answer was good and true and came from his heart. 'All this and more,' he added, 'no less the other children of our poor clan.'

The bard did not reply to this. In the silence, I dared to raise my eyes and saw that he gazed, as it seemed to me, in deep contemplation.

My father seized the opportunity to press the matter further. 'I know the Darini are not accounted much in this worlds-realm. As a clan among clans—even within our tribe—we are least and our name is lower than any other. This is because of our lord and the lord before him. Though we have no claim to dignity, some of us still have pride. For the sake of—'

'Enough!' roared the druid, his voice echoing back from the high timber wall of the fortress.

At this the great one climbed down from his horse. He stalked to where my father knelt and stood over him. 'Get up on your feet.'

My father rose and stood before him.

'What is your name?'

'Ardan mac Orsi,' he answered.

The druid nodded and placed his left hand upon my father's heart. Then, raising his right hand, he held it above my father's head and in a voice to freeze the marrow in the bone, he said, 'For the humility and respect you have shown me, Ardan mac Orsi, I tell you the truth: your sons will be kings and the champions of kings.' He lowered his hand and touched my father's brow. 'This, I have seen. This, I have spoken.'

'I am honoured, lord.'

'You say rightly, friend. Yet, as everyone knows, with honour comes obligation. This day you must give me one of your sons.'

My father gasped. His mouth opened and closed. When he at last found his voice, he said, 'This is a hard thing you ask of me—sooner ask the mountain to give up its gold.'

The druid smiled at this.

'The cost is greater than I can bear,' my father pleaded. 'How could I choose such a thing?'

To my surprise, the bard's piercing eyes swung to me. 'This is one of them, I think.'

My father glanced at me and with a gesture warned me to stay back. 'Yes,' he allowed hesitantly. 'This is Conor—oldest of the three.'

The druid's eyes narrowed as he observed the ruby stain that discoloured my cheek, and the merest lift of a dark eyebrow gave me to know I had been judged and found wanting. 'Not him,' he said, dismissing me at a glance. 'Show me the others.'

Ach, my blood boiled—as it so often did when anyone made bold to mention, much less deride, my disfigurement. Writhing with embarrassment, I lowered my eyes and stepped aside as my father summoned Liam and Rónán. Of my brothers, Liam is a year younger but almost as tall and strong as me, and Rónán is four years younger still.

The bard took one look at the two of them standing barefoot in the dust of the road and stretched out his hand toward Rónán. 'The youngest shall be mine.'

I saw my little brother's eyes grow wide with alarm, and I started forward. 'Take me!' I said, starting forward. 'Take me instead.'

'Conor! Stay back,' shouted my father. He then turned his face to the sky and drew a deep and heavy breath. 'Is there no other way?'

'Tears are not a becoming ornament for a warrior,' the bard observed. 'Why so sad?'

'How not? You take away my truest treasure.'

The druid smiled again and gently shook his head. 'Think you now, who would not give dross for gold? Cheer up, man. This day, you give me a brat. Tomorrow, I give you back a bard.'

This is how it came to be that little Rónán rode off clinging to the great druid on his splendid red steed. Later that same day, King Eochaid, known henceforth as the Tight-Fisted, was pulled from his noisome hall and thrown out of the fortress; the gold torc was torn from his throat and the gates barred against him. His grasping avarice had secured the doom of our long-suffering people, and every last clansman turned his hand against him without pity.

Three days later, the Black Ships came. In their thousands they came, and Eirlandia sank beneath wave upon wave of the invading Scálda warhost.

Thus, the world is changed—not with a sword, but with a word.

1

Conor stood easily in the fore rank of the warband, leaning on his spear as he watched the enemy traverse the wide green expanse below. The long grass rippled in waves across the broad valley floor, like an inland emerald sea stirred by the progress of the dark shapes moving swiftly across its surface. 'Where *do* they get all those horses, brother?' he asked the warrior next to him.

'Their women birth them,' replied Fergal. He spit into the turf at his feet. 'That is the only explanation.'

'The beasts come from Hibernia,' announced Eamon a few paces away. Tall and lanky, with a long face and massive hands, he was Ardan's oldest friend and foremost of the king's hearth companions, and saw himself as a counsellor and guide to the younger warriors; he prided himself on his wide-ranging knowledge. 'They are wild and free for the taking.'

'Free or dear, I mean to take one as a prize before the day is done,' Conor vowed.

'One only?' said Fergal. 'I will have six at least.'

'Aye,' agreed Conor amiably, 'that would be the way of it. You will need six of your horses to rival the one I shall get.'

Those nearby chuckled at this, and even Fergal smiled.

From their vantage point high on the ridge overlooking the plain, the Darini warband waited to receive the decision of their king. Conor dipped his hand into his sparán, the little leather pouch at his belt, pulled out a scrap of bósaill, and tucked it into the side of his cheek. He chewed slowly, savouring the salty flavour of the tough, sun-cured beef as he watched the dark shapes moving across the plain. Then, lifting his face to the clean, cloud-spotted sky, he drew the sweet air deep into his lungs. The sun was warm and bright and the wind was fair from the west. Away to the south, the bright silver-blue band of the sea shimmered and gleamed against the high green hills on the far side of the bay where the Black Ships had landed. Those hateful vessels still filled the southern bays, Conor supposed; the Scálda infested the broad shallow waters of the far southern coast just as their squalid settlements blighted the southern hills and inland meadows of the territories the invaders had claimed for their own.

Conor felt the sun on his back and caught the bright glint of the spear blade in his hand; he tightened his grip as the deep red stain that disfigured the left side of his face began to prickle and throb—as it did when emotion ran high, or something extraordinary was about to happen, but always before a battle. Conor rubbed the strawberry blemish absently, and wondered why the Scálda moved with such speed. What drove them? It seemed to him that they flew with reckless haste, as if being chased, yet he could detect no sign of pursuit. But then, who could fathom the crooked mind of such a race of swarthy, bloody-minded brutes?

Common wisdom held that Scálda could be rash, but stupid they were not; nor were they inclined to allow themselves to be goaded into foolish mistakes. Even so, it appeared to Conor that they streamed headlong and heedless into the pinched gap that formed the only outlet at that end of the valley. Most unusual, Conor decided. 'See how they run,' he observed to no one in particular. 'Did you ever see anyone fly to Toothless Badb's bleak hall with such ardour?'

Donal, standing with Conor and Fergal, gave a derisive

snort. 'Do you think we should tell them about Red Badb's fair sisters?'

What could be better just now, thought Conor, than standing with his two best friends on the brink of battle? Here was long-limbed, fair-haired Fergal, always ready with a quip or jest; and dusky Donal, shorter than either of them, but broad of chest and well muscled in shoulders and thighs, never one to miss a cup or a fight. Both men, like Conor and all those of the warrior caste, were clean-shaven, save for extravagant moustaches: Donal's was long and luxuriant, almost covering his good-natured smile; Fergal's, like Conor's, was well-trimmed, drooping down only a little at the sides.

'Why tell them and spoil the surprise?' mused Fergal. 'Ach, nay, let them find out for themselves what delights await them in the halls of the dead.'

It had been a quiet summer—with only one other clash so far—and the raiding season was almost half over. The king and his warband had been out for most of a week and this was the first raiding party they had encountered. Still, the enemy were far north of the borderlands and that could not be allowed to go unpunished.

'Silence, brothers—hear me.' It was Liam, the battlechief. He had been talking to the king and the plan of attack was now decided. 'Two branches—one to remain here, and one at the gap'—he gestured with the point of his spear to indicate the place he meant—'just there, where the dale narrows between the rocks.'

Liam glanced around, gathering the nods of the warriors before he continued. 'Second branch will take the gap and fill it. When the enemy have halted to trade blows, branch one will rush in and take them from behind.' He eyed each warrior in turn to make certain they understood, then said, 'You here—I give you first choice. Which do you prefer, the first branch or the second?'

A brief discussion ensued. There were merits to either side of the choice, as well as drawbacks. These were duly pointed out and the deliberation began. Liam listened for a moment, then said, 'Be quick about it, or the dog-eaters will be out of sight before you decide.'

'If it's horses we want,' Eamon pointed out, 'attacking from the rear offers the best chance.'

'Done.' Liam turned and hurried away, saying, 'You lead the first branch, Eamon. I will lead the second.'

'Meet you in the middle,' Conor called out.

'Ha!' sneered Liam. 'Just see you do not kill any of our men by mistake.'

As Liam returned to the king's side, Fergal observed, 'Your brother does not think much of you.'

'He is the king's battlechief and champion,' replied Conor with a shrug. 'Should he treat me better than another now?'

'That is wide of you,' said Donal. 'I would not bear the barb so lightly.'

Conor held his tongue and jabbed the ground with the butt of his spear instead. The spear was a veteran of seventeen battles; a well-made weapon, it had a lethal leaf-shaped blade of heat-tempered iron affixed to a stout shaft of smoothed ash wrapped at the head and middle with straps of rawhide as an aid to grip against the sweat and blood of the fight. Conor called it Bríg—in respect of its strength and valour. The sword at his side he called Gasta, and in Conor's hands it was indeed an object to be feared.

'Everybody knows *you* are the best warrior,' offered Fergal. 'Any king worth his torc would welcome your sword above any other.'

Donal saw Conor's jaw tighten at the glancing allusion to the unsightly blemish and knew it was time to change the subject. 'Well, if anyone gets a horse today, it will be Conor.' He gave his friend a slap on the shoulder. 'There won't be a better blade on the field today.'

'And you, brother, are a very head of wisdom,' Conor replied, happy to step away from a subject that still held the power to cloud his better moments. 'But it will take more than flattery to pry the bridle from my hand. Let us see if just this once you two can match your skill at words with swordplay.'

'Watch and be amazed!' replied Fergal with a grin.

The warriors of the second branch, twenty-seven in all, departed on the run, leaving the fifteen of the first branch to wait and ready their attack when fighting started. Conor and his swordbrothers watched the Scálda racing across the plain, making straight for the valley's narrow neck. Owing to the speed of their passage, the enemy line was long and staggered. To Conor's expert eye, the riders did not appear to be wary of any danger; they raced headlong into the trap.

Even as he watched, the first enemy raiders thundered into the gap between the rocks. Conor and the others counted off the enemy as they passed into the narrow gorge. Fergal muttered, 'What are they waiting for? The dog-eaters will be through the pinch and out before a single blow is struck.'

'So impatient,' remarked Eamon. 'Our battlechief knows well enough how—'

Before he could complete the thought, the ambush began. The first Dé Danann spear flashed out, striking an enemy mount through its outstretched neck. In full stride, the horse's forelegs collapsed, hurling its startled rider to the ground.

Before the first warrior ceased tumbling, a second missile had taken another horse and rider. A third spear sang through the air—and a fourth, fifth, and sixth—in such swift succession that they struck as one, each taking down a rider and his mount.

'Ach,' sighed Fergal, 'not the horses . . . please, not the horses.'

'Worry not, brother,' said Donal, 'there are plenty more besides. You'll have your pick.'

'Be ready . . . ,' called Eamon, his voice rising. He pointed with his spear to where the headlong flight of the Scálda was already faltering. The oncoming riders, unable to avoid the animals on the ground, pulled up hard and were immediately ploughed into by the next tranche pounding in behind. Scálda in the trailing ranks, unaware of the danger up front, galloped into the heap. Chaos spread like fire across the grassy plain. 'Now!'

Up, over the crest, and down the slope the warriors of the first branch flew to the fray. Conor paced himself, keeping a step or two behind Eamon, letting him lead the attack. There was nothing to be gained by showing up a swordbrother, and much to be lost—especially when naked blades were involved.

Dé Danann warriors were not as big or heavily muscled as their Scálda counterparts, but whatever they lacked in stature and bulk, they more than made up in speed and agility. They closed on the foe with uncanny swiftness and half a dozen more riders lay on the ground with spears in their backs before the rest knew they were under attack from the flank. The speed of the second assault sent panic rippling through the already disordered foe and the battle became a rout.

For reasons Conor could not discern, the Scálda seemed more interested in escape than defence. Thus, what might have been a satisfactory contest deteriorated into a slaughter. Most of the raiders simply fled the field, leaving the Dé Danann to claim the victory, and Conor himself clutching the reins of a handsome young stallion with a fine dappled coat of purest white and russet red; the irregular coloured splotches reminded Conor of the blemish on his own skin. That—added to the fact that it was clearly a splendid specimen of its kind: strong and straight of limb, fluid in motion, with a deep chest, powerful hindquarters, and a broad noble forehead—instantly endeared the animal to him.

'Be easy now, handsome,' said Conor, taking hold of the bridle strap and stepping close. He stroked the stallion's forehead and stared into the deep brown eye. 'I will call you Balla, and we will be the best of friends.' He had just about succeeded in calming the agitated beast when he heard the rapid thump of hooves on the turf behind him.

He spun around as a lone rider charged: a swarthy brute, with long, matted hanks of thick black hair, his face frozen in a rictus of rage and hate, an expression enhanced by a livid scar that ran from brow to chin—an old wound that rendered him one-eyed and ferociously ugly. He wore no battle cap or helm which the Scálda were sometimes known to do, but his rough leather tunic was tricked out in small triangular iron plates, and he carried a large round shield rimmed in silver with the painted image of a coiled snake—the device of a chieftain, Conor surmised. Leaning out from the saddle to lop off a Dé Danann head as he passed, the Scálda chief made a wide sweep with his ragged blade. Conor was ready and ducked low, raising his sword to parry the next thrust. But it did not come. Instead, the Scálda, intent on joining the retreat, sped on by without a backward glance.

It was then that Conor saw the woman.

She was sitting behind the Scálda chief, and that she was his prize there could be no mistake. Her hands were bound with braided leather and she was secured to her captor by a length of crude iron chain that encircled her slender waist. Conor had never before heard of the Scálda taking hostages, but neither had he ever seen a woman so strange, so beguiling in appearance, and so utterly helpless.

The gleaming lustre of her raven-black hair, the exquisite

cast of her pale features, and the crystalline depths of her blue eyes were by no means the first thing he noticed, nor that which made him stop and stare in slack-jawed wonder. Nor, indeed, was the prodigious extravagance of her garments the first thing Conor noticed; his impression was of a flash of scarlet and blue and gold. All these were things Conor would remark on later, and consider at length.

In that first glance, however, it was the stately set of her head, the firm cast of her mouth, and the implacable dignity of her posture—despite the obvious extremity and futility of her position—that caused him to stop and stare. Erect, dignified, defiant, she radiated not only supreme courage, but also absolute hatred for the creature that had captured her. And the look of pleading entreaty that she gave Conor as she swept past pierced him to the quick. Yet . . . and yet there was something more than an emotional tug of recognition or sympathy, something passing strange and beyond Conor's ability to comprehend, something alien and other.

For, in that fleeting instant, Conor felt a physical jolt from the woman's intense glance, a thing he had never experienced before—as if he had slammed headlong into a wall, or taken a hammer blow to the chest. The impact caused his heart to skip and lurch and rocked him back on his heels even as a word formed in his head: *Faéry*.

The strangeness of the encounter rooted Conor to the spot; before he could move, the Scálda chieftain and his fair captive were gone, leaving Conor flat-footed and staring as they raced away to be lost amidst the turmoil of the retreat.

2

'Fergal!' shouted Conor. 'Did you see that?'

Holding tight to the reins of his new-won prize, Conor picked his way over and around the bodies of dead and dying warriors and beasts. An unnatural tranquillity reigned over the field now, broken only by the moans and cries of wounded men and creatures.

'Did I see what?' asked Fergal, wiping blood from the blade of his spear with a handful of grass. 'Did I see the seven Scálda champions I met this day? Aye, I saw them and sped them on to pay my respects to the Hag Queen Badb.' He threw away the grass and stooped to wrest another handful from the turf. 'Aye, I saw that right well.'

'Ach,' replied Conor, 'then you will have missed the best sight of all.'

'And what was that?' asked Fergal, rubbing down the spear shaft. 'Was it you dawdling behind the battle line leaning on your spear and sucking your teeth?'

'On the day you see that, brother,' sniffed Conor, 'you will know that one of us is in the Otherworld.'

Tossing the grass away, Fergal smiled. 'What is that pitiful animal you have there, brother? Could that be the horse of your prideful boast?'

'None other,' replied Conor, reaching up to pat the stallion's neck. He looked around. 'But where is the herd of horses you were going to win? You won't be telling me your labours have been in vain?'

'Far from it!' Fergal turned and gave out a whistle. 'Donal, bring the horses. Let us show Conor the spoils a true warrior can acquire with his skill.'

Conor looked across to where Donal came leading three good-looking mares toward them. Two of the beasts had trophy heads of Dé Danann warriors tied to their manes by their braided hair. 'Is that the only mount you could get, Conor?' he said as he came to stand beside Fergal.

'A man can only ride one horse at a time,' Conor told him. 'And, as you can plainly see, I choose to ride the best.' He caught sight of the trophy heads then, and his voice hardened. 'Take those off and see them properly buried,' he ordered. 'I will not have our dead defiled by those toad-sucking bastards.'

Donal nodded and, passing the reins to Fergal, began untying the grisly trophies. Eamon, leading a sturdy black mare and a brown stallion with white fetlocks, joined them. 'Here, now! It seems to me that we have the beginnings of a worthy herd.' He looked approvingly at the prize animals. 'Right worthy.'

'Did any of you see the woman?' asked Conor. He went on to describe the captive he had seen bound and chained to the retreating Scálda chieftain. He mentioned her exceptional beauty and the unspoken cry for help he read in her enchanting eyes. He did *not* say he thought she was a faéry.

'And here was I,' said Eamon, 'thinking you had eyes only for your Aoife.'

'True enough,' allowed Conor. 'But did any of you see the lady?'

They all shrugged and shook their heads. 'A Scálda woman on the battlefield? I would remember that, I think,' remarked Fergal.

'Ach, aye,' agreed Donal, 'a sight like that would be well worth remembering—*if* it happened at all.'

'It happened,' Conor declared. 'But no Scálda ever had eyes like that, nor skin pale as cream, nor hair like midnight, nor lips like—'

'You there!' shouted Liam, striding up. 'Tell me, have you lazy idlers seen any of my warband? If they were here, they would be helping to strip the enemy of weapons and valuables.'

'We were just about to begin,' Fergal told him. 'We had first to secure the horses.' He waved a hand to indicate the animals they had taken. 'What do you think? A few more battles like this and we will all be riding.'

'Aye, and that would be a grand thing, would it not?' replied Liam. 'But, seeing as I am warleader, I will take these off your hands and thank you for them. They will make a fine gift for the king.'

The warriors glanced uneasily at one another. 'Ach, no,' complained Donal. 'You cannot be taking away our horses.'

'How not?' said Liam. 'When *you* become chief of battle, then you can decide how best to divide the spoils, brother. Until then, it is my right, and I have made my decision.' He lifted his chin in defiance of any more complaining. 'Bring all you find to the foot of the mound. See you make short work of it. The king would sleep in his own hall tonight.'

'So would I, Liam,' replied Donal. 'Am I like to a king, then?'

The battlechief glanced at him and, unable to decide whether he was being mocked, snatched the reins from Fergal's hand. Ordering Eamon to follow with the rest, he led the horses away.

On a rise at the edge of the battlefield King Ardan stood waiting with the ardféne, his hearth companions; they were friends of his youth, his swordbrothers, men who had been with him since the time of Eochaid when Ardan was merely a member of the small Darini warband. Now they were his council of advisors and, at sight of the horses, they already had their heads together.

'We will never see those beasts again,' sighed Fergal.

'Maybe the king will give them back to us in the dálin,' suggested Donal. Depending on his mood, the king sometimes honoured the exceptional effort of particular warriors by returning the more valuable items in the division of spoils known as the dálin.

'More likely the king's hounds will grow hooves and we can ride them instead,' grumped Fergal, kicking at the turf.

'Take heart,' said Conor, clapping hand to his friend's shoulder, 'that is three fewer mouths you will have to feed. Besides, with animals like that, you'd soon be up to your chin in muck. Consider yourself lucky.'

'Aye, it is lucky I am,' Fergal agreed sourly. 'Lucky like the toothless dog at the feast.'

With grudging reluctance, they turned to their work, helping to collect the plunder. Conor moved slowly among the corpses, recoiling now and then at the sour stench of blood and bile rising from the freshly dead. The enemy's weapons were of only limited use: Scálda shields were heavy and round, whereas Dé Danann shields were lighter and rectangular, affording more versatility and protection; and Scálda blades were likewise inferior in many ways. Still, they all contained useful metal that could be melted down and recast into better blades and tools. The other valuables—bits of gold or silver or jewelled ornaments—were likely stolen from their many and various victims. These would be added to the prizes to be meted out in the dálin and, as the king saw fit, for the benefit of the rest of the tribe.

Any wounded enemy found still clinging to life were swiftly sent on their way to wherever the Scálda went in death; injured Dé Danann, and there were blessedly few of these, had their wounds carefully tended by Muirac, a druid from Carn Dubh who sometimes accompanied Ardan's extended sorties, along with two attendant ovates.

While Conor went about his gruesome chores, he thought about the entrancing captive on the back of the retreating horse. What was it about her that touched him so deeply in that heart-clenching moment? Was it the surprise of discovery? The look of desperate pleading on her exquisite face? Her erect and haughty demeanour in sharp defiance of her captive state?

Or was there something more? Something with a hint of enchantment about it? He had heard of the spells women could sometimes cast on men—perhaps this was such a case. Then again, the sight of a beautiful face most always made him feel a little strange—perhaps because of his own birth-born imperfection. A fair and flawless skin always seemed a magical thing to him.

As he combed the battlefield, gathering weapons as he went, Conor asked his comrades if anyone else had seen the woman chained to the Scálda chieftain. No one else had noticed such a thing, it seemed. The very suggestion was considered improbable, if not ridiculed outright. Conor might have begun to doubt himself if not for the image of her pleading eyes now deeply etched in his memory.

He eventually reached the mound with an armful of blades and two heavy shields slung on his back. Quickly dumping the gear onto the heap of gleanings, he hurried over to where Liam and the king were in consultation with the ardféne and a few of the other warriors. The horses were lined up before the king for his appraisal and despite the smiles and nods of approval, there were frowns, too. 'What goes?' asked Conor, sidling up to Fergal.

'Just listen,' hissed his friend.

'My king,' said Liam, raising his voice so all could hear, 'in celebration of your victory today, I am pleased to deliver these horses as a gift. Look on them with pride, and remember the prowess that won them and the generosity of your warriors and battlechief.'

'I knew it!' muttered Fergal. 'He gave away our horses.'

'And claimed the gift as his own,' observed Donal sourly, adding, 'That is low, so it is.'

'Easy, brothers,' advised Conor. 'The king may yet add them to the dálin.'

The king was speaking. 'Was any king better served by his chief of battle?' Ardan asked to the murmured approval of his attendants. 'I thank you, Liam; your gift is well considered. Indeed, these horses will win us great favour when I bring them to the Oenach.'

'What!' whispered Fergal. 'He means to give them away at the council!'

The Oenach—a formal gathering of the lords and chieftains—had been called by King Brecan of the Brigantes and would take place at the time of the next full moon—a little over a week away. As Brecan mac Lergath was ruler of the largest and most powerful of Eirlandia's many tribes, Ardan and his warleader were expected to obey the summons, of course, and the ardféne would accompany their lord to serve as retinue and bodyguard. Few, if any, of the greater warband would be either asked or expected to attend the council. In fact, the assembled lords now prohibited anyone arriving with large retinues as it was seen—and very often proved—a dangerously provocative display. Since the coming of the Scálda, no fewer than three royals had lost lives and lands to devious rivals during such gatherings of their fellows. Thus, the councils were welcomed only with caution and wariness; and this one aroused more suspicion than most, following as it did so hard on the heels of the last one.

Normally, a ruler liked to have a season or two to mend fences and shore up alliances after one of these contentious assemblies.

Conor was happy enough not to have to attend yet another tedious council; the boasting, self-aggrandizing exhibitions gave him a sour belly. But the thought of his brother, Liam the generous battlechief, being lauded for his largess as his father the king gave away the horses won by Conor's blade and those of his swordbrothers fairly made the blood boil. If gifts were to be given then, at the very least, the true benefactors should be recognised in some small way. That was only right and fair.

Conor watched as his father turned to begin organising the collected plunder. 'My king,' said Conor, speaking up quickly, 'with animals as valuable as these, you may require an escort to the council. I place myself at your service.'

Lord Ardan paused and turned to regard his son, a quizzical expression on his face.

'I also pledge myself to aid you in this chore,' volunteered Fergal, and Donal was not slow to echo the offer.

Before the king could reply, Liam turned on them. 'Would you impugn the abilities of the matchless ardféne to serve and protect our king?'

'As *we* were the ones that—' began Fergal.

Conor cut him off. 'Full sorry I am if you feel yourself impugned by such a mild suggestion,' he said, putting a restraining hand on the seething Fergal. 'I merely thought to spare our worthy brothers the feeding and care of these beasts while on the way to the council.' He smiled and inclined his head. 'Yet, if hauling water and handling loads of dung is the very work you crave, then far be it from me to stand in your way. I humbly withdraw my offer of service.'

More of the warband had gathered by now and most heard the exchange; some laughed behind their hands, but others waited to see how Liam would respond before committing themselves to either side of what appeared to be shaping up as a sibling squabble.

Liam's face darkened. His mouth squirmed with displeasure, but before he could counter his brother's sly insult, the king said, 'Your offer is well considered, Conor. You three shall attend the Oenach and the responsibility for the care of the animals shall be yours.'

'But they have no place at the council,' objected Liam. 'Their presence will be seen as—'

King Ardan raised his hand. 'The decision is made. They go with us to tend the horses.'

Liam again tried to voice his objection. 'Fine warriors they surely are, but they can have no place at—'

The king silenced him with a warning flick of his hand. 'I have spoken. That is the end of it.' He turned and gestured to the heap of Scálda weapons and valuables. 'It grows late. It will be dark before we reach the ráth. Bring the spoils. I will make the dálin tomorrow.'

With that, the king and his hearth companions moved off, leaving Liam fuming with indignation.

'He had that coming to him,' surmised Fergal as soon as Liam's back was turned.

'That is what happens when you overreach yourself.' Donal pronounced this as a judgement.

Liam appeared to overhear, or at least sense that the three were talking about him. He swung around and glared at them, making his anger known to one and all.

'Say no more,' Conor advised, keeping his voice low. 'I challenged him before the warriors and won. How would *you* feel, eh?' He turned and started off. 'Let us be about our business, lest we give our battlechief cause to punish us for his humiliation.' Having won the skirmish, Conor quit the field.

'What are we to do when we get to the council?' Fergal asked, falling into step beside him. 'What then?'

'I cannot say,' Conor confessed. 'We are going—that is enough for now. We'll think of something when we get there.'

Rónán

I cried last night . . . again. There are five of us in this house. The two older boys mock, but the two younger ones know how it is with me. I have been here seven moons. Cabiri, the filidh of Willow House, tells me that the time for mourning is now past and that I must look to the future. 'If you can see the shape of things to come,' he says, 'and then put yourself into what you see, you will find yourself there.'

I don't know what that means. All I know is that I miss my home; I miss my da, and Liam. Mostly, I miss Conor. Though he is my brother, and four years older, he is my best friend.

'This is now your home,' the druid chief told me on that first day. 'We are now your family.' He lifted me down from his fine horse and set me on my feet. He put his heavy hand on me and said, 'Look around, son. The houses you see are your ráth, and this grove is your fortress. The boys and girls you see going about their tasks are your brothers and sisters. Be good to them. Treat them as you would your blood kin and they will do likewise.'

He pinched my chin and made me look at his eyes. 'I am Morien, and I am your father now. I am your teacher, your master. You are my son, my pupil, my slave. Heed me in all things and you will gain wisdom and knowledge and power.'

He stooped down to look in my face. 'Do you understand?'

I nodded—but he cuffed me on the ear. 'Do you understand me?'

'I understand, my lord,' I told him, my voice shaking, for I was that much afraid of him. He says he is my father, but he is not.

'See that little clot of dirt?' He pointed to the ground at our feet. 'Pick it up.'

There were many such little lumps of earth lying about and I did not know which one he meant, but I bent down and picked one up and gave it to him.

'Hold out your hand,' he said. And so I did.

He put the dirt in my hand said, 'This bit of raw earth is you, my son—not much to look upon, useful in its own way, but worthless otherwise. Not so?'

I nodded.

'Close your hand,' he instructed, and I did.

The druid reached out and wrapped his two hands around mine. He held them for a moment and I felt my hand grow warm.

'Hear now,' he said, looking into my eyes. 'If you fold your life into the life you see around you, marvels are possible.'

He released me and said, 'Open your hand.'

I did as he said and the lump of dirt was gone. Instead, there was a little silver ring. I almost dropped it, but Morien snatched up the ring and held it before my eyes. 'In this place, under my care, this is what you will become.'

Shaped like a serpent with its tail in its mouth, the ring looked like a tiny circle of light. I had never owned anything so grand. I could not take my eyes from it. Morien put it on my thumb and smiled. 'Go now,' he told me, 'and discover your new home.'

We came a long way from my ráth to this small steading in the middle of a great forest I don't know where. There are nine houses here—most are only huts of stick and mud, but two are large as a king's hall and made of good cut stone and shaped timber; all of them are roofed with river reed and none have doors that close. Instead, they have only deer hide to keep out the wind and rain. The houses have names, too. Willow House is where I sleep. The biggest house belongs to Morien, for he is our chieftain. He is called the head of wisdom, for he is a very prince among druids everywhere.

The houses are made in a circle and there is a big fire ring in the middle. We have a grain store and two cattle pens. One pen is for the pigs, and one for the two horses our chieftain owns. We do not have any cows just now. Outside the circle of houses is the Sacred Grove, and there is the Watching Pool. On the other side is a field. But we only grow herbs and vegetables. Everywhere else is only forest. There is a cookhouse with a well beside it, and we also have a workshop. One house is made of stone and it is the treasure house where is kept the gold and silver used to make torcs and bracelets for kings and warriors. But we do not make them ourselves.

Our ráth is called Suídaur. There are maybe thirty of us here. Men and women both. There are some who are called ovates and filidh—the lowest ones, I think. We have an ollamh also, but he is very old. Morien is called a brehon—and that is the best of all. Sometimes we have more here, and sometimes not so many. Cabiri says, 'The Learned Brotherhood hold no fixed abode and roam at will through the world. We are welcome everywhere.' He says we can even go visit druid schools and ráths in other lands across the sea—in Cymru and Alba and Gallia. I don't know where those places are, but he tells me I will go there one day maybe. 'We go where the wind goes,' Cabiri says. 'Our welcome is assured in any hall we choose to enter, but we suffer no authority above us save Lady Sovereignty herself.'

I think he means the druid kind have a queen, but I think she lives somewhere else. At least, there is no queen here.

Most days, I do chores. We go about two-and-two. I help feed the pigs and horses. I carry water from the well or sometimes the pool. When the sun is out we pull weeds in the field, or gather in firewood from the forest. The older boys have razors to shave the special druid sign in their hair, but I am not old enough yet. Oh, and part of each day we sit at the feet of Cabiri, or one of the ovates, and try to learn what they teach us. Mostly they only teach us the names of things— trees, rocks, animals, plants—and the orders of belonging for these things, because, as Cabiri says, 'Everything under heaven is alive and everything alive belongs, and everything that belongs is united in belonging to its kind.'

Our filidh goes on like this. Sometimes I understand him. Mostly I do not.

But it is more the way he speaks—not like ordinary men— his words flow like water, or drip like slow honey. Sometimes he sings.

There is much singing!

All of us are singing all the time. We sing songs about plants when we are in the field; we sing songs about water when at the well or pool, and songs about animals when we feed them. Everything we do has a song, or likely many songs, to go with it.

'In this way,' Cabiri says, 'we take our rightful place in the Oran Môr, the Great Music.' The world, he says, is built on a strong foundation of song.

So we sing whatever we do.

Morien calls us Children of Song. And this is not all. On many nights, the banfaíth plays the harp and tells us one of the stories we must all learn one day. We have a banfaíth. She is a druid princess. She plays with such skill it seems like magic. Her name is Credhe and she is Morien's wife and a very great druid herself. She tells us that she is our mother. When she says this, I want to believe her.

My own mother died when I was small. I do not remember her face, only her eyes. They were blue. It was fever, I think, that took her. That is what Conor told me once. After that, other women came—my father's sisters, mostly. My father was part of our king's warband then, and he lived with the other warriors. Only sometimes he came to us at his kinswoman's house.

Then he would tell us of great battles and great victories, and I liked the way he told them. That was before the Scálda came. But they are here now and we must fight them, for they are our great and terrible enemy. They are big as giants and they eat dogs—and children, too, sometimes. If they can catch them out at night. I asked Cabiri about the Scálda and he said, 'Do not say that name in this place. They are a very plague and a pestilence, and they seek to take Eirlandia for themselves. They wish to destroy us and all our people and all our works. But we will never surrender.'

This is why there are so many young ones here now. And not only here in Suídar, but other bard ráths, too. I think this is why Morien came to our ráth that day—to find someone who could come to the druid school. He chose me. This is my fate.

Banfaíth Credhe says we have been chosen to help our people by making more druids. This is a good thing.

Still, I miss my da . . . and Conor.

3

The Hill of Tara was almost within sight when the storm finally broke. Conor had been expecting another confrontation with Liam, but had hoped it would wait until they had reached their destination. Earlier that morning, the royal retinue of the Laigini had passed by on its way to the Oenach, and now, as the ardféne set about making camp for the night, they could see the fires of three other encampments across the valley. Liam seized the opportunity to once again press his argument.

'My lord,' he announced as the warriors gathered for their evening meal, 'tomorrow we will enter Mag Rí. Already we are seeing the retinues of your brother kings and it will not have escaped your notice that your escort is larger than any we have seen so far.'

King Ardan nodded. 'This concerns you does it, Liam?'

'My sole concern is for your prestige, Father. I would not like to see you held in lower esteem because it was thought you were attempting to exalt yourself with an unwarranted display.'

Conor was quick to guess what was coming. Before Ardan could answer, he said, 'Who do you imagine would think such a thing?'

Liam turned, instantly wary; his jaw tensed, yet he spoke with some restraint. 'As we all know, the pride and vanity of some of the smaller kings is easily bruised. We must beware lest we give anyone cause for grievance—unintended as it might be.'

The warriors stopped what they were doing and some moved in closer, gathering around their king—all of them silent and alert.

'That is most considerate of you, brother,' allowed Conor graciously. 'Yet, it seems to me that if the sight of three extra warriors excites such a grievance, then these imagined kings of yours must hold themselves very small apples indeed.'

Liam's moustache twitched, fairly bristling at Conor's subtle jibe. 'You have no say in this,' he replied. 'You would be wise to keep that babbling mouth of yours shut.'

Despite the king's frown, Conor charged ahead. 'It is no secret that you resent the wearisome necessity of us horse handlers.' He put out his hand to Fergal and Donal, who were standing nearby. 'Therefore, we will save your maiden blushes in the presence of these small kings you admire so highly.' Turning to address his father, Conor bowed low and said, 'My lord, we will depart at first light tomorrow and burden your company no longer with our unwanted presence.'

Conor's friends moved in close behind him. Donal gulped and Fergal seized his arm. 'What are you doing?' growled Fergal under his breath.

Ignoring him, Conor said, 'May it go well with you at the Oenach, my king.' He touched the back of his hand to his forehead and, without a backward glance, walked away.

The king sought to call him back. 'Conor—'

'Let them go, my lord,' Liam interposed quickly. 'They have no place here and will only make trouble if they stay.'

King Ardan watched the three younger members of his warband stalk off into the gathering twilight. 'Let it be as you say.'

As soon as they were far enough away from the others,

Fergal wasted no time letting Conor know how he felt about what had just happened. 'Tell me now, Conor—have you lost the little good sense you had?'

'We were this close to joining the Oenach,' said Donal, squeezing his thumb and finger together in a pinch. 'This close! And I hear they have women at these gatherings— dancing girls and ale maidens and—'

'They do not,' said Fergal.

'They do!' insisted Donal. 'Anyway, I meant to find out for myself, so I did.'

'Fret not, brothers,' Conor replied mildly. 'They'll be begging us to return before the sun has quartered tomorrow's sky.'

The two friends stared at him. Fergal pushed out his lower lip. 'Is it certainty or stupidity I see on his face there, Donal?'

Donal, stroking his moustache, replied, 'I cannot say. Nor can I see proud Liam begging for anything.'

'Hear now,' said Conor, laying a hand on Donal's shoulder, 'when Liam learns they must feed and water the animals without the use of the buckets, he will come running after us quickly enough.'

'And why will they attempt the care of the horses without these very useful items?' demanded Fergal.

'Because they are *my* buckets, are they not?' Conor allowed himself a sly smile. 'Think you I would abandon such valuable articles? Never, I say. We will take them with us when we leave. Let the ardféne find their own buckets.'

'Ha!' Fergal barked a laugh. 'Out here? Not likely.'

'They'll be watering thirsty horses with cupped hands!' hooted Donal. 'That I would like to see.'

'Ach, nay,' countered Fergal. 'They'll just bundle feed in a cloak, and take them down to the stream for water—will they not?'

'Aye, and who will lead the noble beasts down to the watering place and stand waiting half the day while they drink? Will it be Liam, or Eamon do you think? Or, maybe Lord Ardan himself,' replied Donal, his tone dripping derision. 'Difficult to do while attending the gathering. Easier to just invite us to return.'

'We *will* attend the gathering, my friends,' Conor assured them.

Night was still stretched full upon the land when Conor and his two friends strapped on their swords, gathered their gear, and, filling their sparáns with hardtack and bósaill, crept away—pausing at the picket line to retrieve the six leather horse buckets. By the time the sun had risen high enough to peer over the surrounding hills, the three were far from their king's encampment. Every now and then, they paused to cast a hopeful glance at the trail behind them; and each time they were disappointed: no horn blower summoned them back; no messenger came running with an invitation to return.

'I begin to suspect they found their own horse buckets,' moaned Fergal gloomily. The three had emerged from a stretch of woodland and paused at the edge of a green expanse of meadow. Regarding the two leather vessels in his hand, Fergal shrugged, and then tossed them into the long grass a few paces away. 'So much for gaining the respect of the tribes with our gift horses.'

Donal threw his buckets away, too, saying, 'We made a worthy attempt—no blame to you, Conor. But it was not to be.' To Fergal, he said, 'Come, brother, at least there is ale waiting for us at home.'

The two strode off together, letting Conor feel their dissatisfaction. Conor watched them walk a few paces, then called, 'If I am wrong, then I will give you my mead portion until the next full moon.'

Fergal cast a glance over his shoulder. 'And if by some wild and vagrant chance you should be proved right?'

Conor lifted his palm. 'Then you will give me your mead portion.'

Fergal and Donal exchanged a dubious glance.

'Both of us?' enquired Donal.

Conor nodded. 'As is only right and fair.' He swung the buckets in his hand and asked, 'But why this hesitation? Can it be your reckless words lack conviction?'

'Done!' said Fergal. 'Our portions against yours. And the mead will taste all the sweeter coming from your cup, brother.' He punched Donal lightly on the arm; they retrieved the buckets they had tossed away, and the three moved on again.

They walked on in silence, crossing the wide grassy meadow divided in the centre by a shallow rill, at the bottom of which ran a willow-lined stream; there they paused to drink and rest a moment. They stretched out on the bank and allowed the morning sun to warm them. They were just rising to leave when they heard the hoofbeats of a rider approaching. Instinctively, the three reached for their weapons and stood ready to meet whoever appeared over the rise of the bank above.

The rider was Eamon. Bearing only a naked sword tucked into his belt, he sat astride one of the gift horses and was clearly relieved to see them. Raising a hand in greeting, he said, simply, 'You are to come back.'

'Welcome, brother,' said Conor. 'Climb down from there and water your mount. An animal of that size must have a prodigious thirst.'

'You would know,' muttered Eamon. Nevertheless, he eased himself down from the bare back of the horse and led it to the stream where it lowered its head to the water. 'Liam is anxious for your return.'

'Ach, well, as to that,' replied Fergal, 'we are not for coming back.'

'Much as we savour the smell of fresh dung, we have better things to do,' offered Donal.

Eamon rolled his eyes. 'Better things to do than sit on your haunches by a lonely brook and watch the clouds drift over your empty heads?' He looked from him to Conor. 'What say you?'

'I think you have your answer. It was made abundantly clear to us that our services were no longer of any value.'

'You have made your point,' the elder warrior told them. He stretched his back and rolled his head on his neck to ease the tension there. 'Come back.'

'What—walk all that long way back only to be sent away again when we come in sight of Tara?' said Fergal. 'A poor bargain that.'

Eamon looked to Conor. 'Your father needs you.'

'He needs us until he reaches the gathering,' countered Conor. 'Fergal is right—why return today only to be sent away again tomorrow? Thank you for your gracious offer, but I think we will go home where we belong.'

'Liam claims the horses for his own, so be it,' said Donal. 'Let him spend all *his* time feeding and watering the animals and good luck to him, I say.'

'Well now, here you have hit on the nut of the matter there,' Eamon said, the shadow of a smile playing about his lips. 'You see, this morning when our battlechief ordered the care of the animals, we could find no suitable utensil to assist in this necessary chore.'

'A very shame that,' replied Donal. 'Even so, I cannot think what you wish us to do about it.'

'Come back, brothers,' said Eamon in a softer tone. 'All will be well. You wish to attend the council. I understand that. If you return with me now, I will see what I can do.'

'You'll talk to the king?' said Fergal.

'Convince him?' added Donal.

'I'll talk to the king and do what I can to convince him to allow you to attend the council—where, I am sure, your services will be properly rewarded.'

Both Fergal and Donal looked to Conor to answer. 'With such assurances as that, how can we refuse?' He grinned at his two companions. 'Brothers, it seems the value of our labours has been recognised at last.' To Eamon, he said, 'Hasten back to our esteemed battlechief and tell him that it will be our highest pleasure to return to our duties.'

The elder warrior inclined his head in assent. Then, gathering the reins, he clambered up onto his mount's broad back once more. 'Will you be very long, do you think?'

'Look for us no later than midday, I should think,' replied Conor.

Eamon nodded. 'I will let them know.' Raising a hand in farewell, he turned his mount and started off.

'What did I tell you?' said Conor as Eamon rode up the side of the bank and away. 'We will yet see our service properly rewarded.'

'You are not going to drink all our mead by yourself now,' asked Donal. 'Are you?'

'To be sure,' replied Conor cheerfully. 'We all know there is nothing sweeter than the mead in another's cup.' He took up his spear and his bundle of gear and started climbing the bank of the dell. 'You should have trusted me.'

'We trust you, Conor,' Fergal called after him. 'It is Liam we doubt.'

Conor crested the bank and disappeared over the top. 'Come on,' sighed Fergal. 'The churn is upturned. Crying about it will not make butter.'

Donal gave a dismissive sniff, took up his gear and buckets, and started up the bank. 'Let him drink your cup first.'

Both warriors reached the top of the bank at the same time, almost colliding with Conor who had stopped, rigid, his attention fixed on something in the near distance. Fergal looked where Conor was staring and saw Eamon on horseback surrounded by five strange riders—all of them wearing horsetail helmets and brandishing long iron spears.

'Scálda scouts,' said Conor as if intoning a curse.

'And they have Eamon at their mercy,' breathed Donal.

'He is a dead man,' muttered Fergal.

'Not yet.' Conor pointed out positions to the left and right, and said, 'You two take either side and attack as soon as you come in killing range.'

'Fly!' He started away at a loping run. 'And Mórrígan fly with you!'

4

Conor was first to reach the circle of enemy riders, and feared he was already too late. Eamon wielded his sword this way and that in a valiant effort to fend off the long iron spears. But it was five against one and the Scálda seemed intent on making rough sport of butchering a Dé Danann warrior caught out on his own. They jabbed at him carelessly, gashing his flesh, and laughing as the blood flowed.

How long this game would continue before the Scálda tired of it, Conor could not say. As he raced nearer, he prayed to every god he knew that he would get at least one sound blow before the stalwart Eamon fell.

In fact, the distraction of the Scálda's taunting game was all the opportunity the three friends needed. Out of the corner of his eye, Conor saw a dark flash arcing through the air and an instant later one of the enemy scouts pitched forward in the saddle, the shaft of Fergal's spear deep in his shoulder.

Donal's cast came but a heartbeat later. A second enemy scout, sensing danger, made a half turn in the saddle to look behind him and that slight movement saved his life. The Dé Danann spear sliced the air, narrowly missing its mark, but catching the enemy rider's mount in the neck just below the ear.

The startled horse shied, then reared, throwing the Scálda

warrior to the ground. Three remained. Grim faces squirming with surprise and rage, the Scálda swung around to engage this unexpected threat and the momentary diversion was all Eamon needed. With a cry, he lashed his mount forward, bolting for the gap left by the fallen rider. He blew by the encircling Scálda, slashing at the nearest rider as he passed. The raider took the blow on his shield and made a desperate counterstrike, but Eamon was already out of reach.

The instant Eamon was free, Conor launched his spear and raced in after it, drawing his sword as he ran. He reached the foe in four quick strides and saw his spear stuck firmly in the centre of the Scálda's shield; he leapt, seized hold of the shaft, and pulled hard. The shield came down, exposing its bearer. Conor, blade in hand, thrust up into the rider's briefly unprotected belly.

The blade struck a metal plate on the armour and slid off. The rider grunted and countered with a vicious chop of his own, knocking Conor's blade sideways. Still clutching the haft of his spear, Conor fell backward, letting his weight drag down his opponent's arm. The Scálda slashed at him but, with his own shield in the way, he could find no suitable angle to strike. Meanwhile, his mount tried to stamp on Conor as he lay on the ground. One of the horse's hooves struck the turf beside his head, and Conor grabbed the beast's leg and held on.

Unable to free its foot, the horse reared and Conor, clinging tight to the shaft of his spear, dragged the rider from the saddle. The warrior fell on top of him with a grunt and, releasing his grip on his shield, struggled up onto his knees, pinning Conor to the ground. He grabbed Conor by the neck and, with one swift movement, drew a long knife from the sheath at his side. Conor, writhing beneath his adversary, saw the cruel blade rise and the downward stroke begin. He blocked the strike with the edge of his sword and kicked with all his might in an effort to dislodge his attacker.

The Scálda snatched a handful of Conor's hair and steadied his head. He raised the long knife again and prepared to slice Conor's throat. As the fatal stroke began its descent, however, the knife blade twisted in the scout's hand and he grabbed his own throat instead. Blood spurted between his fingers in a crimson arc; he loosed a wild roar and half turning, tried to rise.

He managed to drag himself to his feet and then, with a low, guttural groan, pitched face-first to the ground beside Conor.

Wiping blood from his eyes, Conor squinted up as Donal's broad face appeared in the air above him. 'Are you quite finished with your nap there, Conor? If so, we could use a little help just now.'

'My thanks, brother. I was this close to a shave I would not have survived.'

'It was myself I was thinking about,' replied Donal, smoothing his moustache. 'Aoife would have my ears if I let anyone crease that lovely skin of yours. Though why she should care at all is a mystery to me, so it is.'

'Love is blind,' Conor told him. Rolling over and squirming up onto his knees, he surveyed the site. Three of the five enemy scouts were dead, one was captive, and that one appeared badly injured. A short distance away, Eamon was sitting in the grass beside his horse, holding his head as Fergal tended his wounds.

'There were five,' said Conor. 'The fifth one—where is he?'

'Fled the moment the fight turned against them,' Donal spat. 'Coward.'

Conor climbed to his feet, picked up his sword, and wiped

the blade on the body of the slain scout. 'Then we must fly back to camp right away and warn the king.'

'What about this one?' Donal jerked a thumb at the wounded man. The warrior sat hunched over, clutching his stomach, his eyes squeezed shut against the pain.

'Tie him up. We'll bring him with us.' Conor started for where Fergal was attending to Eamon. 'It may be that someone at the gathering can get him to say something useful.'

'And the horses?'

'Do you need to ask?'

While Donal set about securing the three remaining Scálda mounts, Conor moved quickly to Eamon's side and examined the elder warrior's cuts and slashes, the worst of which was a deep gash to his sword arm. 'Nasty,' he observed.

'I've had worse,' replied Eamon.

'Lucky we got here when we did,' Fergal told him. 'Another poke or two and you *would* have had worse.'

'I had them right where I wanted them,' sniffed Eamon. 'Did you kill them all?'

'Three only,' said Fergal, tearing another strip from the warrior's siarc to use for a bandage.

'One we have with us still,' Conor added. 'One got away.'

'Good work, lads,' Eamon nodded. 'It seems you were not asleep during your training after all. Now, you must ride ahead—take word to the king right away. The council should know there are scouts sniffing around the gathering.'

'You speak my thoughts exactly,' said Conor. 'Can you ride?'

'What so—with such a niggling scratch as this?' Eamon lifted his arm, which was now bound with strips of cloth torn from his siarc. 'I could race you back to camp.' He offered his good hand and Fergal pulled him to his feet, where he swayed slightly. 'And what is more—I would win.'

Conor shook his head doubtfully. 'Fergal, take Eamon's

mount and ride to the gathering. Tell them what has happened here and that we have captured one of the scouts. We will do what we can for him—if he will let us. We'll strip the dead, hide the bodies, and follow along with the horses.'

Fergal turned and started for Eamon's horse.

'Be quick about it,' added Eamon. 'There may be more dog-eaters lurking about.'

'Mind, keep a sharp eye on the trail ahead and stop for nothing,' Conor called after him. 'We will join you as soon as we can.'

As Fergal galloped away, Donal came leading a trio of horses. 'Only three?' asked Eamon.

'One was injured in the fight. I thought best to let him go. Likely, he will not last the day.'

'You might have spared him his pain,' suggested Eamon.

'Perhaps you can carry the carcass of a dead horse upon your back, but I cannot,' Donal, replied. 'As it is, the beast will go to water and likely die there. If we're lucky, he won't be found should anyone come looking for him.'

Conor agreed and, handing the reins of the horses to Eamon, he went to examine the captured scout's wounds, while Donal set about collecting weapons and valuables from the enemy corpses. Although the scout resisted Conor's help, he accepted a piece of cloth to press against the wound to staunch the blood. Conor stripped him of his armour and searched for hidden weapons, then left him to himself and went to help Donal. They piled the dead onto one of the horses and Conor led the animal back to the rill where he found a secluded nook, dumped the bodies, and then rode to the edge of the wood where Donal and Eamon were now waiting.

They bound their captured spy and bundled him onto one of the horses, and, with a last look at the glade—little trace remained to indicate the battle that had just taken place—Conor gave a nod to Donal and they rode on into the wood. They soon picked up the trail and followed it all the way back to the Darini encampment where King Ardan and his retinue, having packed up, were just getting ready to move on.

At their approach, one of the ardféne glanced up and announced their arrival with a shout. As Conor and Donal helped Eamon down from his mount, King Ardan welcomed them and one of the warriors called out, saying, 'Trust Conor to leave empty-handed and return with horses and a captive!'

A grimace of distaste creased Liam's face, and he said, 'Trust Conor to stir up trouble where there was none—and wound a comrade as well,' he added, indicating the injured Eamon just then climbing down from his mount.

'It was not Conor who attacked me,' Eamon replied, 'but if not for him that dog-eater'—he jerked his head toward the wounded scout—'and his friends would have made a corpse of me this day.'

'I'm sure we are grateful for your safe return,' said Liam, adopting a more lenient tone. 'And grateful, too, for the increase of our stock. The horses will make a fine addition to the king's gift.'

'I would have it no other way,' replied Conor grandly. Touching the back of his right hand to his forehead in salute, he greeted his father and then said, 'As you see, we bring not only horses, but one of the Scálda scouts as well. Fergal has warned you of the danger?'

Ardan nodded. 'He has. I have sent Gaen on ahead to inform those already assembled at Tara. We go to join them directly.'

Camp had already been struck and the Darini resumed their march, moving easily along well-travelled paths. The sun was low in the west by the time they came in sight of the sacred mound rising in the near distance. The camps of other kings were spread out on the three plains surrounding the ancient meeting place. Smoke from numerous cooking fires made the air silvery and heavy with the scent of burning wood.

Even from a distance, Conor could see a sizeable group on the flattened top of the ancient gathering place. Ardan's message had been delivered, he guessed, and was even now being discussed. The Darini delegation found a place below the hill and, while his men set about establishing their camp, Ardan summoned Fergal, Donal, Conor, and two others to attend him; Eamon, insisting his wounds were not enfeebling, was also allowed to join them. 'We will go up now and see how the kings have greeted news of the spies and what they mean to do about it.' To Donal, he said, 'Bring a horse—the spotted stallion is best, I think.'

Conor heard the command and groaned inwardly. *No . . . not the stallion. Please, not my Balla.* But, aware that other eyes were on him, he set his jaw and said nothing as his prize was loosed from the picket and led away.

The company joined one of the many pathways leading to the top of the hill; Donal, leading the gift horse, fell into step beside Conor. 'How have the kings greeted our report?' he asked, keeping his voice low. 'I don't expect the thought of Scálda scouts sneaking around the protected lands made anyone leap for joy.'

'Nor do I,' agreed Conor. 'And why are there Scálda skulking about at all? That is what worries me.'

'You think maybe the dog-eaters somehow learned about the Oenach?' said Donal. He rejected the prospect with a shake of his head. 'Not likely, that.'

'Not likely,' echoed Conor. 'Unless we have a traitor among us.'

* * * *
5

In the centre of the imposing eminence of the Hill of Tara stood the remnants of Ráth na Rí, the Stronghold of Sovereignty. Once the fortress of the great High Kings of Eirlandia, all that remained of that storied time was the great circular ditch and the Pillar Stone known as the Lia Fáil where gatherings and kingmakings took place long ago. There was also a massive stone barrow tomb of age beyond reckoning, erected by a race long ago lost to memory and reputed to be the burial place of King Nuada, first king of the Dé Dananns, or perhaps the father of the race, Donn himself, whose footprints were said to be embedded in the Rígad Stone. On that sacred stone, each of Eirlandia's high kings had been sworn and enthroned—back in the days when a supreme king ruled the island. Over time, other structures had been added, as need and custom dictated: a large circle of wooden posts topped with a roof of reed—the original purpose of which had been forgotten, but now functioned as a meeting place when the weather was foul; a great fire ring for the ceremonial fires the druids venerated; three houses to store the food and drink for the official gatherings, and several small grave mounds of unknown nobles—one of which was reputed to be that of King Samildanach, the Many Favoured.

Assembled within the encircling ditch, a triple rank of perhaps fifty warriors and no fewer than eight lords crowded the perimeter of a wooden platform. Though it had been four, or maybe five years since Conor had attended one of these gatherings, he recognised most of the early arrivals. Of those he knew on sight, there was Rochad of the Gangani, a dour, mirthless fellow ruling a dour and mirthless tribe, always dressed in drab, colourless garb as if in perpetual mourning for his lost kingdom. Next to him stood Lord Alamaich of the Luceni with a few of his advisors; they, at least, displayed the general penchant for bright colours and expensive cloth favoured by the other chieftains: siarcs of bright saffron yellow and short summer cloaks of soft sea green, close-cut breecs the colour of copper, ochre, and sorrel. Surrounded by his warriors nearby, arms over his paunch, dressed all in red, stood hook-nosed Credne, Lord of the Cauci, a stiff-necked, garrulous old moaner, no mistake, but a lord who knew how to look after his diminished clan.

To a man, they all wore the emblem of kingship: the torc. Whether crafted in twisted strands, bands, or rolled into fat hollow tubes of silver or gold, the neck ornament gleamed at every lordly throat. Nor was that all—there were bracelets and armbands and chains and brooches of every size and description a smith could devise, and each and every ornament polished until it gleamed.

Outshining them all, up on his raised platform so he could look down upon all other lesser lords, stood Lord Brecan, King of the Brigantes. Legs spread and arms crossed over his chest, and a thick golden torc around his throat, he stood and surveyed the crowd arrayed before him. Brecan carried no weapons, but had a ceremonial obsidian knife stuck in his wide leather belt from which hung a richly tooled sparán. His dark hair, streaked with grey, was plaited in an elaborate double braid at the side of his square head, giving him a look at once august and slightly vain, and the trailing ends of his long moustache were braided, too. He wore a flame-coloured siarc with blue embroidered knotwork, heather-coloured breecs, and soft leather brócs; a green-checked cloak, fixed with a handsome gold cassán, lay in neat folds on his shoulder and hung down over his chest to partially hide his substantial belly.

His aged druid, the wizened and crusty Mog Ruith, stood beside him, a stern and disapproving presence, dressed in a faded red cloak over a much-worn green tunic of rough woven cloth.

The outer ring of onlookers parted to admit Ardan and his attendants to the conclave. King Brecan, assuming the part of the gracious host, welcomed the newcomers warmly. He stepped to the edge of the platform, reached down and gripped Ardan by the forearms in the warrior's embrace, and said, 'Hail and welcome, Lord Ardan, may you and your people prosper with all the good fortune you deserve. Please, take your place among us that we may all benefit from your astute counsel.'

'Lord Brecan, I give you good greeting and bring a gift to honour your long and loyal guidance of the Oenach.' He signalled to Donal, who led Conor's fine red-and-white–spotted stallion into the circle and to the foot of the platform where he handed the reins to King Brecan. This caused a muted murmur of appreciation to flutter through the assembled ranks. Not even Brecan himself brought gifts like this to a council gathering—and everyone there knew it.

'I hope you will think well of the Darini when you ride,' continued Ardan. 'Long may our tribes continue in friendship.'

'I accept your lavish gift, brother,' replied Brecan a little stiffly, but with a nod of acknowledgement. 'As a sign of amity and peace between our peoples, I shall indeed esteem it greatly. Moreover, I will remember your generosity.' At this he cast a stony glance at the other lords standing nearby—as if to reproach them for neglecting similar good manners.

King Ardan placed his hand on his chest and bowed to both the king and his druid; the gift horse was led away and Ardan waved his men to range themselves behind him in the inner circle of onlookers.

The formalities concluded, the king raised his hands in a grand gesture to the assembled lords and said, 'Tomorrow the Oenach begins and we will meet together in council. But tonight—tonight we feast and drink, and renew the bonds of friendship and goodwill. Until then, my friends, I bid you return to your camps and your preparations.'

Ardan spoke up. 'A moment more, Lord Brecan, if you please. We sent a message of some importance to the council ahead of our arrival. I would know whether this message was received.'

'I believe it was,' Brecan replied. 'Something about catching a few Scálda scouts or spies—was that it?'

'Indeed, my lord—five of them. My men discovered them and attacked them. A warrior of my ardféne was injured.' Here he indicated Eamon, standing beside him.

Brecan's brows lowered in a thoughtful frown. 'I am sorry to hear it.'

The king's druid stepped forward just then and said, 'Your messenger told us of these spies and we have been chewing over the implications of this matter. The king will bring it before the council tomorrow.'

King Brecan smiled and nodded in satisfaction as if that should preclude any further debate. 'There now, you see,' he said. 'All is well in hand.'

The group began to break up. A few of the lords who held Brecan's favour, or wished to, remained for more private conversation. Others began to move off, but none had gone very far when a lone voice sang out.

'Why this unseemly retreat, lord king?'

Conversation ceased. Everyone turned to look at the man who dared question the king's decision.

'Conor!' hissed Donal. 'What are you doing?'

Brecan parted those around him with a gesture and took a step forward to address his questioner. 'Who is this?'

'My lord, I am Conor mac Ardan.' He stepped forward and made the sign of obeisance.

'You accuse us of retreat?' said Brecan, his tone even but edging toward irritation.

'Was that an accusation?' said Conor lightly. 'Forgive my bluntness, lord. No doubt I was confused by the abrupt dismissal of our concerns and blurted out the first words that came to me. I am sorry if you felt yourself accused.'

Conor's outburst had caught the attention of many still lingering on the hilltop. They returned to their places with renewed interest. 'No more, Conor,' said his father in a low, urgent voice. 'This is not the time.'

'What do you want, warrior?' demanded Brecan. 'If you have something to say, say it now because you won't be allowed to speak in council.'

'It was myself and my friends who fought the enemy scouts and sent my father that message of warning. This I think you know. Yet, knowing this, you gave us short shrift when we came to join your discussion. Is this the way a great lord treats those who have done him good service?' He put out a hand to the handsome spotted horse standing nearby in the care of one of Brecan's attendants. 'And this after we have brought a fine and costly gift to grace your stables—a prize won in battle by the edge of my own blade?'

'We have determined that any question regarding the Scálda spies can wait,' declared Mog Ruith in an attempt to save his king the indignity of being questioned by a mere warrior of the rank. 'Rest assured, clansman, the presence of these spies—if spies they be—will be discussed before the assembled lords tomorrow.'

'But tomorrow,' countered Conor, 'I will not be allowed to speak—as I am so courteously reminded.'

'Conor, that is enough,' said Ardan. 'Come away.'

Brecan, frowning now, demanded, 'What is it that you want?'

'Only this,' replied Conor, 'I would like to hear what others think about the enemy sniffing around the edges of the Oenach. It seems to me that this is a matter of some urgency—at very least, one that requires more serious attention than given here.'

'There were spies. You caught them. They are dead,' the druid intoned. 'Where is the urgency?'

'In truth,' said the king, his tone softening somewhat, 'we have already given the matter ample scrutiny. Indeed, we were talking about it just before you arrived.' He appealed to some of his client kings for support. 'Is this not so?'

There were nods and mumbles of agreement all around.

'Well and good,' replied Ardan, stepping up beside his son. 'Yet, seeing as it was my men who discovered the scouts and subdued them, perhaps you would not mind sharing the fruits of your private conversation.'

Brecan raised a hand to his druid and said, 'Tell him.'

Mog Ruith drew himself up and said, 'If we seemed curt, it was only to spare you the displeasure of a half-digested meal. Yet, since you insist, I will tell you that your message was thought by many to be false, or perhaps, mistaken.'

'You think we lied about this?' Conor felt the blood-red birthmark prickle as his temper mounted. 'Who among you would call us liars?'

'Conor!' hissed his father. 'Step back.'

Eamon reached out and put a restraining hand on his arm, whispering, 'Remember where you are, lad.' Donal moved to his side and whispered, 'He's right, brother.' Conor took a grudging step back.

Ardan, appealing to his fellow lords and chieftains, said, 'I can assure you one and all that there has been no mistake. Neither have we given a false report.'

'I am certain you meant well.' Brecan waved away the allegation as if swatting a bothersome fly. 'But the Scálda are always slinking around. It probably means nothing. Anyway, we shall never know.'

'What if I told you we have brought one of the enemy scouts with us,' replied Ardan. 'Would that make a difference?'

This announcement caused a muted sensation in the ranks.

'You took a Scálda prisoner?' The speaker was one of Ardan's good friends, Lord Cahir of the Coriondi. A stout, bullnecked man with short grey hair and a red face, he turned to entreat the assembled lords and warriors. 'We must talk to this captive at once. Does anyone know the Scálda tongue?'

Despite much muttering and mumbling, no one stepped forward claiming to possess this skill.

'The language of the Scálda is a cursed difficult thing. Not a man among us can make sense of it,' King Brecan said when the murmuring died away.

'Perhaps one of *your* clan knows the rudiments of their speech,' said Cahir, addressing Mog Ruith.

'Alas,' replied the druid, 'that, too, is unlikely. Even so, I will send word to Carn Dubh and ask if anyone there has acquired the necessary ability. If so, we will soon know. Until then, whatever we might say now would be merest speculation and hardly worthy of the deliberation it deserves.'

King Brecan spread his hands as if to indicate there was nothing more to be done. 'We will await an answer from the Learned. Until then, I think we should avoid leaping blindly to any conclusions. Would you agree?'

'Indeed,' Ardan replied. 'We will abide your decision and

wait until all the kings are gathered tomorrow. We will bring the Scálda captive with us then.' Ardan turned and started off. Eamon, still holding tight to Conor's arm, made to follow and, with a last begrudging glance at the Brigantes king, Conor allowed himself to be led away.

The Darini contingent made its way back to their camp on the plain where Liam and the rest of the ardféne were waiting to hear what had transpired up on the hill. Lord Cahir and some of his men accompanied them, and Ardan invited his friend to sit and share a cup of mead. While the warriors talked, the chieftains passed the cup. After they had sipped a little, the cup was refilled and the Coriondi king offered his appraisal of what had happened at the meeting before the Darini arrived.

'Ach, well,' mused Cahir, 'that was very odd—in my view, at least. Your man here'—he indicated Gaen, who was standing close by with Eamon and Conor to hear what was said— 'your man can tell you the report of spies was greeted with alarm by some of us, but Brecan seemed to be at pains to question it.'

Ardan looked to Gaen, who said, 'That he was, my lord. Brecan made it clear to everyone that he did not believe me.'

'He said this?' Conor asked, somewhat aghast. 'He openly contradicted a king's messenger?'

'Nay, nay,' Cahir replied, 'Brecan is more canny than that. He merely laughed and said he thought the Darini had been keeping close company with the ale vat and were now seeing spies behind every tree.'

'The sly old hound,' grumbled Liam. To his father, he said, 'He as much as called us all liars.'

Cahir licked his lips, reached for the cup, and took another sip of the sweet honey liquor. 'Brecan said that it had been a peaceful summer in the south with only a few minor skirmishes along his borders. There has been no raiding at all.'

Gaen nodded. 'It was more the way he said it—as if this somehow proved our report could not be true.'

Ardan frowned. 'Little wonder that he did not greet our arrival with much warmth.'

Cahir agreed that there was more to the incident than he knew, then asked, 'But why was he at such pains to deny it? That is what puzzles me.'

'With three Scálda horses, an injured man'—Conor put out his hand to Eamon—'and a captured Scálda, Brecan can deny it no longer.'

'We shall see what we shall see.' Cahir returned the mead cup to Ardan and climbed to his feet. 'Find me at the feast tonight and we will drink together, eh?'

Ardan rose, too, and took his friend by the shoulder. 'You speak my mind as if it was your own. Until tonight, brother.'

When the Coriondi had gone, Conor said, 'I smell a filthy rat.'

Liam nodded in agreement. 'By your leave, my lord, I will take Eamon and visit some of the other camps, talk to the battlechiefs and see if anyone else thinks the same.'

'What, and alert Brecan Big Breecs of our suspicions before we know what he is about?' Conor shook his head forcefully. 'Not the best idea, I think.'

'You know better, I suppose?' sneered Liam. 'Then, tell us, what would *you* do?'

'Do nothing. Say nothing. Any suspicions we may have, we will keep to ourselves—but we will also remain alert and listen to all that comes our way.' Conor looked to his father. 'If word gets back to Brecan that we suspect him of . . . of . . . of I don't know what, but whatever it is, he will hide it. Worse, he might move against us somehow.'

Ardan nodded. 'Conor is right. Until we know more, we will pretend all is right and well.' To Liam, he said, 'Tell the men to say nothing of this to anyone.'

Liam stalked off, leaving Conor and his father alone. The king glanced around at the Hill of Tara, now in shadow, a great dark expanse looming over them like a storm cloud threatening on the horizon. He suppressed a shudder and pushed his feeling of foreboding aside.

6

Vats of ale and tubs of mead had been set up in the centre of the council hill, near the Lia Fáil, that ancient sandstone pillar the druids held in almost rapturous esteem. For Conor, the so-called Stone of Destiny might as well have been named the Pissing Stone. 'Destiny is what a man makes with his own two hands,' he told Fergal as they shouldered their way through the throng to plunge their cups into the dark, frothy ale for the third time. 'No chunk of rock has power over a man's fate.'

'Unless that chunk be hurled from a sling,' remarked Fergal cheerfully.

Conor gave him a sideways look. 'Brother, I do believe you are drunk.'

'No more than you. Even so, you will not catch me speaking ill of the Lia Fáil.'

Conor laughed and shook his head. They walked on, easing through the throng where they took their places and waited for an opening at the vat. While others were preparing for the evening's festivities, both on Tara Hill and elsewhere, they had spent the day tending the horses and guarding the Scálda prisoner. When not feeding, watering, walking, or grooming the animals until their coats gleamed, they were standing watch over their injured prisoner who, in fact, required little enough attention. 'Is he not the most wretched creature anyone ever saw?' was Donal's observation.

The captive spent most of his time inert, hunched over his wound, sometimes moaning softly and rocking back and forth. Since his capture, he had refused all food and only accepted, from time to time, a little water. 'Is he thinking we'll try to poison him?' sniffed Fergal. 'He should know better than that. Why, it would be a waste of poison.'

Conor regarded the suffering Scálda curled like a sick animal on the ground and concluded that Donal was probably right: a more miserable being would be difficult to imagine. Even so, when his heart lurched toward pity for the fellow, Conor reminded himself of the charred Dé Danann corpses in the scorched farms and settlements where the Scálda raided and the trophy heads and hands hanging from Scálda belts and bridles, and all compassion fled.

Thanks to Eamon's intervention, the three had been released from their duties for the night and allowed to come up and join the feast. Donal had gone off in search of the serving maidens and dancing girls he fancied were to be found, leaving Conor and Fergal to plumb the depths of the ale vats. As they stood waiting for their turn, more warriors pressed in behind them and, owing to the crush, Conor could not fail to overhear what they were saying.

'. . . aw now, Barae, you would not know a faéry from a foot rag,' said one of the men.

Conor glanced over his shoulder. There were three hulking warriors standing a little too close behind them. All were robust, meaty men with the splayed bushy moustaches, side braids, and blue slash-mark tattoos of the Eblani tribe. And all were ruddy faced from the ale.

'So now, when was the last time *you* saw one?' retorted the warrior called Barae. 'Since you seem to know all about them. When did you ever meet one, eh?'

Conor turned around. 'Forgive a stranger, but am I hearing that you have seen one of the faéry kind?'

'It seems to me you that what you're hearing is none of your affair,' retorted the tallest of the three.

'Leave off, Duad,' said the one called Barae. To Conor, he said, 'Ach, aye, I saw a faéry woman and I will fight anyone who says otherwise.' He thrust out his chin belligerently. 'What have you to say about it?'

Fergal put out a hand to the affronted Barae. 'Easy now. We're all friends here.'

'And who are you to stick your oar in, eh?' demanded the one called Duad. 'You can kiss my rosy pink—'

'Friends,' said Conor quickly, 'I see your cups are empty. Allow us to fill them for you and we can all sit down and enjoy a cup of ale. Why quarrel when we can drink?' He relieved Barae of his wooden cup and nudged Fergal, who collected the others.

'Why are we filling *their* cups?' muttered Fergal as they pushed their way through the swarm around the vat. 'Bignosed Eblani—*they* should be filling *ours*.'

'It never hurts to be friendly,' chided Conor. 'Besides, they have something I want.'

'It's all that faéry woman of yours again,' he said, 'Aye, it is. Don't bother to deny it. What makes you think that lot will tell you anything worth hearing?'

'I won't know until I hear what they have to say.'

The two jostled their way to the ale vat, dipped their cups into the dark, foamy liquid and, unable to resist, took a deep draught, and then proceeded to refill all the cups once more. With sweet dark liquid slipping over the rims of their wooden vessels, they threaded their way back to where the Eblani warriors were waiting and handed the dripping vessels around. 'No man who drinks with another can be a stranger,' Conor announced grandly. 'I am Conor mac Ardan, and this is Fergal mac Caen of the Darini.' He raised his cup. 'We share a drink as friends and brothers!'

They all guzzled down a deep draught, and then Duad said, 'Darini, eh? You are the ones who caught the Scálda spy.'

'Is that true?' asked Barae, suspicion edging his tone even as the ale slurred his words.

'Our lord says it is a ploy to defy King Brecan's authority,' declared the third warrior. He took a pull from his cup and wiped his long moustache with the back of his hand. 'A low trick to make yourselves look important.'

'A curious trick, it seems to me,' reflected Conor evenly, 'when the truth is so easily proved.' He fixed the tall warrior with a firm and steady look. 'Now that we know what your lord thinks, what do *you* think?'

The warrior glanced away. 'I don't say one way or the other. I'll wait for the council to decide.'

'Wise man,' said Conor. 'But I can assure you it is no ploy. It was Fergal here who caught the enemy scout.'

'Aye, I did,' confirmed Fergal. 'There were five of them together. They attacked one of our lord's ardféne and would have killed him, too, if we hadn't arrived to fight them off. Killed three and captured one. The last got away.'

'Ha!' sneered Duad. 'If we had been there none of those dung dwellers would have got away.' He elbowed his comrade; the warrior nodded with a knowing smile.

'I expect you are right,' conceded Conor lightly. 'But it was five of them on horseback to three of us on foot and, truth be told, we felt sorry for them that they should be so badly outmanned.'

Fergal laughed and added, 'Did I mention we also captured three horses? Though I expect *you* would have captured ten.'

'Will your king bring the Scálda scum to the council tomorrow?' asked Barae.

'He said he would, and so he will,' Conor replied. 'Though,

unless someone can be found to speak that crude tongue, I think we will learn little from our captive.'

The Eblani warriors nodded appreciatively and then busied themselves with their cups. When those were finished, Duad offered to refill them again; his comrade and Fergal went along, leaving Conor and Barae together. With the others gone, Conor wasted no time. 'I want to hear about the faéry woman,' he said.

Barae regarded him closely. 'Why?' he asked, his tone guarded.

'Because, my friend,' said Conor, lowering his voice and leaning close, 'I saw one, too.'

Barae's dark eyes darted right and left. 'You did? Where was it? When?'

'You first,' Conor said.

'There is little enough to tell.' He pulled on his moustache so as to compose his thoughts, then said, 'I was out hunting—myself and four others. We came to a part of the wood—near the southern border of our lands, it was. We do not normally hunt there for all the trouble it causes, but that day we did. I made a hasty cast at a little yearling roebuck in the deep brake, missed, and went to retrieve my spear. As I was looking for it, there came to me the most delightful music any man ever heard—this man, at least.' He glanced at Conor, as if willing him to understand. 'How long I stood there, I cannot say. But when I finally stirred, I parted the branches and there she was with her harp cradled on her lovely knee.' He fell silent, remembering.

'What happened then?' asked Conor.

'There was a noise—not me, something else—and she turned to look. Then, quick as the blink of a bird's eye, she's up and away. But, just as she turns, she sees me and I see a terror there—a power of terror. The sound comes again and

I look to see what has frightened her. When I look back, she is gone. It was only a pig rooting in the underbrush, mind. But the lady fled as if the Hounds of Gurgan were on her . . .' His voice caught and cracked at the memory. 'I would give my left eye to see her again.'

'I know what you mean, brother,' Conor told him. 'It is that much the same with me.' He explained how the Darini warband had encountered a fast-moving enemy force and attacked. 'The battle did not last long,' Conor concluded; 'we cut down a few of them and the rest fled. That is when I saw her—on the back of a horse, chained to a Scálda chieftain.'

'She never was!' gasped Barae. 'Chained like a slave, you say?'

'She was indeed,' Conor assured him. 'And the look she gave me was full of such longing, such pleading . . .' He paused as the vision of that expression on that lovely face overwhelmed him anew. 'I never saw the like.'

'And was she very beautiful?' asked Barae.

'Aye, she was,' replied Conor. 'More beautiful than my poor tongue can tell.'

'And do your swordbrothers believe you?'

'They do not,' answered Conor sadly. 'Not a word.'

'Ah!' sighed his new Eblani friend knowingly. 'But, hear now, since coming to the council you are the second person to speak of faéry captives to me.'

Conor's glance quickened. 'Two, you say? Who was the first?'

'Ach, well, I thought it just some idle talk I heard when we were making camp.'

'Who? What did they say? Do you remember?'

Barae nodded. 'It was one of the Venceni, I think . . . aye.' He stroked his moustache thoughtfully. 'No! It was one of the Ulaid. This one and another were talking about seeing a faéry as they were passing by. I asked them to tell me what they knew, but they said they had heard the tale from someone else.'

'What was it? What did they hear?' asked Conor impatiently.

Barae shook his head. 'Only that they heard the Scálda had captured a queen of the fae and were keeping her at one of their strongholds in the south.'

'Who told them this?' asked Conor.

'I don't know.' The warrior shrugged. 'A druid maybe.'

Conor pursed his lips and stroked the strawberry stain on his cheek. 'They were Ulaid, you say?'

'Just so.' Barae gazed at Conor for a moment in silence, then said, 'Do you think there is something to the tale then?'

'Possibly,' mused Conor. 'Who can say?'

'Here now,' called Fergal, returning with the two Eblani, 'these cups need drinking, and I cannot do it all myself.'

'You can, you know.'

Fergal grinned. 'Ach, aye. But I did not like to boast.'

As they drank, the evening stole upon them and smoke from the cooking fires wafted the scent of roasting meat and fresh bread through the hilltop assembly, and warriors started drifting toward the fire pits where, owing to the generosity of King Brecan, a dozen or more cooks were busy putting the finishing touches to a feast for the three hundred or so tribesmen and their lords.

In the largest fire pit, three young bullocks were smoking over a bed of glowing embers; in a second smaller fire pit five fat hogs were crisping to a golden brown; in a third, seven sheep sizzled away, the juicy fat sputtering on the coals. A rich-scented silver cloud spread over the entire hilltop and the cooks, stripped to the waist and armed with long forks and basting ladles, stood by to turn the spits and baste the meat.

'I'll have one of those,' said Fergal, indicating a whole half pig. He sucked his teeth and inhaled deeply as he gazed upon the roasting meat.

Conor nudged him and pointed across the pit to where warriors were already gathered to collect the first carvings as soon as the cooks began slicing. 'This way, brother, they are getting ready to serve.'

They threaded their way around the outside of the fire ring and plucked wooden trenchers from one of two large heaps. Beside these sat wicker baskets full of barley bread; they helped themselves to several small loaves, then pushed in behind the front ranks waiting for their food. After a long, slow shuffle, they reached the serving place and both received a fine slab of roast pork and a shank of mutton. They retreated with their trenchers in search of a place to eat in peace— making sure to pass by the vats one more time before settling down to sate themselves on the succulent meat and good fresh bread.

'Ach, so,' said Fergal, after the first pangs of hunger had been appeased, 'what do you think our generous lord Brecan is about? Why hold another Oenach so soon after the last?'

'Need you ask? He imagines himself high king of Eirlandia—what better way to show it than by making everybody come running at your every beck and call?' Conor dabbed at the grease running down his chin. 'The grand and mighty lord, throwing himself around and making big before the world.'

'Well,' replied Fergal, lifting his cup, 'I will eat his meat and drink his ale with the best of them and no complaint.'

'All this'—Conor waved a hand to indicate the mass of men enjoying the feast—'it comes at a price. Never forget that.'

Fergal wrested meat from a bone with his teeth, chewed for a while, then said, 'Full sorry I am your father gave him our best horse—and we got no glory for it neither.'

'There was no need to mention that.' Conor shook his head and sighed, then drained his cup. 'I named him Balla, you know.'

'Cheer up,' said Fergal. 'Maybe the next one you get will be better still.' He wiped his now-empty dish with a scrap of bread and popped it into his mouth. 'I think a bit of beef is wanted here.' He stood. 'What about you, Conor?'

Conor held out his trencher. 'Only if it is no burden to you, now.'

Fergal trundled off and Conor stretched out on the grass and gazed up at the night's first stars already kindled in the blue-black expanse above. Full of good ale and tasty meat, he closed his eyes and let his mind wander where it would. Almost at once, it wandered straight into the thicket of his deepest suspicions. If the Scálda had captured one of the fae—a queen no less—what else might they soon possess? The secrets of faéry magic? Faéry armour? Faéry weapons?

If the enemy should gain even one of those things, there would be no stopping them—an outcome that did not bear thinking about.

Ardan

I do not know what made me run after him that day. And if I *had* known all that would flow from that rash act, would I have run anyway? It is a question I have asked myself a thousand times through all the years that have followed. In truth, I cannot say.

Ach, now, I was younger then—with a young man's heart and a young man's head. Everyone knows the way the heart can so easily rule the head. Truth to tell, this is what happened on the day my people call the Day of the Druid. But, know you—I was desperate. Our tribe was suffering. Something had to be done. And when the druid chief called down his curse upon our sorry heads, I could not let it stand. I ran after him.

I ran after him and I begged him to foreswear his curse. On my knees I begged him. He could not call back the word once spoken, but his cold heart warmed a little and he granted me a boon instead. He gave me a prophecy and a hope. He said my sons would be kings and champions. And, great druid that he was, he spoke the truth.

Even so, it was no gift bestowed on me that day. He took my youngest son away and a piece of my heart went with him.

If the boy's mother had been living still, she would never have allowed it. Druid prince or no, she would have bled and died before they took her sweet maíni from her arms. But, me . . . well, I did what I did. If any man knows better, let him answer: What choice did I have? Something had to be done to save our tribe. A sacrifice was needed. But, oh, it was a hard, hard thing.

Little Rónán went away that day, and before the sun had set, old Eochaid Tight-Fist was torn from his darksome hall and driven from Dúnaird. I never heard where he went, or how he fared—nor cared to know. The next day, by the acclamation of the tribe, I ascended to the throne in his place. Though I was shamed and disgraced by my grovelling on my knees in the dirt, the hearts of my people were moved—no less from pity than from deep relief that our long suffering beneath Eochaid's stinting rule was over. They made me king, and I have ruled every day to now. Mine has not been an easy reign. The Scálda have made certain of that.

The joy of our release was still sweet and fresh when the Black Ships arrived, swarming Eirlandia's southern coast. I have heard it said that the sea could not be seen for the enemy ships spread upon it. They came ashore—wave after wave, like a ferocious storm tide—and swiftly overran the Seven Kingdoms of the South. The Coriondi fell first and fled north—as did the Osraige, Cauci, and Menapi after them. The hapless Uterni and Velabri were all but wiped out. The brave Gangani allied with the Luceni and resisted for an entire year before succumbing the next raiding season. The remnant of those tribes fled north and the few clans remaining are clients now of the Brigantes, the Auteini, or the Bréifne.

The next years were years of war and want. Evil rained from the skies and seeped from every rock, it seemed—on and on, and still the deluge came. Those first battles took a great toll. The number of lives lost is beyond counting. The land has been ravaged and raped, and even the sheep and cattle have suffered the predation of the insatiable Scálda raiding parties that continually harass the borders. They take livestock, slaves, and weapons. What they cannot carry off, they kill. They are not human beings, they are beasts— more ravenous than wolves, and just as vicious.

Even so, they are proud of their strength and hotheaded. They can be beaten. Well I know it. We worked like slaves to staunch the blood flow; we turned back their incessant raids and eventually established a borderland—a wasteland, a wicked, dangerous place where neither man nor beast is safe. Alas, if not for the ever-mounting numbers of the enemy and the ceaseless bickering and backbiting of our own kings the Scálda might have been vanquished or pushed out long ago. That they are still here, still a plague upon this green land, still breathing the free air of Eirlandia is a wound in every true heart.

And, by the god who made me, I do feel it.

7

With heavy heads from feasting and drinking too well the night before, Conor and his friends woke to greet a dreary dawn. A heavy dew made every surface damp and lent a chill to the early morning air. But, by the time King Ardan and his ardféne were ready to take their places at the gathering, the sun had begun to burn away the wrack, and patches of blue could be seen peeping through. Despite Eamon's best efforts, neither Conor, nor Fergal, nor Donal were to be included in the formal proceedings. Liam made certain that they knew their place—and that place was not among the assembled lords on the Hill of Tara.

'You will stay here and tend the horses,' Liam told them. 'That is the only reason you are here, after all.' He looked them up and down. 'Or, have you forgotten?'

'How could we ever be forgetting,' complained Donal, 'when you so thoughtfully remind us every spare moment of the day?'

'No need to thank me,' Liam replied lightly. 'Just knowing that these valuable animals will receive the best of care at your hands is thanks enough.'

'At least let Conor go with you,' Fergal argued. 'He can bring us word of what goes on up there.' He jerked his chin in the direction of the hilltop.

'Far be it from me to deprive you of the company of your

good friend.' Liam smiled and shook his head. 'Nay, brother, you would think ill of me long before the sun crested midday were I to do such a low thing as that.'

'What about the Scálda captive?' said Donal. 'You will need an extra hand to guard him, will you not?'

'When *you* join the ardféne—should your fortunes ever improve—you can attend the council. Until then, you watch the horses.' He gave a flat chop of his hand to cut off further conversation and hurried away to take his place among those making their way to the hilltop.

'For a truth, I would think no more ill of him than I do now,' Donal sighed when the battlechief had gone.

The three watched as the royal retinue merged with those of other kings on the winding hillside path leading to the summit. They looked around at the silent camp and the picket line of horses patiently waiting to be fed and watered.

'You should go up there even so, Conor,' said Fergal.

'You should,' agreed Donal.

'We're to stay here. That was the agreement and that is our chore today.'

'Ach, aye—but it does not take three brave and able men to tie the feedbag on a few long-legged beasts.'

'See here, Conor, we'll take good care of the horses,' Donal said. 'You go.'

'Go and look after our interests at the council,' Fergal added.

'We have interests at the council now?'

'Aye, should anyone question how we fought off the attack and captured the enemy spy, you will be there to bear witness to the truth,' said Fergal.

'Eamon is there and his injuries alone bear ample witness.'

'Aye, but what if they should doubt our good Eamon, eh? Have you considered that?'

Conor gave Donal a pat on the cheek, saying, 'I yield to your persuasion, brother.' With that, he started off at a trot.

'Bring back word now!' called Fergal.

'And ale,' added Donal.

Conor reached the gathering by a circuitous route, winding around the hill and approaching the assembly at an angle from behind. As before, the lords and chieftains and their advisors gathered shoulder-to-shoulder one with another within the encircling ring. That was as it should be. But, in the centre of the ring, on his specially constructed platform, sat King Brecan enthroned in a high-backed chair in the manner of a king of kings—an honour which, by Conor's reckoning, the ambitious nobleman had not earned and did not deserve. Beside the seated king stood his druid, the grim, sour-visaged Mod Ruith in his best white robe and leather hood of bleached deerskin. In his hand he held his rowan rod topped with a gold cap shaped like the spread wings of an eagle.

Seeing the two of them together, holding court as if all the world owed them a duty of fealty, brought the bile to Conor's throat. He swallowed hard, choked it down, and spat into the grass. But the bad taste lingered. He crept closer, easing in among the onlookers and keeping well out of Brecan's view. He located his father and Liam at the foot of the platform, and made sure to stay out of their sight, too.

He listened for a while and, if the sight of Brecan putting on airs filled him with disgust, what he heard upset him even more.

The Scálda captive knelt on the edge of the platform in front of Ardan and the Darini contingent. Miserable, sick, and shaking with fear and fever, he looked half dead—as, in fact, he undoubtedly was. But, though the Scálda captive had been produced as promised by his father, to all appearances the problem of spies tracking lords to a royal assembly had, apparently, been set aside. Conor, arriving only a little late, was surprised. When he asked a warrior standing next to him, the warrior explained that since no one could be found to talk to the captive, his value as a source of information was worthless. Therefore, the enemy's presence was deemed to be of no importance and whatever he and his fellow spies had been doing was now beyond recovery and unworthy of further discussion.

Conor did not see it that way. To him, the very idea of spies venturing so far into protected territory was a potent danger— and that they should be sneaking around a high council made it doubly so. Was it merely luck or chance that brought them? Or, had the enemy been given advance knowledge of the Oenach? Did no one else think such questions merited a full and forthright airing?

He glanced around at his fellow warriors and the lords ranged around the foot of the platform. Did none of them feel the least outrage at this audacious incursion by the enemy? And then he heard Mog Ruith declare, 'Let the captive be taken to Lord Brecan's ráth and held in exchange for future favours should any of our people fall foul of a Scálda raiding party.'

There was much nodding agreement from the lords all around and the matter was summarily dropped as Brecan began talking about the need to increase production of grain by clearing certain tracts of woodland for planting. Was *this* why they had been summoned to an Oenach? To discuss farming?

Angry now, Conor pushed himself forward to the edge of the platform, the words already forming on his tongue. 'My lord Brecan,' he called loudly. 'Forgive a lowly warrior of the ranks, but it seems to me that the presence of this spy requires greater consideration.'

'Conor!' Liam hissed from his place beside Ardan. 'What are you doing?'

Ignoring him, Conor said, 'There are questions to be answered.'

'You again.' Brecan frowned heavily. 'I should have thought Lord Ardan might teach his son something of respect in the presence of his lords and masters.' Casting his gaze around the assembled kings and warriors, he appealed to them directly. 'It is my judgement that the fate of this Scálda filth need no longer concern this gathering.'

'That much is clear,' replied Conor, holding his ground. 'Your lordship seems to be at pains to rebuff any claim this captive might have on our attention. Why is that?'

Brecan visibly stiffened at this allegation. 'I need not justify the decisions of the council to a warrior of the rank—no matter how insolent and ill mannered he may be.'

'Perhaps not, your lordship,' said Lord Ardan, coming to the defence of his son, 'but perhaps there are those among our brother kings who would care to hear more. I number myself among them.'

At this several voices—friends of Brecan, to be sure—shouted for the council to move on to other matters. But others, louder and more insistent, called for answers to Conor's questions.

Brecan's frown deepened to a belligerent glower. 'Never let it be said that the king of the Brigantes failed to allow a hearing of any subject, even the most trivial and insignificant . . .'

Before he had even completed the thought, Conor was on him. 'Am I to believe, great king, that the honest concerns of our people are trivial and insignificant?'

'I said nothing of the kind, as many here will attest,' countered Brecan. 'But since it seems nothing will prevent you, ask your questions and let the council judge whether they are fit to answer.'

Conor made bold to step upon the platform, but kept his

distance from the king in his thronelike chair. 'Though I am merely a warrior of the rank, as you say, I must confess I do not know which alarms me more—that one in authority should be blind to the more obvious implications of this enemy intrusion, or that you hold the presence of enemy spies deep beyond the boundaries of the protected lands to be a trivial affair?'

Several Brigantes warriors jostled forward to pull Conor from the platform. Eamon made ready to prevent them, but Lord Brecan waved them off instead. 'You want to know how the spies slipped past our borders—is that it? Why ask me? Ask *him* if you can.' The king thrust a finger at the Scálda scout, who was now quietly moaning as he lay on his side at the edge of the platform. He turned with a superior smile to his druid. 'I do believe it would be more beneficial to address a stump in a bog.'

Several of the Brecan's supporters laughed at this and called for Conor to step down. Two even reached out to pull him from the platform, but Eamon shouldered his way to them and, after a quiet word, they desisted.

King Ardan stepped forward. 'The question,' he said, raising his voice to be heard over the hubbub, 'is not *how* did the spies get past our borders, but *why* were they following a king and his ardféne to the Oenach?'

'And why you believe that to be a matter of no concern?' added Conor.

Brecan shook his head. 'Do you expect me to answer such things? How should I know? And since we cannot ask *him*'—he indicated the captive again—'we may never know.'

'I do not expect an answer from you, my lord,' replied Ardan smoothly. 'But I expect an airing of the issue before the council where we can all express our opinions. That is only prudent.'

'It is a waste of breath,' insisted Brecan. Rising slowly

from his chair, he put out his hands in appeal to the gathered lords. 'Does anyone here believe this gathering is in danger of imminent attack?'

No one made bold to speak out.

'No?' said Brecan, a note of triumph edging into his tone. 'Then, let us continue with—'

'A moment more, my lord.' It was Ardan's ally, Lord Cahir, wading into the debate. 'I beg my brothers to forgive a slow, old plodder, but whether we are under imminent attack—or not—seems to me much beside the point.' He, too, stepped up on the platform and turned to appeal to the gathering. 'The question asked was not about possible attacks, but about the significance and implications of spies roaming so deeply and freely through our protected lands during an Oenach.' Turning back to Lord Brecan, he said, 'That, I believe, is the real question.'

'Then, by all means,' intoned Brecan, adopting a weary air, 'feel free to ask the captive for yourself. Let him tell you what he knows. That is the only way you will receive an answer to these vexing questions of yours.' Once more, he flung out his hand toward the wounded enemy scout.

Cahir turned to regard the captive, who was now completely inert on the platform. 'That will be most difficult, I think.'

'You see!' Brecan threw out his hands as if demonstrating some sort of vindication of his stubborn position. 'As I said, we can learn nothing because you do not speak his language.'

'Not so,' replied Cahir, 'it is because he is dead.'

Conor looked at the unmoving body. Their valuable captive had quietly expired while the king argued and prevaricated. That, Conor reflected, was most unfortunate—but far from a complete disaster.

'We have lost nothing,' declared Conor, standing over the deceased Scálda. 'The fact remains that the spies were here and that one of his number escaped to tell their masters what they discovered.'

'That is unfortunate. But, tell me—what did they learn?' said Brecan, defensive again. 'Eh? What did they learn that they did not already know? Answer that if you can.'

'That is beyond answering now,' Conor admitted.

'It is beyond answering,' added Ardan, 'because we do not know what it was they were sent to discover—the strength of our numbers, perhaps? Or, the placement of our settlements and strongholds, the distances between them, our fields and how they grow, where water can be found and grazing for horses, the lay of the land itself? All these, it seems to me, would be useful for an enemy intent on mounting an invasion very soon.'

'Or,' added Conor, 'perhaps they had another purpose in mind.'

'Go on,' urged Cahir. 'You and your friends were the ones who caught them. Tell us what is in your mind.'

'Could it be,' ventured Conor, 'that they were sent to discover the location of the council itself? It occurs to me that finding out where the lords of Eirlandia met would be useful to someone preparing a future attack.'

'When we were all together and at our most vulnerable, you mean?' said Cahir. 'Why, the Scálda could wipe out all the lords and battlechiefs at a single stroke. The attack would be over before any of us could lift a finger to stop it.'

'Bah!' cried Brecan in exasperation. 'You are making more of this than is merited by the very few facts in evidence. The truth is we do not know, and now will never know what the enemy was doing here. We must turn away from what has happened, and look instead to what we can accomplish in days to come.'

The king returned to his chair and resumed his place, the grand monarch once more, taking control of the proceedings.

Conor, accepting there was nothing more to be gained by arguing, made a curt bow, stepped from the platform, and pushed his way through the press of the assembly. Whatever happened at the council would happen without him. He had spoken his mind; there was nothing more he could do. So, he left the hilltop and started back down the path to rejoin his friends in camp.

He was halfway down the steep-sloping path when he heard a call behind him. 'Here now!' someone called. 'Stop a moment.'

Pausing, Conor glanced over his shoulder to see three warriors he did not recognise hurrying down the hill toward him. One of them carried a spear—in defiance of the ban on weapons on the council hill. Something in the narrow set of their eyes did not inspire trust. He hesitated, then continued on.

'We want to talk to you,' called another of the three.

'What about?' Conor replied, still moving.

'What was that you were saying at the council just now?' called the one who had spoken first, the obvious leader of the group.

'I have nothing more to say,' Conor told them. He kept his pace, but was soon overtaken as the warriors ran to join him.

'But we have something to say to you,' said the leader.

Conor paused and as he turned, he was struck from behind by the shaft of a spear. The blow hit the back of the knee; his leg buckled and he fell. Before he could squirm out of the way, the next blow found his ribs and stole the breath from his lungs. Instinctively, he doubled up to protect himself and caught another jab in the ribs followed by a crack on the head as the three warriors joined in the beating, raining down punches, kicks, and clouts.

Twisting on the ground, Conor kicked out with a foot and toppled one of his attackers. He managed to snatch hold of the spear shaft and yanked down hard, momentarily wresting the weapon from its owner. He made to rise, but the third warrior reared back and gave him a swift kick to the head. Blood-red stars exploded in his eyes, obscuring his vision. The weapon was pulled from his grasp and the beating resumed with a vengeance. Pain jolted through him with every thump. One particularly vicious kick aimed to take his eye. Conor absorbed the blows as best he could, but the world grew dim around him and he had almost passed beyond knowing when he heard a familiar voice cry out somewhere below him.

'You there! Leave off!'

One of the warriors shouted something back, and then, mercifully, the beating stopped.

'Back away!' commanded the voice and a moment later Fergal was there beside him. Conor opened his one good eye and saw Fergal crouching beside him, sword drawn, and Donal standing over him, spear lowered. 'What is wrong with you lot? Eh? Three against one and that one unarmed?'

'We only wanted to talk,' said the leader, backing away a step. 'But he wouldn't listen.'

'Nor will I,' replied Fergal, 'your talk is too rough.'

'Cowards,' snarled Donal. 'Creep away now while you can still walk.'

'And if we don't?'

'Then stay and talk to my blade.' Donal moved forward, ready to strike.

'Calm yourself,' said another of the warriors, also backing away. 'We're going.'

'Ach, aye,' Donal told him, 'and if I ever see any of you again, blood will flow.'

'Just you tell your friend there'—the leader pointed at Conor on the ground—'that King Brecan is not a dog to be whipped by any upstart spear-polisher. Remember that.'

The three departed then, and Fergal raised Conor into a sitting position. Conor tried to get to his feet, but was reduced to breathlessness by another wave of pain. 'Easy, brother,' said Fergal. 'Rest a moment. They won't come back.'

'If they do, they'll regret it.' Donal bent down and, looking into Conor's face, said, 'That is going to hurt.' Conor reached up and touched his cheek; his right eye was already swelling shut.

'What did you say to them anyway—to make them so angry?' wondered Fergal.

Conor shook his head. 'I challenged high-and-mighty Lord Brecan before the gathered lords,' he moaned.

Fergal glanced at Donal and shook his head. 'I hope you think it was worth it.'

'Challenging Brecan before the council.' Donal shook his head. 'What were you thinking? Or, were you thinking at all?'

'Brecan is slippery as any eel in the lough.'

'And did you not know that already?'

'I wasn't the only one,' Conor said, feeling his arm and wincing at the touch. 'Also Cahir and Ardan—they both tried to get Brecan to admit that there is some foul purpose in play.'

Donal squatted down in front of him and reached out a hand to his cheek. 'I don't like the look of that eye. I expect Aoife will like it even less.'

'She loves me as I am,' grunted Conor. He lay back with a groan.

'Brecan's men, eh?' said Fergal, glancing back up the hill. 'We'll have to think of some way to return the favour.'

'Leave it alone for now,' said Conor. 'Their time will come.'

'Well,' said Fergal, 'let's get you back to camp and see what damage they've done you.' Together, he and Donal levered Conor up and onto his feet and, as they made to drape his arms around their necks, Conor gave out a shriek of pain and promptly vomited. 'It's that arm there,' said Fergal. 'It must be broken.'

'Wait till Liam learns about this,' sneered Donal. 'Bastard Brigantes.'

8

'It is your own fault. You had no right to speak in council. Perhaps this will teach you to keep your place.' Liam's tone was cool and critical.

'We can but hope,' allowed Conor. He lay on the ground outside his father's camp tent on a bed of river rushes overspread with an ox hide. His head ached. His ribs and shoulder hurt. His eye throbbed and his arm was hot to the touch; he feared it was broken. Fergal and Donal stood beside him, still seething at the Brigantes' treatment of their friend.

'What did you think would happen?' said Liam. 'He is a king, after all.'

'That is no reason to ambush a brother,' said Fergal.

Liam turned on him. 'Were you there? No? Then stay out of it.'

'We were there when they attacked him,' Donal pointed out. 'And lucky, too. They would have done worse if we hadn't put a stop to it.'

'See?' said Liam, appealing to his father. 'I said it was a mistake to bring them. I knew nothing good would come of it.'

Ardan waved aside the comment, but was no more inclined to sympathy than his battlechief. 'What made you think you could confront Lord Brecan before the council?'

'I thought,' groaned Conor through gritted teeth, 'that the

Oenach was where men of honour could meet to speak their minds without fear of reprisal.'

'You were wrong,' said Liam. 'You should have known better.'

'King or no,' said Fergal, 'it seems to me that Brecan has overreached himself.'

'What do you know about it?' demanded Liam.

'I know that sending three to attack one—and him unarmed—is unworthy of any man of honour.'

'Shameful,' concluded Donal.

'Well, thanks to your friend here'—Liam indicated the wretched Conor on his rough bed—'we've enough trouble now without you two stirring the pot.'

'Enough—all of you!' rumbled Ardan, growing weary of the bickering. 'We do not want a battle with the Brigantes over this. But I agree'—he nodded to Fergal—'Brecan has gone too far. I will bring the matter before the council tomorrow and demand an answer for it.'

'I fear that would be a mistake,' said Conor, rousing himself at last. 'Say nothing to anyone about this. We will keep this to ourselves.'

'But the attack was meant to silence you,' Fergal pointed out.

'Then we will be silent—and bide our time.' Conor appealed to his father. 'Brecan has many friends in the council. Go against him alone, and we can but fail. To challenge him properly, we will need the help of the other lords—or at least as many as can be made to see reason.'

His father considered this for a moment, then announced, 'Conor may be right. We will say nothing for now, but I will begin seeking among the other tribes for those who view Brecan's ambition as a threat to us all.' Ardan told his injured son to rest and recover his strength, then moved off to speak to Eamon and his ardféne.

'Fool,' sniffed Liam before taking his leave of Conor. 'This is your own fault. You poked your nose into the hornet's nest and got what you deserved.'

Liam stalked off, shaking his head at the stupidity of his brother. Fergal glared after him and Donal spat onto the ground. Conor saw their disapproval and said, 'That was frustration speaking just then,' Conor counselled. 'Liam doesn't mean half of what he says.'

'Ach, aye,' observed Donal, 'but it is the half he *does* mean that worries me, so it does.'

'He'll come around. But I am sorry to leave you to care for the horses on your own,' said Conor, quickly changing the subject. 'It means more work for you.'

'No matter,' replied Fergal, 'we won't be going up to the council anymore anyway.'

'At least,' added Donal, 'the animals welcome our company.' He gave Fergal a nudge. 'We'd best go and see to them.'

The two left him then, and Conor remained sprawled on his bed, hurt and dejected, watching his clansmen at their chores, but mostly just feeling aggrieved that his ill-considered confrontation had not only failed, but had landed him in such difficulty and discomfort. His father spoke to Cahir about his son's injuries, and the Coriondi lord sent his druid to see what could be done to ease Conor's pain and aid his healing.

The bard was an upright man, old as an oak stump and thin as a willow rod, with a hawk nose set in a narrow face framed by a scant fringe of snow-white hair, his druid tonsure long since eroded away by the years. He wore a thin cloak and long belted siarc the colour of autumn leaves on the turn, and breecs of the same material bound with leather laces to his spindly shanks; from his wrist dangled a heavy gold bracelet of the kind kings often give to champions and valued advi-

sors, and a slender torc of twisted silver hung around his
wattled throat. The old fellow carried a leather satchel, battered and bulging, on a strap around his shoulder, and a
small three-legged stool; a knife with a blade of black stone
was tucked into his belt. The druid arrived unannounced,
spoke briefly to Ardan, and then set to work. 'I am Mádoc.
How are you?'

'I am Conor, and I am as you see me.'

'Ach, well, hold still.' The bard seized Conor by the chin
and proceeded to inspect Conor's angrily swollen eye, damaged limbs, and bruised torso, prodding here and poking
there, making Conor flinch and grit his teeth. 'Are you spitting
blood?'

'Not so much,' replied Conor.

'Pissing blood?'

Conor shook his head. 'I don't think so.'

'Headaches?'

'Only where they cracked my skull.' Conor lifted his fingers to the lump on the back of his head.

The druid touched the lump lightly and shrugged. 'What
about those ribs?' he asked, pointing to the bruise spreading
across Conor's chest.

'It hurts if I breathe too hard.'

The druid nodded. 'Arm and ribs,' he mused, stroking his
long chin. 'Anything else?'

Conor thought for a moment. 'No.' He glanced at his swollen arm. 'How bad is it?'

'I've seen worse,' Mádoc concluded.

'Happy news.'

'Now be quiet while I treat you.' He rose and went to fetch
some supplies, returning a few moments later with a wooden
bowl of warm water and a small roll of clean white linen.
Then, perched on his stool, he drew from his leather satchel
bits of this and that; he wet a scrap of linen and began

carefully cleaning the bruise around Conor's eye. Next he bound the swollen mass with soft damp moss mixed with dried herbs of elderflower, camomile, and dandelion root. That finished, he turned to Conor's chest and arm.

'I do not like this.' Mádoc, holding the arm as if it were a length of kindling wood, lowered his head and sniffed the tissue.

'Is it broken, do you think?' asked Conor. 'You would tell me if it was.'

'If the bone was truly broken, you would not need me to tell you.' He placed a dry palm on the warm, flushed skin. 'Does it hurt very much?'

Conor winced at his touch. 'It burns with a vengeance.'

'That is probably for the best.'

'Well, I'm glad of that—for I would hate to think I was enduring this agony to no good purpose.'

'The bone has been deeply bruised, perhaps even cracked—likewise your ribs. Fortunately, your bones are young and not old and brittle or they would be in pieces. Still, I will bind your arm, but you must refrain from using it as much as possible.'

'For how long?'

'For as long as it takes.'

'Are you really a druid?' Conor asked.

The old man regarded him with a grudging look. 'I was an ollamh . . . once—a long time ago.'

'But not now?'

He shook his hoary head. 'I am my lord Cahir's chief advisor. That is all, and that is more than enough for an old man.'

'What happened? Why did you leave the Learned Brotherhood?'

'Not that it is any concern of yours,' replied the once-druid tartly, 'but I grew weary of the endless pomp and pageantry, and self-important preening—few nuggets of truth hidden in a mountain of empty ceremony and bluster—and all to maintain a feeble hold on their precious authority.' He made a sour face. 'Bah! You wouldn't understand.'

'More than you think,' Conor muttered.

The old ollamh gave him another canny look, and proceeded to wrap the injured forearm with strips of wet linen lined with shavings of willow bark; he then bound the entire limb to Conor's chest with more strips of linen to render the limb all but immobile. 'Tell me about what happened to you,' he said, tying off the binding strips. Conor gave a cursory account of the disagreement at the council and the subsequent attack by Brecan's men—and expressed the opinion that such things ought not happen between brothers of the sword and spear, and never at an Oenach.

'Hmph!' snorted Mádoc through his nose.

Nothing more was said, but Conor could tell the old man was deep in contemplation of what he had been told. Mádoc finished and rocked back on his stool, surveyed his handiwork, and pronounced himself satisfied with the result.

'That's it?' said Conor, regarding his arm with some misgiving. 'That's all you can do?'

'All?'

'What about my ribs?'

'You are young. You will heal.'

'A very prodigy of a physician,' sighed Conor.

'Just refrain from sudden movements. That means no fighting. In a few days, you will hardly notice the pain at all.'

'I thank you, Mádoc.' Conor relaxed and lay back once more. 'I am sure Lord Ardan will reward your good service.'

The old man inclined his white head in a slight bow, and said, 'A little information would be reward enough.'

'That is readily supplied. What would you like to know?'

'You claim that you were set upon by Brigantes warriors

for your impertinence in questioning King Brecan before the council.' Mádoc folded his hands and cocked his head to one side. 'Yes?'

'So it would seem,' Conor admitted. 'They were Brigantes at least.'

'Perhaps so,' allowed the druid. 'Yet my lord Cahir also questioned Brecan but was not set upon or attacked by anyone.'

'I am just unnaturally lucky.'

'What do you think it means?'

'Why ask me? I'm just a fool poking the hornet's nest.'

'Even so, here I am—asking you all the same,' replied Mádoc. 'What do you think it means?'

Conor paused to consider a moment, then said, 'I am thinking that Brecan intends to seize the high king's torc. See how he behaves—summoning everyone to a special Oenach so that he can lord it over all the others—up on his platform in his big chair and his arrogant druid looking on. And when we raise a matter of real concern—'

'The Scálda spies?'

'Just so,' said Conor with a sharp nod. 'When I try to alert the council to the danger, Brecan says it is of no consequence. Scálda spies! Of no consequence!' Conor's face contorted in a grimace; his outburst sent a stab of pain through his chest. 'Well, Brecan is jealous of anyone who might try to ruin his plans. That much is clear.'

Mádoc's glance grew keen. 'We have not had a high king in Eirlandia since Artuin mac Datho, and that was more than ten generations ago.'

'As long ago as that?' said Conor.

'At least.' Mádoc bent to his satchel and began putting away his medicines and herbs.

Conor sensed some hesitation in the old man's tone. 'But what?'

'Think you now,' replied Mádoc, his voice falling to a whisper, his tone sombre. 'Eirlandia has not faced a foe like the Scálda for ten generations, either.'

'And this alone gives Brecan the right?' Conor scoffed.

'Your words, son. Not mine.'

Conor stared at the white-haired man before him for a long moment, trying to decide what else he was withholding.

Mádoc seemed to read the trend of his thoughts. 'You took a beating and others did not. Think! What does this tell you?' A puzzled expression wheeled across Conor's face, but before he could reply, the bard lost patience. 'Bah! Life is not long enough to wait for you to blunder into an answer.'

'You speak to a fool—so everyone tells me—what do you expect?'

Mádoc sighed and shook his head. 'You saw something you were not supposed to see.'

'I saw only what everyone else saw up there. I saw—'

'Not *up there* . . .' The druid jerked his head in the direction of Tara's hilltop. 'Before—when you fought the Scálda spies.'

'Fergal and Donal saw them,' Conor replied, 'and Eamon, too—he was attacked and would have been killed.'

Mádoc shook his head wearily. 'Aye, to be sure. But they were not up on the platform confronting Brecan before the whole assembly. *You* were.'

'There is some hidden purpose here—is that what you mean?'

Mádoc nodded with satisfaction.

'But that's what I've been saying all along!' protested Conor.

'Ach, so now you have confirmation. You have the proof of your mistrust in the bruises you carry.'

Conor allowed that this might be so, and said, 'But I cannot see that this leads us anywhere.'

Mádoc laughed and shook his head. 'No, you would have to be a druid to see where this leads.'

'Can you? Can you see where it leads?'

Suddenly serious, Mádoc leaned forward. 'Do you trust me?'

Conor looked into the intense dark eyes. 'I trust you as much as I trust any man,' he answered truthfully.

'Hmph!' said the bard again. 'There speaks a suspicious man—a wary and skeptical man.'

'If so,' Conor observed, 'perhaps I have earned my suspicions.'

Mádoc regarded him for a moment and then smiled. 'Yes, by the purple bruises on your flesh, perhaps you have earned the right to your suspicions. Even so, if you will put at my command what little store of trust you still possess, we will undertake a work to lay bare Brecan's plans to usurp the high kingship. We will expose his schemes for all to see and thereby end them.'

He fixed Conor with a firm and steady gaze. 'Will you trust me, Conor mac Ardan?'

Unable to discern what he was being asked to do, Conor hesitated. 'I might . . . I suppose.'

'It will mean great hardship, and even greater peril. . . .'

Conor's brow creased in thought.

'And certain death if we are discovered.'

'Ach, well—that is alright then. And, here, I was afraid you were going to say that it might be dangerous.'

'Mock if you will,' Mádoc grumbled. 'But we must act swiftly.'

'How swiftly?'

'Even now—and hope that we are not already too late.' Mádoc's tone was grave and pitiless. 'Our lives may be forfeit, but Brecan must be stripped of power or he will become invincible—and all Eirlandia will pay the price.'

'Put like that,' mused Conor, 'a fella would have to be a fool to accept.'

'Aye.' Mádoc's faded eyes framed a grim smile. 'And you, my son, are the very fool for this chore.'

Aoife

Twice I should have died. Three times, if you count the day our ráth burned. I was among the few who escaped the flames. Alanna and Bradyn, my older sister and brother, did not. They were at work in the fields when the Scálda came. I never saw them again. We never said our farewells. My father, Deaglán, escaped with us, but was among the warriors who fought to defend our retreat. The last I saw of him was, sword in hand and shield on arm, embracing my mother and telling her to go and he would find us, but he never did.

The Scálda took everything. They came out of the south and ran over our lands. Like hornets spilled from a hive they came—killing and burning everything in their path. I do not believe they are men at all.

We fled north, my mother and me, along with the survivors of our tribe and those of other tribes of the south—there were Velabri, I know, also many Uterni, and maybe some others. I was but ten summers, and my view of the world was very different then. I thought our ráth the safest place in Eirlandia, and that our warriors were all mighty. I was wrong.

We walked many days, stopping here and there, but always moving on. Along the way, the survivors were taken in by other tribes. My mother and I found our way to the Darini because she thought she had some kin among them. On account of this, we were welcomed and slowly folded our lives into theirs. Dúnaird became our home.

Before the Scálda came, before flames and death filled all the land, I was learning to become a druid—a banfaíth, perhaps, a healer and singer for my people. I may have been only ten summers in the world, as I say, but already my fingers were skilled at the harp and pipe. My teacher was Tirnanon, who many thought the greatest ollamh in the land. Even now men say, 'His harp could calm the angry sea, and silence the singing stars.' And I was his best pupil, or so he said.

Since the king in our new home had no filidh or even an ovate to fill his hall with music, I was chosen be his harpist. Young as I was, I soon rose to become Chief of Song in Lord Ardan's ráth—but this only because there was no one else.

Ach, but I race ahead of my tale. In those first days, before I had even met the king or anyone else, my mother and I turned our hands to whatever chores needed doing. We fetched wood and water, helped the women render fat to make soap and candles, fed the goats and geese, and milked cows.

That was how I fell into peril the second time.

On that day when death again hovered at my shoulder, there were no flames of warning, no shouting or fighting, no spears or swords or blood poured out on the ground. I was helping to feed the cattle and paying but little heed to the animals in the pen. The bucket was heavy. I slipped and fell in the mud and my flailing drew the attention of a young bull. Too late I saw it. The creature charged with head lowered and sharp horns displayed. Unable to move, I screamed and closed my eyes.

When I opened them again three heartbeats later, there was Conor—standing between me and the bullock, arms outstretched, dodging from side to side and shouting rude insults at the beast in order to draw it away. The trick worked.

The animal chased Conor around the pen—I laugh to think of it now—until the young bull tired and men came to throw a halter around its thick black neck and lead it away.

Conor ran to lift me back onto my feet and we were friends from that moment, I think. We have been friends, and more, ever since. Indeed, over the next years we pledged our lives, each to the other, many times. So now, this autumn, at the Lughnasadh festival, we are to be married.

Yes, I have loved him that long.

* * * *

9

'Do you trust me, Conor mac Ardan?' the wily old druid asked. Why the question had been posed was still not apparent to Conor; the fact that it had been asked not once, but twice over, puzzled him greatly. And the question continued to pester him over the next two days as he limped around camp waiting for the Oenach to finish so they could all go home.

Conor himself would not go up to the council again—even if allowed. What would be the point? Showing his battered face at the gathering would only earn him another thumping—not that a beating would deter him necessarily, but what would be the point?

'It was a mistake to come here,' Fergal observed glumly as he refilled the bucket from the river that snaked along the edge of the wood and formed the boundary to Mag Coinnem, the council plain.

'We came to tend the horses,' Conor told him. 'We're tending them.'

'But that's *all* we do!' Fergal growled. 'You forget, we also came to see our part in the gift horses recognised and rewarded.'

'And there aren't even any dancing girls,' muttered Donal.

'Were we promised serving maids and dancers now?' Conor said.

Fergal set the bucket aside and began filling another. 'Ach, well, everything has gone rancid now anyway, and we are to leave tomorrow.'

This was news to Conor. 'How do you know? My father told you this?'

'Aye, he did. I asked him if he wanted us to bring any horses up to the council today. He just said he was not inclined to generosity.' Fergal picked up two overflowing buckets. 'As it is, we go home tomorrow and take our horses with us.'

'All but the best one,' said Conor, 'the one we gave Brecan.'

'Save the one we gave Brecan.' Fergal nodded to Donal and, buckets in hand, they started back to the picket line.

Conor limped after them. 'But the council ends tomorrow?'

'I did not say that,' replied Fergal. 'Ardan just said we are to be ready to leave in the morning.'

'What if the Oenach is not concluded?'

'How should I know?' replied Fergal. 'I'm just a stable boy now.'

Later, when Ardan and Liam and the ardféne returned to camp that evening, Conor hobbled to his father's tent and begged an audience. 'A word, Father, if you will.'

'How are you feeling, son? You seem to be moving about more freely.'

Conor acknowledged that this might be so. 'Mádoc tells me that I am young and will heal. I suppose we must trust to his wisdom in these things.' He paused and then said, 'I am hearing a rumour that we are leaving the Oenach.'

'Aye—unless something prevents us,' confirmed the king. 'I want to be far away from here by this time tomorrow.'

'Whether the Oenach is concluded or not?'

'This gathering has been for nothing,' complained Ardan;

he rubbed a hand across his face as if to wipe away the exasperation Conor saw there. 'Lord Brecan proposes an issue to be discussed, and this we attempt—only to be told in the end how we are to think and what we are to do.' He slouched into his camp chair. 'He treats the council as his personal retinue, and the Council Ring his private audience chamber. I am not his kitchen céile to be commanded. We are leaving.'

'Do you think that wise, my lord?' asked Conor. He moved to stand before his father.

'It's better than staying here and prancing to whatever tune Brecan decides to call next.' He slammed his hand against his knee. 'I will not stand by and watch that puffed-up cockerel strut about as if he owned the yard.' He regarded his son's anxious face. 'This troubles you?'

'What does Liam say?' said Conor.

'Liam agrees with me, to be sure. He is even now instructing the men to be ready to strike camp at daybreak. I would think you, above all men here, would approve—no? Just look at yourself, boy.'

'For a fact, I am most eager to put Tara beyond my sight,' Conor told him. 'Yet, it seems to me that leaving before the Oenach has ended will give Brecan an excuse to raise his hand to you.'

'He would not dare,' huffed Ardan. 'I am a king within my rights.'

'I think this puffed-up cockerel already dares a very great deal.' Conor touched his bruised eye lightly. 'And that with impunity. I think he would not hesitate to move against you. Who would stop him?'

Ardan exhaled heavily in frustration. 'Well, then . . . what? What would you advise?'

'Merely to behave as all the other lords. Give Brecan no

cause to suspect you or catch wind of your displeasure. See the Oenach through to the end and thereby remain blameless in the sight of your brother kings.'

'I will think about this and discuss it with Liam and Eamon.' He shook his head. 'Two good men injured because of this. What a mistake.'

Conor offered an awkward bow and took his leave. As he stepped to the entrance to the tent, his father looked up. 'Was there something else?'

'Only this,' replied Conor as a thought occurred to him. 'Fergal says we are to take the gift horses with us when we go.'

'Aye,' replied Ardan, 'I mean to keep them—unless you have a better idea.'

'Do keep them—all but one, and give that one to Cahir. A friend should be rewarded when he stands with you. And we need all the friends we can get.'

Ardan accepted the suggestion and told Conor to go and choose one of the animals for the Coriondi lord. 'Thank you, son,' said the king. 'You have given me sound advice and I will consider it—be certain of that.'

Liam and Eamon came in to attend the king, and Conor went out to choose from among the five remaining horses which to give away. He moved along the rope line, observing them one by one. He ran his hands over their coats and stroked their fine, strong flanks, speaking soft words to them. Having spent enough time with the animals, he thought he knew them and had a good idea of their respective temperaments, strengths, and likely weaknesses. The grey stallion was quick, but headstrong; the chestnut mare was biddable and smart, but a little thin in the hindquarters; the red roan was even-tempered and unexcitable, strong, but not among the swiftest; the brown stallion was young and spirited, and needed a good deal more training; and the larger tawny bay was steady on her feet, with good long legs and a deep chest.

After appraising each in turn, Conor decided that the larger bay would be best; a good gift, which would be gratefully received, and they would be saved having to train the beast. In any case, it was more the gift than the horse and he knew Cahir would be pleased. He explained his decision to Fergal and Donal, and asked them to make the tawny-coloured mare ready for presentation to the Coriondi lord, while he lay down to rest, exhausted by the exertions of the day.

The council lurched on for another day, and then Brecan announced that the time for talking was ended. He thanked the lords and their advisors and warriors for their good service and then said, 'As a token of the high value I place on the sage counsel of my brother kings, I would like to give you each a gift.' He gestured to his druid, Mog Ruith, who stepped forward with a small leather bag, which he placed in Brecan's outstretched palm. Then, one by one, he called the kings to him and, dipping into the bag, brought out a silver ring that he bestowed on the attending lord, saying, 'Let this be a sign of the loyalty and friendship between us and our people.'

When the rings had been dispensed, Brecan stood up from his chair and strode to the edge of the platform. He raised his hands above the gathered lords and said, 'I wish you all a safe and pleasant journey home, and a bounteous harvest. Farewell, brothers, until we meet again at the Samhain Oenach.'

The gathering broke up then, and the lords, eager to begin their homeward journeys, quickly dispersed—not all, it seemed, in the best humour. Some of the kings were heard to grumble as they departed the Hill of Summoning. 'He thanks us for our service?' muttered the Eridani lord. 'Are we his céile boys now?'

'He says he values our counsel?' said another. 'And is he making decisions now for everyone?'

'If that is the way of it,' muttered his companion, 'why were we even summoned?'

Conor sensed the undercurrent of rancour when his father and the ardféne returned much earlier than expected. He quickly learned the reason for everyone's irritation and went to his father, who was deep in conversation with Liam, Eamon, and some of the other lords. 'So now,' said Conor when his father and the other lords had moved on, 'did Brecan show his hand at last?'

'Nay, nay, he is too canny for that,' Ardan huffed. 'But he let us know we stood lower than himself in his eyes.'

'At least it is over,' Liam said. 'We won't have to suffer his arrogance any longer.'

'He gave out rings,' groused Eamon. 'Who is he to be dispensing silver trinkets as if he is celebrating a great conquest? He goes too far.'

'Does everyone feel this way?' asked Conor.

'They do not,' declared the king with some force. 'And that is a problem. Brecan's antics have won enough favour among the weaker lords to justify his grand view of himself.' He shook his head again. 'Silver rings . . . a gift for a sweetheart, or a child.'

They talked a while longer in this way and then, having exhausted a distasteful subject, Ardan turned to his son and said, 'Did you choose a horse for Cahir?'

'I did, my lord. I think the big bay mare will please him.'

'Well and good. I asked him and his ardféne to come to us tonight. We will share a cup and I will give him the horse then.'

'I wait upon your word.' Conor took his leave and went in

search of Fergal and Donal to tell them how the Oenach had ended, and to prepare the young bay for giving away—they combed and braided the mane and tail, and brushed the coat until it gleamed.

All was ready for Cahir and his men when they arrived. The sun had just doused itself in the western sea, sinking below the horizon in a blaze of crimson and gold when the doughty lord, accompanied by four warriors of his ardféne and his chief advisor, Mádoc, entered the camp. They were given good mead to drink, and Ardan did his best to create a buoyant and convivial atmosphere, but the simple celebration failed to kindle much by the way of mirth or warmth. No one, it seemed, possessed either heart or will for much merrymaking. Time and again, the talk turned back to wily Lord Brecan and his schemes. Even the presentation of the gift horse—which Ardan conducted with heartfelt sincerity—did little to lift the company's spirits. More mead was drunk, a little food taken, a song was sung, and the Coriandi departed with promises to return the favour one day soon.

The next morning, however, they returned. The Darini were busy striking camp and eager to be away when the Coriondi reappeared. With a woeful expression, Lord Cahir strode into the camp and brusquely asked to see Ardan, who greeted his friend and asked what was the matter—for, from the look on his face, there was clearly something wrong. 'I will tell you soon enough,' Cahir replied tersely. 'Though you will wish I had said nothing—I cannot keep silent.'

'Come aside with me and let us talk,' said Ardan. 'The difficulty, whatever it may be, will certainly yield when two unite against it.'

'Thank you, my friend,' replied Cahir, 'but what I have to say must be said in the hearing of all your men and these of my own.'

'Speak then, and have it out.' He told Eamon to summon

his ardféne to attend him. As soon as they were all gathered around, he said, 'Here now, what have you to say to us?'

Cahir drew a heavy breath and, looking around the tight circle of faces, said, 'You all know me to be a fair and honest man—at least that is my dearest hope—and I expect those I trust to be fair and honest with me. It is because of this that I come before you today.'

A hush settled upon the little gathering as everyone strained to hear what he would say next. Cahir allowed the silence to stretch a little longer, and then said, 'You, my friend, have a wicked thief in your camp.'

Ardan professed amazement at this revelation. 'This is a serious accusation,' he said. 'It cannot be one of my men that you suspect?'

'I wish it was someone else,' replied Cahir unhappily. 'With all my heart I wish it.'

'What has been stolen?'

At this, the Coriondi king looked to his chief advisor; Mádoc stepped forward and, holding up his bare arm, said, 'Three days ago at this time, I possessed a bracelet of gold—a token of honour I have worn for many years.'

'I think I know the item,' replied Ardan.

'As you can see, I wear it no more.' He turned this way and that to show he lacked the bracelet. 'My gold has been stolen from me.'

'I am grieved to hear it.' Ardan glanced around his retinue, and was met with blank, unswerving stares all around. 'But I cannot see why you think the absence of this cherished ornament can have anything to do with anyone here. Is there no mistake?'

'I would that it were otherwise,' allowed Mádoc judiciously, 'and yet, I think, there is one standing here among us who knows the answer to that.'

The former filidh turned and, extending a bony finger, intoned, 'Conor mac Ardan, I accuse you of theft, and call you to answer for your crime in the hearing of your brothers this day.' He thrust out his chin. 'What have you to say for yourself?'

10

Conor, his mind numb, the accusation still ringing in his ears, gaped at the old man before him. *Impossible! How could anyone think he was a thief?*

'Me?' was all he could think to say. The crimson patch on his face tingled with the shock and embarrassment. 'You point at *me*?'

Grim and gaunt, Mádoc fixed him with a pitiless stare. 'Yes, even you, Conor mac Ardan.'

'You accuse me of taking your bracelet?' Conor, his mouth suddenly dry, looked around to see every eye on him and not a few expressions as astonished as his own. Turning away from the accusing finger, he appealed directly to his father. 'My lord, I know nothing of this theft—if theft it be. On my life, I swear it.'

'Do *not* swear by anything you care to lose,' roared Mádoc. 'Do not do it!' Drawing himself up in his outrage, he cried, 'I accuse you and the charge will be proved. Before these witnesses, the accusation will stand.'

Conor, almost deafened by the roar of blood in his ears, heard himself say, 'Go on, then, prove it.'

Ardan stepped forward, interposing himself between the two. 'Let us not be overhasty. Before this matter goes any further, I think it only fair to remind everyone here that a heavy tribute will be exacted for a false accusation.' Looking squarely at Cahir, he said, 'Do you want to proceed, my lord?'

Cahir looked to his chief advisor, who, implacable in his outrage, merely nodded.

'Then so be it.' He gestured to the old man to continue.

'Rest assured, lord king, the proof you require is easily obtained.' Turning to Cahir, he said, 'Choose one of your men to assist me, and let King Ardan do the same. Then we will see what we will see.'

Cahir appointed one of his ardféne—a solid and thoughtful man—but before Ardan could choose, Eamon stepped forward and volunteered his services. 'Allow me, my lord,' he said, stepping forward, 'if no one has any objection.'

Ardan accepted both men, and looked to Conor for approval. 'I am content,' he said, still thinking that, since he had stolen nothing, nothing could go against him.

The two men stepped forward and stood together. And, Mádoc, satisfied that all was in order, said, 'Show me where you keep the cups and serving vessels.'

All the camp furniture and utensils had been stored away in wicker baskets to be loaded on the horses for the trip home. Among the baskets was one that contained the beakers and eating bowls, along with other small items. Eamon, who had supervised the packing, pointed out the basket and, at a nod from Mádoc, Cahir's man lifted it and carried it to where the company stood looking on.

'Empty it onto the ground,' commanded Mádoc, and this was done. The articles formed an untidy pile on the grass. Examining the heap from a little distance away, he said, 'That jar—there'—he pointed to a large pottery water jug—'pick it up and give it to him.' He pointed to Eamon.

The man bent down and, shoving aside a few bowls and cups, brought out the chosen jar and held it up, then passed it to Eamon. The movement produced a hollow, rattling sound. Eamon shook the jar and the unmistakable clatter told everyone that there was an object inside.

'Break it,' instructed Mádoc.

Eamon gave a little shrug and let the jug fall from his upraised hand. The earthen jar landed with a thud and cracked in three places. With his foot, he broke those pieces into smaller bits. A glint of gold flashed up from the shards of pottery in the grass.

'There!' cried the old man, pointing to the gleam of metal. 'Show me—and show the others. Let everyone here see what you have found.'

Eamon pushed aside the potsherds and retrieved a gold armlet. He took it between thumb and finger and held it high for all to see.

'That is my bracelet,' Mádoc said, his voice loud with condemnatory triumph. He directed Eamon to show it to Cahir, who confirmed that it was indeed the same ornament he had given to his advisor years ago.

The Darini looked at one another in amazement. King Ardan was not yet convinced. 'While I accept that this may be your property,' he allowed, 'and that someone must have put it there seems undeniable, it does not follow that that someone must have been Conor. Anyone might have packed that basket.'

'Indeed, my lord,' agreed Conor loudly, 'anyone at all.' He looked to Eamon for support, but both appeared wavering and doubtful.

'True enough,' replied Mádoc. 'Let me ask who then packed the basket?' He passed his gaze around the circle of onlookers. 'Hmm? The question is simple enough. Who among you packed that basket for leaving?'

No one made bold to answer; each either looked at his feet or at his neighbour. It was Eamon who broke the silence. In a voice of deep regret, he said, 'Sorry, Conor. The truth will be told in the end.' To Mádoc he said, 'I helped oversee the striking of camp. It was Conor who packed up the cups and bowls and such.'

Conor could not believe his ears. 'Eamon—what are you saying?'

'Silence, thief!' Mádoc snapped. To Eamon, he said, 'Did you see him with the jar?'

'I did,' replied the warrior with some reluctance. 'But I did not see him with the bracelet,' he added quickly.

'Did you not?' said Mádoc, his voice a sneer. 'Well, only a fool would let himself be seen with his stolen goods in his hands. He deceived you as he has sought to deceive everyone else.'

'Conor?' said Ardan, appealing to his son. 'What do you have to say to this?'

Staring at the incriminating evidence as if in a trance, Conor replied, 'What have I to say? Only this—how is it that Mádoc knew exactly where to look for that bracelet of his? It might have been hidden anywhere. How did he know it would be in that jar?'

'You ask this of a druid?' sniffed Mádoc.

'Former druid,' said Conor. He pointed to the armband. 'Let this *druid* tell, if he can, how this crime was accomplished, for I cannot.'

'That is easily told,' replied Mádoc. 'At my lord's request, I came to this camp to treat the injuries this man received at the hands of the Brigantes. Many here would have seen us together.' He flung out a hand in appeal to the company. 'As is my custom, I removed my gold in order to wash and bind his wounds. This I did—and it is beyond doubt that while I laboured, he took my bracelet for himself and hid it in the very jar I used to bathe him. In this way, my possession was stolen from me.' The old man's gaze was stern as he surveyed the unhappy faces around him. 'As you yourselves have witnessed, the crime is exposed and explained. I demand justice.'

'Conor,' said Ardan, looking to his son. 'The evidence of your crime demands an answer.'

'What can I say? If I protest my innocence, I risk adding the unjust charge of liar to my shame. But if I acknowledge guilt, then I am lying to myself—and that I will never do.'

Ardan stiffened at the words, yet his voice was steady as he turned to Mádoc and asked, 'What justice would you accept?'

'Nothing less than the full weight of the law,' sniffed the druid. 'I appeal to the Cáin Nuada.'

This caused a murmur among those present who knew something of the legal code set forth in the decree of King Nuada. 'That is a heavy weight to bear for a crime such as this,' Ardan said. 'Your ornament has been found and returned to you, the theft exposed and the thief humiliated. Perhaps this would suffice to satisfy you for the slight distress you have suffered.'

Mádoc drew himself full height. 'Never! Are we to believe you would tolerate a known thief to live among you as a companion of your hearth? Noblemen and warriors must forever remain above reproach.' The druid shook his grizzled head slowly. 'The crime is grave enough. That it was perpetrated by a trusted member of your retinue at an Oenach is cause enough for the full penalty to be rendered.'

Ardan, unwilling to accept the verdict, searched among the company for any to speak a word of mitigation for his son. But no one stepped forth. Therefore, with a heavy sigh and a heavier heart, he replied, 'Let it be as you say. What does the Cáin command?'

Mádoc turned to Lord Cahir and the two spoke briefly for a moment; then the king said, 'The accusation has been made and theft demonstrated. Though the thief has not confessed, his guilt is manifest—therefore the punishment is clear. The thief, when a member of a royal household, must be cast out of his ráth at once, and under pain of death not to return for three years from the date of his crime.'

Ardan put out a hand to his friend. 'You would have me make of my son an outcast?'

'The law is clear,' replied Mádoc gravely. 'He must be banished from the tribe.'

Conor, who had been listening to this with mounting disbelief and anger, could barely absorb what had just taken place—as if it were happening in a dream, or to some other hapless wretch. 'Outcast?' he whispered, feeling his birthmark tingle and burn as anger mounted. He turned in appeal to Eamon, still standing over the broken pottery; the elder warrior would not meet his gaze, but looked down at the ground instead.

'Come,' said Lord Cahir. 'It is hard enough—do not make it harder still with needless delay. The thing is best done swiftly.'

Ardan, seeing no way out of this predicament, drew a deep breath and addressed his son. 'Unless you can offer a better explanation for this crime, I have no other choice but to declare your guilt.'

Conor, rigid with anger, spat, 'I will not answer their lies, nor confess to something I did not do.'

His father shook his head sadly. 'I am sorry. It is out of my hands.'

'Father, I—'

Mádoc turned on him. 'Do not think to add to your disgrace with tears.'

'Tears!' shouted Conor, the blood-tinged birthmark throbbing with fire. 'How little you know me if you think an unjust accusation and excessive punishment will break me or reduce me to weeping. Though mountains fall upon me, I will not be crushed.'

'Conor mac Ardan, you have been found guilty of this crime in the judgement of your brothers,' said Lord Cahir, invoking the ancient law. 'You are forthwith cast out of the warband, and out of the ráth of your people.'

The Coriondi king turned to his friend to ratify the ruling. Ardan swallowed hard and, after a moment, said, 'Go where you will, my son. If you can find anyone to take you in, lodge there and serve in whatever way is given you. At the end of three years, return to us . . .' He lowered his head. '. . . . if life is left in you and you so desire.'

Full angry now—filled with righteous rage at the gross injustice perpetrated against him—Conor nevertheless held his temper in check. Mouth hard and jaw set, his ruby birthmark searing his cheek, he removed the sling from his arm, tossed it away, and, with some difficulty, strapped his sword to his side; he retrieved his shield, cloak, and spear and strode resolutely to the picket line of horses, and untied the first one on the line—the grey stallion.

'You cannot be taking a horse!' began Liam, starting forth. 'They belong to—'

Ardan threw an arm across the chest of his battlechief to restrain him. 'Let him have the beast,' said the king. 'It is the only help I can give him.'

With some little difficulty owing to his injuries, Conor clambered up onto the horse's back. He picked up the reins and paused to look his last upon those who had been his friends and family. 'I would bid you all farewell,' he called, his voice cracking, 'but for the injustice served me this day, the words would stick in my throat and choke me dead.'

With that, the outlaw wheeled his mount and rode west in the direction of the sea.

11

Stunned by the speed of his descent into exile, Conor rode for the coast. By the time he reached the plain, however, he had begun to impose a rough order on the chaos of his thoughts and feelings. That he had been made the victim of a colossal injustice was manifestly evident, but railing against it would not serve him now. Instead, he funnelled his energy into one paramount desire: to see Aoife one last time.

Thus, as soon as he was beyond sight of Tara's kingly mound, he pulled up hard and waited to see if anyone followed. 'Not to return on pain of death . . . ,' he muttered. 'Well, let them try to keep me away.'

The grey stallion chafed the ground with a forehoof, as if eager to be away. Conor's lips curved into a grim smile and he reached down to pat his mount's finely muscled shoulder. 'You're angry, too, aye?' He stroked the animal's gleaming coat. 'Then come, Búrach,' he said, naming his mount for the rage coursing through his veins at that moment, 'we're going home.'

He rode all day and most of the night, stopping only for water and to rest his mount and, occasionally, for Conor to ease the pain of his injured arm. Conor slept in fits and snatches—sheltering in a copse here, a spinney there—and pressed a reckless pace. The grey responded to all Conor asked of him, and more, and Conor's admiration of the beast grew with every hill and valley and stream ford they crossed. Owing to the speed of the horse, no less than to the determination of the rider, they completed the journey, riding through the gates of Dúnaird some little time before sunset on the third day.

Conor's clansmen were surprised to see him—mounted and alone, and battered as he was—they naturally feared that some disaster had befallen the king and his ardféne. Conor quickly assured them that all was well and that Ardan and his retinue would arrive in a day or two. 'I was sent ahead,' he explained simply, 'on account of my wounds, to bring word of the gathering and ready the king's welcome.'

Before he could say more, old Hano, one of the tribe's elders, pushed himself forward. 'So, you bring news, eh?' he called. 'Tell us, then, how went the Oenach?'

Conor offered a somewhat shaded account of what had taken place at the gathering. He told about catching the Scálda spies, the fight and capture of one of them; and gave a highly biased account of the overbearing Lord Brecan's odd behaviour; and he mentioned one or two other bits of more mundane business. He told them as much as he thought they would like to know—pointedly leaving out any mention of the incident that had led to his being branded a thief and forced into exile. Of that, he breathed not a word.

'Was there a fight, then, Conor?' asked another of the elders, indicating the young man's bruises.

'Aye, there was,' he replied, and related how he was attacked by Lord Brecan's men in reprisal for speaking above his rank at the council. He concluded, saying, 'If I never attend another Oenach, it will be all the same to me.' Conor promised to tell more later and then, glancing around the group but failing to find the one face he most wished to see, he asked, 'Where is Aoife?'

'Ach, I expect she is with that brown cow of hers,' replied one of the women as people began to disperse. 'It is calving any moment now, and she is that anxious over it. You'll find her in the byre, so you will.'

Conor thanked the woman and hurried off to see his beloved, threading his way along the narrow paths between lodges and dwellings to the small shed built up against the wall at the far side of the fortress. Ordinarily, the cattle remained in their pens outside the ráth, but sick animals or any requiring special care were brought to the birthing byre. On his way, Conor greeted all he met, saying it was good to be home and that no doubt he would have more to say tomorrow—all the while knowing that by tomorrow he must be far away from Dúnaird.

The sun was slanting low in the west as he approached the hut. He put his hand to the wattle door and paused to listen. Someone was speaking within . . . no, not speaking . . . singing. The voice was Aoife's, no mistake, and she was singing to the cow. Conor smiled and then he joined the song.

Aoife, startled, rose up on her knees and turned her head as he pushed open the door, letting in a flood of light that illuminated his lady in a golden glow. And, oh, his breath caught in his throat. She was so very lovely. How was he to live without her?

Conor fought down the lump in his throat and simply gazed, drinking in the sight of the dark-haired young woman he would soon be missing. This would be the last he saw of her for a very long time, and he wanted to remember her just this way: her shapely form wrapped in a simple green tunic held at her slender shoulder by a silver leaf casán—the brooch he had given her as a betrothal gift, a simple girdle of corded buckskin around her waist, her hair gathered in back to fall loose, bare feet tucked neatly under her long mantle. . . . It was an image to impel a bard to song.

'Conor!' she cried, jumping up. 'Is it you?'

'It is myself,' he said. 'I am back.'

'But I did not hear the sounding iron.'

'The others have not yet returned,' Conor said when they parted. 'Just me. I came on ahead. I could not wait one day more to see my love.' He moved into the shed. The cow lay on its side, the great swollen dome of its belly heaving with every breath. It rolled a big brown eye at his intrusion.

'Why did—?'

Conor silenced her question with a kiss. She moulded her body to his and returned the kiss with the ardour of the bride she hoped to be. Winding her arms around him, she gathered him in a lover's embrace, which promptly drew a sharp gasp of pain.

'But what is this?' Putting her hands to his chest, she pushed back and held him at arm's length, taking in his battered face for the first time. 'You're injured! My love, what happened?'

'There was a discussion,' he said. 'It is nothing.'

'It is *something*,' insisted Aoife, 'I never heard of any mere conversation leaving such bruises on flesh and bone.'

'Ach, well, you have never been to Tara of the Kings, I suppose. The discussions there are often conducted with fists and clubs. It is much the quickest way.'

Lifting a hand to his discoloured cheek and eye, she said, 'Does it hurt very much?'

'Now that I am here with you, I feel better already.'

She peered at him doubtfully, then embraced him again, gently, and led him into the byre. 'Sit with me and rest yourself,' she said. 'I will go fetch some mead and we will—'

'A moment, my love,' he said, 'come out and walk with me a little. I have that much to tell you.'

'But the calf—'

'The calf will wait a while yet. Come—' He held out his

good hand and took hers. They walked together into the last of the dying day's light.

He led her out through the small postern gate to the fields and pastures beyond the ráth's high timber wall. The air was soft, rustling the dry stalks of grain in the gentle evening breeze; the trees at the far end of the field were alive with the clack and chatter of rooks flocking to their night roost.

'What's wrong, Conor?' she asked.

'Should anything be wrong?'

'Aye,' she said, 'and can I not tell when something troubles this man of mine?' When he made no reply, she asked again, 'What is it? Tell me.'

'You know me well, Aoife,' he said after a moment. 'And you trust me, no?'

He heard in his own words those of Mádoc, who had asked him the same question not so many days ago: *Do you trust me?* Well, that was a trust misplaced.

'Trust you?' said Aoife. 'Only with my very life and the lives of our children yet to be born,' she said. 'But you know this—or should know it—without the need of asking.'

'But I do ask it,' he said, 'for I fear you shall soon have cause to doubt me.'

Aoife stopped walking. 'Conor mac Ardan,' she said gently. 'I have pledged my life to yours for good or ill a hundred times if once, and I will honour that pledge to the grave.' She searched his worried face as she said this. 'I only hope you will do the same for me.' Conor nodded, and lowered his eyes from the intensity of her gaze. 'What has happened, my love?'

'I have been exiled.' He did not mean to be so abrupt about it, but in the moment could not find a better way to say the hateful words.

Aoife's smooth brow creased in a frown of concern. 'I do not understand.'

'Nor do I,' he sighed. 'Nor do I.'

'Exiled . . .' She reached for his hand and pressed it hard as if to make better sense of the word. 'You mean outcast?'

'Just that,' he said, nodding, and then unwound for her the whole sorry tale—beginning with his rash challenge of the Brigantes king at the council, the beating he had endured because of it, how the druid Mádoc had tended his wounds—and then, two days later, accused him of stealing and hiding a valuable gold bracelet.

'He never did!'

'And this before my father and Lord Cahir and all the men. Everyone heard the accusation and, if that was not bad enough, they all saw the evidence of the crime as well.'

'But there is some other explanation,' Aoife insisted. 'There must be.'

'There is,' Conor assured her. 'But whatever that explanation may be, it lies beyond my reach. I know I did not take Mádoc's gold bauble, but I could in no way prove my innocence and nothing I could say made any difference. And so I am banished from the tribe. Not to return for three years. . . .'

'No!' Her hands flew to her mouth.

'I could not let you hear this from someone else. I had to see you and tell you myself.'

'Three years . . . ,' she said with a gasp, holding back the tears welling in her eyes.

'Even now I should be far away from here. I am forbidden from returning—on pain of death they said.'

Suddenly aghast, her eyes went wide. 'Conor, no—then we must leave at once! If they find you here—' She made as if to run.

Conor remained unmoved. 'I do not ask you to come away with me.'

'There is no asking. We will leave now—this instant,' she said, pushing away the tears with the heel of her hand. 'I will go and—'

'Aoife, no!'

His voice was sharp as a slap. She stared at him, dumb with shock.

'I know you would gladly share my portion—whatever that portion might be,' he said, gentle once more. 'But the next years will be hard years. I do not know if I can find a tribe to take me in. Many will not. Likely, *most* will not. And I refuse to make you an outlaw with every hand raised against you.'

'Together we would have a better chance,' she insisted. 'We would find a way. We would—'

Conor was already shaking his head. 'I could not protect you, Aoife,' he said gently. 'And I could not live if you suffered for this injustice. It is bad enough for me, but for you it would be worse. No one will look upon you with anything but scorn and contempt.'

'Think you, I care about that?' The defiance in her voice touched him and his heart lurched heavily in his chest.

'Maybe not,' he managed to say, 'but I know *I* could not live with it.'

'No more could I live without you here,' she said. 'So, if it is not to be here, then it will be somewhere else. I care not a whit what anyone might say.'

'But I care,' Conor told her. 'I could not bear to see how men will treat you when they think you are banished with me. With everyone assuming our guilt, we will be treated like lepers—wherever we go, worse than lepers. I can face my exile if I know that you are safe and well, and keeping the hearth flame alight for me.'

'What about *my* exile?' Aoife said, her voice trembling, 'I will be exile to all happiness and light. I will be exile to ease and pleasure. I will be exile to any thought or hope of peace—never knowing whether you live or lie dead in the ground.'

'You must endure your exile, then, even as I endure mine,'

replied Conor, cupping her face in his hand. 'Let us not each add to the misery by letting the other see our desolation and wretchedness.'

Aoife lowered her head in resignation, but said nothing.

'But I am not gone yet,' he said, moving his hand down her arm to take her hand. 'Let us spend one last night together and make a memory that will last until I return and we can marry.'

She nodded, squeezed his hand, and allowed herself to be led back to the ráth. They had no sooner closed and barred the postern gate when they heard the frenzied, insistent clanging of the sounding iron—a strip of solid metal used to announce the arrival of a visitor or sound the alarm.

Conor halted in midstep. 'Someone's coming.'

'What if it is your father and his warriors?' Aoife gasped. 'Oh, Conor! What if they have caught up to you?'

'I can't see how,' he said with a shake of his head. 'But maybe some of the others. Let's see.'

They hurried to the yard and arrived just in time to see a rider in a grey cloak and blue mantle gallop through the gate and into the yard. Conor, hiding behind a corner of the building, peered around the wall and saw the stranger rein up outside the hall. 'Can you see who it is?' whispered Aoife. 'Is it Liam or one of the warriors?'

'No . . . ,' Conor groaned and fell back against the timbered wall. 'I almost wish it was.'

'Who, then?'

Conor did not answer; instead, he drew a deep breath, pushed away from the wall, and stepped boldly out into the open. 'You!' he called. 'There will be no welcome here for *you*.'

'Conor!' The rider, stiff from his long ride, extricated himself somewhat awkwardly from the saddle and slid ungracefully to the ground. He stood for a moment kneading the muscles of his back. 'I am glad to find you.'

'What are you doing here, Mádoc?' demanded Conor, advancing with slow menace toward the old man.

Members of the clan, called by the iron, poured into the yard from all sides and warriors spilled out from the hall. They saw the druid and one of them, Iucar, an elder left in charge during the king's absence, made to welcome the distinguished visitor. 'Greetings in the name of King Ardan,' he called. 'Please, come and be—'

Mádoc waved aside the speech with a quick gesture of his hand and said, 'Your welcome is acknowledged and gratefully received. But the terrible urgency of my task prevents me from accepting. I cannot stay.'

The people quailed at this. Most, if not all, well remembered the last time a druid had appeared on horseback and had refused to stay.

Conor pushed forward. 'What do you want?' he demanded, his voice flat, uncompromising.

Mádoc turned and regarded him blankly across the distance—as if the answer was too obvious to require comment.

'I am waiting,' intoned Conor. 'And there is little now to prevent me from running my spear through your lying old guts—so answer and be quick about it. What are you doing here?'

Conor took another step nearer, bristling with anger. 'If you value your life, old man, speak!'

'What do I want?' The old bard blinked in confusion. 'You, Conor mac Ardan. I have come for you.'

Rónán

Today, I stood at the door of Rowan House and saw dawn's deft fingers tint the sky with red gold, and I thought, *This is my true home*, for I have lived in this place longer than any other I have known, and the people here are more kin to me now than any blood kin have ever been.

Twelve years have I laboured in the groves of wisdom and tilled the fields of song. I know the March of the Seasons and the Grand Procession of the Stars; I know the Braided Way, and I know the Law of Three, the Broad Arrow, the Cleansing of the Cauldron of Being. I can sing 'The Cycle of Lesser Tales' and play them on the harp.

I can read the signs of the wind and rain, and anticipate the ebb and flow of the sea; I can invoke the covering of clouds and mists; I can see three paces beyond the veil of time, hold a moment in my hand and release it according to my will. I can heal seven times nine diseases, set the broken bones of man and beast, and I know the preparation of potions for inducing sleep and wakefulness, love and aversion, for easing pain and causing death. What is known of faéry magic, I know—how to pierce their mystical deceptions and thwart their charms. I know how to identify faéry poison and the antidotes to each.

I know the Nine Sacred Names and the worship of the Ollathir, the All Father, he of the Swift Sure Hand, Champion of the Gods, and his consort, Mor Rioghain, Goddess of Sovereignty and Queen of the Gods. I know the invocation of Dagda, the Just and Good; the placation of Badb, Queen of the Shadow World; and the appeasement of Elathan, Brigitis, and Cromm Cruach, the Bent One.

I understand the meaning of the seven, and thrice holy nine, and the power of three and the mystical twelve. I know the eight stations of the wind and where the snow and rain resides. I know the location of the Isle of the Everliving, the Isle of Promise, and how to find Mag Mell and Emain Macha, and I know all the tribes and territories and provinces of our fair homeland in the Region of the Summer Stars.

All this, and so much more I know. I have mastered the learning set before me, and my toil has brought a bounty of fruit in due season. Now is the harvest time and at the next equinox, I will join the Learned Brotherhood. No longer an ovate, I will be a druid.

When I have received my robe and belt, my rod and sparán, I will be sent to the great school at Carn Dubh to continue my training in the discipline of my own choosing. A weighty matter that; it has occupied my mind these last three years. Many a night I have sat with Morien or Cabiri, my best friend. Both have advised me in their way, and I value their counsel above any other. Together we have searched the many paths open to me. 'Your playing on the harp and pipe is second to none,' Cabiri has told me. 'Perhaps it is a master of song and satire you should be.'

'A physician and master of elixirs is always in great demand,' Morien said one day. 'Not everyone is suited to it, but you are adept, Rónán. You have the healing touch.'

Another time, they said, 'You are unsettled. You want to help your tribe. Have you considered becoming a master at law? Maybe you should become a brehon.'

'Another few years and who knows?' Morien told me

recently. 'Uniting all your gifts and achievements you could become an ollamh.'

And so it goes. But even as they advise, they remind me that the choice must be mine and mine alone, for it will shape the rest of my life, and perhaps the lives of many—not least my tribe.

Until then, I continue my work here in Suídaur, teaching some of our newest residents—those of Willow House. They call me Rónán the Shrewd and think me a very head of wisdom. This is because they are very young and easily impressed. Even so, I tell them that once I was like them: anxious, frightened, knowing nothing but loss—the loss of home and kin, of all the things previously cherished.

'The world is far larger than what you have seen from the threshold of your mother's hut,' I tell them. 'Be patient and learn what is placed before you, and you will find that every man will be your brother and all creation will be your home.'

This, I truly believe.

12

'What were you thinking?' shouted Conor.

'I asked you to trust me,' Mádoc replied. 'You said you would.'

'Stupid old man! Have you any idea what your idiot meddling has cost me? Have you even the slightest notion what it means to be made a criminal and an outcast? Do you know what you've done?'

'If I had betrayed you, why would I have gone to all the trouble of saving you?'

'When was that?' snapped Conor. 'When did you save me? Was it when you accused me of stealing your precious bracelet? Or was it when you had me exiled? No? Maybe it was when you insisted on enforcing the punishment on pain of death? Was that you saving me? Enlighten me if you can.'

'I saved you tonight from your father's men,' explained the former druid wearily. 'They will arrive at Dúnaird this very night—perhaps they are riding through the gates even now.'

'Not so!' countered Conor. 'They couldn't possibly get there so fast.'

The druid made no reply. Conor, in exasperation, cried, 'Stop! I grow weary shouting at your back this whole time. I agreed to come with you and you agreed to explain. Well, here I am. Explain!'

Mádoc reined up and allowed Conor to come along beside

him. The two sat for a moment, listening to the far-off sigh of the waves on the shore carried on the sea breeze. After repeated appeals and warnings, and a hurried farewell kiss from Aoife, Conor had been persuaded to accompany Mádoc; the two had left Dúnaird just before sundown and had been riding ever since. Night was full upon them now as they worked their way south along the winding coastal path—slowly, lest the horses stumble in the dark.

'Liam and Eamon and one other left the Oenach only a short while after you departed,' said Mádoc, breaking the silence at last. 'I thought it safest to assume they made good speed, the three of them, and will soon arrive in Dúnaird if they are not there already.'

'You know this how?'

The druid sighed. 'I know because I was there when your father commanded them to go and not to spare the horses. It is my belief that, knowing you as he does, it was in his mind that you might try to return to see Aoife. He told Liam and Eamon that when they reached the ráth they were to bar the gates against you—that way they would not have to kill you. They could simply refuse entry to you. You father was trying to save you from yourself.'

'They would not have killed me,' Conor maintained, though with less conviction than he might have hoped.

Mádoc shook his head. 'If they had found you in the ráth they would have been duty bound to kill you because, friend and brother or king and lord, they would have had no other choice lest they take the punishment onto themselves—and likely Aoife as well for aiding you.'

'Hmph,' muttered Conor. 'If my father wanted to protect me, he might have done better to defend me against your false accusation. I never stole your gold and you know it. Outcast! Where am I to go? How am I to live? I could die out here—and probably will, thanks to you!'

'I did only what I had to do. I do not apologise for that.'

'Too late for apologies, old man,' Conor told him in a tone of ripest scorn. 'I ask you again—what were you thinking?'

Mádoc turned in the saddle and regarded him with a wounded expression. 'Conor mac Ardan, you amaze me. How can you not have seen instantly why I had to do what I did?'

'Not seen? Perhaps it is because being condemned before my brothers and made an exile to my own people slightly clouded my discernment. Or, then again, maybe it is because your plan—whatever it might be—is so cunning as to be obscure and incomprehensible to any and all but yourself alone.'

'Enough!' roared the old man. 'If you were not so blind-stubborn determined to nurse the full measure of your grievance you would see the danger staring you right in that stupid face of yours. Anyway, the fault is more yours than mine. You brought this on yourself.'

'My fault!' cried Conor. 'How is this my fault?'

'Your provocation of Lord Brecan gave me very little room to work. You alerted him to the possibility that his schemes might be vulnerable to discovery. The Oenach was about to end. There was no time—whatever I did had to be done swiftly and it had to be public—while the kings were still present to hear about your banishment, and spread the word. In short, you had to be removed.'

'You removed me, no mistake,' Conor snapped. 'However can I thank you?'

Ignoring him, Mádoc continued, 'With you out of the way, Brecan may just be satisfied that you are no longer a threat and he need trouble himself no further on your account. And you,' he concluded, 'you are now free to move at will throughout Eirlandia without anyone taking any notice of you or the least interest in your affairs.'

'That is a freedom I can well do without,' Conor countered. 'In your inscrutable wisdom, you have arranged it so that while I may be free to go where I will, I am constrained on every side. Outcasts are despised and rejected by all decent, right-thinking men. So now, though I can travel, I cannot go anywhere!'

Conor's voice resounded among the unseen rocks around them. The risen moon peered above the line of hills to the east, casting a thin light over the narrow trail. Conor saw the old bard awash in a silver, spectral gleam, his white hair like a fine mist floating around his head. The breeze soughed in the distant pines, and Conor shivered with a sudden chill. 'Are you truly insane now?' he asked quietly. 'To have thought that this was in any way a good idea, you must surely have lost your mind. Three years, Mádoc! Three years in exile before I can even think of returning home. I was to be married at Lughnasadh. You have ruined my life.'

'Ruined your life,' sneered Mádoc in a mincing voice. 'Listen to you. I will tell you about ruin, shall I? You whine about leaving home and your beloved Aoife, about marrying, about soiling your spotless honour. Let me tell you there is no honour in death and the dead do not marry. You mourn the loss of your home and your woman? If we fail to stop Brecan, you can forget about ever going home. Your home will be nothing but a mound of cold ashes. You can forget about Aoife, too—or perhaps visit her grave, *if* there is anything left of her to bury when the Scálda finish with her.'

'Stop it!' snarled Conor. 'Stop saying these things.'

'Today I merely say this,' Mádoc told him. 'Tomorrow it is real.'

Conor stared at the old druid. Silence stretched taut between them.

'Bah! Sooner teach a pig to play the pipes than teach you to see what stands naked and dancing before you.'

'What, then? What do I fail to see?'

'Did the beating you received from Brecan's men teach you nothing?' The horses jostled uneasily, anxious to be moving once more. Mádoc became insistent. 'Think! Why did they attack you?'

'We've already discussed this,' complained Conor.

'Tell me. I want to hear you say it.'

'They attacked me because Brecan is vanity itself stuffed into a pride-bloated skin. I questioned his integrity before his brother kings and made him look a fool,' answered Conor. 'That's why he had me beaten.'

'You may think you made him appear foolish,' replied Mádoc, his tone dripping scorn, 'but, in truth, I suspect the proud king was grateful for your ill-advised challenge.'

'A strange way to show gratitude,' Conor muttered.

'Aye, grateful—because your impudence concealed the real reason he wanted you silenced. Should anyone question what happened, they would merely think that you over-reached yourself and so Brecan's men decided to teach you a lesson.'

'That was reason enough for me.'

'Ach, just throw yourself in the sea and be done with it.'

Conor's brow lowered in thought. 'Brecan's real object was to keep anyone from prying into the presence of the spies so close to Tara?' he mused aloud. 'And that was why he was so indifferent to our capture of the Scálda spy. Brecan made small of our discovery in order to allay concern. But I would not let the matter rest.'

'Finally,' sighed Mádoc. 'Now ask yourself this—what if the Oenach itself was not the reason for the summons?'

Conor stared hard into the darkness as if he might somehow penetrate this mystery by force of will. 'Brecan merely wanted to lord it over us—to make everyone jump to his command. What other reason could there be?'

'Think!' Mádoc's voice was quick and sharp as a slap.

'I *am* thinking—but you talk in riddles and who can—'

'You, Conor mac Ardan, stumbled over it when we first met. How have you forgotten?' The druid waited for him to arrive at the answer and then, losing patience, lifted the reins and urged his restless mount to walk on, leaving Conor in frustrated silence.

'Wait!' Conor called, thought for a moment, then followed, reining up beside his prickly companion. 'So, tell me—what did I say?'

When Mádoc did not deign to reply, he said, 'We were talking about Brecan and . . . Nay, you asked me what I thought and I said . . .'

'Aye, I did, and what did you say?'

Conor cast his mind back to that conversation. The druid had just finished binding his arm and asked for information: He wanted to know why had Brecan commanded his men to silence Conor. What did it mean?

'You asked what was meant by Brecan's men attacking me,' answered Conor as the memory came back to him, 'and I said I thought it was because Brecan had eyes on a high king's torc—and you agreed. You said we had to expose his schemes and end them. You said Brecan had to be stripped of his power, or else—'

'Or else what?'

'Or else,' replied Conor, recalling the words exactly, 'he would become invincible. . . .'

'Aye, to be sure. And how would he do that?' asked Mádoc.

'I don't know,' Conor said. 'Anyway, the other kings would never allow it. They would unite in their outrage and rebel against him. They would resist.'

'If you say so,' granted the druid.

'The other kings would never acknowledge Brecan's sovereignty. Even with the backing of his client kings, he could not stand before the combined forces of the other lords.'

'Well, you know best.'

'The kings would never allow it,' he insisted, loudly, 'unless they were forced to it. . . .'

Invincible! The word broke fresh upon him as a new and terrible vision formed in his head: Brecan as high king with the help of the Scálda.

Conor pulled hard on the reins, bringing Búrach to a halt. Mádoc's warning of only moments ago took on an ominous cast . . . *If we fail to stop Brecan, you can forget about ever going home. Your home will be nothing but a mound of cold ashes. You can forget about Aoife, too—or perhaps visit her grave, if there is anything left of her to bury when the Scálda finish with her.*

'That is why the kings were summoned to the gathering'— Conor whispered the words to himself as the meaning came clear—'to allow the spies freedom to move about the land.'

Conor flicked the reins, urging his mount to close the distance between himself and Mádoc once more. 'Brecan in league with the Scálda,' he said, still trying to fathom that possibility. 'With the support of the enemy, he can claim the throne—is that what you mean?'

The old bard nodded. 'A thought we will keep to ourselves.'

'We cannot let that happen,' Conor told him, his voice charged with alarm. 'We have to stop him.'

Mádoc returned a thin, mirthless smile. 'You got there at last. There may be hope for you yet.'

* * * *

13

Sunrise found the two riders approaching the edge of a dense woodland many miles inland and south of Dúnaird. Exhausted from lack of sleep—as well as all that had happened to him and all he had learned in the last few days—Conor dozed, slumped over, reeling on the back of his horse. From somewhere far away, he heard someone whispering his name. He roused himself enough to lift his head and realised Mádoc was calling him. Búrach plodded to a stop, and Conor looked blearily around to see Mádoc a few hundred paces behind; he was studying the dark line of trees rising before them in the near distance.

'What so?' asked Conor, stifling a yawn.

Mádoc made no answer, so Conor asked again.

'Shh!' hissed Mádoc. 'Listen.'

Conor paused, but his weary ears heard only the whisper of the western breeze sifting the broom and long grass along the track, and somewhere, far away, three dull clicks—the sound of two sticks struck together . . . a pause, and the sound repeated.

'Ah!' said Mádoc with satisfaction. 'There it is.'

'What was that?'

'The signal. All is well. We may proceed.'

Conor, tired as he was, did not question any of this as he surely would have if not aching to remove himself from his mount, lie down, close his eyes, and forget the last few days had ever happened. Mádoc, who seemed impervious to fatigue, picked up his reins and rode on. Conor allowed him to pass, and then followed listlessly, returning to his dozy, slumping sleep. As they drew nearer the tree line, Mádoc stopped again; the aged ollamh reached out, took hold of Búrach's bridle, and pulled the grey to a halt. Conor felt the horse stop and woke again in time to see a pale flicker of movement on the trail ahead.

'Mádoc!' he whispered. 'Someone's lurking in there.'

Mádoc regarded him with a curious glance. 'I should hope so. That will be our céile.'

'We have a servant?' said Conor.

'We do.'

They rode on until the trail entered the wood and, as the canopy of branches closed over them, a slender boy stepped from the shadows. No more than nine or ten summers old, with large dark soulful eyes that looked out beneath a wild thatch of black hair—more like the feathers of a flustered bird than the locks of a well-groomed child—he appeared at once innocent of all experience and wise beyond his years. He was dressed in a simple yellow tunic and breecs, and very tall, slightly oversized brócs that had obviously been made for a bigger boy. He neither smiled nor offered any greeting.

Conor acknowledged the boy with a silent open-palmed salute, which the boy returned. 'This is Huw,' said Mádoc. 'He will tend the horses and camp.'

'Greetings, Huw. I am Conor.' The dark-haired boy regarded him with an open, interested stare, but made no attempt to reply. 'Not one for simple courtesy, I take it?' sniffed Conor.

'He is deaf and mute,' said Mádoc. Throwing down the reins, he slid from his mount and stretched the ache from his back and legs. 'And even if he could hear and speak, he would not likely understand you. He's Cymry.'

'Cymry, eh?' Conor mused. Their cousins across the Narrow Sea were odd, and perversely difficult to understand. As the boy moved to take the bridle of Conor's mount, a black pony emerged from the shadows—one of the mean-tempered, stubborn little half-wild beasts that roamed the rugged, cloudbound Cymru hills of western Albion. Stout, stub-legged, and spiteful the animals were; in Conor's opinion they were not worth the trouble it took to keep them.

Huw grabbed the bridle and Conor dismounted; he took a moment to knead the muscles of his shoulders and massage his injured arm, wishing now that he had not thrown away the sling quite so hastily.

'Here, let me look at you,' said Mádoc, stepping before him. He took Conor's arm and gingerly applied his fingertips to the wound, pressing it gently, and then gazed into Conor's bruised eye for a moment and felt the bruise there, too.

'Well?' asked Conor when he finished.

'You'll live,' he said, turning away.

'Where are we?' Conor gazed around, recognising nothing. The wood looked strange and, having dozed, he had no firm idea how far they had travelled.

Mádoc did not deign to reply, but made a series of motions with his hands, and Huw turned and led them off the trail and through the trees where, after a short walk, they came to a clearing—little more than a wide place among the trees—in the centre of which stood an earthen mound of the sort used by charcoal makers. Next to the mound was a round leather tent, and before the tent a stone-lined fire ring with glowing coals ready to be kindled, a brass basin of water, and fleeces spread upon the ground. Conor stood, reeling on his feet as he looked around.

'Leave the horses,' Mádoc said, joining him. 'Huw will take care of them.'

A grateful Conor smiled and nodded his thanks, then staggered to the nearest sheepskin and collapsed. When he opened his eyes a few moments later, the sun was full up and filling the dell with warm midday light. A fire blazed and stew bubbled away in a black caldron at the edge of the fire ring. Someone was humming nearby and, across the clearing, Huw had stretched a picket line between two trees and was hauling water to the horses in a leather pail.

Conor sat up and turned his head in time to see Mádoc deposit the quartered carcass of a skinned hare into the murmuring cauldron. 'That smells good,' he said, his voice dry and cracking slightly.

'Greetings and good day to you,' said Mádoc, interrupting his song. 'This will suffice until we get something better.' He cocked an eye at Conor. 'When was the last time you ate anything?'

'I don't know—yesterday or the day before.' Conor yawned and kicked off the rough woollen cloak someone had thrown over him; he stood and stretched, then winced as he overstressed his injured ribs.

'Well, that will not do,' Mádoc told him. 'From now on we eat whenever we can, for we never know when the next meal will come.'

'I won't argue with that.' Conor looked around the camp. 'Are we staying here, then?'

'Only one more night. You can use the rest and another day to heal. We will move along tomorrow morning . . .' He paused and added, 'One way or another.'

Conor heard the slight hesitation. 'Why? What are you expecting?'

'Perhaps nothing.'

Conor rolled his eyes and shuffled from the camp. He

walked a short distance into the wood to relieve himself, and then went to find the little willow-lined stream where Huw was drawing water. He shed his clothes and waded into the chilly water, washed himself, and then climbed back onto the grassy bank to sit in a patch of sun to dry. Every now and then a nearby willow would shed a leaf that would spin down to alight on the water and be swept away by the smooth-flowing stream.

That is me, he thought, *a leaf spun round and carried off to who knows where. . . .*

Was there any moment in the last many days that he might have pulled himself from the flow—a moment he might have stepped out of the relentless race of onrushing events? If there had been such a time, it had passed without causing so much as a ripple. And it was far too late for such thoughts now. 'Three years!' he sighed, throwing back his head. He was already missing Aoife, missing his swordbrothers—and this was just the first day. How was he to endure the thousand to follow?

Suddenly aware that he was being watched, he sat up and glanced quickly around to see Huw standing behind him, holding a cloth bundle and regarding him with a curious gaze. Conor lifted his hand and beckoned the servant to continue with his chores. 'Do not mind me, boy,' he said, knowing the lad could not hear him. 'I'm just sitting here feeling sorry for myself.'

Huw stepped nearer, unfolded the cloth, and produced a clay bowl, a pair of scissors, a knob of green soap, and a razor. He smiled shyly, and placed these items on the grass beside Conor. 'Is Mádoc trying to tell me something?' he said. The boy ducked his head and hurried away. Cheered by the druid's thoughtfulness, Conor spent what was left of the morning bathing, shaving, and trimming his moustache; he returned to camp a much better man than had left it.

The stew was not yet ready, so he went to the picket line to spend some time with the horses. He pulled up a handful of sweet grass, tied it in a knot, and offered it to Búrach, pressing his face against the splendid grey's head while the horse nuzzled his hand. Conor offered him another knot of grass and while the animal ate, he stroked the long neck and shoulders, whispering in low, gentle tones, telling him what a handsome, strong creature he was and how much he valued his strength and grace and endurance. Next, Conor examined the legs and hooves, checking for any sores or injuries, then inspected the creature's body from head to tail and saw that Huw had rubbed Búrach's coat and combed his mane; he appeared well fed and watered. With a final affectionate pat on the rump, Conor moved on to Mádoc's mount—realising for the first time that it was the gift horse he had chosen for King Cahir: the big bay mare. With a coat of deep brown with a black mane and tail, it was a sturdy, dependable animal—a good choice, as it turned out, for their purpose. 'Has Mádoc given you a name, my girl?' he said softly, looking into her big, liquid eye. 'No? Well, then, I will call you Drenn—for you are surely a stout friend.' He repeated his examination of the horse, pausing to feed it a knot of grass before moving to the pony. The testy little beast nipped him on the hand, so Conor left it alone, saying, 'Just for that, I will call you Íogmar. Maybe then you will think twice before biting the hand that feeds you.' Conor concluded his inspection and decided that young Huw had done his work well. Satisfied that the animals were in good hands, he returned to the fire to wait for the stew.

Mádoc sat on a low three-legged stool with a bowl of brown batter between his knees. 'All in order?' he asked as Conor resumed his place cross-legged on the sheepskin.

'Take care of your horse, and he will take care of you,' Conor replied, watching the old man pinch off a small lump and slap it back and forth between his palms to form the dough into a flat patty that he gently placed on one of the hot rocks of the fire ring.

'Bairgen,' Mádoc told him, indicating the little loaves. 'Small bread.'

'Small is better than nothing,' Conor replied. 'I didn't know druids could cook.'

'In druid schools where there are few céile,' Mádoc told him, 'the young ovates must all lend a hand in the cookhouse. We quickly learn the ways of pot and fire.' He regarded Conor with eyebrow raised. 'Have *you* ever cooked anything?'

'Aye, once or twice,' Conor replied. 'I wouldn't starve, anyway.'

Mádoc snorted through his nose and continued moulding the little round loaves. He finished and set the bowl aside; from another bowl he took up a handful of leafy herbs, tearing them deftly between his fingers and dropping them into the steaming pot.

Conor yawned and lay back on his elbows. After a moment, he said, 'So now, if we believe Brecan has made a pact with the Scálda, how are we to prove it? And, assuming we can find this proof, what are we to do with it?'

Mádoc pushed out his lower lip and stirred the stew with a long stick. 'The last part is the easiest,' he said at last. 'We will take our evidence to the Ard Airechtas.'

Conor repeated the name; it meant nothing to him. 'Who is that?'

'Not a who—a group,' corrected Mádoc. 'It is the Oenach of bards, you might say. The high and noble gathering brings druids from all the tribes and clans of Eirlandia. Every kingdom is represented and all bards are bound by its decisions.'

'So we take our proof to this druid gathering,' mused Conor. 'What happens then?'

Mádoc lifted his bony shoulders. 'Who knows? Who can

say what they will decide? But whatever their judgement, it will become law throughout the land—and all must obey. The Learned Brotherhood will see to that. But, as you ask, if presented with compelling evidence of Brecan's treachery, I expect the members of the Airechtas would see the danger and act accordingly.'

Conor mulled over this eventuality and shook his head slowly. 'I cannot see that grasping traitor accepting any decision that would thwart his plans. He would simply ignore whatever the druids said and go his own way.'

Mádoc's hand ceased its circular motion over the pot. 'He would not dare.'

'What would stop him?'

Mádoc cocked his head to one side and regarded Conor with curious disbelief. 'Where do you think the power of a king derives? Where does his sovereignty reside?'

Conor shrugged. 'In the point of his spear? In the might of his arm or strength of his warband?'

'Ha!' scoffed Mádoc. 'Spoken like an ignorant warrior.'

'Why do I even bother?' huffed Conor, slouching back on his fleece.

Mádoc went back to stirring the stew. 'Listen, then, if you would know. The power of kingship resides in the word of the druids. See here, it was long ago decided that sovereignty was far too potent an elixir to be left in the cups of individual noblemen, so it was given to the bards for safekeeping. We who are not beholden to any lord or king, and who are ourselves excluded from kingship, are the caretakers of sovereign power. Thus, the Learned Brotherhood alone has the authority to raise a lord to kingship,' he concluded. 'Or, equally, to depose him should the need arise.'

'The people choose their kings,' replied Conor. 'Each tribe chooses the man best suited to wear the torc.'

Mádoc shook his head.

'That is how my father was chosen,' Conor told him. 'I know. I was there.'

'The tribes may raise up the man they choose,' Mádoc replied, 'but the choice must be confirmed by the bards, who can either grant or deny the choice. Most often, they grant it. Only rarely do they take it away once it has been given.' The old druid looked at Conor as the young man turned this over in his mind. 'Were you raised by goats that you do not know this?'

'Our tribe had no druid to instruct us in the obscure ways of your learned clan,' Conor said.

'That is no excuse at all.'

'Anyway, it seems to me that kings behave however they will—regardless of whatever the bards might say.'

Mádoc simply sighed and shook his head. 'You have so very much to learn—I wonder if you should live long enough.'

Conor, annoyed by the turn of the conversation, bit his tongue. He lay back and stared up at the patch of blue sky he could see through the trees overhead. When he tired of that, he rose and left the camp, following the trail to the edge of the wood where he stood gazing out at the green hills to the west. Cupping a hand to his eyes, he scanned the empty hills where, after a cursory sweep of the horizon, he turned his face to the sun and felt its warmth wash over him. He stood for a while, bathing in the light, and then returned to camp. As he turned, however, he caught a glimpse of movement. He stopped and scanned the hills again—and saw a somewhat mottled shape moving on the track, still far off.

Instinctively, he stepped aside, melting into the shadows. He watched, holding his breath, and soon discerned that two riders—armed with spears and bearing shields on their backs—were definitely coming toward the wood. Conor turned and hurried back to where Mádoc was tossing little bread loaves into a straw basket. Huw emerged from the tent with a stack of wooden bowls and a spoon.

'Someone's coming!' Conor announced. 'Two men on horseback—armed. They're still some way off, but they'll be here soon enough.'

Mádoc received this news calmly—so calmly, in fact, that Conor repeated the message and said, 'What are we going to do?'

'What do you want to do?'

'We should hide.'

'Good idea, son. You go hide.'

Conor rolled his eyes. 'What do *you* mean to do?'

'Invite them to eat with us.'

'But, we don't—' began Conor. 'They might be—'

'Everyone must eat,' Mádoc intoned, 'weary travellers most of all. And we have more than enough to share.' He made a sign to Huw and the boy ducked back into the tent to retrieve more bowls.

'Well,' decided Conor, 'they may not be after your head, but I value mine.' So saying, he disappeared into the wood.

Mádoc watched him go, then gave a smile, and took the bowls from Huw and placed them on the ground beside him. Soon, he heard the sound of horses on the trail and the voices of the riders as they conversed along the way. He rose and followed the track to the edge of the wood to greet the strangers.

Conor, from his hiding place down among the bracken at the edge of the camp, saw Mádoc leave and, after what seemed an interminable interval, he heard voices and, in a moment there appeared in the glade two exhausted riders leading tired mounts, and Mádoc chatting easily to them.

Conor climbed to his feet and emerged from his hiding place.

'There you are!' called one of the visitors.

'Were you hiding from us, then?' said the other, and both men laughed.

'Very funny, I am sure,' replied Conor. Nevertheless, he smiled and hurried to embrace his friends. 'Fergal . . . Donal, glad as I am to see you,' he said, gripping them each in turn with his good hand, 'I must ask how do you come to be here?'

'Well, we all know how much trouble you can stir up when left to yourself,' replied Fergal. 'So we've come to guide you in the straight path.'

Conor, amazed and gratified, gazed into the faces of his friends and said, 'But how did you know where to find me?'

'Mádoc here made it clear enough before he left us at the Oenach where a body might search if they were looking to find someone.'

Mádoc beamed with pleasure at the reunion. Conor said, 'You knew they were coming! Why didn't you tell me?'

'I did not know,' replied the old man simply. 'I merely mentioned in passing where I was going and that I would remain here for a day or so should anyone choose to join me.'

'We had no idea what he meant by that,' said Donal, 'but marked that he said it, so we did.'

'But when we got back to Dúnaird and heard that you and Mádoc had been there together,' said Fergal, 'well, we guessed what had happened and decided to see if we could find you.'

Conor shook his head at his friends, revelling in their trust and loyalty. 'How did you convince Liam to let you leave?'

'We just told him we were going hunting.'

'We maybe forgot to mention we were hunting for *you*,' added Donal.

'And he let you take Ossin and Grían?' said Conor, indicating the horses.

'They have names now?'

'They *all* have names.' Conor pointed to the Fergal's roan stallion and said, 'That is Grían. And Donal's fine black-legged dun is Ossin.' Turning back, he added, 'I cannot think the king would let you have two of his best for an errand such as this.'

'Ach, now, Donal did not think to ask him.'

'And why would I?' replied Donal, 'when I thought it was *you* that asked him.'

Fergal gave a fishy smile. 'The way I see it, Liam did not say we *couldn't* take them.'

The two laughed then, but stopped when Conor said, 'You won't be able to go back, you know. Not after they realise what you've done.'

'As to that,' replied Donal, 'there will be no joy in Ardan's hall until you return.'

'We might as well stay with you now that we're here,' said Fergal, 'the better to make sure you get home in one piece.' He smiled and then, digging into the sparán at his belt, he brought out a scrap of cloth. 'Your lady said to give you this if we happened to find you.'

Conor took the scrap and unwrapped it to reveal a silver leaf casán—the brooch he had given Aoife to seal their betrothal. He glanced a question to Fergal, who merely shrugged as much to say, *Women, eh? Who can guess what they're thinking?*

'Thank you, brothers,' said Conor, putting his good arm awkwardly around their shoulders. 'It is more than I deserve.'

'You're right there, so you are,' agreed Donal with a grin. He looked to the fire ring where Huw was just then lifting the cauldron from the coals. 'See now, that smells good. When do we eat?'

14

The weather changed during the night and they woke the next morning to heavy grey clouds. By the time they had broken fast and struck camp, rain had begun leaking from the swollen sky. The dense woodland through which they travelled offered some slight protection, but as the day wore on, the rain increased. By midday they were soaked to the bone. Wet and weary, they stopped early to make camp for the night and built a big fire beneath an old oak in the hopes of drying out a bit. Rain continued through the night, however, and by morning they were as cold and wet as ever. Nor did things improve much over the next few days.

Braving blusters of wind and gusts of rain, wrapped in their wool cloaks or beneath their fleeces and shivering in silent misery, they pushed ever southward—through lands of tribes they knew and into those of tribes known only by name. They passed through open heathland thick with gorse and broom, and forests of oak, larch, or ash, skirting peat bogs and marshes, and pausing only to rest the horses or hunt when opportunity arose.

At some of the settlements they were welcomed, their animals fed and watered, and, in exchange for the news they brought, the travellers were treated to a good meal and a dry place to sleep. But, the farther south they pushed, the more unfamiliar the land became, the holdings fewer, meaner, and less welcoming—sometimes only offering food for them and water for their animals. They crossed many rivers, the names of which they could only guess; they traversed grain fields ripening to the harvest, and sometimes saw farmers, but any approach or attempt to converse proved futile. At first sight of the travelling party, the locals fled.

'Can they not see we mean them no harm?' asked Fergal, watching a group of field hands scurrying for the safety of a nearby beech wood. Having caught a glimpse of the warriors at the far end of the field, they fled.

'They have learned to fear strangers,' Mádoc observed morosely. 'Nor can I blame them.'

'Are we that close to the Scálda territories, then?' asked Donal, who, having left behind familiar lands, now had only the haziest notion of where they were or how far they had travelled.

'Aye,' replied Mádoc, 'we are that close.' He raised a hand to indicate the cloud-veiled hillscape looming across the wide valley sloping away before them. 'At my best recollection, that ridge on the far side of the valley marks the border, and after that the lands the Scálda have stolen.'

'You don't know?' asked Conor, his voice betraying a touch of irritation. 'We've come all this way and you don't know where we're going?'

Mádoc merely shook his head. 'When was the last time you were here, eh? Where we're going no Dé Danann has been for a very long time.'

Dark clouds roiled low in the southern sky, and the wind sighed mournfully through the damp-leafed copse around about. Conor regarded the long, undulating line of the ridge as if it marked a foreign land. For, though the Scálda mounted raiding parties deep into northern territories—mostly during spring and summer—the rest of the time they more or less confined themselves to the south, ever increasing their strongholds and settlements. It was as Mádoc said: after the coming of the Black Ships, no one Conor knew had ever been farther south than that dark line of hills looming in the distance. Within his own memory, the southland had become a place untravelled and unknown.

The ollamh turned to the warriors ranged behind him. 'Once we cross the valley, there will be no turning back.'

'Turning back, is it?' enquired Fergal. 'We didn't come all this way for turning back.' He turned his gaze back toward the distant ridge. 'Still, a fella could wish we didn't have to go there at all.'

'Ach, and why *are* we going there anyway?' asked Donal.

'Did Mádoc not tell you?' Conor could see by the look on Donal's broad face that he had no idea. 'You mean to say you've been travelling all this time without any hint of where we were going or why?'

Donal shook his head. 'Mádoc said Conor needed help.' He shrugged. 'That was enough for me, so it was.'

'And me,' said Fergal, 'Donal promised there would be ale and dancing girls.'

Conor laughed and shook his head, breaking the gloomy mood that had settled over him. Reaching out a hand, he gripped Donal by the arm. 'Brothers, if I had a thousand more like you, there would be no Scálda left in Eirlandia.'

'Why *are* we going?' wondered Donal.

'Tell them, Mádoc,' Conor said. 'They should know.'

'We go to learn whatever can be discovered of the enemy's strength, their numbers, how they marshal their forces, how they build their strongholds and fortresses, the number and location of their settlements, where they harbour their ships—anything could help us build an advantage for the battles to come.'

Hearing this, Conor gave Mádoc a sharp glance, and started to object. But, Mádoc cut off his interruption. 'Getting all that will not be easy, mind. From now on we move at night,' he continued, ignoring Conor's lowering brow, 'the better to avoid unfriendly eyes. We must go quietly, with all care, and observe and remember all we can.' He looked around the copse. 'We might as well make camp here.'

'If that is the way of it,' said Fergal, glad for the chance to dismount. 'I'll be needing a nap.'

'Aye to that.' Donal slid down from Ossin. 'And a little something to eat. Huw, lad!' he called, though he knew the boy could not hear him. 'Let us build a fine fire and cook something tasty, eh?'

'There will be no fires,' Mádoc told him.

'Ach, now, that is very harsh,' complained Donal. 'How are we to warm ourselves and cook our meat?'

'We don't. From here on we must become as ghosts.'

'We're almost ghosts already,' Donal muttered, and set about unpacking their gear. 'Just a little fire, then?'

Mádoc relented, saying, 'Just a small fire—and do enjoy it for it will be the last.'

They made their camp among the purple leaves of the beechy grove. Huw and Donal set about making a fire to warm them and cook the last of a haunch from a deer taken two days ago. Huw cut the venison into small pieces to be mixed in the pot with dried peas and barley, and flavoured with ramp. While the food was being prepared, Conor took Búrach and Ossin; Fergal gathered the reins of Grían, Drenn, and little Íogmar; they led the animals deeper into the wood and tethered them so they could graze, then put up a picket line nearer the camp. That done, they constructed a simple shelter from the leather tent—nothing more than a roof held up by sticks and bent-over saplings. These chores finished, they spread their sheepskins on the ground beneath the canopy and, after fetching water from a nearby brook, Fergal sat back to wait for the porridge. Conor went in search of Mádoc and found the druid sitting on a rock, intently studying the landscape to the south—as if he might read something in the ragged line of rocky hills rimming the horizon.

'Why didn't you tell them the truth?' said Conor.

'Eh?' said the old man, stirring.

'You know what I mean. Donal and Fergal—why didn't you tell them?'

'What I said was true enough.'

'Aye, true enough as far as it goes—but we both know that was never far enough.'

'They were satisfied. It was enough for them.'

'We are asking them to risk their lives,' said Conor. 'You should have told them.'

'If I had said more, I would have been speaking only our suspicions, doubts, and fears. Trading on such things only increases them and, believe me, nothing good can come of that where we're going.'

'Then at least tell me,' Conor said. 'If proof of Brecan's treachery is what we want, why are we going into Scálda territory to find it?'

'Where better?'

'Go to Brecan himself. He's the one deceiving everyone.'

'What do you think you would find, eh? He would be at pains to cloak his deception by all possible means. Or, perhaps you think to confront him in his hall—yes? Do that and it will be the last thing you do.' Mádoc drew a breath and puffed it out. 'But, see now, the Scálda will have neither desire nor necessity to hide the alliance—if it exists. For them it is a triumph to be celebrated—and, if we are very canny, we will see signs of that.'

Conor sat for a moment, trying to fathom this reasoning. At last, he shook his head, saying, 'If you don't tell them, I will.'

Mádoc opened his mouth to object, then hesitated and, looking back to the dusky hills across the valley, said, 'You will do what you think best.'

Conor left him then, and a short time later, Donal called them to eat; they shared a hearty, filling meal and then lay down to rest and wait for night to steal across the valley. Conor slept fitfully and woke in a sullen mood under a low, heavy cloud wrack. He snapped at Donal—and then quickly apologised. Donal only grunted in reply. Fergal said nothing at all as they broke camp and readied the horses. The prospect of entering hostile territory had put everyone on edge, Conor concluded, the animals as well.

When the gear had been packed on Huw's pony once more and everyone mounted, Mádoc called for their attention. 'Be wary of all you see and hear,' he told them. 'Until we know more about how the Scálda range themselves, we must assume that they are watching. Make no mistake, my friends, they will kill us if they catch us.'

'Unless I kill them first,' boasted Fergal. But his voice lacked all conviction.

'All the same, keep your eyes open and your wits about you.'

Nothing more was said, or needed saying. They rode out—a single file of riders staying close together—with Mádoc at the head of the line, followed by Fergal, then Donal, and Huw on the pony, with Conor bringing up the rear. The warriors carried their spears at the ready and shields unslung. They rode in silence, picking their way slowly across the fields and through the orchards that filled the wide valley. Unable to see the trails, if there were any trails at all, they had to nudge their way along by feel alone. Eventually, they reached the far side of the valley, and paused to rest the horses before beginning the long climb up through groves of nut trees lining the lower slopes leading up to the ridgeway. While they waited, ears attuned to the night sounds around them, the overcast thinned and the clouds began to break up, allowing the light of a spectral moon to trickle down, coating every branch and leaf with a slippery silver sheen. Though it did little to illuminate their way, they continued on in better spirits for the gentle light, eventually gaining the ridge top where they paused again. One look into the darkened slope on the other side and Mádoc broke the silence, saying, 'I think we've gone far enough tonight.'

'But the night is only half through,' Donal pointed out. 'We still have plenty of time before sunrise.'

'Look down there,' instructed the ollamh. 'Tell me, what do you see?'

Donal squinted into the darkness. 'I don't see anything.'

'Exactly,' replied Mádoc. 'And that is why I think we must stop. We dare not risk blundering into an enemy ráth or holding.'

'He is right,' Conor said. 'We should wait until we can determine how best to proceed.' He turned his horse toward the downward slope. 'Come, we will find a place to make camp—but not up here where we can be seen.'

In a coombe below the crest of the ridge, they made a low lean-to of the tent among the rocks and, securing the animals down the slope and well out of sight, they settled back to wait for the sun to rise. Huw served a modest meal of bread and dried meat, and they rolled themselves in their cloaks to doze until daylight. Conor was the first to stir. Seeing the others were still asleep, he crept quietly from the shelter and climbed to the top of the ridge for a view of the other side. Dawn was showing a dull, ruddy glow in the east by the time he gained the spine of the ridge and stopped to look down. What he saw stole the warm breath from his mouth, for it was a charred wasteland as far as the eye could see: nothing but dead earth and ashes.

Whole forests had been set ablaze; the blackened skeletons of trees—trunks blasted and limbs burned to stumps—dotted the scorched landscape. The ravaged hillsides were pocked with shallow craters and mounds of broken stone. Fields had been put to the torch and the ground gouged and ripped. Scattered over the valley floor were the remains of settlements and small holdings, levelled, the houses pulled down and foundations scattered, high timber walls and stout protecting gates wrecked and burned. Nothing hale or whole was left standing. All was either black with soot and smoke, or grey with ash. What once must have been fertile fields and forest was now but a wilderness, a bleak and barren desert of destruction. Here and there brambles and nettles struggled to reclaim a patch of ground, theirs the only green showing.

Conor was still staring at the wasteland, trying to fathom the extent of the ruin and the terrible rapacity behind it, when Mádoc appeared beside him. 'I expected it would be changed,' he said, his voice cracking.

'This is not a change, old man,' he said, his voice the quiet calm before the storm breaks. 'It is annihilation.'

The old druid seemed not to hear him. 'I did not know it would be . . .'—he lifted a limp and empty hand to the grim panorama before him—'that anything could be this bad.'

'The creatures that did this are not fit to live beneath the blue sky of heaven,' Conor declared. 'While I draw breath in this worlds-realm, I will not cease fighting while any of them remain in Eirlandia.'

Fergal and Donal joined them just then. 'How?' whispered Fergal, his face grim and pale. He shook his head and turned away. Donal gazed in silence at the great swath of devastation, stunned to silence.

One by one, they returned to their crude camp, where Huw had laid out the last of the cold venison and leftover porridge. 'We will move on after we've eaten,' said Mádoc. Fergal opened his mouth to speak, but the druid anticipated his question, adding, 'Pointless to travel at night. There is no one here.'

They ate their unhappy meal in silence, and then broke camp and resumed their journey beneath a low sky of heavy grey clouds. They rode slowly, picking their way down the ruined slopes into the wasteland, a nightmare realm as grim and dead as the cinders crunching beneath the hooves of their horses. The air was rank with the scent of stale smoke and rot, and left a bitter metallic taste in the mouth. No one spoke.

They proceeded into the lowlands that stepped away in ever-lowering slopes from the height of the ridge and soon came upon the dull, irregular depression of an empty lough— a wide, barren gash in the valley floor. A channel had been cut through the bank at one end, allowing the water in the lake to drain away into the valley beyond, flooding the fields and settlements downstream. Even from a distance they could smell the sour stench, for the bottom of the ruined lough was a quagmire of slime and reeking sludge. Grim-faced, they moved on.

All that day, they saw no wildlife; not even crows or buzzards traversed the sky. At one place, they crossed a riven field and came to one of the nearer settlements; nothing remained but heaps of ash and the tumbled, blackened spars of collapsed roof beams; corner posts jutted up from the debris like misshapen spears. Sometimes, amidst the destruction, they saw the green shoots of a stunted bush or tree, occasionally a brave little patch of grass caught the eye, stark against its drab surroundings.

Conor kept his eyes on the far horizon, but every now and then some object would claim his attention: the rim of a shield; here and there, sword blades bent out of shape by the heat; a smoke-grimed cup or bowl that had otherwise escaped destruction. And once, what he thought was the round base of a pot turned out to be a fire-blackened skull. On closer inspection, there were fire-chewed bones everywhere.

As they rode farther into the deadlands, Conor thought he heard someone singing. He listened for a moment and then urged his mount forward to draw even with Mádoc. He saw the druid's lips moving to a bleak and mournful melody barely uttered.

'A song, Mádoc?' he said. 'You think of music in the face of . . . of this?'

'I sing because I have no more tears,' the bard replied. 'It is a charm against evil—the most powerful one I know.'

'Sing on, then,' Conor told him. 'I will uphold you.'

Mádoc did sing on—all the way through the valley and to the banks of a river where they stopped to rest and water the horses. They dismounted and Donal gathered the reins and led the horses to the water's edge where he stopped—making no attempt to let the animals drink.

'What now?' asked Fergal, joining him a moment later.

'The water is foul.' He pointed to a stream that was little more than a scum-crusted ooze. There were dead fish floating and in the mud at the water's marge.

Fergal squatted down for a closer look. The water was a putrid grey, and held a strange oily sheen. He dipped a finger into the sluggish flow and lifted it to his nose. He sniffed gingerly and then poked out his tongue.

'See now, you're not—' began Donal.

Fergal touched the drop to the tip of his tongue, tasted, and then spat. By this time, the others were watching, too.

'Well?' said Conor.

'It tastes of rotten eggs, or rust . . . rock. . . .' He wiped his finger on the bare ground. 'Something like that.'

'Then we move on,' said Conor.

At the next burned-out settlement, they paused long enough to search the ruins for a well—and found one beneath a heap of stone that had once formed the rim. After shifting some few of the larger stones aside, they were able to lower Huw's leather pail down on a rope and bring up potable water for themselves and the horses. 'At least the dog-eaters did not think to poison the well,' observed Donal.

'Why would they bother?' asked Fergal. 'No one would be crazy enough to come here.'

'*We're* here.'

When all had drunk their fill, the company moved on without stopping until the sun dropped beneath the low cloud ceiling. For a time, the stark barrenness of the landscape lay exposed to the true light of day and was, if possible, even worse. The horror of the day, grown more tangible with every blighted field they crossed and every violated fortress they passed, solidified into a vile and malevolent force that owned the air above and the soil below.

When the brief light began to fade, they found a place to make camp, choosing a flattened area in what might once have been a cattle enclosure at the foot of a denuded hill; they erected the tent and tethered the horses close. They lit no fire—what was left to burn?—and gnawed on trail bread and scraps of bósaill from their provisions. Talk dwindled into dismal silence as each found what solace they could in their private thoughts. They slept in fits and starts, snatching at slumber's elusive peace, and woke to another dismal day beneath dull, dirty cloud.

A half day's ride through the barren waste brought them

to what appeared to be the farthest extent of the destruction. On a rising slope across a scoured valley they glimpsed a woodland, still green and whole, apparently untouched by the damage inflicted on all that they had passed through.

Upon reaching the edge of the wood, they paused. 'At last,' sighed Fergal, casting a last glance at the deadlands behind them. 'We're through the worst.'

'From here on,' Conor said, 'we must be on our guard. We don't know how close we may be to Scálda strongholds—we must assume there are enemy warriors about.'

Donal rode into the wood, returning a short time later to report that it was safe to proceed; they resumed their foray. When the light began to fade, they had made camp in a tiny glade a fair distance into the green woodland. Though the heavy sky began leaking a cold drizzle over them, and they did not dare to risk a fire, they nevertheless welcomed the cleansing rain.

Some little time after dark, as Donal and Huw were settling the horses for the night, Huw came running back to the tent. He made an excited motion with his hands, and Mádoc stood abruptly. 'Where?' he said aloud. The question was accompanied by a gesture and a sign. 'Show me.'

The boy darted away again, with Mádoc close behind.

'What was that now?' asked Fergal.

'Let's see.' Conor hurried after the two and found them with Donal at the edge of the glade where the horses were tethered—all three merely standing there, looking at something. 'What? What is it?'

'Up there,' said Donal, raising a hand to the sky.

Conor looked where he was pointing and saw a faint reddish glow reflected on the low overcast sky.

'Is that—' began Fergal.

'Fire,' said Donal. 'A big one.'

'Half the forest must be on fire,' suggested Fergal.

'Either that, or we are very close,' said Conor. He looked to Mádoc, and added, 'I think we know where to look for the nearest Scálda settlement.'

Liam

They were wrong to let him live. The elders knew best. Nothing good would come of it, they said. Why endanger everyone for the sake of an ill-omened infant? The welfare of the tribe is at stake. So they argued, and they argued truly.

By right custom, common sense, and the greater good of the tribe, Conor should have been placed on the midden heap the day he was born, or thrown to the scavenging animals outside the ráth. But our mother would be having none of that! She wanted him alive, her firstborn son, and fought to save him. Fierce as a wildcat and spitting mad, fresh from the birthing bed, our mam refused to let anyone touch her baby boy.

'Look at its face!' they cried, the old wives and elders, pointing to the ugly crimson mark that stains Conor's cheek and throat. 'That is the mark of evil! A curse! It must be cast out.'

'So, you say!' she raged. 'And have none of you ever had a spot on those perfect skins of yours?'

'This is different,' they shouted. 'That child is marked for destruction. You let it live and it will bring destruction down on us all. Better that one should die so that all may live.'

Everything that happened and was said that day is well known among the clans of the Darini, and the story is often told and the outcome argued over—usually in times of hardship or threat.

But on that fateful day, Ciara looked to her husband for help. Our da was so deeply shocked by the scarlet birthmark that disfigured his precious son that he found it hard to rise to the infant's defence. I say this not to blame him—anyone else would have done the same. Even so, seeing his wife in such agony stirred the warrior within him. He came to her aid and threw the midwives and elders out of the birthing hut, slammed the door on them, and defied anyone to challenge him.

The matter did not end there, of course.

The clansmen, upset and anxious now, took the decision to the king. Fortunately for Conor, Lord Eochaid was so far sunk in his cups that he would not be roused from his hall. So, when the elders brought their complaint to him, he merely lifted his ale-sodden head from the board and said, 'Ach, well, he won't be the first Darini with a defect. Let the lad live if he will.'

Those early years passed, and our mam weathered this hardship as well as she could. She was ever at pains to defend her blighted child, always protecting him, worrying, watching over him. By the time I came along, the pattern was firmly set and though I was born clean-skinned and healthy, I received little of her affection or care. Likely, she had none left over to give me. I may be wrong in this, but for a fact I never felt the warmth from her that Conor endlessly enjoyed.

In any case, the weight of that disfigurement weighed on her, preyed on her, and I do believe it wore her down and weakened her so that by the time Rónán came along she no longer had the strength or will to live and died a few days after he was born.

I was too young to understand this at the time, to be sure—but I have brooded over it through the years. Aye, and a blind man could see that Conor's birthmark was ever a concern of the clan. That never changed. Any misfortune set the tongues wagging, and certain folk readily lay the hardship, whatever it might be—from a sick cow to summer drought—at Conor's feet.

Truly, some of the old folk even blamed Conor for the invasion of the Scálda! Daft, I know, but old ways run deep. Thanks to our da, Conor became a warrior—and a good one, too, give him that—but even then some of our clan yet begrudged him his life. Indeed, the fact that he could wield a blade like a whirlwind only made him all the more dangerous.

Fortunately, for Conor—he is never less than fortunate, mind—by the time the Scálda invasion had settled into a standoff many of the elders who so opposed his life had given up their own, so there were few left to raise the old complaint. Most folk had long ago resigned themselves to Conor's odd looks and, for good or ill, accepted him as he was. Aoife surely did. Strange to say, but I don't think she has ever even noticed that vile red stain. Certainly, it has never made the slightest difference to her glowing opinion of him. To hear fair Aoife tell it, Conor was the sun and stars and the soft sea breeze all in one and could do no wrong.

To those who point the finger and accuse me of dishonouring my blood kin, I can only say that until they have come of age in the shadow of a brother who soaks up all the air and light in every room he happens to enter, they should bite their flapping tongues. Who among them know the disappointment and frustration of being always overlooked, always coming second, always ignored, disregarded, unnoticed—and this because you are *not* blemished and disfigured!

Whatever another would have done in my shoes, I can tell you Conor's presence made me try all the harder—I stayed longer on the training field, I toiled at weapons craft until I could no longer hold a spear shaft or sword hilt. If I could not run faster, I ran farther. I climbed higher and swam more treacherous waters than any of the other boys who took the warrior path. I made myself into a man who could fight fearlessly and well. I listened to my elders tell of battles won and lost, and learned from their triumphs and defeats. In the years since taking up the shield, I made myself the best. No one gave me anything. Everything I have achieved is on the strength of my own arm alone.

And when an injury forced Eilhon, our serving warleader, to step down and a new battlechief was appointed to take his place, it was me that Ardan chose, not Conor. That was the happiest day of my life.

I have heard it said that the king was only giving in to outmoded belief, bowing the knee to the long-accepted custom that says a blemished, injured, or impotent man can neither lead nor rule. But that is not true. Not true at all.

The king chose me because I was the best choice. It is as simple as that. Custom did not come into it, and I will fight the man who says otherwise. Conor may be quick-witted in a fight, aye—and his luck is always with him. Ach, but he is too often rash and reckless, and never coolheaded in the battle heat. Add to that the fickleness of men—for, when the time comes to engage the enemy, it will not do to have any warrior doubting his battlechief, or hesitating at the last moment because he distrusts the ability of the one who leads him into the fray.

Conor could never lead men into battle because there will always be those who cannot bring themselves to wholly trust a blemished man. My father understood this—and understood, too, that a king has a greater duty to seek the best for his tribe and that is why he chose me. That choice has never rested easily with Conor. So be it.

So long as Conor bears the evil stain on his face for all the world to see, he will never rule so much as a pig wallow. For good or ill, that is the way of it.

Am I sorry he is gone? Truth be told, I am. The warband has lost a good swordhand. As I say, Conor swings a fine blade—and just now the Darini need every single warrior we can get. He will be missed.

All the same, the churn is upturned and it is no use crying about spilt milk now. He brought this trouble on himself, and there is the good of the tribe to consider. The life of the tribe comes first and we will all have to accept that, and accept the fact that Conor is gone and never coming back. Aoife, too, will accept that. Sooner or later, she will see the folly of waiting for someone who will never return.

15

After seeing the red fire glow in the sky, sleep proved elusive for the travellers. Their fevered imaginations filled the night with strange howls and yelps, horn blasts and rumblings in the dark. They woke early and ill rested to a fresh wind driving the clouds away and blowing damp, grey mist from the east . . . and something else: the taste of salt air on the tongue. If any trace of smoke remained from the night before, it was carried away on the wind. The change in the weather only enhanced the fretful, fidgety mood in camp. Even silent Huw went about his chores with lowered brows and a truculent frown.

'We are that close to a Scálda settlement,' Conor said as they broke fast on more dried beef and trail bread softened in water. 'I say we go and see what we came to see and then get out.'

'I agree,' Donal chimed in quickly. 'We cannot be sitting around here all day.'

'The sooner we're done,' Fergal put in, 'the sooner we can be on our way.'

'Listen to yourselves,' Mádoc grumped. 'Have I not said we must be patient? We cannot allow our unease to make us less wary.'

Both Fergal and Donal looked to Conor, who sat thumbing the red stain on his cheek. Finally, he said, 'I do not suggest we go charging off into the wood like a pack of wild pigs. Donal and I will go alone and locate the Scálda settlement, see how it lies and how it may be guarded. We find out all we can and then return here to discuss among us what we have learned. Is that wary enough for you?'

'We should go at night lest they see us,' said Donal.

'Are we cats, then—that can see in the dark?' said Fergal.

'If we keep quiet and stay off the trails,' Conor replied, 'no one will even know we're around.'

'Well and good,' said Mádoc with an approving nod. 'But I would urge one additional precaution—that we remove ourselves from here. Clearly, we are too near the enemy and might easily be discovered.'

To forestall further discussion, Conor quickly agreed. 'Where shall we go?'

In reply, Mádoc sniffed the wind. 'Smell that?'

The others tested the breeze.

'Salt air,' replied Fergal. 'Are we near the sea, then?'

'Nearer than you know,' replied Mádoc. 'In this part of Eirlandia there are sea cliffs along the shore. And where there are sea cliffs, there will be—'

'Caves,' said Conor, guessing the drift of the druid's thought. 'Right so, first we find a sea cave and make that our hold.' He turned to Fergal and Donal, adding, 'And *then* we go spy out the enemy settlement.'

This plan was approved and they broke camp quickly, doing their best to hide any sign of their having been there. Once the tent was stowed and the gear packed away, Huw and Mádoc led the horses from the picket, and Donal took a leafy branch and swept the ground to raise the flattened grass; Fergal and Conor gathered the horse dung and scattered it among the nettles in the undergrowth. Then, satisfied that only the most discerning eye would notice their tracks, they took their mounts and made their way eastward through the trees, following the salt tang on the wind. A short ride brought them to the coast. The woods thinned to a band of low, stunted scrub and, beyond that, a leaden expanse, so flat and dull and grey it was difficult to distinguish where the sea ended and the sky began.

The cliffs were steep and sharp, but here and there along the coast the high bluffs stepped down in low terraces. They took the nearest of these down to the shore—rough shingle of slate pebbles and grit. The tide was out, so they had no difficulty making their way along the coast, keeping close to the base of the cliffs the better to remain out of sight from above. They worked south along the cliff face and, when they had gone a fair distance without finding a suitable place of refuge, they turned around and proceeded the opposite way until they came to a ruined headland. The towering rock stacks had tumbled into the sea some ages ago and the shore was strewn with boulders big as houses and seamed with deep crevices like fingers. In one of these reaches, they found a fair-sized hollow—as if a giant had scooped out the stone with a cup. The floor formed a ledge a step or two up from the shingle, and it lay a fair way above the high-tide mark so that the nook stayed dry.

'This will make a decent shelter,' declared Mádoc. 'We stay here.'

Seeing how dry and secure was their stony stronghold cheered the warriors, and they set about establishing themselves in the cave without grumbling this time. As soon as Íogmar was unloaded and everything carried into the cave, Conor surveyed the situation and said, 'We will leave you to finish here. Donal and I will take a look around hereabouts. We won't be gone long.'

'I'll go with you,' offered Fergal.

'Someone must stay behind and protect the camp,' Conor told him. 'Today, that is you.' So saying, he and Donal climbed onto their mounts and returned to the cliff top and the fringe of scrub wood lining the coast to the south.

'We saw the fire to the west of us, I think,' Donal pointed out as they proceeded toward the shelter of the wood.

'Aye, but I'm thinking we should explore the coast a little while we are here—just to get the measure of the place. There may be fishing camps nearby.'

Donal agreed and led the way along the cliff top; he had not gone far when he reined up. 'A fishing camp like that one, Conor?' he asked, pointing down to the beach far below.

As he spoke, the sun poked through the clouds and shone full on the shore below where lay six small boats roughly size of the leather curraghs the Dé Danann fishermen built; nearby, two of the larger Scálda ships lay on their hulls. The sails of one of the ships had been stretched over the mast and pegged to the sand to form a rough shelter. Some way farther up the beach, they saw more ships and beyond those, still more—covering the strand and lining the entire length of the cove.

'Badb take me,' muttered Donal, 'there must be a score of them at least!'

They dismounted and hunkered down in the rough saw grass growing on the bluffs. They watched and after a while, two men emerged from beneath the sailcloth shelter. Dressed in long, knee-length siarcs and baggy breecs, the two ambled up the beach along the line of ships, pausing now and then to inspect one or another of the vessels before moving on.

'Guards maybe?' concluded Donal. 'Not fishermen, I think.'

Conor agreed and, looking the opposite way up the coast, saw with some relief that the beach ended at the foot of a massive sea cliff thrust out into the sea. 'At least our camp is cut off from them here,' he said. 'They won't see our cave from down there.'

When, after another lengthy watch, no one else appeared on the beach, Donal and Conor remounted and resumed their scouting foray, moving quickly across the scrubland to the cover of the woods. Once within the shelter of the trees, they slowed and turned south, slowly working their way ahead with quiet caution. The sun quartered the sky and they began to see signs of habitation: beaten paths and wider trails carved into the wood, timber cut down and removed, brush cleared. 'We're getting close,' observed Donal, pointing to a wide and well-rutted trail. Here they stopped, dismounted, and led their horses into the brush; they tethered Ossin and Búrach to low branches so they might graze while waiting.

Conor and Donal crept back to the trail and knelt to examine the ruts. 'They used wagons and teams here,' observed Donal, pointing to the wheel marks and hoofprints in the chewed-up earth.

'Hauling timber, I'd say,' offered Conor; he picked up a piece of tree bark as big as his hand, and indicated more of the same scattered along the way—along with twigs and branches.

'For building a stronghold, maybe,' suggested Donal.

'Let's see.'

They reclaimed their mounts and proceeded along the edge of the trail. In a little while, they glimpsed, in a clearing beyond the trees, a fortress with uneven walls made from unworked tree trunks. What the walls may have lacked in regularity was made up by their substantial girth; the gaps between timbers were crammed with what appeared to be a mixture of mud and straw, giving the place an odd motley appearance. Smoke from at least two fires formed a dark haze above the settlement, building to a dirty cloud before dissipating on the wind.

Conor and Donal crept as close as they dared, then lay down among the wet ferns and myrtle to observe and learn what they could of the place. The first thing they marked was that along the entire length of the walls crouched tight clusters of crabbed huts made of mud and sticks. From these, Scálda women came and went intent on their daily chores; some carried their brats wrapped up like bundles on their backs, and others toted baskets of stuff—though neither of the spies could determine what the baskets contained.

'They cannot be living in those pig stys,' muttered Donal.

'Shh!' Conor hissed, and gave him an elbow in the ribs for good measure.

They maintained their watch through midday and, as the sun began its long slide into the west, Conor indicated he wanted to move and view the ráth from the opposite side. They withdrew quietly, edged back into the wood, and then slowly, painstakingly, worked their way around the fortress where they were able to get a view of the gate, which was wide and low and nearly as stout as the walls.

A road of pounded earth issued from the fortress and as the two spies resumed their watch, there came a team of horses dragging a number of trimmed logs—thin birches and slender hazels. Another team, coming close behind, dragged scavenged oak limbs, dried and broken. Conor took this to mean that the trimmed timber was for building, and the dried oak for fuel. He raised his eyes to the twin columns of thick smoke billowing steadily from the heart of the settlement. To Donal's questioning glance, he whispered, 'Blacksmith forges?'

Donal shrugged.

For a long while nothing more happened. No one came or went from the settlement, but just as Conor was getting ready to suggest they move again, he heard the slow, steady clop of horse hooves on the road. Conor put a hand out to Donal, pulling him down into the brush. 'Someone's coming,' he whispered.

They waited, and in a moment a large, heavy wagon came lumbering around the bend and into view. Pulled by a two-horse team, the vehicle's sides had been let down and the flat-bed loaded with what appeared to be iron hoops—dozens of them, all bound together in stacks half a man high. The team, led by a driver with a whip walking alongside the lead horse, bumped along to the gate and rolled into the fortress. A few moments later, four men appeared and hauled the massive gates closed—cutting off any glimpse inside the stronghold.

When nothing else happened, Conor backed away from his post, motioning Donal to follow, and the two made their slow way back to where their horses were hidden. 'What are they doing with all those hoops?' said Donal as soon as they were mounted and away from the settlement.

'I don't know,' replied Conor. 'Shield rims, maybe?'

'If those were rims for shields,' said Donal, 'a fella would have to be a giant to carry one, so he would. Do you think they have giants now?'

'Not likely.'

Donal glanced around the wood, and then at the sky. 'We'll be losing the light soon—we should get back and tell the others what we've seen.'

'Aye, we will,' Conor said, 'but first, I want to see where that road leads.'

They made a wide circuit of the ráth and then worked their way back to where the road curved away to the west through more heavy woods. Keeping out of sight of the road itself, they followed it some distance until they saw another thick dirty column of smoke rising into the sky directly ahead—this one easily twice or three times the size of the first, indicating a very large fire. 'There,' said Conor. 'I think that's what we must have seen on the clouds last night.'

They dismounted, secured the horses as before, and continued on foot toward the place marked by the dark pillar of smoke. Closer, they began to hear the distinctive ring of hammer on anvil. The land rose away from the road, and Conor followed the rise, keeping the smoke in view, edging nearer by degrees until they came to a place where the surrounding wood had been cleared in a great swathe from the immediate hillside—and all the nearby hillsides as well. Whole trees had been hacked down and dragged away. The sound of the hammers was louder now, and it was coming from just beyond the crest of the hill before them. 'Whatever they're doing,' suggested Conor, 'they're doing it over there.'

With that, he started off at a low, crouching run toward the hilltop. Dropping onto his hands and knees as he neared the crest, he crawled forward and lay on his stomach to look over the other side. The entire hillside had been dug out and carted away, quarried for the red rock under the earth. The excavation had created a wide basin, on the floor of which stood a roofed platform abutting an enormous beehive-shaped structure made of stone; from an opening in its top belched smoke and flames and sparks, while all around the great stone hive toiled a score of large-boned, swarthy men, naked save for leather clouts around their waists and brócs on their feet. They moved with the slow, methodical rhythm of men used to and well suited for their drudgery. More labourers worked at smaller fire pits supplied with bellows; others plied a range of anvils.

Donal and Conor took all this in without a word. While they watched, another wagon appeared on the road and entered the enclave; pulled by a team of four, it contained a load of red rock in large wicker baskets. This cargo was dumped onto a mound at the edge of the platform, and the vehicle was then loaded with iron hoops just like those they had seen at the first stronghold. The wagon departed and, as the sun slid down behind the trees, Conor gave Donal a nudge and retreated from the hilltop.

Once safely under the cover of the trees, Conor said, 'We have seen their forge and quarry, and something of what they are doing.'

'Right so—but what are they making? That would be worth knowing.'

'You speak my thoughts exactly, brother,' said Conor. He glanced at the sky; the light was fading fast in the deep wood. 'But that must wait. We should start back. Mádoc and Fergal will be wondering what happened to us.'

'Aye to that,' agreed Donal. 'I tell you the truth, all this spying sits ill with me.'

'Something warm in your belly will cheer you,' said Conor, swinging himself onto the back of his horse. 'Let's go see what Huw has cooked for us.'

'Ach,' replied Donal with a sniff, 'with our luck it'll be sea-grass and limpets or some such. The horses eat better than we do.'

'And complain less also.' Conor pulled the reins and turned his mount onto the wooded path.

'They've got nothing to complain about,' replied Donal, following Conor's lead. 'See me home in one piece, and I'll never complain about anything again.'

'If only,' replied Conor with a laugh. 'Then our time here will not have been ill spent.'

* * *
*   *

16

That night, safe within the stone walls their sea cave, with a small fire to cheer them and beds of saw grass spread with the sheepskins, the travellers ate the peas and barley porridge Huw and Mádoc had prepared and discussed what Conor and Donal had seen. Outside, the waves washed the shingle, tumbling the pebbles with a constant low rattling, and the sough of the wind among the high rocks could be heard above the crack and tick of their driftwood fire.

'They are smelting ore and making iron,' Donal said, breaking a piece of dry bairgen into his porridge, 'that much is certain. But it is not weapons they are making just now.'

'Tell me more about the hoops,' said Mádoc, tilting his bowl to his mouth.

'What is there to tell?' replied Conor. 'They are hoops—empty bands of metal, curved into a circle and joined—hundreds of them.'

'Why do they want all those hoops?' said Fergal.

They discussed the various possibilities, but the list was short and none of the suggestions seemed likely. In the end, they looked to Mádoc for an answer. The druid rubbed his grizzled head, put his thumb in his mouth, and closed his eyes and chewed. A few moments passed, and then he gave a little shiver, opened his eyes once more, and spat. 'The mystery remains,' he told them. 'I am sorry.'

'Then we will have to learn the answer another way,' said Conor. 'We'll go back tomorrow and see if we can find a way to see into that settlement of theirs.'

'I'll go with you,' volunteered Fergal. To Donal, he said, '*You* can stay here and guard our rock.'

'Both of you should go with Conor,' said Mádoc. 'Huw and I can look after things here. We saw no one on the beach today, and there will be no one tomorrow, for it will rain.'

'Then it is settled.' Conor raised his bowl and gulped down the last of his gruel, then wiped his mouth on the back of his hand. They talked of other things then, and as Huw took the bowls and pot outside to wash, Donal induced Mádoc to tell them a story. The old druid complained that it had been so long since he had sung anything, it would be a very poor song. But Fergal and Conor took up the appeal and at last persuaded him to sing. The old druid sat searching his memory and decided that a song to remind his listeners of what they were fighting for, and why, would be no bad thing. After a moment, he said, 'Hear then, if you will, the "Tale of the Coming of Danu to Eirlandia."'

The warriors lay back on their fleeces to listen, and the old druid closed his eyes and, in a low and somewhat shaky voice, began. This is what he sang:

'In former days, in the Birthing Time, there was no man—nor yet any woman—in Eirlandia. No voice had been heard on the soft sweet air, save that of rooks and robins, seagulls and sandpipers, and all the other air-sowers. No footprint had been seen on the soft sweet earth save that of the bear and badger, and the ox and otter, and all the other field and forest creepers. Never a word had been spoken, never a hearth fire kindled, never a cup of ale offered in friendship, never a comely smile imparted, and never a sword stropped in anger. As it was in Eirlandia—called Ériu then—so it was in Albion, in Prytain, in Cymru, and all the other lands un-known and unseen by any now alive to see them.

'How long was this former time, the time of Birthings and Beginnings? A day only? A year? Or ten thousand of the same, who can say? For when there is no one there to know it, to measure its length, to count each rising of the sun and each setting, each spring and autumn, summer and winter, and notch them on the counting stick, what does it signify?

'Even so, all things come to an end and so the time of beginnings ended, too. And this is the way of it:

'One morning, when the sun rose in a pearl-pink mist, there came a great ship to the sparkling shore of green Ériu. It came out of the west, from beyond the Region of the Sum-mer Stars, from Tír Tairngire—that some call the Land of Promise, and made landfall at Cúan Díthrab, on the western coast. And on that boat were the three loveliest maidens ever to set foot on Eirlandia, for no ladies of greater beauty have ever been known from that day to this. The first to come ashore was Áine, Badb the second, and the third was Danu. All were dressed in shimmering gowns of purple-blue edged in silver, and all wore mantles of gold bright as sunbeams; their long hair was coiled and braided with threads of silver and gold and tiny bells so that each movement made a tin-kling music pleasant to the ear; around their waists each wore a girdle woven of strands of gold and doe leather. Sandals of white bronze kept their tender feet from the rough ground.

'Radiant and smooth were their noble brows, and proud and glowing were their eyes—green for Áine, black for Badb, and blue for Danu—and clear as the crystal all. Their cheeks were fair to look upon, and their teeth like a clutch of pearls between lips as red as cherry wine. White as the fresh-fallen snow of one night was the skin of their smoothly rounded bodies, and so also their gently mounded breasts.'

The warriors smiled at the description of the maidens, and each closed his eyes as old Mádoc's voice found its rhythm in the song's remembered cadence. He took a sip of water, and continued:

'Next from out of the ship came fifteen serving girls, slender as willow wands, with russet hair and wide dark eyes, and each arrayed like the queens they served. Behind the serving girls came seven dogs of the hunt, with chains of silver upon them, and a golden apple on every chain. Name a colour and it was upon those dogs. Seven hunters with horns of silver and gold came next, and many-coloured were their garments, and yellow was their hair. Next came three druids with clean-shaven heads and torcs of silver at their throats, their mantles likewise many coloured, and each carried a staff—one oak, one ash, one rowan; and each staff was topped with a gem the size of a swan's egg—one emerald, one ruby, one garnet. These wise bards were attended by three harp-players in spotless green cloaks with harps of gold set with amethyst and moonstone. Three nines of warriors came next from out of the ship. Their shields were of copper with rims of bronze, and their spears were long, cold iron topped with blades that caught the sun for brightness. Each warrior was as strong and as skilled as the next, and each one a champion and kingly to look upon.

'The three queens walked upon the strand and searched abroad to see what kind of land they had come to find and all decided that it was a splendid place where their design could flourish. For they had come from the blessed isle of Oiléan Gainithir with a grand ambition; and the plan was this: to birth a noble race unto themselves among the mortals. For, as yet, none of the three had taken a king to be her mate.

'With their noble retinue, they walked here and there about

Ériu, looking for the best place to build their ráth. Such was the fragrance that came from their garments when passed that it was like being in an apple orchard, and flowers sprang up in the footprints of their passing. At length they came to the foot of a solitary hill that was stately and high and surrounded by three wide plains, and seeing it, Danu said, "Here I will establish my ráth and build my lodging place. I need look no farther, for I know I will never find another as good as this. The hill I will call Druim Caín, and Teamhair shall be my palace."

'And it is that hill and ráth we know as Tara. The two other queens were jealous of their sister's choice, but neither was willing to quarrel over it because each had a separate desire. So, Áine said, "You have made an excellent choosing, my heart. May it go well with you here. But I will not stay with you, for I cannot be out of sight of the silver-glinting sea longer than half a day, and so it is to a broad and comely shore that I shall go, seeking wherever it is to be found." Her sisters agree that this, for her, would be best.

'Then Badb said, "Far be it from me to dispute your decisions, my sisters. But I hope you will understand when I tell you I cannot abide too long away from the trees and shrubs, and fruit and flowers of the fair woodlands. I see that Ériu has many great forests and it is there I know I shall find a place worthy of my stature, and there I shall build my palace."

'The other two agreed that this would be a fitting place for her, and readily offered to help her find the home of her desire. Once this had been decided, all were in harmony once again and all petty envies forgotten. While they had been about their deliberations, their retinue had erected three tents and a spacious canopy blue as the windswept sky beneath which they set up a table filled with all manner of sweet and savoury dishes good to eat. There was sweet mead and ale to drink and wine without stint, for never was a cup placed empty upon that table but that it was instantly filled again with whatever beverage its holder might desire.

'The queens sat down to eat and while they ate, the harpists played, and with delicate music in their ears, they talked. Long it was they talked, and found themselves discussing many subjects, but chief among them was where they might find husbands to be kings to rule with them in Ériu and produce a mighty race. . . .'

The old druid's voice had slowed and here it faltered as his head nodded on his breast and he fell fast asleep. None of his listeners noticed, for they had long since preceded him.

17

The wind rose during the night and the travellers awoke the next morning to a fitful rain and a driven sea spewing foam along the shore. Conor awoke first; he moved to the mouth of the cave and looked out. 'Not a day to be stirring much outside,' he murmured.

'This won't last,' Mádoc said as he joined him. 'But it may allow you time to get in place without being seen.'

'There's that.' Conor went out to relieve himself and see to the horses. Huw and Fergal had strung up the leather tent as a roof over them, but it failed to keep off the worst of the rain. The poor animals were wet and miserable. 'Here now, Búrach, all will be well soon enough,' he whispered, stroking the jaw of his mount and promising he would soon be grazing in fields of long green grass. He moved on to Drenn and made the same vow, repeating it to Grían, Ossin, and Íogmar in turn, petting them as he spoke to give what comfort he could before returning to the cave where he found Fergal and Donal breaking fast on hardtack and dried beef; he stuffed some into his sparán and the three departed shortly after, taking all the horses with them—including Drenn and Íogmar the pony so that they could graze along with the others.

'See you bring us back something for the pot,' called Mádoc as they rode off. 'If that is not too much trouble.'

'We will,' said Donal, strapping on his sword. 'If it's not too much trouble.'

The three riders made their way up to the top of the bluff and proceeded at once through the scrubland and into the wood. Donal led the way among the dripping trees to the Scálda stronghold with Conor behind, and Fergal leading the two extra horses. They were still some distance away from the enemy settlement when the rain stopped and the clouds began to clear somewhat; they paused at a brook for water and found a place where the animals could satisfy themselves on the long grass. They tied the horses to a tether line attached to the base of an alder tree, and then proceeded the rest of the way on foot, picking through the thick-grown brush beneath spreading elms and ash. Upon approaching the Scálda stronghold, they paused to listen and, hearing no sounds that might alarm, began working their slow, stealthy way to the vantage point Conor and Donal had found the day before.

'Not much to look at,' said Fergal as they came in sight of the timber walls. 'Big, though.'

'You stay here,' Conor told him, 'and can keep an eye on the road as well. Mark all who come and go.'

'Where are you two going?'

'To get a look inside,' Conor replied, 'and see if we can learn what they're making in there.'

'Are you fair certain you don't need me to come with you?' Fergal asked.

'We won't be gone long,' Conor said. 'Then we'll go to the forge.'

'Well, see you don't get caught. I would not like to have to fight the entire Scálda warhost to get you out.'

'We're not about being caught,' Donal said. 'It's you falling asleep you should worry about.'

The two crept away and soon disappeared into the dense

foliage. Fergal watched the road and the settlement; after a time he saw the smoke begin to billow and rise in the still air, and even imagined he heard the ring of hammers as the Scálda smiths resumed their work. But nothing stirred from the mud huts clustered hard against the outside walls of the ráth. Meanwhile, the sun continued to burn through the clouds, bringing out the shadows of the wood.

He was watching the far edge of the fortress from where he sat and, sensing a flicker of movement, glanced back to see Donal dart across the gap between the forest and the outer wall. He trained his eyes on the place, but saw nothing else. A short time later, he heard a faint rumbling in the air and, a few moments after that, a wagon appeared on the road. A vehicle with large, sturdy wheels, it was loaded with the strange iron hoops Conor had described. There were two Scálda drivers attending the wagon, one leading the horses, and another walking beside. The night's rain had left the road a quagmire and the four-horse team strained against their yokes. 'Better work for an ox,' muttered Fergal, heartily disapproving of how the noble animals were being treated.

After the wagon passed, all remained quiet—until he heard the soft brush of feet through the grass behind him. He glanced around to see Conor creeping up on him, and Donal a few steps behind.

'Did you see anything?' asked Conor.

'One lone wagon on the road is all—carrying more of those shield rims, or whatever they are. What about you? Were you able to get a look inside the ráth?'

'Aye, we did, but there was not much to see,' Donal answered. 'A few small forges, but mostly just houses and storage huts of one sort or another.'

'Did you see any warriors?'

Donal shook his head, and Conor replied, 'None that we could see. Those working here seem to be mostly craftsmen and labourers—maybe fifty or so in all—including women and their young. But, whatever they're doing with all those hoops, we can't tell. Let's go look at the forge.'

The three removed themselves cautiously from view of the settlement, and returned to their tethered mounts. They remounted and moved off through the trees, located the road and followed it, alert to any Scálda who might be travelling on it. By the time they reached the cleared hillside, the forge furnace was in full spate, spewing black smoke and cinders into the air. They watched and listened until they thought it safe to proceed, then crept closer and, as before, peered over the crest of the hill and down into the excavated bowl of the hillside below.

All was more or less as Conor and Donal had seen the day before: the great furnace roared and fumed; the company of smiths pounded hot metal on their anvils, filling the air with the clanging ring of raw iron being tortured into shape. Wagons of rock ore appeared at intervals and were unloaded, and empty wagons trundled away. This activity continued steadily and without interruption, or even much variation. The three watched this activity with a dread fascination, knowing that such intensive labour was not for the idle amusement of the Scálda chieftains. There must be a dire purpose to it that defied ready explanation.

Since nothing else seemed likely to happen and, having seen what they came to see, Conor signalled his companions and the three withdrew from their lookout.

'Have you ever seen the like?' asked Donal once they were safely down the hill once more and on their way to collect the horses.

'And where would I have seen it?' said Fergal. '*No* one has ever seen such a thing in Eirlandia.'

'What *are* they making?' wondered Conor. They rolled up the picket line, stowed it away, and remounted. 'I say we follow the road a little and see what else we can find—maybe learn where those wagons go.'

They continued along the road as it wound through light woodland and low hills, with a keen eye for any sign of movement up ahead. As they rounded a bend and started a long climb up a shallow slope, Donal hissed, 'Someone on the road!'

They scattered into the dense bush beside the road, hid the horses, and waited. Soon they heard the creak and rumble of another wagon on its way to the forge. Unlike the others they had seen, however, this one carried baskets of what looked like bread and others that contained cabbages and turnips, along with earthenware jars—of the sort used to contain liquids. A second wagon, similarly laden, followed close behind. 'Supplies for the workers maybe?' Fergal guessed.

'I wouldn't mind a bit of whatever's inside those jars,' said Donal, and received a sharp look from Fergal. 'Why the fish face now?'

'You would drink anything those dog-eaters brewed?' asked Fergal in a tone of disgust.

'I'm that parched I would even drink something *you* brewed, brother.'

'Quiet!' whispered Conor. They waited, and when no more wagons or carts appeared on the track, the three scouts continued on. The road remained empty, and seemed to go on and on. They were just about ready to turn back when Fergal saw what looked like the timber walls of another settlement rising above the trees on a hill a short distance ahead. As before, they moved off the road and worked their way slowly toward the settlement. They found a secluded place well out of sight to tether the horses, and moved in closer on foot, flitting silently from tree to tree until they came to a field made from cleared woodland and, beyond the field, a protective earthwork and ditch. The ditch had been dug around the foot of a low hill, banked high on the outside, the hollow filled with sharpened stakes, brambles, and stinging nettles. Here they stopped, and hunkered behind a thorny hedge to observe the fortress.

That this was a major Scálda stronghold was obvious from the first glance. The walls encompassed the entire tops of two low, conjoined hills, giving it a commanding view of the countryside round about. Irregular in shape, the walls— constructed of whole tree trunks, trimmed of limbs and branches, and planted upright—undulated along the uneven ground between the crown of one hill and the other. The gates were whole trunks of pine trees bound together with wide iron bands. And, what is more, those gates were open.

One look at the daunting size of this structure was enough to impress. None of Eirlandia's tribes could boast a ráth of such size, though perhaps Lord Brecan with his outsized ambition dreamt of such. In all, the fortress was easily twice as big as any Conor knew. Yet, as he looked on, it occurred to him that, imposing as it certainly was, the stronghold seemed very coarsely, even crudely made. There were gaps in the walls—some of them wide enough to admit a man—spaces where another timber might have been placed, but had been left void. The resulting holes had been filled in with wattles made of sticks and mud—the same material the Scálda used in building their rude huts. In all, it gave the very strong impression that the fortress, for its imposing size, had been constructed in haste and the defects left uncorrected.

'They think themselves invulnerable,' Fergal concluded after taking in the structure. 'They may be right.'

'Nay, brother,' said Conor, examining the walls closely. 'For all its size, it is an ill-made thing. Why, it looks like Donal built it after a night in the cups.'

Donal gave him a dark look, but agreed that the walls at

least appeared hastily constructed and with little care or craftsmanship.

'This way,' said Conor. 'Let's see if we can find a better view.'

The three edged around the circular ditch, angling for a glimpse inside the walls. The road curved around the base of the hill, passed over a narrow bridge across the ditch, and rose to form a long ramp leading up to the gates, which opened onto a sizeable yard. There were large wooden buildings and many of the rough-made mud huts they had seen before, but dominating the centre of the settlement was an enormous structure with a high-pitched roof covered in flat stone slabs taken from the shore. The eaves of this building reached almost to the ground, and a pair of high doors, covered in a patchwork of horsehide, gave access to the central yard.

'That must be the hall,' suggested Conor. Several ragged, dirty children roamed the bare earthen space in front of the hall while, among them, men loaded provisions onto another of the wagons. Smoke from cooking fires drifted through the yard and seeped out from the gateway, wafting down the side of the hill.

'Like swine, the lot of them,' sniffed Donal, 'and smell of it, too, so they do.'

'Ach, aye,' agreed Fergal. 'And what's this now?' He pointed west along the road where a party of Scálda warriors—four mounted, followed by three more on foot— had appeared. All bore arms, but their shields were slung, their swords sheathed; a few also carried iron spears carelessly propped on their shoulders, and some had crested helmets tied to their sword belts.

The small warband moved up the ramp, thumped across the bridge, and entered the fortress where they were greeted by one of their own who emerged from the hall. The riders dismounted and stable hands came to lead the horses away; the new arrivals trooped into the hall.

The three watched a little longer, and then Fergal said, 'Have we seen enough?'

'Aye,' said Conor, 'as much as we're going to see. 'Let's go back and tell Mádoc what we've discovered. I'd like to hear what he thinks.'

They crawled back from the earthen bank and just as they turned to make good their retreat, Donal whispered, 'Wait! Someone's coming!'

They halted, flattening themselves to the ground. In a moment, they heard voices. Conor inched his way up to peer over the edge of the ditch bank. Out on the road he saw six Scálda—not warriors this time, though they carried spears. Dressed in dark leather tunics, they carried the carcasses of gutted deer on birch poles, two-by-two.

'Hunters,' Conor said. 'Six of them.'

'Somebody will eat well tonight,' sighed Donal. 'But not us, I think.'

'Ach, see now,' said Fergal in a strange, half-strangled voice, 'somebody will ride.'

Conor glanced at him and then followed his eyes to where Fergal was looking. Following the first group came four more of the hunting party—each leading a horse—the last with a pony in tow.

'No . . . ,' groaned Conor. 'No, no, no. . . .'

'But, I don't—' began Donal, and then abruptly stopped. 'Badb's breath!' he growled through clenched teeth. 'They've got our horses!'

18

The three Darini watched in helpless disbelief as the Scálda hunters led their horses over the bridge, across the ditch, and up into the stronghold. That they *were* their horses and not some others, was certain enough. If there could be another such as Búrach, Drenn, Ossin, or Grían, then the presence of Íogmar, Huw's stubby little Cymry pony, removed any doubt whatsoever. Conor saw his prized grey stallion disappear into the ráth and so, too, any hope of an easy retreat. With a low groan, he sank down, rolled over on his back, and lay gazing emptily up at the cloud-filled sky, cursing their luck.

Losing their mounts was bad enough, but in having discovered the animals, the enemy was now alerted to their presence. Conor could well imagine the hunters boasting of their find and informing their leaders that there were intruders nearby. And who were these intruders? Dé Danann . . . possibly spies. Any moment, Conor expected a Scálda search party to come boiling out of the fortress to sniff out their trail. They would be discovered and . . . he did not like to think what would happen after that.

Fergal slumped down beside him, and Donal stared up at the ráth as if willing the horses to come galloping back to them.

'If we go now,' Fergal mused, 'and if we run—'

'What?' muttered Donal. 'So we can be hunted down in the wood?'

'We might get back to the cave before the Scálda find us,' said Fergal, finishing the thought.

'And what then?' demanded Donal, frustration sliding toward anger. 'They will trap us in the cave, so they will.'

'Better there than here,' replied Fergal, his temper rising to match Donal's. 'Maybe Mádoc can do something. This was all his idea, after all.'

'*He* didn't lose the horses!'

'Did *I*?' snapped Fergal. 'It was just stupid, rotten bad luck.'

'Stupid is right—'

'Quiet! Both of you!' Conor shoved himself up into a sitting position. 'Listen to you—yapping like dogs scrapping over a clean-picked bone. Shut up and let a man think.'

The two subsided into a prickly silence and stared at Conor. Finally, Fergal said, 'We've got to do something. We can't sit here much longer and wait for them to find us.'

'Here's what we're going to do,' Conor told him. 'We're going to get those horses back.'

'Brother, I do think you have not grasped the difficulty here,' Fergal suggested. 'How do you propose to accomplish this impossible feat?'

'I expect the Scálda will search for us,' said Conor. 'So I would do if it was my ráth with spies creeping about. As soon as the searchers depart, we go in.'

Fergal stared at him. 'Ach, aye,' he replied with a knowing nod, 'and that must certainly be the worst idea you have ever had.'

'You are right there, brother,' added Donal. 'Maybe the worst idea *anyone* ever had.'

'Is it that you expect the entire stronghold to go running

off in search of us?' said Fergal. 'If not, the rest will remain inside—hundreds of them!'

'Or, maybe you expect us to fight them all,' said Donal.

'The search party will ride out,' insisted Conor. 'And they will be away some little time. We will use that time to get into the fortress and find the horses. When we have found them, we take them back.'

Fergal and Donal looked at each other, shaking their heads. 'It has finally happened, brother,' said Fergal. 'Our Conor's mind has collapsed under the strain of thought.'

'Sadly so,' agreed Donal. 'Ach, well, it was only a matter of time.' To Conor, he said, 'Are you completely insane, now?'

'Scoff if you must,' replied Conor evenly. 'But the last place they will think to look for us is inside their own strong-hold.'

'What about the guards?'

'Do you see any guards?' replied Conor. 'The gates are standing open. They know themselves to be secure here—so far away from the deadlands and the Dé Danann territories. If there are no guards at the gate, there will be none inside the fortress.'

'If they suspect spies are slinking around, they will be wary,' Donal pointed out.

'Then we must be warier still,' Conor countered. 'The only way we're getting our horses back is to take them.'

The force of Conor's conviction carried the argument. Both Fergal and Donal admitted with some reluctance that Conor's plan, foolhardy as it most assuredly was, would be better than trying to outrace a body of mounted warriors in the tangles of the forest. At least, it had the advantage that, if against all odds it should succeed, they would have their horses back.

'Right, so,' said Fergal after they had pledged themselves to the scheme, 'how are we to do this impossible thing?'

Conor told them his hastily conceived plan and the three of them hammered at it until all were content with the shape and utility. Then they hunkered down to wait.

The sun sank lower in the west and still no party of frenzied searchers issued from the stronghold. Doubt crept in and certainty wavered. 'We could have been back in the cave by now,' Fergal muttered.

'Without our horses, mind,' Conor told him.

'What if they don't come out?' asked Donal. 'What then?'

Conor was saved having to answer by the hollow thump of hooves on the bridge. Fergal, who was closest, slithered his way to the top of the earthen bank and peered out.

'How many?' asked Donal. When Fergal did not reply, he asked again, more insistently. 'Well? How many?'

He continued to observe for a moment, and then slid back down the bank. 'A score at least,' he reported with a grin.

'A score, you say!' said Donal, much impressed. 'They must truly desire our heads to adorn their stinking hall.'

'Aye,' agreed Fergal. 'And I would not be surprised if the one in the lead was the battlechief himself—the horse he rode and the way he rode it—a man who held himself very grand anyway.'

'It took them long enough.' Conor glanced at the sky. 'It'll be dark soon enough and they'll be back.'

'After you, brother,' Fergal told him.

Crouching low to stay below the protecting bank, the three proceeded to make their way around the base of the hill, looking for a gap they might exploit to get inside; and, as they had seen before, these were plentiful enough and they quickly found such a place on the eastern side where the sticks-and-mud filler used to close the space between tree trunks had collapsed and pulled away, exposing a fair-sized breach.

'There,' said Conor, pointing to the place. 'That will do.'

'Squeeze through a tiny hole like that, now?' said Donal. 'It would be easier to throw one another over the top.'

'First we must get across the ditch,' observed Fergal. To Donal, he said, 'Or, maybe we should throw one another across that as well?'

Donal gave a snort and said, 'Follow me and try not to get lost.' With that, he was up and over the bank of the ditch, and all but swimming through the nettles and brambles with Conor and Fergal in his wake. They crossed the ditch and darted to the shadow of the timber wall. 'There now, was that so difficult?' he said, dabbing blood from the scratches on his hands and face, and picking bits of broken briar from the snags in his clothes.

Pressing themselves tight to the fortress wall, they drew their swords and worked away quietly at the wattle-and-daub filling the gap, pulling off loose chunks of crumbling material, widening the hole until it was large enough to admit them. Donal, the biggest of the three, had to be pulled through without his sword belt and cloak. Once all were through, they took refuge behind the nearest mud hut and paused a moment to watch and wait. All remained quiet in this the outer perimeter of the settlement, so they proceeded to make their way along the wall of the fortress, flitting from building to building as quietly as possible and keeping to the shadows.

There were no Scálda around, as this part of the ráth seemed to contain only storage huts of one kind or another— some small, some larger, and several that were very large indeed; the smaller ones lacked doors, but the larger ones had wickerwork doors of woven laths and branches. Carefully working their way around the border of the ráth, they came to one of these larger storehouses, and, as they rounded a corner, saw two Scálda tribesmen approach bearing a basket laden with something heavy. Conor and his companions ducked out of sight and the men went into the large storehouse.

They did not stay long, but soon emerged empty-handed and went away again. Curious now, Conor signalled to the others that he wanted a look inside. So, creeping around the edge of the building, the three flitted across the narrow path, snatched open the flimsy door, and darted in. It took a moment for their eyes to adjust to the dim light inside, but what they saw made them stare in disbelief: wheels!

They gazed around the room in puzzled disbelief at rank upon rank of narrow wheels, leaning against the walls in rows ten and twenty deep. Here, then, were the hoops they had seen being made at the forge and transported on the wagons. They were used to form the iron rims of the wheels. The three moved to one of the nearer wheels to examine it more closely. Made of long ash spokes joined to a hub of oak, the wheels were thin and fairly light in weight—too thin and light for a wagon—each was exactly the same and a little better than waist high.

Fergal shook his head and Donal shrugged. Conor moved to the door, glanced out, and, seeing no one about, moved on, keeping to the narrow pathways at the rear of the buildings; some of these they looked into, but saw only tools, or weapons store and, in one, baskets of grain. At length, they came to what they imagined was the Scálda king's hall. Conor pressed himself against the wall and glanced around the corner. There, hard against the longer side of the hall, stood a small, sturdily built shed. Unlike most of the huts they had seen so far, this one was all of timber and had a wooden door. They moved cautiously closer and, on hearing voices, pressed themselves against the wall to allow several clansmen to pass by. When the path was clear again, they continued along the side of the hall in the direction that the clansmen had gone and heard more voices—raised, raucous laughter and what sounded like cheering. At the far corner of the hall, Conor stopped and motioned for the others to stay back and, peeking around the edge of the building, saw an expansive central yard and in it a crowd of Scálda—men mostly, but many women and children was well—and a body of warriors gathered in front of the hall. They were watching one of the warriors riding around in a small two-wheeled cart.

This vehicle was pulled by two horses, running fast, and the driver, standing upright and holding the reins, was making wide and uncertain circles, sliding almost sideways with every turn—much to the ecstatic delight of the crowd. A dense haze of dust hung over the yard . . . and then Conor saw what it was that raised such a cloud: the fast careening cart was dragging something . . . a person.

A gale of laughter erupted from the yard. Conor felt his stomach tighten and his birthmark began to burn with rage. He fell back. Donal pushed forward into Conor's place and observed for a moment, then returned, his face dark and angry. Fergal had a look next—a swift glance out into the yard, and then back. Eyes close, he mouthed a silent curse.

Another gale of laughter brought all three to peer around the building's edge. The wheeled cart spun in a tight circle and the rope around the shoulders of the dragged man went slack; the body rolled and stopped—just in time for the wheels to turn and pass over him as the cart completed the turn. The thin iron wheel caught the victim in the middle of the back. The cart bounced high, and the man screamed in agony as his back and ribs broke and the thin iron-rimmed wheel severed his spine.

The doomed man writhed screaming in the dirt, his agony bringing more laughter, jeers of jubilation. The driver leapt down from the cart and, drawing a small knife from his belt, seized his broken victim by the hair and sliced off a chunk of his scalp, which he waved to his spectators before throwing the bloody scrap to some boys as a trophy. Lifting his face to the sky, he loosed a wild whoop and fell upon the screaming man. Kneeling on his helpless victim's broken back, the Scálda proceeded to hack off the captive's head. It was slow, bloody work, for the knife was small. The man's cries subsided as death released him from his agonies.

The Scálda continued chopping and slicing with his small knife until at last the victim's head came free. The butcher rose, bloody to the elbows, to display his gruesome handiwork to the crowd. Leaping back into the cart, he paraded around the yard with the dripping head of his victim lofted high as if some great victory had been won. The Scálda roared their approval and cheered.

And while the cheers rang out, Conor pointed beyond the grisly scene and the laughing crowd to the far corner of the yard. There, away from the commotion in the centre, stood their horses: Búrach, Drenn, Grían, Ossin, and Íogmar, tethered to iron rings set in the wall.

Some of the older boys of the tribe were now taking turns kicking the corpse and hacking off pieces of flesh with their little knives and throwing the bloody bits at one another. Others made a game of kicking the severed head. The Scálda warrior stood looking on for a moment, then joined his swordbrothers gathered outside the hall, and all went inside. Men ran forward to take the two-wheeled cart away and the crowd began to break up. Several men started toward the rear of the hall where the three intruders stood watching.

Conor glanced around. There was no place to hide, and the entire length of the hall to run. Conor snatched at Fergal's sleeve, turned, and fled back the way they had come.

They reached the hut attached to the hall and, as the Scálda warriors came around the back side of the hall, Conor threw himself at the door to the hut, shoved it open, and leapt inside, drawing his sword as he crossed the threshold. Fergal and Donal tumbled in after him, their weapons at the ready.

The interior of the hut was dark and empty. Flattening

themselves against the wall on either side of the door, they waited with breath abated until the warriors passed by outside. They heard the voices grow louder as the Scálda approached, and then grow fainter as they moved on.

Conor let out his breath and, as his gaze swept the room, froze. Fergal glanced at his face as Conor extended a hand and pointed to a far corner of the room where, in the dim light of the storeroom, cowered two of the most extraordinarily beautiful women any of them had ever seen . . . save Conor. He, at least, *had* seen one of them before.

'It's her!' gasped Conor, his voice strained by disbelief. 'The faéry queen.'

Aoife

On the night Conor rode out of Dúnaird, I wept—selfish, bitter tears. To my shame, I did not think of him and what he might be feeling as he left his home and hearth-mates. I thought only of myself and the hurt I was enduring, and would endure for the next three years. I know he did not steal the druid's gold ornament, but I thought he had acted rashly at the council and brought this judgement on himself somehow—little sparing a thought for me. Oh, but men are such thoughtless creatures and it is women who suffer for their foolishness.

The next morning after Conor left, Liam and Eamon and one other appeared—to ward against Conor's return. When they learned Conor and Mádoc had already been there and gone, they would say nothing but to wait for the king. The day after that, Lord Ardan and the rest of the ardféne returned to the ráth—downcast and oppressed by all that had taken place at the gathering. My lord Ardan did not wish to speak of it, and others would not for fear of going against the king. But, Eamon, good Eamon, took me aside and told me what had happened to make everyone behave so. He told me all, and my heart went out to my Conor, my love—and I cursed my selfish tears, and cursed my faithlessness for doubting him. When I heard that Fergal and Donal were making plans to leave the ráth, I went to them. 'Give this to Conor with my love,' I said. Unpinning my casán, I pressed it into his hand.

'We are only going hunting, you know,' Donal said with a sly grin.

'Aye, I know,' I told him, 'but if it should happen that you see him somewhere along the way.'

'If we happen to see him,' Fergal replied, dropping the silver casán into his sparán, 'I will deliver it into his hand.'

'With all my love.'

'To be sure, my lady, with your love.'

It was some little time later—four days, maybe five—after Fergal and Donal had gone, that Liam approached me. I had played and sung for the king and the warriors in the hall and, as I was putting away my harp and gathering my cloak, the king's champion pulled me aside and said he had always treasured my way with song. He was glad to have a chance to tell me this as, he said, he had always meant to do.

He told me many other things of this sort and I do confess it was flattering to hear him speak so. If I were another woman, and if my heart did not belong to his brother, very likely I would have looked upon our battlechief as a prize to be sought, for is he not a fine and handsome man?

Liam said, 'Conor is never coming back. You must know that. As much as it pains me to say, I fear it likely that he will meet his end out there. . . .' He waved a hand to the unknown beyond the fortress walls. 'You will want for a companion and father for your children.'

My heart quailed within me to hear him speak so. 'I have no children,' I told him. 'As we both know very well.'

'But you could,' said Liam.

'Aye,' I granted lightly, 'with the man I love.'

'He is gone, Aoife. He has left you behind. And, much as we might regret it, that is a fact.'

I looked him in the eye and though I wanted to spit at him, I made a modest reply. 'But, see now, Liam, I do not think his leaving pains you at all, nor do you regret it half so much as you pretend.'

'Little you know me, my lady,' he said. He raised a hand to my hair and stroked it. 'Think about what I said. We will talk again soon.'

I slept ill in my bower in the corner of the hall. Knowing that Liam was somewhere beneath the same roof made me fretful and unsettled, and I lay awake thinking about all the things I might have said to him . . . about how as younger brother he always and ever sought to usurp Conor's place, first as battlechief and warleader—which would have been Conor's by right if not for the blemish of that unsightly birthmark—and now Liam tried to take Conor's place with me. But I would not be having that. Nor would I spend another night under the same roof with him, so the next morning after the warriors had broken fast and trooped out to their weapons play, I went to the king. He was sitting in his kingly chair, while one of the handmaids shaved him. Dé Danann men shave. We are not like the savage kind, but clean-shaven. Most shave themselves, but a lord has servants to do this for him and they seem to like it. Eamon stood looking on and both appeared to be in good humour.

'My lord,' I said, dropping to my knees before him. 'I crave a word and a boon.'

'Ach, now, Aoife,' he said lightly, and smiled. 'Only speak the word and if it is agreeable to me, you shall have the boon.'

'I would like to go to the Women's House,' I said. The young woman at the razor—my friend, Uina—glanced a warning at me.

'To visit?' he said, somewhat puzzled. 'You need not ask my permission to visit the Women's House.'

'Not to visit, my lord,' I said. 'To stay.'

'What so?' The king opened his eyes and raised his head, waving Uina aside. He stood, wiping his face with the offered cloth. 'Here, stand up on your feet and tell me what has happened to make you ask such a thing. Are you unhappy here in the hall?'

I stood and tried to smile. 'Nothing like that.'

'Then why do you wish to leave?' He fixed me with a kindly, fatherly look. 'Tell me. Has anyone of my ardféne treated you unworthily?'

'It is no one thing, my lord king. Know you, the ardféne are the best of men and never a lady need tremble on that account. But a young woman sometimes desires the company of other women. . . .' I saw the frown of doubt tugging at King Ardan's mouth and my words dried up.

Eamon saw me floundering and leaned forward and whispered to the king, 'Older women, I expect, who can tell her *things* she needs to know.'

'Eh?' He glanced at Eamon, who nodded knowingly. Understanding came to him and he blustered, 'Aye, aye . . . to be sure.'

Eamon smiled at me and said, 'Still, you would come to play and sing, would you not?'

'Gladly,' I reassured them. 'I have no wish to give up my place as my king's Chief of Song. I will sing and play as ever I have so long as it pleases you, my lord.'

'Well, then,' said Ardan, 'I see no reason why you cannot have the boon you seek.' He put his hands on my shoulders and said, 'Do as pleases you best, dear one of my heart. But know there is always a place for you in my hall so long as I draw breath.'

I thanked him, bowed, and turned to go, my heart lighter already.

'Aoife,' he said, 'we must all bear Conor's absence as best we can.'

'My lord?'

'But I tell you the truth, I yearn for the day when I can call you daughter.'

Ach, my sweet man. How could I have doubted he would grant me anything I asked?

I went to him and, taking his right hand in both of mine, I kissed it and then ran from the room lest he see my tears. Though, if you had asked me why I was crying I could not have told you.

19

Conor stared at the two faéry women huddled in a dusky corner of the storehouse. They were dressed in simple shifts of glistening material—one emerald green, one deepest scarlet—and both wore simple corded belts of braided gold over a thin sleeveless gown of shimmering blue adorned with elaborate filigreed figures in black. The faéry unknown to Conor had hair so pale and fair it was almost white, in contrast to the one he thought of as the queen, whose long, tangled locks were deepest black—just as he remembered from that first passing glance: chained to the Scálda chieftain fleeing the battlefield. This was in his mind as he stepped into the room. Instinctively, he raised a finger to his lips and shook his head to discourage the captives from crying out. He tucked his sword into his belt and took another step nearer, raising his empty hands. 'Please, we mean you no harm,' he whispered.

'Faéry,' mouthed Fergal, nudging Donal, who was gazing at the women in amazement. Donal turned wide eyes to Fergal, who only pointed in reply.

Conor moved closer to the captives, and they shifted nervously; the green lady placed herself between him and her queen. 'We mean no harm,' he said, his voice a barely audible whisper.

The women stared at him in fearful silence.

'Do you understand me?' he asked. 'We can help you.'

The queen made a motion with her hand and eased past her would-be protector and whispered, 'I understand. She does not.' She indicated her companion. 'She has not the skill.'

Conor grinned and nodded. Pointing to himself, he leaned close and spoke into her ear, saying, 'I am Conor mac Ardan.' Indicating Fergal and Donal, he added, 'These men are my friends. We are here to help you.'

The faéry nodded and replied, her breath warm in his ear, 'I am Rhiannon.' She put a hand on the woman with her, and said, 'This is my maid, Tanwen. Can you take away the iron?'

'The iron?' asked Conor.

'It hurts,' said the faéry queen. 'We can do nothing because of the iron.' She pointed to the chain that passed around her waist and that of her companion.

Conor motioned to Fergal and Donal, and pointed to the iron chains binding the women. He made a breaking motion with his hands. Fergal nodded and, while he and Donal made a quick search of the storeroom, Conor moved to the women and examined the chain that bound them. It was stout, well made, and attached to the wall by a large iron ring driven deep into the timber.

Fergal looked into baskets and Donal lifted the coverings of some of the jars; he sniffed the contents of one of the vessels, his face crinkling in disgust, and turned back, shaking his head. Conor, meanwhile, had found a weakness he might exploit. For, though the chain was solid enough, the spike holding the iron ring to the wall was not; moreover, the join fixing the spike to the ring that held the chain was large enough to admit the point of a blade. He drew his sword and, under the fearful gaze of the faéry women, forced the tip into the gap and tried to prise the joint apart. The first attempt failed, but Conor motioned Fergal to help him. Donal moved to the door and looked outside, then nodded for them to continue. Fergal and Conor bore down with the sword; the blade began to bend. Conor tightened his grip and they applied still more pressure. The tiny gap widened a fraction and Conor, drawing breath, put all his strength into the effort.

Both sword and ring snapped at the same instant; the blade tip broke off, the chain fell to the floor. Replacing his now-broken blade, Conor quickly untangled the chain and unwound the heavy links. A moment later, the scarlet queen and her maid stepped free of their iron bonds.

Donal, pulling his head back into the room, hissed at them. 'Someone is coming!'

Rhiannon moved quickly into the centre of the room. 'Stand with me,' she said. 'Here.'

The men hesitated. Footsteps sounded on the path outside.

'Do as she says,' ordered Conor, taking his place beside the women. Fergal and Donal joined him, and all five stood huddled in the centre of the storeroom. In a voice like leaves rustling in the wind, Rhiannon uttered a strange incantation and traced an intricate motion in the air with the long fingers of her right hand. Tanwen shivered as with a chill, her eyes shining in the dim light of the room as she placed a hand on her lady's sleeve.

Rhiannon turned to the others. 'Touch my gown.'

Conor, hesitantly, put his hand to the lady's arm; her flesh beneath his touch was cold. He looked to his still hesitant companions. 'Do it,' he commanded. Fergal and Donal each took a bit of cloth between their fingers.

At that moment, voices were heard outside the storeroom door.

'Say nothing,' instructed the queen in a tense whisper. 'And do not move.'

The door to the storeroom burst open and two Scálda warriors, spears ready, stepped into the storehouse. Their eyes swept this way and that, and they seemed puzzled by what they saw. They looked at each other and at the room again—staring, as it seemed to Conor, directly at the place where he now stood. Then, abruptly, the two departed, banging the door behind them.

'They didn't see us,' breathed Fergal in a tone of amazed relief. 'They looked right at us and didn't see us.'

'We are covered by a charm of veiling,' explained the queen. 'All who touch my belt and all we touch are hidden from mortal sight. They think we have escaped. But they will return and the magic will soon fade.' Her voice was calm, but there was pleading in her eyes.

'We have horses,' Conor told her. 'All we need do is reach them. Will the charm last that long?'

Rhiannon gazed at him, desperate and uncertain.

'Then we must hurry.'

The queen nodded and began untying the corded belt around her waist; she wrapped one end around her hand and then passed it to Conor; he took the belt cord and passed the length to Fergal, who did likewise and handed it on to Donal and the lady Tanwen. He then led them to the storeroom door. He cracked open the door and looked out. Then, looking back, he nodded and stepped over the threshold out.

They moved into the path in a line, each behind the other, each holding tight to the faéry queen's braided belt. With hurried steps, they made their way to the fortress yard. There were still many Scálda about, some of them warriors, and these were clearly agitated as news of the captives' disappearance raced through the ráth. Conor paused at the corner of the hall, drew a breath, and, with a nod to the others, stepped boldly around the corner and out into the open yard.

There were no cries or shouts of discovery; indeed, their passage went unnoticed. Conor proceeded along the outer perimeter, staying close to the wall to avoid as much as possible the few Scálda still milling about in the yard. As the fugitives moved across the entrance to the hall, however, the doors suddenly swung open. Tanwen gasped in fright and Donal put a hand to her mouth to silence her and received a nip for his trouble. With mounting apprehension they watched a score or more warriors charged into the yard. Conor caught a glimpse of the one who he thought of as their chieftain: the great swarthy brute he had seen fleeing the battlefield that day they won the horses. The same ferocious sneer, the same livid scar that cleft his face and left him a one-eyed grotesque—there could be no doubt—it was to him that the faéry queen had been chained. Rhiannon stiffened as the Scálda chief paused and turned to stare straight at them, an expression of bewildered confusion swarming across his wicked features. Seeing nothing, he swung away again and dashed on, shouting orders to his men.

The Darini horses remained hitched to a post at the far corner of the hall where Conor had seen them. Still clinging to the golden cord, they made their awkward way to the tethered animals where, with some little difficulty, they succeeded in getting themselves and the faéry women mounted without either releasing their grip on the queen's belt or arousing the notice of the enemy—now agitated and distracted by news of the escape. Conor put Rhiannon on Búrach, and Donal took Tanwen on Ossin; Fergal took the reins of Grían and of the two spare horses. Taking Búrach's bridle, Conor plucked up his courage, and led the stallion around the perimeter toward the wide open gate, doing his best to avoid the confusion in the centre of the yard. The escapees had almost reached the gate when a wild cry resounded behind them. Conor threw a glance over his shoulder. A Scálda woman was pointing at them and shouting.

'The charm is fading!' cried Conor. 'Fly!'

He swung himself up onto Búrach behind the faéry queen

and lashed the grey to speed. Three swift paces carried them to the gates . . . three more and they were racing down the ramp toward the bridge over the ditch. Conor reached the bridge first and thundered over it with Fergal leading the other horse and pony right behind. Donal and the green lady came after. As soon as Fergal crossed the bridge, Conor reined aside. 'Keep going!' he shouted. 'Get back to Mádoc and warn him! I'll try to lose them in the forest.'

He was still speaking when he heard a cry from behind. He glanced around to see Donal clutching his side, trying to stay upright on the galloping horse. Scálda warriors were pouring out of the stronghold; many brandished spears, and some were throwing them. He urged the grey forward and reined up beside Donal. 'I'm cut!' Donal groaned through teeth clenched hard against the pain.

Conor reached out to steady his wounded friend; he gave Donal a shove to push him more firmly onto his mount, and Tanwen screamed. Her face, already pale, now lacked all colour; her features grew slack and her eyes became glazed. On its way to Donal, the Scálda spear had pierced her, too— and the slender iron shaft still hung from her back. Conor made a grab for the spear to pull it out, but Donal shouted, 'Leave it! I can ride.'

'Follow Fergal,' Conor told him. 'Ride for the trees. I'll meet you back at the cave. Go!'

Conor slapped the rear of Donal's mount, sending him on his way. A cry of rage sounded behind him and Conor looked back. The one-eyed chieftain stood in the gateway, spear in hand. The Scálda chief roared out a challenge to him and drew back his arm to hurl the spear. Conor tightened his grasp on Rhiannon and, with a shout, wheeled Búrach and leapt away, heading off in the opposite direction from Donal. The Scálda chief, seeing that he was taking the road leading around the base of the hill, directed his warriors to give chase.

Spears and rocks sang through the air, but Conor kept his head down, and the grey stallion flew.

Upon reaching the rear of the fortress, Conor swerved off the track and made for the near line of trees across the open field. The ground was soft and Búrach's hooves bit deep, flinging clots of dirt high behind them. The Scálda still heaved their spears, but the stallion's speed rendered the chase futile and they reached the shelter of the wood well ahead of their pursuers. Conor gave Búrach his head, allowing the stallion to choose the quickest path through the trees. The angry cries and shouts of the Scálda diminished until at last Conor felt safe enough to pause and scan the trail behind them; not the least flicker of movement among the thick-grown trees and brush met his eye, nor could he hear the sound of any pursuit. After a moment, Conor resumed their flight, but at a much slower pace to allow his winded mount to catch its breath as they pushed on deeper into the wood. Shortly, they came to a part of the forest Conor had passed through before. He found their former trail and made directly for the coast.

When at last Conor deemed it safe to stop, the shadows were beginning to stretch long and the sky was blushing pink and orange. He reined Búrach to a halt and turned around to listen; except for the sound of trickling water mingled with birdcalls, he heard nothing. So, sliding from the horse, he reached up to help the lady down, saying, 'We will rest a moment. I think there is a stream nearby. We can get some water.'

'I need nothing,' Rhiannon replied. She slid from the horse into his arms.

Conor gazed up into her face, struck as before by the perfection of her features. Suddenly aware that he was staring, he released her and stepped quickly aside. 'Well, I need a drink—and so does Búrach. It will be dark soon—too dark, at least, for following hoofprints through heavy brush. The Scálda will have to give up for the night.'

'They will renew the chase tomorrow,' Rhiannon pointed out.

'That is a worry for tomorrow.' He gathered the reins and led the grey through a thicket of elder and plum, and soon came to a brook—narrow, but deep and clear running— between two mossy banks. Conor gave Búrach to drink, then knelt down on the bank and, cupping water to his mouth, eased his own thirst. Finished, he rose to the sound of gentle, melodic laughter.

'You laugh at me?' he said.

'I have never seen horse and man share a drink before,' the faéry told him in a lilting accent, more like song than speech. 'We would think it perverse and unnatural.'

'I see it pains you,' replied Conor, embarrassed and some-what piqued by her response, 'to have been freed by a per-verse and unnatural fellow such as myself. I am sorry for your discomfort.'

'You think me ungrateful?'

'I think you rude.'

She held her head to one side and gazed at him with her eyes of liquid blue. After a moment she smiled. 'I like you, Conor mac Ardan. You will do.'

Before he could think what to say to this, she continued. 'Only return me to my people and you will see how grateful I can be.' These words were spoken lightly, but with serious intent; she meant them and, perhaps, something more.

'As to that,' said Conor, reaching for the halter of his mount, 'we must first make good our escape. I do not think the Scálda will rest until they have found us.'

Rhiannon shivered and glanced over her shoulder as if she feared that even now the foe was creeping up on them. 'I will die before I allow those animals to take me again.'

'They have not found us yet,' said Conor. 'Come, we are losing the light. Let us see if we can find Donal and Fergal—they will not be far away.' With that, he remounted and, putting out his hand to pull the lady up behind him, they set off once more.

Twilight came quickly to the forest, and it was hastening on toward night when they finally reached the coast and paused to see if—against all odds—they had been followed. Seeing and hearing nothing but the wash of the sea and the wind scouring the rocks of the headland, they dismounted and Conor led the way down the winding coast path to the strand, which was now falling into darkness. They came to the cave and were relieved to find Grían, Drenn, and Íogmar tethered outside. So as not to startle anyone within, Conor gave a low quavering whistle and waited. He repeated the signal and was answered; an instant later, Fergal emerged from the cave and jumped down onto the beach.

'Conor!' he called. 'Right glad I am to see you. Mádoc is here. There is food and drink.' Glancing past Conor, he said, 'Where is Donal?'

'He has not returned?'

'He was with you.'

'Nay, brother.' Conor frowned and looked back along the beach as if expecting to see Donal arriving from that way. 'I told him to follow you. He was wounded—and the lady with him.'

Fergal looked up to the cliffs above. 'I'll retrace my steps and—'

'I'll go.' Conor was already running to Mádoc's horse; he loosed the tether line. 'You stay here.'

'But—'

'If there is a fight, they will need a fresh blade. You are rested. You stay here.'

'What if they have been captured again?'

'If they have, I will find out soon enough.'

Mádoc appeared at the mouth of the cave, gesturing wildly. Fergal ran to him. 'Here, give this to him—' The druid held out a small flask and pressed it into Fergal's hand. 'If Donal is wounded, give him that to drink. It will revive and awaken strength.'

Fergal hurried back to Conor's side and handed over Mádoc's little jar. Rhiannon, who stood looking on, stepped forward as Conor swung himself up onto the brown mare's back. 'I will go with you. They are wounded and you will need help.'

'I will go more quickly alone,' Conor told her, tucking Mádoc's potion into the sparán at his belt. 'It is better that you stay here—lest I am forced to rescue you again.'

The lady accepted this, but said, 'At least, allow me to send you with a charm to help you see in the night.'

Conor nodded his assent.

'Close your eyes,' Rhiannon told him. She moved close and, raising her two hands before her face, she spoke softly into the palms of her hands, and then breathed on them and placed them over Conor's eyes. Her touch tickled Conor's skin like the brush of snow on a winter's day. She held him for a long moment, and when she removed her hands it seemed to Conor that the night had vanished, replaced by a strange luminescence—not night, but not day either—a curious half-light that banished shadows and bathed everything in a pale silvery glow as if washed in liquid moonlight.

'It will last until sunrise,' she told him.

'Can you see yet, Conor?' asked Fergal.

'I can, brother,' he said. He pulled on the reins and the mare jigged sideways. 'If Donal and Tanwen can be found, I will find them.' He paused, and added, 'But if I have not returned by sunrise, flee this place and ride north for the borderlands.'

'See, now, if you—' began Fergal.

'Do it,' Conor told him, starting away. 'If I am still alive, I will make my own way back.'

Fergal raised his hand to wave him away. 'Fare you well, brother. We will watch for you until sunrise—and then we are gone.'

Satisfied, Conor nodded, then urged the druid's mare into motion, quickly fading into the darkness of the narrow coastal path.

20

Upon gaining the cliff top once more, Conor headed for the line of trees to the west that marked the forest edge. He thought he knew the way Fergal had taken, and planned to retrace his steps in the hope of finding Donal along the way. The night sight granted by the charm made it possible to see the track clearly—and many other things as well: a small herd of deer darting across the trail, and a family of wild pigs led by an old boar rooting through the undergrowth; he saw ferrets and even a wildcat—creatures who, like himself, cherished the cover of night to escape their foes.

Every now and then he stopped to allow one or another of the nocturnal creatures to scurry past; he also stopped to listen. It might have been his imagination, but seeing so well in the dark—it seemed like daylight to him—he also thought he could hear much better, too. He listened for sounds of pursuit, but also for any sounds a wounded man and faéry might make as they lay injured in the wood.

Hearing nothing but the scuttlings, gruntings, and rustlings of animals disappearing into the brush, he hurried on. He rode until the moon stood overhead, bright as the midday sun but casting no shadows. His path had taken him almost to the first Scálda settlement—the ráth of the craftsmen—and a thought occurred to him that Donal might have been captured and taken into that evil place.

No, he decided, Donal would never allow that to happen. Wounded or not, he would fight to the last breath rather than permit himself or Tanwen to be taken. A Darini warrior would sooner cut his own throat to protect his friends, or safeguard their whereabouts, than fall into the hands of an enemy in pursuit. Thus, Conor's thoughts bent inevitably toward finding a pair of dead bodies.

As he came in sight of the Scálda forge settlement, he reined up. Uncertain whether to continue on, or turn back and try another path, he paused to consider the best course. Perhaps he should have let Fergal come along. Two could cover more ground than one, surely, and Fergal knew the way he had come. In the end, he decided that he would ride on a little farther before turning back and trying another path.

He found the track he had used earlier to bypass the fortress and came to the hollow where they had hidden the horses while they advanced on foot to observe the forge works. And there, standing calmly, asleep, stood Donal's dun-coloured mare, Ossin. So unexpected was the sight, that Conor jerked back on the reins, causing his own mount to balk, nearly throwing him into the bramble hedge. He slid to the ground and ran to the waiting animal. Taking the bridle, he quickly examined the animal for injuries, and found none. 'Where is your master?' he said gently, stroking Ossin's black muzzle. 'Where did he go, eh?'

Tying the reins to a branch, he began walking around the animal in a wide circle and at once almost tripped over a body on the ground.

Donal lay on his side, curled around his wound. In the strange faéry night sight, it seemed to Conor that his friend's flesh was pale as chalk. He crept forward, knelt, and reached a tentative hand to the expected corpse—only to find that the flesh, though ghostly, was warm and somewhat damp.

'Donal,' he said softly. 'Can you hear me, brother?'

He gave Donal's shoulder a gentle shake, speaking low and close to the fallen man's ear, and succeeded in rousing him a little. Donal gave a moan and his eyelids fluttered open. 'Conor? Is it you?'

'I am here, brother. All will be well.'

Donal coughed, and said, 'I am cold, Conor . . . cold and . . . so tired.'

'Can you sit up?'

'Let me . . . let me rest . . . a little . . . rest. . . .'

'You rest while I look at your wounds.'

Conor rolled the injured warrior onto his back and then levered him upright. The movement brought a groan of pain and coughing. 'Ahh . . . ,' groaned Donal. 'Ahh . . . it hurts, Conor. It hurts.' He coughed again. 'Go on . . . without me . . . go.'

'Shh.' Conor hushed him. 'Do not talk so. I came to find you. Now we must get you safe away.' Reaching into his sparán, he produced the potion Mádoc had given him. 'Here,' he said, pulling the stopper from the mouth of the flask. 'Drink some of this. It will restore your strength.'

Donal nodded and reached for the little jar. His hand trembled so much that Conor tipped the vessel to his friend's mouth; Donal swallowed, gasped, and coughed—then took another drink.

'Easy there,' Conor told him, pulling away the container. 'Save some for the lady.' He looked around, but did not see her anywhere nearby. 'Where is she?' When Donal did not respond, he gave his friend a little shake to keep his attention. 'Donal?' he asked again. 'Where is Tanwen?'

Donal raised his head and looked around as if seeing Conor for the first time. 'Conor . . . you're here.'

'Yes, I'm here. Come, we must get you back to the cave. The faéry woman—Tanwen—what happened to her? Where is she?'

Donal turned a confused, wondering gaze to the woods. 'Where am I?'

'Donal,' said Conor, 'look at me. Tanwen was with you. Where is she?'

Donal shook his head as if to clear it. He seemed to come more to himself as the druid's elixir began to exert some effect. 'Tanwen?'

'Yes. She was with you. What happened to her?

'Over there, I think. . . .' He gestured vaguely back along the trail, and then winced and doubled over with pain. 'She— she fell . . . ,' he choked. 'I could not hold her anymore.'

'Sit there a moment.' Conor hurried to where Donal had pointed and, a few dozen paces along the trail, found the crumpled form of Tanwen lying on the trail. Strangely, she was not as she had last appeared. Instead of the alluring young beauty, he beheld a shrunken, shrivelled carcass of desiccated flesh and bones held together with brittle skin like parchment—like someone long entombed in a burial mound of the ancients.

The once-fair Tanwen was dead; nothing could be more obvious. Still, to reassure the living if nothing else, Conor placed a hand on the bare spindle of her arm—only to have the solid-seeming flesh melt away beneath his touch. Skin, bone, hair, and cloth—all that made up the corpse—simply collapsed into ashes. And then, like snowflakes scattered on the wind, the pale residue swirled up into the air and vanished, leaving nothing behind but the faint outline of her body in the grass.

Conor stared at the spot for a moment, contemplating what he had just witnessed, then shook himself and returned to Donal. 'I found her,' he said. 'Tanwen is dead.'

'Ach, no,' Donal sighed, half in pain, half in regret. 'I should have been quicker. She would be alive if not for me.'

'Not so,' Conor told him. 'She would be alive if not for a

Scálda spear. We can do nothing for her now.' He stooped to lift his wounded comrade, gathering Donal under his arms. 'But come, if we do not care to share her fate, we must be away.' He offered the flask to Donal once more. 'Drink the rest of it and let's get you on your horse.'

With the help of Mádoc's potion and Conor's muscle, Donal was able to get to his feet and stagger the few paces to his waiting horse. Donal allowed himself to be manhandled onto Ossin's back and they started off, Donal slumped over the neck of his mount; Conor, riding beside him, held him in place with a firm hand on his shoulder to make certain he did not slide off again. Dawn had etched a rose-coloured line on the grey sea horizon when they finally reached the coast. With the coming of the day, Conor's enchanted night sight quickly faded, but enough remained to see the path leading down to the shore, now a black expanse in the dim predawn light. 'We made it, brother. Wait here and I will fetch Mádoc and Fergal.'

Donal made a sound deep in his throat, which Conor took to mean he would ride the rest of the way, but the wounded warrior was nearly unconscious by the time they reached the dark shingle. The tide was coming in and restless waves splashed the horses' fetlocks as they came up the beach. Conor called out as he approached the cave, and Fergal, who had been watching all night, hurried to meet them. Mádoc followed hard on his heels and, while Fergal and the druid lifted the unresisting Donal down from his mount, Huw came running to secure the horses. Conor, all but swooning with exhaustion, breathed a heavy sigh, and then followed them into the cave where Mádoc and Rhiannon were already hovering over Donal's wound.

Rhiannon glanced up quickly as Conor entered the cave. 'Tanwen?' she said.

Conor merely shook his head, and said, 'I am sorry.'

She stifled a cry and bit the back of her hand. Then, with a visible effort, she straightened and turned back to the task at hand. Fergal laid a hand on Conor's shoulder and said, 'You should eat. We have some gruel, and Huw has caught some fish.'

Conor turned dull eyes on him. 'We cannot stay here. It will be light soon and the Scálda are sure to find our trail.'

Fergal nodded. 'Eat something, brother. Restore your strength and we will decide what to do.'

Conor heeded this advice. Settling himself at the fire, he filled a bowl from the pot and slurped the salty gruel, then picked at a bit of roast fish. 'That is better,' he said, pulling off flecks of white meat from the feathery bone.

'I've been thinking,' said Fergal, 'we could maybe evade the Scálda if we kept to the shore near the cliffs out of sight from above.'

'Maybe,' allowed Conor, licking his fingers, 'until we came to rocks or a headland we could not get around.' He pulled off another bit of fish, and said, 'I say we take one of the Scálda boats.'

Fergal regarded him doubtfully. 'Leave the horses behind? Even so, we would never all fit in one of those. They are too far too small.'

'I'm not talking about a little fishing boat,' Conor said. 'We'll take one of the big ones.'

'A Scálda ship?' Fergal's eyebrows rose. 'Do you know how to sail a ship now, brother?'

Conor sucked the fishbone clean and tossed it aside.

'How do we get it into the water?'

'We have horses,' Conor said. 'We'll use them.'

Fergal's lips twisted into a dubious frown.

'Think you now, it makes sense. Donal is in a bad way. Even

if he could ride, horses would be too slow.' He watched Fergal weighing the idea in his mind. They were still discussing whether this plan might possess even a remote possibility of success, when Mádoc rose and came to them. 'I have done what I can for Donal,' he said, keeping his voice low. 'The bleeding is stopped, but he is very weak. I have given him a draught for the pain and he will sleep now.'

'We cannot stay here,' Conor told him. 'The Scálda will be on our trail soon.'

'Donal should not ride,' Mádoc said. 'If he is to survive, he must rest.'

'Let him rest on the ship.'

Mádoc glanced at Fergal, who said, 'Our man here is saying we should take a Scálda ship.'

Mádoc did not object outright. He asked how they would get it in the water and Conor told him; the druid frowned as he considered the idea. 'You should get started,' he concluded. 'It may take longer than you imagine. Huw will pack our gear and I will prepare Donal to travel.'

Leaving the cave, Conor and Fergal hurried to the horses, unhitched Drenn, Grían, Ossin, and Búrach, and, leaving little Íogmar for Huw to load, rode up the shore to the fishing camp they had seen two days before. There was no one there, so they went to work. 'We'll take that one,' he said, pointing to the first of the ships in line and closest to the tide mark. 'If we roll it over, we can drag it into the water.'

That is what they did. From the coils of rope stashed beneath the half-deck that covered the front half of the vessel, Conor tied four goodly lengths to the mast and threw them to Fergal, who fashioned loose halters. Then, each taking a pair of horses, they coaxed the animals to pull. But these were not workhorses, they were creatures bred to speed and battle. None were accustomed to working together with others under harness. Búrach kept trying to lead, and Ossin would not follow, but insisted on going her own way. Fergal's stallion refused the halter; Mádoc's bay mare was the only of the four to adjust herself to the task. By shouts and threats and sweet entreaties, they at last succeeded in rolling the vessel onto its keel. Conor climbed over the side and, with his damaged blade, cut the lines and hurriedly retied them to the high prow. Meanwhile, Fergal led the four unruly horses around to the front of the ship and tried to keep them in line. Returning to the strand, Conor unstrapped his sword and laid it on the beach so that it would not get drenched in salt water, then waded into the surf to help Fergal entice the horses into the waves.

Fergal, holding on to Grían's halter, shouted, 'Hie-up!' and urged the horses forward. Step by step, the skittish animals entered the cold, swirling water. Conor, standing between Búrach and Ossin, had all he could do to keep them from bolting and retreating to the beach. The stallion did not like the water and bucked, which made the mare shy and dig in her hooves, refusing to move. Again, the air rang with threats and supplications and promises of future pleasures. The ropes sighed and complained, and the belly of the ship grated against the pebbles. One hard-won step at a time, they dragged the vessel forward. Fergal was all but chest high in the waves before the keel had even touched the water. 'Shorten the ropes,' he called, 'or we'll be drowning ourselves!'

'Wait there!' Conor shouted, and sloshed his way back to the beach and onto the deck once more. Fergal backed the horses to slacken the lines and Conor drew in the extra length and quickly retied them. He dropped over the side and into the water; he took up the halter again and gave Búrach a slap. 'Hie!' he cried, and the grey heaved forward.

'Hie!' echoed Fergal, pulling on Grían's halter. 'Hie-up!'

The horses strained against the ropes and the upswept keel touched the water. 'Again!' Conor shouted. 'Once more!'

Fergal, up to his shoulders in the wave surge, drove the horses deeper into the wash. The keel groaned on the shingle and a little more of the ship eased into the water.

'Again!' cried Conor. 'We're almost there.'

'Wait!' shouted Fergal above the slap and dash of the surf. 'That's as far—' He broke off as a big wave broke upon him, lifting him off his feet and dumping him onto his backside. Fergal clung to the halter rope and came up spluttering. He heard Conor shouting, 'Enough! The tide will do the rest. Let's get the horses aboard.'

Conor took hold of the rail and scrambled up over the side. He found the boarding plank and heaved it over the side, secured by ropes to cleats on the side of the ship. Then he ran back to help Fergal coax the animals aboard. If getting them to pull together was difficult, getting the contrary creatures to walk up that strip of narrow planking was impossible. The ramp refused to remain stationary, swerving and bobbing as the waves lifted and tilted the ship. Conor watched as Fergal tried to force a skittish and reluctant Grían onto the boards. 'Blindfold him,' he shouted. 'Don't let him see it.'

'Right so,' replied Fergal. 'And with what do you suggest I blindfold him?'

'Your siarc, brother. Use your siarc.'

'I have a better idea. Let's be using *your* siarc, now.'

Conor did not argue, but stripped off his siarc and tossed it to Fergal, who tied it like an apron around the top of the roan stallion's head, shielding the animal's eyes. Conor got on the ramp and, taking hold of the halter, half led and half pulled the unwilling animal onto the deck. The same operation was repeated with each of the others in turn. Búrach was last and as he stepped onto the swaying deck, Huw appeared with Íogmar. The fully laden hill pony showed up his bigger cousins by clipping smartly up the ramp.

'Go get Mádoc!' Conor shouted. 'Huw and I will secure the animals.'

Fergal turned and ran back to the cave, splattering seawater as he went. Conor and Huw gathered the horses' halters and tied them to a loop of rope fastened to the mast—not an ideal solution, but the best they could devise with what they had on hand. Next, they stowed the camp supplies under a net fixed to the forward platform and, that done, Conor raced back to the cave where Fergal and Mádoc struggled over the slippery shingle with Donal slung between them using his cloak for a sling. Rhiannon came behind, carrying Mádoc's staff and satchel. With Conor's help, they soon had everyone aboard and Donal settled as comfortably as possible in a nook beneath the forward half-deck.

The sun had risen above the horizon, burning a hole in the low-lying sea mist. Conor cast a searching look at the cliff tops towering above them—no sign of Scálda searchers yet—then he and Fergal put their shoulders to the stern and shoved. The ship moved more easily this time; the incoming tide had lifted the vessel. 'Once more!' shouted Conor. 'Then get aboard.' They gave one last heave and the hull floated free at last. They clambered aboard and pulled in the ramp.

'What next?' asked Fergal.

'Let's get the sail up.'

Mádoc came out from attending Donal and told them how to unfurl the sail, which was wrapped around the mast, and then showed them how to set it on the long spar attached to the mast. He then directed Conor to put out the rudder oar and explained how to ply it to steer the ship. 'Fergal will hold the guide ropes,' he said, 'and you will steer. Just try to keep the sail more or less square to the wind.'

They were still discussing how to do this when, against every expectation, the sail bellied out and the shallow-hulled craft began to float out into the bay.

'You must remain vigilant,' Mádoc warned. 'From the little I know, the wind will pull the harder once the vessel has reached deep water beyond the shadow of the headland, and good luck to you.'

'What else?' asked Conor.

'That is all I know,' replied the druid. 'We have exhausted my small store.'

Conor perched himself on the tiny pilot's bench beside the steering oar; gripping the length of use-polished oak, he set his eyes on the thin line of waves he saw forming farther out. The shallow-keeled vessel bounced as it hit the rough water. The sail slacked and snapped; Fergal pulled this way and that on the spar lines until he found the wind again, and the ship lunged ahead.

Once beyond the wind shadow of the headlands, the sea smoothed out; the sharp prow parted the green waves and sent the spray flying. In a little while, the cliffs and bluffs of the headland had shrunk away to little more than a low-lying bank behind them. Conor called out to Fergal, 'I think we are out far enough. I don't want to lose sight of land. I will turn the ship.'

Fergal gave him a wave and prepared to wrestle the sail. It took several attempts—they kept losing the wind—but at last they managed to coordinate their efforts sufficiently to bring the prow around; the vessel swung onto a new heading and proceeded on a shaky course along the coast.

Rhiannon came to stand beside Conor. 'You are doing well,' she told him. 'You and your man—you could be sea-men yet.'

'I will be content to remain a warrior,' Conor replied.

She smiled. 'Either way,' she said, 'you will be needing this.' She held out his still-damp siarc to him. 'It will soon be dry.'

Conor, who had been too busy to notice the lack, released

his hold on the rudder momentarily and drew the siarc over his head, then struggled one-handed with the laces.

Rhiannon reached out, deftly tied the laces, then let her hand rest for a moment on Conor's chest. 'Thank you for saving me,' she whispered, leaning close.

'You have thanked me already,' he told her.

'And I will go on thanking you for the rest of my days— long or short as they may be.'

Conor lowered his head in embarrassment. 'I am sorry I could not save Tanwen. But, if I should ever find any more of your people made captive by the Scálda or anyone else, I will do all I can to free them. I give you my solemn vow.'

Rhiannon smiled sadly and, placing a finger beneath his chin, lifted his head once more. 'My lady Tanwen will be properly mourned and her life celebrated by my people. She was dear to me and nothing will fill the empty place she has left in my heart.'

'I am sorry,' Conor said again.

The faéry released him. 'No,' she said. 'You must not feel sorry for her. Those of our race see death—hateful as it must be—as a release from the endless cycle of our years. While we do not seek it, we recognise it as a dark friend who opens the door to the next life, a higher life and a better one than we have known before. That is why we both mourn and celebrate the life that the All Wise Mother has given.'

'I would have brought her body back,' Conor told her. 'I would never have left her there for the Scálda to find.' He shook his head, remembering how the corpse had disintegrated at his touch. 'But there was nothing left—nothing at all.'

The faéry gave a sad smile. 'I know. That is how it is with us. In death our true age is revealed. Those of us who have lived long . . .' Her voice trailed off. 'There is nothing left. It is better that way.'

Conor merely nodded.

She mistook his simple acceptance and said, 'You think me coldhearted.' Before he could object, she continued, 'Mortals always do—they think us callous and unfeeling. They say our blood is cold and it freezes the warmth of our hearts. They think us cruel. They know nothing about us.'

Conor regarded her steadily. 'I do not think you coldhearted.'

She appeared to comprehend that this was so. 'Then, perhaps, you are a mortal I can trust.'

She left him then, and Conor sat for a while thinking about what Rhiannon had said and watching the sail; Fergal eventually succeeded in finding the best angle to catch the wind. He breathed in the clean sea air and then turned for a last look behind them.

His heart sank like a stone dropped into the salty deep.

There, blossoming on the horizon, were the red sails of another Scálda vessel in swift pursuit.

21

'Rhiannon! Mádoc!' Conor shouted. 'I need you!'

He shouted again and the lady hurried aft from her place with the stricken Donal at the prow; Mádoc followed a moment later, lurching unsteadily, holding to the rail all the way to the stern. 'Can a man have no peace?' he said, his face clenched as if he had eaten something rotten.

'I would not disturb your peace for all the world,' Conor told him. 'But I heartily doubt the Scálda behind us would be so considerate of your sweet slumbers.'

'I am trying to keep Donal alive,' growled the druid. 'Scálda?' He cast a glance over Conor's shoulder at the pursuing vessel.

'We must get more speed from this craft,' Conor said, thrusting a hand at the Scálda ship behind them. 'How—how is it done?'

Catching sight of the enemy ship, Rhiannon fell back a step; her hands fluttered like lost birds and, turning an anguished face to Conor, said, 'I don't know—our seamen, they know such things, but I do not.'

'What about a charm? Do you have any magic for speed over water?'

'I am sorry.' Shaking her head, she glanced again at the Scálda ship and backed away. 'You must do the best you can. I am sorry.'

Conor watched her scurry back to the shelter of the platform, then turned to Mádoc, who was staring at the enemy ship with half-closed eyes. Conor followed his gaze: he could now make out the mast and the shape of the hull beneath.

'Well?' said Conor. 'Can you do anything?'

Mádoc opened his mouth to reply, but the ship lunged into a wave just then and Mádoc grabbed for the rail as bile gushed up his throat. He spat over the side and hung there, head down, heaving.

'Fergal!' Conor shouted. 'We have trouble.'

'Eh?' Fergal cast a glance over his shoulder, and Conor pointed to the ship looming on the horizon. He took in the sight, then looked back to Conor. 'Tell me what to do and it will be done.'

Turning back to Mádoc, Conor said, 'Well? Can you do anything?'

The druid straightened; wiping his mouth with his sleeve, he said, 'Can I do anything? How little you know the power of an ollamh.' He paused, his wrinkled face crumpled in thought. At last, he said, 'Do nothing. Only watch what I can do.' So saying, the druid hobbled back to the prow to rummage around in the camp supplies.

Conor looked around. The enemy ship was now close enough to make out the dark shapes of warriors crowding the deck. 'Mádoc!' he shouted. 'They're getting close.'

The old druid returned with his leather satchel and with Huw in tow: the latter carried the cooking cauldron. He directed the boy to put the cauldron against the stern post and then, with a gesture, sent him back to the prow. He then dipped into his druid bag and withdrew a small parcel wrapped in birch bark and tied with a leather string. Huw returned with a bundle of kindling and a flint and iron striker and, while he busied himself lighting a fire in the pot, Mádoc, eyes closed, cradled the little bark-wrapped parcel be-

tween his palms and breathed silent words on it. At least, to
Conor, it appeared that was what he was doing; the old man's
lips moved and he exhaled, but no words reached Conor's
ears.

While Mádoc made his incantations, little Huw worked
away and soon had a small blaze going inside the cauldron.
It smoked somewhat and the smoke was snatched away by
the wind. Conor, meanwhile, kept an eye on the Scálda chase
vessel, which seemed to gain on them with every rise and fall
of the waves. But still the druid stood with his eyes closed,
speaking to the parcel in his hands.

Fergal, standing at his station, fought to keep the ungainly
square of cloth filled by pulling the spar ropes first one way
and then the next; he called back over his shoulder, 'What is
happening back there?'

Conor turned to the druid. 'Mádoc? The Scálda are getting close.' He could see individual warriors leaning out from
the ship behind them, spears in their hands, which they thrust
and lofted, eager for the first opportunity to make a throw.
'Mádoc! Did you hear me?'

The druid made no reply, but remained in his rigid pose
seemingly lost to the world. Meanwhile, the Scálda pursuit
drew swiftly, inexorably closer.

'Did you hear me, Mádoc?' said Conor, raising his voice.
'The Scálda are almost upon us now.'

Mádoc lowered his hands and, casting a sour glance at his
interruption, said, 'I heard you the first time. Do you think
this is easy?'

'I think it slow.'

'Then *you* do it!'

'Mádoc, please—' said Conor, gesturing to the ship behind
them. He could now hear the shouts and jeers of the Scálda
warriors. 'Just do your work.'

'If you will allow me. . . .' He turned and, seeing that the fire Huw had made had burned down to hot embers inside the cauldron, Mádoc knelt before it and, with a last word spoken to the parcel, dropped it onto the glowing coals.

The little bundle smouldered for a moment and burst into flame as the dry birch bark ignited. It burned brightly for a moment and then subsided. Conor saw the flames die and felt his hope die with them. He prepared for battle. Grabbing Huw by the arm, he pulled the boy to his station and put the steering oar into his young hands. 'Hold the course,' he told the boy. 'Keep it steady.'

Then he ran forward to fetch his sword and see if he could find something to use as a shield.

'Now what?' called Fergal as Conor flashed past him.

'I'm getting our weapons. We will soon need them.'

'It comes to that, eh?' said Fergal, risking a hasty look over his shoulder. 'Aye, it comes to that.'

Conor dived under the low platform where Rhiannon sat huddled over Donal's inert form. She had her long hands on his body—trying to keep him from being rolled and tossed by the movement of the ship.

'I need my sword,' said Conor. 'Gasta—where is it?'

Rhiannon regarded him for a moment. 'I saw no weapons among the things from the cave.'

Conor rocked back on his heels. What had he done with it? He had it with him the whole night through . . . right up to the time he had waded into the water in the frenzied effort to launch the ship. And that was when he and his sword had parted company; the renowned blade lay even now on the black-pebbled, wave-washed shingle—forgotten in the haste to launch the ship. Conor muttered a curse for his carelessness. That sword was a stout companion through many battles and he would miss it sorely—and likely very soon. He hurried back to the stern.

Mádoc's ministrations had not achieved much, if

anything—aside from producing a quantity of pale, silvery smoke and a foul stench. The charm—if that was what it was—had made no appreciable difference. He took his place beside Mádoc and drew his knife.

The druid saw the blade in Conor's hand and said, 'Will you fight an entire shipload of Scálda warriors with a knife?'

'If I must.'

Mádoc favoured him with an approving gaze. 'You do not lack for courage, Conor mac Ardan—good sense, maybe, but not courage.'

'Be about your business, bard—and let me be about mine.'

They watched the Scálda ship for a moment as it feinted slightly to the landward side of their vessel—a preparation, Conor assumed, for making their attack.

'As soon as they are close enough, they will throw spears,' Conor said. 'You and Huw get below the platform. Fergal and I will collect what weapons we can and—'

'So impatient,' huffed Mádoc. Drawing a deep breath, he turned his face toward the Scálda ship and, stretching both hands above the cauldron, cried, 'Behold!'

The smoke issuing from the rim of the bronze pot suddenly thickened and changed, becoming less smokelike and more vaporous. The substance flowed up over the rim of the cauldron and spread over their feet and across the deck. Huw, his eyes wide, backed away from the pot as more and more of the stuff poured out, bubbling up so fast that the entire deck was soon awash in thick, grey-white fog.

Almost at once, the hull filled up; dense white mist spilled over the rail and down the sides of the ship, building and cascading like a waterfall, spreading out onto the sea in rushets and rivers that grew as they spread, gathering and multiplying, building and rising. Very soon a solid bank of fog grew up between the two ships; the bank became a barricade and then a wall and still it grew, mounding and mounting until the sun was merely a dim white spot and the sea could no longer be seen.

'Go and drop the sail,' Mádoc instructed. 'With a little luck, the Scálda may pass us by.'

'And then?'

'And then we shall see what we shall see.'

Conor hurried forward to help Fergal wrestle down the sail, and the vessel coasted for a while and then began to drift on the current. 'Do you think it will work?' asked Fergal, gazing skyward as the last patch of blue sky faded from view.

'I think it is working already,' said Conor. 'Listen . . .'

The shouts and jeers from their pursuers had diminished greatly; what had been plain and clear was now muffled and indistinct, and seemed to come to them from a distance. The ghostly fog continued to build and deepen until the voices of the foemen were shrunken small and very far away. Even as they stood listening, the voices passed from hearing and an unnatural silence descended upon them, broken only by the waves lapping against their hull.

Mádoc came to where Fergal and Conor stood listening. 'This will last until evening,' he said. 'We will remain out of sight until then.'

'All well and good,' said Conor. 'Only now we are becalmed.'

'Nor can we see to steer our way along the coast,' Fergal pointed out.

'Is this gratitude?' Mádoc huffed. 'Next time we will let the Scálda catch us. Perhaps you would prefer that.'

'Peace, druid,' said Conor. 'You have saved us with your craft. I merely look ahead to the completion of our escape.'

'Think you then,' grumbled the bard, 'when the fog diminishes we can flee under cover of darkness.'

'Make passage in the dark?' Fergal shook his head at the thought. 'That lies beyond my abilities as a seaman.'

'You have no abilities as a seaman,' Conor told him. 'But Fergal is right. How will we navigate by night?'

'Others do it,' Mádoc replied, moving away. 'It is therefore not beyond the wit of men—even dull warriors.'

The day passed by slow degrees; the sea remained calm and quiet. Conor soon tired of watching the fog and succumbed instead to sleep, making up for the rest he had missed the night before. He roused himself just before sunset and rose to see that the unnatural fog had thinned in the sky directly overhead. A landward breeze was blowing, shredding the vapours, and soon the ghostly outline of a distant shore could be made out.

'The fog is clearing fast,' Fergal said, joining him at the rail. 'We will soon be able to put up the sail again.'

'Any sign of the Scálda ship?'

Fergal shook his head. 'Neither scrap nor scrape.'

'Nothing at all?'

'Only a few gulls.'

'Let's put up the sail and make use of the light we have left.'

Together, they moved to the mast and, each taking hold of line, hauled the heavy red cloth and spar to the top. Then, leaving Fergal to man the ropes, Conor took up his place on the steersman's bench and, as soon as the wind caught and the great sheet billowed, the vessel began to move once more. They had drifted very far out to sea and it was all Conor could do to steer them back toward the coast. He tried to keep the prow on a northeasterly course, but this proved more difficult than previously. Every time he managed to guide the ship to the north, they lost the wind; and when he regained the wind, the vessel headed farther away from the shore.

Fergal, frustrated at the ropes, kept calling for him to keep a steady course. Meanwhile, twilight deepened around them and darkness swept in from the east. Soon they could not see to navigate at all. Conor called Fergal, Rhiannon, and Mádoc to him and said, 'If any of you know how to pilot this ship in the dark, keep that knowledge to yourself no longer—else we shall have to lower the sail again and wait until morning.'

'And hope the Scálda do not reappear with the dawn,' Fergal put in.

The others looked at one another, and when no one offered any advice, Conor said, 'Then we haul down the sail. With any luck we may not drift out of sight of land during the night.'

'What about the charm for seeing in the dark?' asked Conor.

'I have spent the charm this moon and must wait for the new moon to renew my powers.'

'Moon!' cried Mádoc as if stirring from sleep. 'We need neither charms nor potions to see in the dark. There will be moon enough tonight.'

'And if the clouds come back?' said Fergal.

'Then they come back,' replied the druid. 'We will take what we are given and make the most of it.'

Mádoc

Victory is sweet—but does often leave a bitter aftertaste. Like strong mead in the cup, its golden allure carries a sting once that cup is drained. This, I reflected, is the lot of human beings in this worlds-realm. There is no arrival without a departure, and all progress is measured by how much has fallen away.

This is in my mind as I sit in the bottom of this wretched ship and watch helpless as the stricken Donal struggles to maintain his grip on life. He is dying because of me—not that I hurled the spear that pierced him, the enemy had seen to that. But I had sent him into the enemy camp to verify a whim I'd had.

Ach, well, somewhat more than a whim, I'll own, yet far less than a certainty. I was curious. There was that in the air and on the land that did not sit well with me and put my teeth on edge. Lord Brecan's summons to the Oenach, coming when it did so quickly after the last one, concerned me, aye, and the strange mood of the gathered royals and their attendants once we reached Tara told me I was not the only one. But there was something more, a thing I could not name. I do believe this unnamed cause worked in me and worked in me until it provoked a gnawing, nagging conviction that things were not as they seemed.

The ill feeling pricked and needled. I watched all that took place and pondered on the meaning behind what I saw as if trying to discern the substance of the tree by the shadow cast on the path in the moonlight. There are some among the Learned, I have heard, who can descry the movements of hidden shapes and events. Alas, I am not one of them.

But the fact remains that I remained restless and twitchy from the moment I set foot on Tara's hallowed soil until I heard that one of the Darini had been attacked by three Brigantes. Hard on the heels of this report followed the rumour that the luckless warrior had drunkenly insulted the Brigantes king and his hearth companions; or that he had gambled, lost, and refused to pay; or that he had tried to steal a gold cup from one of the camps when the nobles were at the gathering.

Rumours all, as I say, and all of them, to my way of thinking, equally suspect. So, when my lord Cahir asked me to go and tend the wounded warrior, I was more than keen to hear what this Darini warrior had to say. That he had challenged Lord Brecan before the assembled kings, he confirmed, and believed that this was why he had been set upon—to silence and discredit him, and dissuade him from asking any more awkward questions. Conor mac Ardan—aye, he was the king's son—told me he believed that greedy, ambitious Brecan Brigantes aimed at making himself High King and, in the moment he spoke those words, my own suspicions quickened. I glimpsed something of the substance from the shadows I had seen.

That is why I chose Conor to help me—that was something of a whim, I admit—but my sense of his integrity did not lead me astray. However, since he was the one attacked by Brecan's men, I needed a way to get him to myself and removed from further contention as a threat to Brecan and his plans, whatever they might be.

For this, I took up one of the rumours already in the

wind—that Conor had stolen something of value from an unattended camp. A thin tale, I know, but serviceable at least. Hiding my bit of gold was not difficult and once that was done, all the rest followed much as I expected.

Did I feel bad for him? Did I feel a pang of remorse for disgracing that brave and noble spirit, and heaping ignominy on that blameless head? Not at all.

Well, perhaps a portion of regret. But to serve a banquet, a bullock must die. Conor's warrior pride was my sacrificial calf.

I could not have found a better collaborator. Thanks to Conor and his stalwart friends, I now have evidence that something new and dangerous is stirring in Eirlandia. The presence of the Fair Folk and the toilsome making of the Scálda war carts points to something dire beyond the naked ambition of a puffed-up lord, aye, beyond anything I imagined. I cannot see its shape yet, but thanks to those three fearless Darini spearmen I have confirmation to lay before the Coinemm of Brehons.

What we have discovered will be discussed and argued over, I have no doubt. Alas, this is the weakest part of our assault. The Learned Brotherhood possess enormous power, but they have grown miserly in their use of it, and their isolation has blinded them to the suffering of our people.

This—this alone is what drove me from their exalted ranks. I watched the Scálda steal our land while the druids stood by and shook their shaven heads in dismay. When the incessant preening and posturing of our learned leaders grew too much to stomach, I left the grove.

Eirlandia was in a chaos of upheaval in those days. It seemed the whole island was on the move, with many tribes and the remnants of tribes fleeing the unstoppable Scálda onslaught. I travelled from camp to camp, listening to harrowing tales of destruction and death, aye, but also great heroism.

I searched among temporary camps and established strongholds alike for a lord I might serve and guide.

In Lord Cahir I found a nobleman who valued a druid's counsel and would listen. At the time, Cahir was still finding his feet. He had not been king but a few months before the arrival of the Black Ships. Raw, untried, and almost overwhelmed by the unforeseen challenges that seemed daily to multiply, he needed my guidance and, I like to think, came to value it. Through this ruler, I was able to wield the better part of a druid's power to good purpose. Through Cahir, I grew to better understand the ways of kings and lords—how they think, how they see the world, the breadth of their influence, and their limitations.

To be sure, there are always limitations—even the greatest monarch among them is hedged about with a multitude of concerns, expectations, responsibilities, and obligations—each of which must be successfully negotiated if he is to succeed. Thus, compromise is ever the order of the day, and then having a druid as chief advisor can be a boon. The kings of old recognised this and most would not venture placing a foot upon the coronation stone without one of the druí by his side. These days, few lords can entertain such a luxury. And the Learned Brothers, even knowing this, do little enough to help.

Shame, I fear, wears a druid's robe and disgrace, a druid's torc.

Yet, there are some—like Lord Brecan, to give him his due—who yet uphold the time-honoured ways. He has ever had a druid by his side. Whatever you may think of Mog Ruith, you will never find a more loyal servant to any king. This is not to say that I approve of either one of them, mind.

From the first, I considered Brecan mac Lergath little more than a prancing pony—tricked out in gold and richly coloured cloth, and surrounded by sycophants who doted on every word. I thought him ambitious, self-regarding, petty, jealous of his imagined stature among the tribes. I saw in Lord Brecan one of those nobles who flatter themselves that they are mighty rulers descended from the Dagda himself and whose every action is worthy of eternal celebration and every utterance the essence of poetry.

I also considered that his occupation of the throne would be brief. The Brigantes have always been known as a moderate, sensible tribe. Surely, they would not suffer such a puffed-up pretender for long. Sooner or later, they would tire of his expensive tastes and his grasping, overweening ways. When his people saw him for what he was, they would throw him over.

Yet, the man persisted. The years passed and, rather than losing faith and support, his esteem among his fellow lords and nobles only deepened. Brecan's standing grew apace and his stature in the Oenach increased. In ways I could neither explain nor understand, Brecan of the Brigantes became the preeminent lord of Eirlandia, and is now well on his way to gaining the high king's torc.

This is not to say that Brecan is loved by one and all. There are those—Cahir and Ardan among them—who cast a worried, wary eye upon the Brigantes lord's inexorable rise. I share their concerns, so I do, and the longer grows Brecan's shadow, the more I distrust him.

Thus, when I began hearing of Brecan's restless travels, those furtive forays along the borders of his realm, I made it my business to find out more. Now, many a king likes to ride to the hunt, and every one of them makes a circuit of his lands from time to time—but not like Brecan, who seemed to ride out every few days with only a scant handful of his most trusted men to attend him.

Who was Brecan meeting? And why?

These questions plagued me for a season or two, and the

more I brooded, the darker my suspicions became. Then Conor appeared. The eldest son of Lord Ardan, he had his father's distrust of the Brigantes lord, and even dared to make his voice heard in the Oenach. What happened next could not have been conceived in another age and time: Lord Brecan had him beaten.

Whether the king ordered it, or warriors of his warband took it upon themselves to enforce their lord's will, made no difference. Incredibly, the incident passed without causing so much as a ripple, but when I learned of it I knew the time had come to discover Brecan's intentions.

Conor believes my method clumsy and ill advised, and perhaps, given time, the plan to remove him from suspicion could have been better. But I had no time. I had to act quickly and so I seized the first tool that came to hand. In this, at least, I am vindicated. For we have learned much in these last few days—enough, at least, to confirm my darkest suspicions that something of great and terrible consequence is about to be unleashed. There is still much to do, but we have made a start. I have every hope that soon, very soon, we will learn the secret that Brecan mac Lergath knows and has laboured long to conceal.

22

Manannán mac Lir, god of sea and sky, smiled on the stolen ship and the canny audacity of its pitiable sailors. The moon held sway most of the night, sinking into cloudy obscurity only a little before dawn. With the clouds came a heavy mist that rose from the surface of the water and drifted on a freshening wind. Conor, on the pilot's bench, steered steadily north, following the coast; Fergal, working the ropes, tried to keep the sail full so the craft could maintain a fair forward speed. But it was a fight. The inexperience of the seamen made even simple tasks difficult. It had been a long, tense night and both men were tired.

Nor were they the only ones fighting fatigue. It took all Huw's considerable know-how to keep the horses calm and quiet, and Mádoc remained occupied with the wounded warrior below the half-deck.

'How is Donal?' asked Conor when Mádoc came to view their progress along the coast.

'He is in a bad way.'

'No change then.'

'We must try to get him to shore as close as possible to Carn Dubh—they might be able to help him there.'

'If I knew where that might be,' Conor told him, 'I would happily comply.'

'Do you not know it? I am surprised.' The old druid looked

out across the sea at the slowly passing shoreline. 'I fear our friend will not survive a lengthy journey over land.'

'What is this Carn Dubh that makes it a good place to go?'

Mádoc regarded him curiously. 'Truly, you do not know?'

'Truly, I do not. Nor will I, unless—'

'A druid school—the oldest in Eirlandia,' replied Mádoc. 'It's also the largest druid settlement, and there will be an ollamh or two who can do more for him than I can do on this cursed ship. On my oath, the very sails reek of Scálda to me.'

'Show me—' Conor made a sweep with his hand toward the long, undulating line of the coast in the near distance. 'Show me where to steer, and I will do my best to take us there.'

Mádoc frowned. 'How should I be knowing where to steer? I have never approached the place from the sea.'

Conor sighed, and with some exasperation, said, 'If that is the way of it, I fear we must make landfall where we can—be it close to Carn Dubh or far away.' He cast a glance around the empty sea round about. 'And that soon, lest the Scálda find us.'

Muttering, Mádoc moved off; he paused to speak to Huw and, patting the boy on the shoulder, continued on, making a circuit of the deck. Conor watched as the druid began to pace—three slow, deliberate steps—from one side of the ship to the other and back again. Head down, sight turned inward, back and forth he paced, pausing now and then, shaking his head, and then resuming. Once, he paused and put his thumb in his mouth and chewed for a long moment, then resumed his pacing.

After a time, Conor lost interest and turned his attention to the coastline once more, searching for any possible haven. He was fairly certain that they had travelled far enough north to have passed out of Scálda reach. He gently nudged the vessel nearer the shore—the better to see any settlements, dwellings, or fishing camps. This, he thought, might indicate a bay or cove where they could make landfall. He called to Fergal and related this intention. Fergal, dull with fatigue, replied that he would do his best.

The sun showed a dull ruddy glow low on the eastern horizon—like that of a hot iron trying to pierce sack cloth; and with the sunrise the wind shifted around to the south. Conor, plying the steering oar, eased the vessel onto a gently veering course that would bring them closer to the coast. Slowly, the ship adjusted to a new heading, and the wind fell away by degrees as they drew nearer to land and their progress slowed accordingly.

Conor was scanning the rock-bound shore when he felt a silent presence. He turned to see Rhiannon watching him—as if she had suddenly materialised from the sea.

'Lady, I did not hear you,' he said, rising from the steering bench. 'How is Donal?'

'He sleeps.' Her deep blue eyes studied him closely. 'How do you fare?'

As if in answer to the question, Conor yawned. 'I am as you find me.'

'Then it is a tired man I see before me.'

Conor shrugged. He did not feel inclined to say more.

'So that is how it is.' She offered a strange little smile, and half turned away. Conor thought she would leave him then but, swinging back quickly, she extended her hand—palm flat, fingers spread wide—and put her hand to his forehead. Instantly, Conor felt a surge of energy and the oppressive lethargy fled; his limbs became lighter, his vision keener; the mental fog dissipated; wit and perception became sharp once more.

She removed her hand and smiled again, but it was clear to Conor that something had gone out of her—some part of her strength and stamina had entered him.

'I thank you,' Conor told her. 'But if you had told me, I would have asked you to give the charm to Donal instead.'

Rhiannon's smile deepened and touched her eyes. 'Your care and thoughtfulness is laudable. What can be done for your friend and swordbrother has been done. And it will be done for Fergal, too.'

Conor watched as she moved to where Fergal stood at the spar ropes; there Rhiannon performed the same charm for Fergal. The effect was not only swift but, seen from a distance, amusing: the tall warrior staggered back and then jerked upright, shook his head vigorously, raised first one knee and then the other, and clapped his hands. Conor chuckled to himself. Dead on his feet one moment and dancing the next—never had he seen such a thing.

'Are you well, brother?' he called.

Fergal grinned and waved at him.

'I thought you might like some help. You were looking a little tired.'

'If you see me tired, brother,' Fergal replied, 'you will know that you are dreaming. I have never been stronger.' He put his head back and drew a long deep breath. 'It must be the sea air.'

'Aye,' agree Conor, 'it will be the air.'

He was still speaking when Mádoc shouted. 'Scálda ships!'

23

Conor spun around and scanned the dull green-grey sea. Rising mist obscured the horizon, but in the dim light of dawn he could just make out two dark hulls to the seaward side and still some way off. He turned back to gauge the distance to the shore and made a swift calculation; the Scálda ships were, he thought, about as far from them as their vessel was from the coast. With any luck, they might reach shore before their pursuers and escape on horseback into the forest—providing they could find a landing place.

'Fergal!' he called. 'We're making for land.'

Fergal saw the red-sailed ships and loosed a groan of exasperation; he tightened his grip on the spar ropes. 'I thought we had lost them,' he shouted back.

'They haven't caught us yet,' Conor told him, and turned his attention to the shoreline.

The eastern coast was rough and rocky, but with a few coves and narrow bays where landfall might be possible. Conor swept his gaze along the tumbled cliffs and steep-walled sea bluffs until at last he spied what appeared to be a suitable landing place: a small rock-bound cove with a pebbled beach. Hard by this inlet was another—little more than a gap between two large stone headland bluffs that stood like ruined towers or the broken feet of giant effigies—a slender cáel providing a channel for an upland stream.

He shouted to Fergal, pointing at the narrow opening. 'There! We make for the cáel.'

Fergal acknowledged the decision with a wave, and Conor, throwing the steering oar wide, shouted, 'Turn!'

Fergal plied the ropes—loosing one and hauling on the other. The full-bellied sail spilled and emptied.

'Too much and too fast,' called Fergal. 'We've lost the wind.'

The ship continued under its own momentum, but slowed quickly and soon sat dead in the water. Conor cast a hasty glance at their pursuers; the Scálda vessels came on apace, their course unaltered. 'Mádoc! Hurry! Take the oar,' he shouted; jumping down from the pilot's bench he ran to where Fergal was struggling with the ropes, trying to swivel the spar to allow the sail to recapture the breeze. The druid took his place at the steering oar to watch as Conor and Fergal worked the ropes—twisting the spar first one way, then the other, and back again in an effort to find the wind. After several futile attempts, the limp cloth at last puffed out and the vessel began to move once more.

The ship swung onto its new heading and even collected some small part of its former speed. Sweating from the effort, Fergal swiped his arm across his face and, looking around to the Scálda ships, declared, 'They know how to sail and we don't. I will fetch our weapons.'

'We may not evade them,' Conor said, watching the twin black hulls; he could see the white froth splashed up by the prows as they cut through the waves. 'Nor can we fight them.'

'What then?'

Conor frowned, his mind racing furiously for a solution. There was none. 'Mádoc,' Conor shouted, 'can you do anything to help us?'

'Given time enough and a few essential materials, perhaps, I might—'

'Mádoc!' snapped Conor. 'Can you do anything?'

The druid glowered at the ships closing fast upon them. 'Alas, no.'

Turning back to Fergal, Conor said, 'We stay on course. Help Huw ready the horses—as soon as the keel touches land, we ride.'

Fergal opened his mouth to object, then closed it again. He handed Conor his rope, and hurried to the mast where Huw stood waiting with the horses.

'Mádoc!' Conor shouted over his shoulder. 'Steer for the gap there—between the rock stacks. We are going to make a run for it.'

The old druid turned his eyes from the oncoming ships to the slender breach between the tumbled bluffs. 'Impossible,' he cried. 'The cáel is much too narrow.'

'Just do it!' Conor shouted. 'We have no other choice.'

'I yield the oar to you,' Mádoc called. 'If we are to survive, you are our best hope.'

Lashing the ropes to the oar post, Conor seated himself on the steersman's bench and took up the relinquished oar. He explained what he intended and ordered Mádoc to help Rhiannon make Donal ready to flee the ship as soon as they touched the shore. 'That will not be an easy thing to do,' the druid told him as he lurched across the deck.

'Nothing ever is,' Conor muttered. 'Just do your best.'

Conor looked to the Scálda ships and saw that they were closer now, as expected, but that their progress had slowed somewhat—the wind fell away for them, too, as their vessels neared the coast. Conor allowed himself a grim smile. *As for the hare, so for the hound,* he thought.

Fergal returned to his ropes and announced that the horses were ready to release on his signal. There then followed a series of frenzied manoeuvres in which Conor did his best to align the prow of the ship with the gap in the crumbling rock wall of the headland bluff—a chore easier said than done for, the closer they came, the harder it proved to keep the Scálda craft on course. Small corrections of the oar produced no effect, and larger movements caused the prow to swing too far to one side or the other. Each lurch brought fresh cries from Fergal, who manfully fought to keep the sail filled. Meanwhile Huw and Mádoc had their hands full with the horses; it was all they could do to keep the frightened animals from bolting and either running amok on deck or leaping into the sea.

Conor glanced back to see that the Scálda ships had so shortened the distance between them that he could see the glint of sunlight off the blades and battle caps of the warriors. He counted heads to gauge the enemy strength, and took some small comfort in the fact that, close as they might be, they were somewhat fewer in number than he had imagined—at least, the ones that he could see. Likely, the pursuers had put to sea with the search party they had, rather than wait for more warriors from the fortress. Nor did he see any horses on board. If only he and Fergal could get everyone onto shore, they stood a good chance of outrunning the pursuit.

Even as this thought was passing through his head, Conor heard the waves breaking on the rocks. Whirling around once more, he saw the cliff base dangerously close on his left-hand side, and the sea flinging gouts of spray and foam into the air. A sea swell passed beneath them, lifting the vessel and driving it forward—and pitching Conor from his perch.

There was no time to think. No sooner had he steadied himself on the bench once more, the next swell was rising beneath them. The rocks loomed hard on the right-hand side and Conor threw the oar to the left as far as it would go. 'Hold on!' he cried, clinging to the shaft of wood. Fergal gave out a growl of despair as the sails spilled and fell slack. Mádoc, grim-faced at the mast, muttered dark oaths and hurled them at the foe behind.

As the next swell gathered beneath them, Conor rose and shouted, 'Get down! We're hitting the rocks!'

Fergal dove for the rail, and Huw embraced the mast. Conor flung himself to the deck and wrapped his arm around the post supporting the steersman's bench as the sea swell lifted the ship and the surge flung the craft forward. There was a fall as the wave passed and Conor thought they might just have eased through. But then he heard a tremendous crunch, and the entire ship shuddered with a terrible rending, grinding shiver.

The deck heaved and bucked beneath him. The ship slewed sideways. Sea and sky changed places. 'Free the horses!' he shouted, throwing off his cloak. He saw Huw struggling with the halter rope and Mádoc diving beneath the half deck platform as for one shuddering heartbeat the vessel seemed to hang in the air.

Another wave smashed the hull against the rock wall, battering its tightly overlapped planks with a shock that jolted the stunned passengers. The vessel tilted and slid, falling back as the next wave struck, spinning the helpless craft sideways. The deck fell away sharply. Unable to hold on any longer, Conor began to slide. 'Rhiannon!' he cried with his last breath as the cold green water closed over his head.

24

The shock of frigid water stole the air from his lungs. Thrashing blindly, Conor fought to find the surface, but could see nothing in the murky, wave-churned depths around him. Then, forcing his limbs to cease their flailing, he held himself still and his body began to rise. He righted himself and, directly above, made out the blurred outline of the hull. Kicking his feet he rose and, upon reaching the submerged rail, grabbed hold and pulled himself into the air. With a gasp, he dashed salt water from his eyes, and looked around furiously.

Fitful waves slapped the broken hull of the wrecked ship; the small portion of the sharply slanting deck that he could see was empty. The next wave slammed into him before he could see more. He went down again and came up coughing and spitting. 'Mádoc!' he called, scrabbling for a handhold on the rail. 'Mádoc! Rhiannon! Fergal!' he shouted again and again, but heard only the thump and crash of the breakers smashing against the quickly splintering hull.

Releasing the rail, he spun around in the water and glimpsed the head of a horse breaking the surface—Grían, Fergal's red stallion. The animal thrashed and plunged, glassy eyes wide with terror, nostrils wide and mouth open, screaming, straining for breath as its forelegs churned the water. Conor whistled to the animal to draw its attention; he started toward it—then saw the blood streaming from the gash in its throat. Conor stopped, treading water. The poor beast sank beneath the surface—only to rise again but lower in the water, its efforts frenzied, but less strong. It sank again, and this time could not lift its head from the water.

'Conor! Here!'

Conor whirled toward the cry, and saw someone clinging to the rocks nearby. 'Fergal!' he shouted. 'Are you injured?'

Before Fergal could reply a wave crashed against the rock on which he clung. The water subsided in streaming white rushets down the black rock face, but Fergal was no longer there.

'Fergal!' Conor shouted again. A moment later, Fergal's head bobbed to the surface. 'Here! Here!' Conor beat the water with his free hand to draw Fergal's attention. The sea swell lifted him and he glimpsed, a little farther off, two horses—one the dun mare Ossin, and the other Búrach, his grey stallion—swimming for the strand.

'Conor!' spluttered Fergal as he swam to join Conor. He reached for Conor's offered hand and Conor pulled him to the rail. 'Donal and Rhiannon—where are they? Where are Mádoc and Huw? Where are the others? Do you see them?'

A savage breaker shivered the wreck just then, forcing the broken vessel higher onto the rocks. A low, grinding moan like that of a great oak being felled sounded from above and the tall mast began to sway precariously. The next wave struck the ruined hull with a thunderous clap and the wreck lurched sideways; the water slid away and the stricken vessel rocked with a tremendous groan of rending timbers.

'Swim for shore!' shouted Fergal. He dived and began swimming away. Tilting precariously, the unsteady mast gave way, splintering from its base; the heavy beam came crashing down, plunging into the cáel with a thunderous splash. The backwash threw Conor against the submerged rail. He gulped down a mouthful of seawater and almost choked on it. Coughing and spitting, he made a last hurried search for anyone nearby, then started for the shore—almost immediately colliding with the body of Grían; the red roan stallion, having succumbed to its injuries, was now floating half-submerged, its struggles over. Conor pushed away from the still-warm corpse and continued on, threading his way amidst the pieces of broken planking, rope, and chunks of debris now floating in the wave chop. Now and again, he knocked against something hard or sharp—a shard of timber or fragment of rail or deck—and once he became ensnared in a coil of rope that threatened to drag him under. The shore stubbornly refused to come any nearer and Conor's efforts grew more desperate until, kicking wildly, his foot struck a rock. Pain streaked through him. He gave out a gasping cry and inhaled a gout of water that burned his lungs, and came up coughing and retching. Sinking down again, he felt stones beneath his feet. Gathering his legs beneath him, he hauled himself upright and stood, finding himself in waist-high water. Still coughing, he hobbled exhausted from waves to collapse on the beach half in and half out of the water, cradling his injured foot. Blood oozed from a bluish scrape beneath which a knot was already swelling. Out of the water now, he shivered with cold in his soggy clothes. Hearing moaning nearby, he turned his head and saw Fergal sprawled on the pebbled strand, wheezing and groaning.

'Are you hurt, brother?' called Conor between snatched breaths.

'Ach, nay—only drenched to the very bones of me, and those are drenched, too.' With an effort, Fergal pushed himself up onto his elbows. 'Do you see there what you did?'

Conor looked where Fergal indicated and saw that the hull had rolled onto its side and, having been driven sideways by the tide surge, was now all but wedged into the breach between the rock stacks—effectively blocking the narrow channel leading into the cove. The Scálda ship in fast pursuit had reached the cáel—too close behind to avoid the wreck—and was now caught up in the disaster. Prevented from entering the cove, the Scálda were desperately trying to disentangle themselves from the wreckage. The shouts and cries of the frantic warriors could be heard as they attempted to get clear. The second vessel had managed to veer off, but was in danger of being swept onto the rocks itself.

'That will slow them down,' Fergal observed. 'But we dare not linger here or they will catch us yet.'

'Not without the others.' Conor looked around the shingle where bits of flotsam were now washing up: snaky lengths of rope and rigging, bits of wood, some of Huw's utensils and supplies—but nothing else. 'We have to find them.' He rolled over and pushed himself up onto his hands and knees and was immediately overcome with a fatigue so powerful that he almost swooned. Black circles wheeled before his eyes and his empty stomach heaved. He vomited bile and fell back onto the beach with a groan. 'Uh . . .'

'The faéry spell is wearing off,' concluded Fergal. 'I do not think I can move.'

Conor closed his eyes and drifted off. A voice came to him out of the air. 'Why are you lying there?'

'Aoife?' he asked.

'Who is Aoife?'

Conor opened his eyes to see that it was Rhiannon standing over him. Her hair was wet and tangled, her brilliant gown a soggy ruin, but her eyes were keen with concern for him. 'Are you injured?'

Conor shook his head. He rolled over and sat up. 'Mádoc and Huw?' he said. 'Have you seen them?'

Rhiannon shook her head and knelt down beside him.

'Donal?' he asked, fearing her response.

'He, at least, is saved.'

'How?' wondered Conor aloud.

By way of reply, the faéry merely pointed toward the wood above the high-tide mark. Donal, pale and unmoving, lay on the shingle. A little farther up the beach stood Ossin and Búrach; of Mádoc, Huw, or the pony there was no sign.

Fergal dragged himself to his feet and shambled over to where they sat. 'We cannot stay here. We have to go.'

'Not without Mádoc and Huw,' Conor insisted.

'There is no time, Conor,' Fergal told him. 'We have to go now—or join them in the grave.'

'We don't know that they are dead!'

Rhiannon glanced at Fergal, who shook his head. 'Look around you, brother; if they were alive they would be here with us.'

'Maybe they are still in the water.' Climbing to his feet, he limped into the waves.

'Wait!' called Fergal. 'Here—' He sloshed through the surf to a hank of rigging rope that had washed up. Returning, he unwound the coil and passed the end to Conor. 'Tie this around you and I will hold you fast.'

Knotting the rope around his waist, he started into the surf once more, shivering as the cold water hit his skin. He drew a breath and launched himself out toward the middle of the bay and soon encountered the body of Drenn, Mádoc's bay mare. The creature had become entangled in the halter rope and drowned; its ruddy brown coat was slick with brine and splotched with bits of seaweed. And from its belly protruded a long, jagged spike of wood, rammed like a spear through the creature's gut. The dead horse stared up at the sky with a wide, black unseeing eye, its head and legs flopping gently in the wash of the waves. Conor drew air deep into his lungs and dived, quickly searching the area in the immediate vicinity of the drowned animal. The muck stirred up from the seabed clouded the water and made it difficult to see; he pulled on the line dangling around the horse's leg and it came free—at least, there was no one attached to it.

Resurfacing, Conor pushed away from the dead animal and swam farther out into the cáel, trying to avoid impaling himself on the splintered chunks of decking lurking in the wave wash. He bumped into the steering oar and held on to it for a moment as he searched the water—but saw no one in amidst the floating wreckage. He heard Fergal shouting something from the shore and, waving a hand in acknowledgement, swam out farther, dodging bits of broken rail and hull. He came upon a section of floating planks—part of the half-deck platform, maybe—and dove under it. There, trapped beneath the planking, was Mádoc.

The old man's eyes and mouth were open, his hands outstretched; he appeared about to give a command, or trying, in death, for something just out of reach. His sparse hair floated around his head in a pale nimbus and his flesh was grey-white as cold ashes. Conor took the proffered hand and gave it a tug. There was no response, not the least flicker of life. The hand was as cold as the water around it.

Conor resurfaced, gulped down another lungful of air, and dived again. Taking hold of the old man's arm, he pulled; Mádoc's head jerked loosely, but the druid's cloak was caught in the tangle of wreckage. Conor pulled again, but the body did not come free. Running out of air, Conor returned to the surface and shouted toward shore, 'I've found him! I've found Mádoc!'

Before Fergal could reply, he dived again to free the trapped corpse. The druid's long cloak was snagged on a spar of splintered timber and, try as he might, Conor could not work him free. Once more, he was forced to return to the surface. Clinging to the half-submerged raft of decking, he drew air deep into his lungs and dived once more. This time, instead of tugging at the body, he went for the cloak and, taking hold of the splinter, broke it off. The cloak came away and the body floated free. Taking Mádoc's arm, Conor swam for the surface, pulling the dead druid with him. He quickly untied the line around his waist and attached it to Mádoc's corpse. 'Pull!' he shouted, yanking on the rope. 'Pull hard, Fergal! Haul him in!'

He had to repeat the message twice more before the body began to move. Once Mádoc was free of the debris, Conor renewed his efforts—searching among the flotsam for little Huw. He dived once and again, trying to see through the murk for the pale shape of a body. Each time he ran out of breath and had to resurface, he dived again, more determined than before, and each time was forced to the surface without so much as a glimpse of the boy.

But he did not stop. He swam farther out, and closer to the ship, which was breaking up, shedding more timber and junk into the cove. He dived again—deeper, longer, and more desperate. He felt his own strength, already low, ebbing away, but he refused to give up. From the beach, he heard Fergal calling to him, but ignored the shouts and dived again, and yet again.

When he came up, it was all he could do to snatch a breath of air and, as he sank back, he felt someone seize his arm. Fergal pulled him up. 'Enough!' he cried. 'It is over. Come back. You help no one by drowning yourself.'

Conor gave in and allowed Fergal to haul him back to the pebbled strand, where he lay on his back panting and gasping. Gradually, as strength returned, he rolled over and heaved himself up onto his feet. Still breathing hard, he staggered to where Fergal now stood over the body of Mádoc. He had pulled the drowned druid from the water and carried him up onto dry land, and arranged the corpse in an attitude of dignified repose. His hands were folded over his chest, his legs were straightened, his ankles placed together, and his eyes were closed. If not for his wet clothes, he might have been simply napping after the events of a trying day. 'That was well done,' Conor told him, then moved on up the beach to where Rhiannon knelt beside Donal.

Conor sank down on the shingle next to her.

'I am sorry about the boy,' Rhiannon said in a voice shaded by sadness.

'His name was Huw,' Conor told her.

'I am sorry.'

Conor nodded and swallowed hard. He put the back of his hand to Donal's cheek; the flesh was cold and, save for the slow stirring of his chest, there was no response. The trauma of the shipwreck and plunge into the sea had reopened the wound in his side; blood seeped through the cloth of his siarc, staining a patch the size of a fist deep crimson.

'We cannot stay here,' said Fergal as he joined them. He cast a look back at the ruined ship, now all but submerged in the mouth of the cáel. The Scálda had succeeded in disentangling themselves from the wreck and were no longer to be seen. 'It is you they want, my lady,' he said, 'and they will not stop until they get you back. We have to go.'

'What about Mádoc?'

Fergal shook his head.

'We take him with us,' said Conor.

'We cannot—'

'We take him with us,' insisted Conor. 'He was a friend, and we do not leave him behind.'

Fergal accepted this and brought Ossin to where Mádoc lay; together he and Conor hefted the body up onto Ossin's back and secured it with a bit of rope so it would not slide off. They covered him with his cloak and then, with Rhiannon mounted on Búrach, they carefully lifted Donal onto the horse, cradling their stricken brother in the faéry's arms. They set off then, Fergal leading Ossin with Mádoc's body, and Conor walking beside Búrach with one hand steadying Donal; they left the beach and entered the wood at the head of the cáel. With a last glance at the all but sunken ship, Conor turned his eyes to the trail ahead.

Rhiannon

Mother's first children, the fairest of Creation, we are the true monarchs of the earth—yet, our time as sovereigns of this worlds-realm is waning. Soon, perhaps very soon, we will withdraw behind the veil of the Otherworld, the better to live out our days in peace and plenty. This, our sages tell us, is for the best. That may be true. Who am I to say?

Still, I do most bitterly despise it.

The mortals are such fragile, fallible creatures. That they should be the chosen inheritors of the land and all its treasures, wealth, and bounty is a continual wonder to me. That the All Mother should allow this calamity to prevail fills me with sadness and, if truth be told, envy. Great the lament! For, while the lesser beings multiply and flourish, spreading their dominance over every order of creation, we slowly diminish. Our numbers fail.

Once, we were mighty; once, we were very gods. It is true that the mortals think us gods and goddesses still. If they only knew how far we have fallen from that exalted height. We gloried in our strength and the Mother's radiance was all our own. But that was a very long time ago. The world will belong to the mortals and their ever-increasing clans and tribes. The human kind will rule in the end. So be it.

The Scálda are not human. They are demons, surely. What manner of demons they may be is a thing too revolting to contemplate. But they are as the pestilence that breeds in the slime and cesspits of the underworld whence they have sprung. Voracious in appetite, full of spite and malice, their small, dark minds—hard and crusted as burned cinders—conceive no virtue, nurture no truth, hold no higher belief than the iron they dig for their hideous weapons. Recognising only hate and fear, they turn every transaction to one or the other. No light of love or beauty penetrates their unfeeling souls.

If we must leave this worlds-realm, then at least we will no longer be forced to look upon the evils they perform. Alas for fair Danu's race! They must live—or just as likely die—in a world tainted by presence of the Scálda and their abhorrent gods of iron and bone.

We of the first children have a choice, but the poor mortal Dé Danann possess no such benefit. If there were but one gift I could bequeath them, it would be to rid Eirlandia of the odious Scálda that they might remember us with the affection of true friendship when we have gone.

25

The four survivors followed a well-worn path inland, little caring where they went just so long as it was away from the cove of the wreck. The sun had scarce quartered the sky when, weary and almost delirious with fatigue, Conor felt Rhiannon's hand on his arm. He shook himself fully awake and looked around. They had passed from the light stands of birch and beech bordering the coast into an older heavier wood of ancient oak and ash and yew. Fergal had stopped a short distance ahead. 'I've found something,' he called, and gestured Conor forward.

Conor glanced at Rhiannon, handed her the reins of his horse, and said, 'Stay here.'

He joined Fergal and found him stopped before an obstruction in the middle of the path. 'What do you make of that?' asked Fergal as Conor came to stand beside him. He pointed to a pillar stone: a tall, thin column of grey rock about the height of a man, the right half of which was painted red, and the left adorned with human handprints in blue. Atop the stone was placed the skull of a wild boar, scoured by the wind and rain and bleached white by the sun, with great curving tusks and ragged teeth; the empty eye sockets had been stuffed with earth from which the curled green tendrils of fern plants emanated.

'Druids?' said Feral.

'Who else?' replied Conor.

The pillar stone marked the the entrance to a small, circular sunlit glade at the far side of which stood a small stone bothy, little more than a hut with a reed-thatched roof; before it, a good-sized fire ring had been established with an iron tripod and large cauldron. Beside the hut stood another, very much smaller round structure made of stone and shaped like an overlarge beehive. The rest of the clearing was given to grass, which grew long and lush. All appeared silent and deserted.

'I don't think there's anyone here,' said Fergal. 'We can rest a while and graze the horses at least.'

Conor agreed and, stepping past the boar's head pillar, they entered the glade. Four more standing stones marked out the perimeter, and each of these was topped by a capstone shaped like an upside-down bowl and painted red. Crossing the grassy expanse, they proceeded to the hut and looked in. The single square room had a floor of beaten earth and bare walls; there were no wind holes or any furniture save for a shelf from which hung a chunk of flint and a tang of iron affixed to either end of a leather strap. The small beehive-shaped building had a small, round wooden door just big enough to admit a man if he entered on hands and knees. Fergal pulled open the door and peered inside. He gave a sniff and then crawled in and, a moment later, backed out again with half a smoked mackerel. 'It's a smokehouse,' he said. 'Someone's been curing fish—there's a rack of them inside.'

Conor pushed past him and looked in. The place reeked of heavy smoke and the rough walls were black with layered soot. Through chinks in the stonework he could see a wooden rack containing a dozen or so flat-splayed mackerel stained orange by the smoke. There was a fire ring in the centre of the house and Conor placed his hand on one of the stones— both it and the ashes within the ring were cold.

'We won't starve, at least,' he said upon backing out again. Fergal handed him a piece of smoked fish and Conor devoured it in two bites, then licked his fingers and said, 'Let's set up camp in the bothy and get a fire going.'

He and Fergal returned to the woodland path where Rhiannon was waiting. They led the horses into the clearing and to the door of the shelter, and then eased Donal down from the stallion, carried him inside, and laid him on the floor. They untied the body of Mádoc and put him at the opposite end of the hut and covered his body with his cloak. 'It is damp in here,' Conor observed.

'Dried bracken would make a fair bed,' Rhiannon told him. 'And a fire would soon warm this place. I will gather the bracken.'

'I'll help,' said Fergal, 'after I see to the horses.'

'I'll get some firewood,' Conor said.

While Fergal tethered Ossin and Búrach with the rope they had used to bind Mádoc's body, Conor went back along the forest path to collect dried windfall wood for kindling. He quickly gathered an armload and had returned to the edge of the clearing when there came a thrashing of branches, of something moving fast through the undergrowth and not caring how much noise it made as it came.

Instinctively, Conor dropped the wood and took up one of the larger pieces to use as a club. He squared off as out from the trail tumbled a short, squat druid. Little more than a mere scrap of a man with an overlarge head, wide mouth, and protruding ears, he was dressed in a green robe with brócs laced high on his bare legs; his druid tonsure was bristly black stubble and in sore need of renewing; the faded blue cloak folded on his shoulder all but trailed behind him on the ground. Red-faced from chasing down the trail, he took one look at the travellers, turned, and shouted, his voice loud and echoing through the trees, 'They're here! I found them!'

The little man took a long look around the glade and said, 'The people with you—one of them was injured, I think. Is he—?'

'He lives, but the wound is deep,' Conor replied, staring at the newcomer. 'Who are you?'

The diminutive druid pushed past him to the boar's head pillar stone at the entrance to the clearing, noting the horses and Fergal who was tending them. 'Your friends—I thought there were more of you. Where are the others?'

'Who are you?' Conor asked again. 'How is it you are here?'

'I am Tuán,' said the man. He made a little bow of courtesy, then started off across the clearing. Conor gathered up the wood he had dropped and hurried after, catching up with him at the door of the bothy. Tuán ducked inside and, kneeling down beside Donal, placed the palm of his hand to the stricken warrior's face and asked, 'Was it the shipwreck?'

'It was a spear wound,' Conor said, dumping the wood by the door, 'from before the wreck.'

The druid nodded and stood. 'You are fortunate to have survived.'

'Some of us didn't,' Conor told him. He indicated Mádoc's body beneath its improvised shroud. With a curious, hopping gait, the druid moved to the body. Stooping low, he lifted the edge of Mádoc's cloak, then glanced up. 'One of the Learned Brotherhood, I see. Who was he?'

'His name was Mádoc,' Fergal said, joining them. 'He was helping us.'

There came a call from outside and the three stepped out of the hut. 'Ah!' said Tuán. He held out a hand to the newcomers. 'Here are my companions.'

Three druids, one of them a woman, advanced across the clearing. Like Tuán, they wore green; the men were dressed in breecs laced up to the knee, with siarcs and short cloaks folded on their shoulders. The woman had a hooded green robe over a mantle of the same colour, gathered in a girdle of pale yellow. All displayed silver torcs, but the foremost bard's torc was larger and made of three twisted strands—one end of which was a bear and the other a stag—marking him as a high-caste druid. Slung over his shoulder was a red-and-yellow-checked cloak. He strode to where Conor stood, raised a hand, and, in a voice like golden mist over a deep calm sea, announced, 'I am Eádoin, Ollamh of Carn Dubh. I give you good greeting. May you find peace and rest from your travails while you are here.'

Conor offered his thanks, and the chief druid continued, 'Tuán you have met and this is Dáithi, our esteemed filidh.' The second druid made a sign of respect and, indicating the woman, the high druid said, 'And this is Gráinne, Banfaíth of Dairefidh, a druid of highest repute and the most accomplished healer among us. She will attend your wounded friend.'

At this the banfaíth lowered her hood to reveal dark hair streaked with white and large, dark eyes that held a look at once gentle and commanding. She stepped close and, placing her hand on Conor's arm, said, 'You are safe within this wood. No harm will come to you here. Trust that I will do all that can be done for your friend.' She looked around. 'Where is he?'

'Just inside,' replied Conor, and stepped away from the door. 'His name is Donal mac Donogh,' Conor told her. 'For his sake, I thank you.'

Gráinne moved past him and went in to examine the wounded man, and Eádoin turned to the warriors and said, 'Your courage is to be commended. Not many would have attempted what you did—'

'And fewer would have survived the attempt,' put in Tuán.

'What is your name, friend?' asked Eádoin.

'I am Conor mac Ardan of the Darini.' He put out a hand to Fergal, adding, 'And this is my swordbrother Fergal mac Caen.'

'Ardan mac Orsi?' asked the filidh named Dáithi. 'Him I have heard of. And you are his son, perhaps?'

'One of them,' Conor replied. 'He has three.'

Before he could say more, the banfaíth emerged from the hut just then, and said, 'I am sorry about the old one, but your friend Donal still clings to life. I will not lead you falsely—his injury is grievous, but trust that I will do all that can be done to save him.'

Both Conor and Fergal thanked her, and Eádoin said, 'I was told there were three of you on the beach,' He looked around. 'Where is the third?'

At this Rhiannon stepped out from her hiding place behind the bothy. Holding a bundle of dry bracken under her arm, she came to stand beside Conor.

One look at her elegant stature, her pale skin and flawless features, and the druids fell back in amazement. 'A faéry!' gasped Dáithi, visibly impressed. Tuán only stared, and Eádoin opened his mouth to speak, but could find no words. Gráinne, however, moved quickly to Rhiannon's side and said, 'We are honoured, lady. May peace attend your sojourn here among us.'

Rhiannon accepted this with simple grace, and replied, 'I am Rhiannon of the Tylwyth Teg, and any kindness shown to me or my people will be remembered and rewarded.' With a nod to Conor and Fergal, she said, 'These men have rescued me from the Scálda to their great cost. I owe them my life.'

Turning to Conor, the high druid asked, 'How is it that you came to pilot a Scálda ship into the bay? That is a tale I long to hear.'

'And here am I thinking you know all about it,' replied

Conor; the faces of the druids swam before him and he stifled a yawn.

Gráinne saw it and put her hand on his shoulder. 'You are
tired and need your rest. Sleep a little, and leave all else in
our care.' With a gesture, she sent Dáithi and Tuán rushing
off to prepare rough beds of bracken beneath the oaks behind the bothy.

'What about Donal and Mádoc?' asked Fergal.

'I will attend Donal,' she told him, 'and, if you allow it,
we will prepare the body of Mádoc for his funeral.'

'I will have supplies and fodder brought from Carn Dubh,'
Eádoin added, waving a hand in the direction of a low rise
just beyond the trees to the north. 'Worry for nothing.'

Conor thanked them both, and he and Fergal allowed
themselves to be led to their rest. 'It appears we were closer
to Carn Dubh than we knew,' sighed Fergal.

'Aye,' agreed Conor, 'Mádoc would be pleased.'

They stumbled to the place beneath the boughs of a great
oak giant where the druids had spread their cloaks over
mounded piles of bracken. A brook trickled from somewhere
nearby, its waters making a pleasant music. Conor sank down,
closed his eyes, and the world drifted away on the gentle
sound of the water as he succumbed, at last, to the peaceful
oblivion of slumber.

26

'Donal!'

The shout brought Conor from a heavy sleep. Battling through a wall of fatigue as through a mud-filled bog, he opened his eyes to find himself in a darkling wood, covered by someone else's cloak. For a moment, Conor could not remember where he was or how he had come to be there; he knew only that he was ravenously hungry and that his bladder was dangerously full.

Raising his head, he looked around. Fergal lay nearby, also covered with a cloak, and still fast asleep. There was no one else around. The shout, then, had been his own. At this realisation, memory came flooding back . . . the sea chase . . . the wreck . . . the druid glade . . . the druids . . . everything. The stone bothy stood nearby and the surrounding wood was alive with the calls of rooks flocking to their night roosts. He dragged his shattered strength together and stood, then staggered a few paces to a nearby tree. While he tended to his business, he caught the scent of smoke and with it the sweet, oily smell of roasting meat. Water instantly filled his mouth.

Greatly relieved, he stepped from the wood and walked around the bothy to find Eádoin and Dáithi sitting on stools beside the fire ring while a young, brown-robed ovate with a ladle and basting bowl was tending three spits on which fine fat hares were now sizzling, and something in the cauldron was beginning to bubble. Across from them, Tuán sat cross-legged on the ground, feeding broken branches into the fire.

'Ah! Here is our man now,' announced Dáithi, his voice loud in the quiet of the clearing.

'Sit with us, please, Conor mac Ardan,' invited the druid chieftain. 'We have been discussing your audacious escape. You and your friends are to be commended for your skill and fortitude.'

'Or, was it simple luck only?' wondered Tuán, breaking another stick. 'What do you think, Conor mac Ardan?'

'I think we make our own luck.'

'Yes, fashioned from fear and desperation, no doubt,' said the small druid, drawing smiles from his Learned Brothers. 'It is a marvel what fear can do.'

'Whether from fear and desperation, luck, or skill—or some admixture of all,' offered the high druid pointedly, 'the fact remains that destiny favours these men.'

'We are *all* children of destiny,' replied Tuán. 'But destiny is not the same as triumph.'

'Sit,' invited Eádoin again. 'Talk with us a while. We would hear more of your escape.'

'Unless you think me too audacious, desperate, and fearful for your exalted company,' replied Conor dryly.

'Take no notice of Tuán,' said Dáithi. Conor watched the savoury juices sluice over the meat, and swallowed heavily. 'He is always contrary. It is his way, but he means no disrespect.'

'Take no notice of me,' muttered Tuán. 'It is my contentious nature.'

'How do you know about the wreck?' asked Conor to no one in particular. 'How did you know to come looking for us?'

'We saw the ships,' replied Dáithi. 'Ever since the coming

of the Scálda we have placed watchers on the coast. One of them witnessed the chase and the wreck of your vessel and ran back to Carn Dubh with a report. When we heard there were survivors, we came to lend our aid and learn what we could of this affair.'

'You followed us?'

'The path from the sea leads here. We guessed you would come this way,' said Eádoin. Indicating the glade and bothy, he added, 'This is our *clóin*—our fish camp and smokehouse. We use it for ceremonies, too, sometimes.'

'I want to see Donal,' said Conor, moving to the bothy. He stooped and entered the little stone hut. Two bronze lamps and a number of beeswax candles illuminated the dark room with a soft warm light. On a bed of bracken, Donal lay covered by a yellow cloak; Gráinne knelt at his side, her hand resting lightly on his chest. Rhiannon sat beside her, hands folded in her lap. The sight was so peaceful, so still, Conor thought Donal must have succumbed at last to his injuries and died.

Gráinne looked up as Conor stepped into the room; she smiled and beckoned him to join her. 'I am glad you have come, Conor.' She reached out and took his hand, pulling him down beside her. 'Do not be troubled,' she said, having glimpsed Conor's face as he took in the sight of the pale, motionless body before her. 'Your friend lives still.'

At the sound of their voices, Donal roused somewhat; he opened his eyes and tried to raise his head. Gráinne brought out a small bowl of brown liquid and, supporting his head with one hand and holding the bowl with the other, she gave him to drink. 'It is beef liquor,' she said. 'For strength.'

Donal swallowed down a few sips, then closed his eyes again and sank back on his bed. Putting aside the bowl, Gráinne pulled back the cloak covering the injured man. They had removed his siarc and applied a sticky green poultice to the wound in his side; bits of moss and other leaves had been mashed up and bound in a paste with camomile, garlic, and honey. With Rhiannon's help, Gráinne now gently rolled Donal onto his side and proceeded to pick off and discard the spent medicine, revealing a nasty red gash with spidery blue-black fingers stretching out from it. The wound was raw and open, and running with a yellowish fluid. Gráinne wiped this away with a soft cloth rinsed in something that smelled of vinegar, and then cleaned the wound and renewed the green poultice.

As she worked, Conor regarded the banfaíth—not young, nor yet old. Full of figure and face, she seemed to exude an air of the wisdom as old and deep as the forest around her, of peace and deep calm; and yet there was something of the night about her: of deeds done in darkness, of secret places, and strange oaths pledged in the light of the moon.

The banfaíth finished dressing the wound, and they rolled Donal onto his back and replaced the cloak. Conor realised he had been holding his breath and exhaled in relief. 'He is very strong—the strongest among us.'

'He is strong, yes, and that is in his favour.' The banfaíth nodded thoughtfully. 'He is also a true warrior, and now he fights for his life.'

Conor stared at the inert body of his friend beneath the cloak. 'Can he be healed?'

'We believe,' said Rhiannon with a nod to the banfaíth, 'that he has been poisoned.'

'Poisoned . . . ,' repeated Conor.

'The Scálda spear was poisoned . . . ,' the faéry explained.

'The blade thrust alone was not enough to harm this much,' Gráinne explained. 'The Learned have had word that the enemy has begun using poison on their weapons. Truly, nothing is beneath them.'

'Can he recover?' Conor asked again.

'We are trying to draw the poison from the wound,' the banfaíth replied, 'but there is only so much we can do without an antidote.'

Conor gazed into her kindly eyes, but felt a chill on his heart. 'If there is anything I can do for him—anything at all, only tell me and I will do it.'

'We will remain with him through the night and see what the morning brings. It is all we can do now.' She gave his arm a squeeze and said, 'You would do well to eat something and rest. Restore *your* strength while you can.'

A gabble of voices sounded from outside, and Conor heard Fergal among them. He thanked the women for their care and, as he rose to leave, he noticed that the place where Mádoc's body lay was empty now. Gráinne saw his glance, and said, 'Eádoin has ordered the body of Mádoc mac Laoire removed to Carn Dubh so his brothers might prepare it for the funeral rite.'

'When?' asked Conor.

'Tomorrow evening at sunset,' replied the banfaíth.

Conor left them to their vigil. Outside, he saw that Fergal had joined the druids and was telling them about the escape from the Scálda stronghold and the sea chase. At Conor's approach, Fergal said, 'It was all Conor's idea, mind. None of us would have survived if not for Conor.'

Shaking his head, Conor took a seat at the fire ring, saying, '*None* of this would have happened if not for me.'

'You saved us, brother. Never doubt it.'

'Huw and Mádoc would take a different view,' Conor replied. 'And Donal would likely agree with them.'

'Why speak of things that are beyond knowing?' said Dáithi. 'What has happened has happened.'

'Fergal was telling us about your recent sojourn among the Scálda,' said Eádoin. 'It was a daring plan. I can only wonder at the reasoning behind it.'

'Ach, now, that was Mádoc's idea,' Conor replied. 'It was in his mind that Lord Brecan of the Brigantes has formed an alliance with the Scálda in order to seize the high kingship of Eirlandia for himself.'

'And if that was true,' said Tuán, 'and such an alliance existed, then you might find evidence of it with the Scálda?'

'That is what Mádoc thought.'

'A grave accusation to place against the name of so great a king,' allowed Dáithi.

'This is why we needed proof,' put in Fergal.

'Rarely has such treachery been known in Eirlandia,' mused Eádoin.

'*If* there was any treachery at all,' Tuán said. 'It might merely have been an old man's delusion, or a misapprehension. Is that not true?'

'We discovered nothing to lay at Brecan's feet, true,' Conor answered. 'But my cracked ribs and bruises convinced me that it was no delusion.'

'Three armed Brigantes against one unarmed Darini,' Fergal spat. 'That such should happen at an Oenach . . .' He shook his head gravely. 'Shameful.'

'This attack took place at an Oenach, you say?' wondered Eádoin.

'For a fact it did,' Fergal declared. 'Donal and I were there to put a stop to it, or they might have killed Conor.'

The druids turned wondering eyes on Conor, who explained how he and Donal and Fergal had caught Scálda spies prowling around the Oenach, and his attempt to bring the matter to the attention of the gathering—only to be rudely dismissed by Lord Brecan when he tried to insist on further investigation. 'I don't think they meant to kill me—only to punish me for speaking out against Brecan and discourage me from meddling any further in the king's affairs.'

'And it is your understanding that this beating came about

as a result of your challenge to Brecan before the assembly?' queried Dáithi.

'I, at least, received that understanding,' Conor replied. 'It is remarkable how persuasive fists and feet can be.'

'It proves nothing,' concluded Tuán. 'Maybe Lord Brecan did not favour the shape of Conor's head—or perhaps the king disliked the scarlet stain on his manly cheek.'

At mention of his ill-favoured birthmark, Conor felt the heat of anger flush through him. 'You are right, of course,' he replied coldly. 'I forget that my disfigurement does often provoke. You are kind to remind me.'

'We are what we are,' said Tuán with a smug little bow. 'The question is, how long will you allow it to hobble you?'

Conor stared at the little toad of a man for a long moment, then turned his face away.

'Now then,' said Eádoin, 'you say that Mádoc's suspicions led you to search behind the wasted land in Scálda territories?'

'Truly,' replied Fergal. 'As Conor said, it was Mádoc's idea. And I believe we were very close to succeeding, but we were exposed and forced to flee.'

'So, in the end, you discovered nothing for your efforts,' said Tuán. 'Nothing at all.'

Rankled at the insinuation that they had indulged in a fool's errand, Fergal said, 'We found two captive faéry women—one of them Rhiannon. We also found wheels—hundreds of them.'

At the baffled glances from the druids, he went on to describe the massive forge fortress and the mine where the Scálda were digging ore out of the hills to construct iron rims for wheels by the score.

'Are you certain that is what they were doing?' inquired Dáithi.

'As sure as I have eyes in my head,' replied Fergal. 'Conor,

Donal, and myself—we watched dog-eaters at the forge, and at the mine, and we saw the finished wheels borne away by the wagonload.'

'Why?' asked the druid. 'Why so many?'

'They are making war carts,' Conor told them, and described the small horse-drawn wagon they had seen being driven by the Scálda chieftain in the fortress yard.

'War carts . . .' Tuán shook his head. 'Has anyone heard of such a thing?'

'I believe I have,' said Dáithi, tapping his chin with his fingertips. 'The Vindelici of old called them *chariots*.'

Conor had never heard of any tribe called the Vindelici, but Dáithi was quick to elaborate. 'In the last age, this noble people flourished across the Great Sea on the plains and hills of Gallia. They were feared by many, and respected by all. Their sages provided a solid foundation that exists to this day in the teaching of the Learned among the Gaels. Even now, there are some who revere them as gods. I do not hold them so high, but only say that they were a mighty race, reigning over all other tribes by the power of trade and their skill at arms. It is said that these Vindelici, under a ruler called Cissonius, brought the chariots—these war carts, as you say—to Gallia.'

'Where did Cissonius get them?' wondered Tuán.

'No one knows,' answered Dáithi. 'Some say they learned of chariots from their trade partners across the southern seas in lands where many such vehicles were known.'

'Ach, I have it now,' agreed Eádoin, nodding his head slowly. 'The Gaels . . . I believe you are right.' He turned his eyes to Conor, his brow creased in thought. 'Hundreds of these wheels, you say?'

'That many if not more. As Fergal said, we saw heavy wagons loaded with rims and at least one storeroom filled with finished wheels—enough for dozens of chariots.'

'Could it be that this is the reason the Scálda have been quiet these last summers?' suggested Dáithi.

'Quiet?' scoffed Fergal. 'You speak as a man who has never held a spear in battle with the dog-eaters.'

'Ach,' nodded Dáithi, 'yes, to be sure.'

'Still, compared to summers past, the swart invaders have been content to harass and harry, but have mounted no sustained assaults,' Tuán pointed out, drawing nods from the other druids around the fire. 'It would seem the enemy have been building their strength and constructing a fleet of these chariots to aid in the completion of the conquest begun these many years ago. That would make sense.'

All were silent for a long moment, and while they sat contemplating the implications of that thought, the ovate rose from his place and announced that the meal was ready. A stew of greens and turnips with onions was ladled from the cauldron into bowls along with portions of roast hare; these were passed around with chunks of dried bread for sopping up the liquid. They ate gratefully, and eventually returned to the discussion at hand.

'It seems to me,' suggested Tuán, 'that this insinuation of treason on Brecan's part is groundless. Apart from gross ambition—as repugnant as that may be—I cannot detect any greater stench to lay at his door.'

Fergal's lip curled in derision. 'I would have thought making war carts was worrying enough to warrant more than a sniff of interest,' he grumbled. 'If Mádoc were here, he would tell you soon enough. It was his distrust and suspicion that drove us into the wasted lands.'

'Do not mistake caution for indifference,' chided Eádoin. 'If we probe a wound, is it not for the purpose of gaining a more accurate assessment of the injury and what may be done to heal it?'

'The nub of it is that you have brought back nothing to link

Brecan to the chariot-building activity of the Scálda,' insisted Tuán.

'That may be,' argued Dáithi, 'but I think you are forgetting the enemy spies our friends here caught at the Oenach—a gathering summoned by Brecan himself.'

'What so?' demanded Tuán. 'That tells us nothing.'

Conor sighed inwardly. Left to themselves, these Learned Brothers could chase a thing from dawn to dusk without ever coming near a capture. He ate his meal, hardly tasting what he swallowed, for his heart was that heavy. When he finished, he thanked the druids for the food and their sustaining aid, then returned to his place beneath the oak, where he rolled himself in his cloak and closed his eyes. Sleep was a long time coming and when it did arrive, it was filled with curious dreams of windswept hills where women danced within a stone circle by the light of a blood-red moon.

27

Conor awoke the next morning ill rested and aching in body and mind. His first thought was to go and see how Donal had fared during the night. He threw off the cloak and climbed stiffly to his feet. Morning sunlight fingered through the mist clinging to the upper branches, and the air smelled of leaves and moist earth. Fergal was still asleep nearby and, at the fire ring in the centre of the clearing, Tuán sat alone beside a cold pot, feeding twigs into the fire to get the water boiling for the porridge. Conor raised a hand in a halfhearted greeting, and went into the bothy.

Rhiannon sat beside Donal, much in the attitude in which he had left her the night before, but her head was bowed upon her breast and her eyes were closed. Banfaíth Gráinne lay in her cloak nearby, also asleep. Not caring to wake them, Conor stood for a moment, taking in the limp hair, bloodless lips, and hollow, ashen cheeks of his swordbrother, and fresh feelings of guilt and futility washed over him. How could he have let this happen?

He turned to go, and as he stepped to the door, the ban-faíth awoke and said, 'Against all our fears, Donal remains in the Land of the Living.'

'But no improvement?'

'Alas, there is no improvement.' Gráinne rose and returned to her place beside the stricken warrior. She drew aside his cloak and put her fingertip lightly to the wound; the surrounding area was still very red, the inflamed area threaded with blue-black tendrils, but seemed not to have grown any larger. She dipped a scrap of cloth into a bowl of water, wet it, and laid the damp cloth on the fevered skin, then replaced the covering and sat back with a sigh. 'No better—but no worse, either. We'll try to get him to eat something when he wakes.'

'Can anything be done?'

The druidess shook her head. 'Not by me.'

'Then who?' said Conor, striking a fist against his leg. 'Eádoin said you were a healer of great renown.'

'Do not be angry,' Gráinne said gently. 'There is yet one hope. I have discussed this with Lady Rhiannon—and she tells me that there exists among her people the possibility of healing.'

'They can cure him?'

'A possibility only,' she allowed. 'It may be there is a remedy for the poison that afflicts your friend. If so, their physicians may know of it.'

'Only tell me the way,' Conor said, gazing at the wasted features of his friend, 'and trust I will go to them and bring back this remedy.'

'No,' replied the banfaíth with a light shake of her head. 'Rhiannon and I discussed this. It is our belief that Donal must himself be brought to the Tír nan Óg so they can examine him. That is now his only hope.'

Conor's ruddy stain began to itch as frustration mounted. 'A stillborn hope, it seems to me,' he said, rubbing the side of his face absently.

'Why stillborn?' The voice was Rhiannon's and it was at Conor's shoulder. He had not guessed she was there, much less that she had overheard them talking. At Conor's forlorn expression, she put a cool hand to the back of his neck and he felt the tension go out of him. 'Do you think I would leave

Donal? Or you? Or Fergal? Or anyone who saved my life from the hateful Scálda and their killing iron?'

'In truth, lady, I do not know what to think.'

'Hear me, Conor mac Ardan.' She held him with her pale blue eyes. 'I will not abandon Donal. And I will never abandon you or Fergal while there is yet breath in my body—or Fergal's, or yours.' She released him then, and said, 'Come outside with me.'

Conor followed her out of the bothy and into the nearby wood. The sun was a little higher and the tall elms and oaks were alive with birds. Rhiannon found a place where the sunlight formed a bright patch on the ground, went to it, and stood there. 'Stay where you are,' she told Conor. 'Neither move, nor make a sound.'

Then, turning her face to the light, she lifted her right hand toward the sky and stretched her left before her. She closed her eyes and began to sing—at least, to Conor it sounded more like song than speech—just a few phrases in a rising intonation. When the song finished, she paused, and then repeated it. Conor watched her and was struck anew by how very lovely she was: the early light struck her upturned face and made her features glow; her night-dark hair gleamed and her blue gown shimmered in the play of light. Once more, Conor was transfixed by the beauty before him and was content just to stand and stare.

Rhiannon repeated the song for a third time and then fell silent. She lowered her right hand, but kept her face raised and her left arm extended. In a moment, Conor sensed a change in the wood around them. While his attention had been on the faéry queen, the birds in the trees round about had grown more agitated, their competing calls becoming louder and more strident. He could hear the flapping and rustling of their wings in the upper boughs and, looking up, saw furtive activity among the quivering leaves: rooks and sparrows, jays and blackbirds and even little finches—all of them hopping from branch to branch and proclaiming their right to a twig of territory.

Then, even as he watched, a great black raven took flight, circled once, and then flew down to perch on Rhiannon's outstretched arm. The creature regarded her with a glossy black bead of an eye, ruffled its feathers, clacked its big hollow beak, and took a nip of the glimmering fabric of her gown. Rhiannon raised a warning finger to the bird, and the creature hopped a little higher up her arm. To Conor's amazement, the raven allowed its sleek head to be stroked while the faéry spoke in low, soft tones to it—her right hand making curious signs and motions over the bird all the while.

When she finished, a look passed between them and the raven spread its wings. Rhiannon raised her arm and, with a last command, launched the bird into the sky. Conor watched it spiral up through the opening in the leafy canopy and quickly disappear above the treetops. The faéry watched the sky for a moment after the bird had gone, and then turned with a smile to Conor and said, 'There—the message has been sent. If all goes well my father will soon receive it and send a boat for us.'

'Your father will send a boat?' Conor repeated. 'Because of the bird?'

Rhiannon laughed and the sound seemed like rain sparkling in the sunlight. 'He will send it because I asked him. I will know if he received the message before this day is out.'

They returned to the bothy then and Rhiannon went in to help Gráinne renew the dressing on Donal's wound. 'If I can do anything . . . ,' said Conor from the doorway.

'Bring us some of Tuán's porridge when it is ready,' the banfaíth told him, 'and a little water. That will be help enough for now.'

At the fire ring, Tuán was just then dropping handfuls of

oats into the pot to get the porridge started, so Conor went in search of the brook that had kept him company through the night, and found it at the bottom of a fern-lined channel not far from the oak where he slept. The stream was shallow and ran to join a bright expanse of water not more than a few hundred paces further on. Conor followed the brook and soon stood at the shore of a fair-sized lough; a bed of tall reeds stretched away to his left, and on his right, a stand of small willows lined a flat grassy bank. The sunlight glinted off the blue, sky-tinted water, and a breeze ruffled the surface in tiny waves that lapped the shore at Conor's feet. Green hills, clothed in morning mist, raised their bare heads above the trees on the far side. Among the tall, swaying reeds, dragon-flies glinted—iridescent sparks in the morning light—and coots scudded about like little black coracles; along the shore-line, swans drifted in slow-moving clouds. The place was so serene, so peaceful, Conor was instantly seized by a yearn-ing so strong it made his jaws ache.

This is how it is supposed to be, he thought. *This is Eirlandia as it is meant to be.*

He stripped off his clothes and waded into the cool clear water to bathe and swim and watch the clouds sail by slowly overhead. When he was clean and refreshed, he waded to shore and shook off the water and dried himself with his siarc, then pulled on his breecs, laced up his brócs, and, with his damp siarc over his shoulder, started back to the clóin. He had only gone a few steps when Tuán stepped out into his path.

'Where are your brother druids?' Conor asked. 'I didn't see them this morning.'

'Eádoin and Dáithi left before daybreak to take word of your discoveries in the Scálda territories to Carn Dubh. Ovate Galin went with them to fetch more supplies for us here.' The squat druid came nearer with his little hopping gait. 'Eádoin is calling for a council to decide what to do. They will return for Mádoc's sending.'

'A council of druids,' Conor mused. 'Will that do any good?'

'We must start somewhere,' replied Tuán.

Conor gave a curt nod, and made to continue on his way, but the little man spread his arms wide, effectively blocking the path. 'It is not your fault that Donal was injured and Mádoc and Huw were killed. I believe in my soul that if you had your way they would still be hale and well, and Eirlandia would be a better place.'

'You mock me, little man?'

Tuán shook his head gravely and bounced up on a fallen log to stand nearly eye level with Conor. 'No, Conor mac Ardan, I only tell you the truth. The world is not yours to command.' He smiled, his wide mouth stretching wider still. 'I had thought a man whose brother was a druid would have a higher opinion of the craft.'

Conor stared at the little man. 'My brother—you mean Rónán? You know Rónán?'

'I know him well. We were many years in Willow House at Suídaur. Morien was our head there, and Rónán used to tell me about his older brothers, but it was you he mentioned most of all.' Tuán held his head to one side. 'When was the last time you saw him?'

Conor had no need to count back through the years—that fateful day was never far from memory. He could see it still: his little brother high up on that fine horse, eyes wide with fear, clinging to the druid who had just called down a curse upon Conor's people . . . and his father standing helplessly by as his youngest son was taken from him—sacrificed for the good of the tribe, but a sacrifice all the same. The pain of that separation had lingered long. 'It has been ten summers—at least that many—although my father got word of him from time to time, and he was brought to visit once. Tell me, how does he fare?'

'Right well. His feet are firmly planted on the path to become an ollamh, or perhaps a brehon. You can be proud of your brother.'

They talked of Rónán then, and life growing up in the druid house. Tuán proved a veritable wellspring of information about Rónán and his progress through the manifold stages of training and practice. Conor came under the sway of the small opinionated druid. By the time they returned to the clearing, he and Tuán were better friends. At the fire ring, they found Fergal awake and watching Galin, the ovate, put apples to bake in the warm ashes. Conor and Tuán sat down to wait for the meal to be ready, and Tuán said, 'Have either of you ever heard of Balor Berugderc?' He looked from one to the other of them. 'Balor of the Evil Eye, they call him.'

Conor shook his head, and Fergal said, 'That is a name I would recall, I think—if I had ever heard it. Who is he?'

'Last year—sometime after the raiding season, we believe—the Scálda warleader was overthrown. His name was Marroc and he had been king over the lesser Scálda tribes since his father Morchan died in a battle a year or two after invading Eirlandia. Marroc was of the Ochthach tribe and his favour has declined sharply, along with the status of his clan, in the last few years. He was vulnerable to a challenge.'

Conor glanced at Fergal, and asked, 'How do you know this?'

Tuán's wide mouth split in a grin. 'The Brothers of the Oak do not spend all our time in groves staring at trees, you know. We have our ways.'

'This Marroc fella,' said Fergal, 'was he killed then?'

'We don't know,' replied Tuán. 'But earlier this year we

began hearing reports that Balor Berugderc—the chief king of the largest tribe known as the Fomórai—had been elevated to the throne. I would not be astonished to learn that Balor is the one building the chariots.'

They discussed this until the meal was ready and Galin began spooning the oat and salt pork porridge into bowls. Conor took a bowl and beaker of water into the bothy for Donal, and returned to the fire ring to eat with the others; when he finished, he put a few handfuls of oats in his sparán and, with Fergal beside him, went to take care of Búrach and Ossin. The horses were tethered beside one of the standing stones at the edge of the clearing; they had grazed the area fairly well, so the two warriors pulled up the tether pegs and led their mounts to the brook for water. While the animals drank, Fergal said, 'They took Mádoc away this morning. Did you see?'

'They took him before I woke up,' Conor told him. 'Tuán said the druids will prepare the body for his sending to-night.'

'Sending?' Fergal regarded him curiously. 'What is that, then?'

'I don't know,' Conor admitted. 'I expect we'll find out.'

After the horses had drunk their fill, Conor and Fergal led them to the lough and into the water; they stood in the shallows, splashing water on the animals' coats and rubbing them down with dock leaves pulled from the nearby bank. Conor gave himself to the task, happy to lavish his attention on the grey and keep his mind off the events of the last few days. While he worked, he spoke to Búrach, calling him by name and telling the handsome beast whatever came to mind; he praised the stallion for his strength and spirit, his speed and noble bearing, and told him about his home at Dúnaird and about Aoife who was waiting for him there. Now and again, Conor dipped into his sparán for a handful of oats and let the stallion nuzzle them from his hand. 'There now, Búrach,' he said, 'you like these oats, I know. See how I take care of you? We take care of one another, aye, so we do.'

The grooming finished, they led the animals to the grassy bank and tethered them among the willows to let them graze to their hearts' content while the two warriors sat and talked and watched cloud shadows move across the distant hills.

The remainder of the day passed peacefully enough, but Conor eventually tired of waiting for Eádoin and Dáithi to return from Carn Dubh and, as the sun began its descent into the west, he walked down the coastal path through the forest to the cove of the shipwreck. It felt good to stretch his legs and move, but as he drew near his destination, he realised there was something in him that needed to see it again. He grieved for Mádoc and little Huw, and in the back of his mind was an unformed thought that he had left something undone on the beach. And so he made his way to the strand, though what he hoped to find when he got there, he could not have said.

He was still high up on the path above the cove when he caught sight of the calm waters of the cáel and the sea beyond. There was no sign of the ship on the rocks, nothing to show what had happened there. He resumed his walk and, upon reaching the top of the strand, saw that the druids had scoured the beach, gathering all the wreckage into a pile hard against the wall of the sea bluff on the far side of the cove; the carcasses of the drowned horses, Grían and Drenn, had been hauled off to one side and covered by the remains of the ship's red sail. The little Cymru hill pony, Íogmar, like his young master, was missing.

Farther down the beach, four young druids, stripped to the waist, were labouring to add timber and driftwood to what appeared to be a low tower. Conor greeted them and asked what they were doing.

'This is for one of our brothers,' the ovate told him.

'For Mádoc?'

'Aye, did you know him?'

'I did. He was a friend of mine.' Conor regarded the structure. 'What about Huw—Mádoc's serving lad? He died, too.'

'I don't know anything about that,' the druid replied. 'Are you Conor? Eádoin told us what happened here. It was a very brave thing you did.'

'Maybe.'

The ovate shrugged and resumed his work, and Conor walked down to the water's edge; he picked his way among the few scattered bits of flotsam and debris that still remained from the wreck. As he sifted through the stuff, he realised he was looking for Huw; half of him hoped to find the boy, and the other half feared that he would. Still, he searched until, overcome by the futility of his efforts and an unutterable pity for the poor lost boy, he sat down on the beach, wrapped his arms around his knees, and let the tears fall. 'I am sorry, Huw,' he murmured. 'Truly . . . sorry. . . .'

The tears and admission expressed the pain of grief Conor felt for the sad deaths of Mádoc and Huw, and his inability to help Donal. The sigh of the waves seemed to echo his sorrow, and he sat for a long time nursing his pain and fell into a reverie as he listened to the ceaseless wash of the water. When at last he raised his head, he saw that the sun was low behind him, casting long shadows of the sea cliffs into the bay. The tide was flowing in and he was alone on the beach. Looking down, he saw something in the wavelets lapping at his feet—a bit of debris, he thought. Reaching into the water, he snagged the leather lace of a shoe—one of Huw's brócs.

Holding the dripping shoe, he rose and, with a last glance out at the empty sea, turned to head back up to the clóin. He had gone but a few steps when he noticed a light in the northern edge of the forest, flickering as it moved through the trees. Conor watched and the light came nearer, and there emerged from among the trees at the northern edge of the wood a young woman carrying a torch; she was dressed in a white robe and blue girdle and her crown was shaved ear-to-ear over the top of her head, marking her as a druid. She paused at the top of the beach, and was soon joined by a procession of bards, both men and women, walking in single file to the cove. Trailing behind the procession came four of their number bearing a simple bier of woven wattles on which rested a corpse in a winding cloth bound with scarlet bands. The corpse-bearers advanced to the water's edge and lay the bier beside the wooden platform, and the rest assembled around it.

Conor scanned the group; there were, perhaps, thirty or more, with Tuán, Dáithi, and Eádoin among them. He walked to where they stood, greeted them, and, holding the wet shoe, presented it to Eádoin, saying, 'I found this. It belonged to Huw.' The high druid took the bróc and turned it over in his hands. Conor added, 'I think it is all that is left of him.'

The chief druid thanked Conor and, turning, handed the shoe to Dáithi with the command, 'Prepare another body for the pyre. Hurry, for the moment draws near.'

While Conor watched, the druids quickly assembled an effigy. Gathering wood from the bier and dried seaweed from the top of the beach, they fashioned a small parcel and tied it with lengths of twine; to this they added the shoe Conor had found and wrapped everything in a piece of a cloak, binding it all together with some of the scarlet bands taken from the larger shroud. When they finished, two body-shaped bundles lay side by side on the strand at the water's edge—one larger, one very much smaller: Mádoc and Huw, together in death as they had been in life.

As Conor looked on, Fergal joined him; Rhiannon and

Gráinne followed a little after, and all four stood together to watch as the high ollamh began the ceremony.

At Eádoin's command, four ovates stepped forward and took up Mádoc's shroud-wrapped body and placed it atop the pyre; they nestled Huw's shrouded effigy beside it. Then, arranging themselves in a semicircle around the pyre, the druids from Carn Dubh began to sing—a strange and melancholy melody with words neither Conor nor Fergal could understand. At their wondering glances, Gráinne whispered, 'It is the Song for the Dead—in the sacred tongue of the bards.'

Like the rising and falling of the sea swell, the voices of the bards rose and fell, intertwining, weaving chains of melody that stretched on and on. Meanwhile, Eádoin turned and faced the sea, searching the dusky water and the slowly dimming sky. At last the moment came and, turning to address the gathering once more, he raised his hands and called in a loud voice. 'Brothers! Cease your sad lament. The time for home-going is at hand.'

The singing hushed and fell away. Eádoin summoned the ovate with the torch; the young woman stepped forward and knelt on the strand before the high druid. 'What do you bring, my daughter?' asked Eádoin.

'I bring fire—the reclaimer and refiner.'

'For what purpose do you bring it?'

'To reclaim the bodies of the dead for the earth,' replied the young woman, 'and to refine their souls for the homeward journey.'

Holding his hands outstretched above the wavering torch, Eádoin said, 'Flame of the Sun, born of the world's first kindling, daughter of the Beltaine blaze, we release you to your sacred work.'

Eádoin stepped aside and the ovate rose and, holding the torch with both hands, she applied it to a clutch of kindling at the base of the pyre. She then moved on to the next side of the low tower and applied the torch, and the next likewise until a small fire burned at each corner. She then turned to the gathered bards and, raising the firebrand, called out in a loud voice, 'This is the work of the flame—to light the soul's journey to the next world, and to purify the flesh for its return to earth. This is the work of the flame.'

She turned and thrust the torch into the centre of the pyre where it sputtered and flared and at last took hold. Wisps of smoke drifted into the still, twilight sky. Soon thin fingers of flame reached up, searching among the logs and branches for places where they might catch, slowly building as piece by piece the carefully stacked timber ignited and burned. When all was alight, Eádoin turned to the assembly and, raising his hands, cried, 'Behold! It is the time-between-times, when the veil between this world and the next is parted. We stand here on the shore neither wholly land, nor yet sea. This is the auspicious time and this the sacred place. Here and now we send our brothers on their homeward journey to the Land of Promise.

'My friends'—he opened his arms wide and smiled—'we fear death as a child fears the closed door behind which unseen dangers lurk. But in death there is no danger, for with it comes the freedom of release and rest and every comfort. I ask you now, what is death that we should fear it?'

The question did not hang in the air very long before Tuán stepped forward. Holding a bunch of six twigs tied with grass, he said:

> *In Death is the death of Pride,*
> *In Death is the death of Ambition,*
> *In Death is the death of Envy,*
> *In Death is the death of Anger, and Wrath, and*
>   *Resentment, for these are the bane of Charity*
>   *and Compassion.*

So saying, he tossed the twigs into the fire. No sooner had he stepped back, than Dáithi took his place before the pyre. Holding out his clutch of twigs, he said:

In Death is the death of Sickness,
In Death is the death of Misery,
In Death is the death of Infirmity,
In Death is the death of Sorrow, and Grief, and every
*   Affliction of Sadness, for these are the bane of Health*
*   and Happiness.*

Dáithi gave his fuel to the flames, and backed away. His place was taken by a young ovate, who, in a high, reedy voice sang:

In Death is the death of Hardship,
In Death is the death of Distress,
In Death is the death of Worry,
In Death is the death of Pain and Hurt and every Harm
*   of heart and mind and spirit, for these are the bane*
*   of Hope and Joy.*

The fire continued to build. The flames leapt high, hungrily devouring the carefully erected pyre, slowly transforming the timber into a golden latticework of fiery embers and the shrouded figures into luminous effigies of light. The ovate put his bunch of six small branches to the fire. The oldest druid in the gathering stepped slowly forward and with trembling hands held his outstretched bundle and, in a quavering voice, called:

In Death is the death of Conflict,
In Death is the death of Discord,
In Death is the death of Hostility,

> *In Death is the death of Hate and Fear and every Evil*
> *under heaven, for these are the bane of Truth and*
> *Wisdom.*

As the last symbolic twigs were consigned to the flames, Eádoin, the Wise Head of Carn Dubh, once again took his place before the pyre. 'In death all things of hindrance, of fettering, and every burden of heart and mind and spirit fall away like the binding cords of the death garment fall away in the purifying fire. The fruits of liberation and true freedom are tasted for the first time, and these, we are assured, will never end.'

Turning to the flames, he said, 'Here, in the time-between-times, we say farewell to the bodies of our brothers, and bid their souls a swift journey to the world beyond this one. And though we may mourn their passing, we are also reminded that they only go before us on the path we all must tread. May they find peace and every comfort in the Land of Promise.'

To this came the resounding reply by the chorused bards, 'So may it be with us all.'

Nothing more was said, or needed to be said. But all stood and watched the fire perform its refining, cleansing, liberating work. The heat of the pyre grew hotter, forcing everyone back a few steps, and still it built until at last the centre of the tower gave way and collapsed inwardly upon itself. One of the bards began a low chant—little more than a hum that rose and fell in waves—and this was picked up by another. One by one, other voices added themselves to the number until the entire cove thrummed with the uncanny sound. When the last bard had joined in, the one that had started the chant turned and began walking up the beach toward the woodland path by which they had come, passing into the night that was now full upon them. He was followed by the second bard, and so on until only Eádoin, Dáithi, Tuán, and the camp ovate Galin were left with Conor and Fergal and Rhiannon to watch the fire.

When the last bard had disappeared into the darkness, Eádoin put out his hand and indicated to the others that they, too, should depart. Lit only by the light from the pyre, they made their way back to the druid glade in silence, still dazzled by the vision of what they had seen. An end had been made, a destination reached, and a new journey begun. There was a rightness about it that satisfied and to add anything more would only be to diminish the perfection achieved. And Conor felt in himself a deep consolation that comforted and cheered him.

28

Conor's feeling of peace and contentment lasted through the night and into the next day. Just after daybreak, Eádoin and Tuán had left the cloín and Conor and Fergal, roused by their departure, found Dáithi and Galin at the fire ring. When they asked where the others had gone, Dáithi explained that they had gone back to Carn Dubh where Ollamh Eádoin was to convene a Coinemm, which Conor thought of as a sort of Oenach of high-ranking druids from across Eirlandia for the purpose of hearing the allegations of treachery against the Brigantes king.

'And if these high druids decide Brecan is guilty,' said Fergal, 'what then?'

'Then the brehons will determine the punishment to be imposed,' answered the filidh. 'Lord Brecan's plan to usurp the high kingship is a threat that must be addressed. And if Brecan has made treaty with the enemy to achieve his ambition, that is a crime that will be answered.'

'Now you sound like Mádoc,' Conor told him.

'I wish I had known him,' replied Dáithi. 'I wish he were here to advise us.'

'So do I,' said Conor—and saw again the funeral pyre on the twilight beach, and felt the peace of that sending.

'I go to help prepare for the council,' Dáithi continued after a moment's silence. 'But Galin will stay here to help keep the camp. I will have more provisions sent down for you and fodder for the horses.'

'No need for that,' said Fergal. 'We are leaving.'

Dáithi looked from one to the other of them. 'When?'

'As soon as Donal's care can be arranged,' Conor told him.

'But I thought he was to be cared for by the Tylwyth Teg,' said Dáithi.

'Aye,' agreed Conor, 'if Lady Rhiannon's father sends a boat.'

Dáithi blinked at them in confusion. 'But he *is* sending a boat. It will arrive today.' He glanced from one to the other of them. 'Did you not know this?'

'I did not,' said Conor, 'I didn't know. Did you, Fergal?'

'This is the first I heard of it.' He looked to Conor, who shrugged.

'But we were hoping you would wait here a little while—should Eádoin call upon you to bear witness to the council. Only a little while, mind, and then you can be on your way.'

'How long?' asked Conor.

The filidh gazed up at the sky as he reckoned the time needed to summon and deliberate. 'I expect,' he replied at length, 'not more than five or six days—seven at most.'

'Six days!' spluttered Fergal, glancing at Conor, who was shaking his head in dismay. 'We can't be sitting here for six days waiting on this council of yours.'

Conor led Fergal a few paces apart and the two held a quick consultation. 'Six days!' huffed Fergal. 'Eirlandia could sink into the sea in six days and those shave-head windbags would still be wagging their tongues over where to sit in the boat.' He puffed out his cheeks in exasperation. 'Your father should hear about all this. The king should be told everything that has happened so he can warn the other lords.'

'And tell them what—that we think Brecan is a devious

bastard and the Scálda are filthy scum? Everyone knows that already. Anyway, we have to take care of Donal.'

'What then?' asked Fergal.

'One of us must go with him. Faéry healers or no, we can't be sending him on his own. It isn't right.'

'What so?' said Fergal.

'You will go with him,' Conor said. 'I'll go to my father and tell him all we've seen and what we suspect. If I hurry, I can ride to Dúnaird and back while the druids are still conferring.'

Before Conor finished speaking, Fergal was already shaking his head. 'Nay, brother, I think you are forgetting that you are exiled from the tribe.'

'That was but a feeble ruse of Mádoc's as you well know—'

'Aye, I know that, but no one in Dúnaird knows anything of the kind—nor will they until someone can explain it to them. The one for that was Mádoc, but he is no longer with us. So, now, that someone must be me—'

Conor opened his mouth to object, but Fergal remained adamant. 'Hear me, Conor, it must be me. Though it saddens me to say it, you are still outcast, brother—on pain of death, remember? If you are caught in Darini lands, much less your father's ráth, they are honour-bound to kill you.'

'But they would *never*—'

'It is foolish to argue. You know I am right,' Fergal insisted with uncommon heat. 'Listen, the solution is simple. I will go to your father, and *you* will go with Donal to Lady Rhiannon's people and see to his healing.'

Conor at last acknowledged the sense of this and, with great reluctance, agreed. The two turned to Dáithi who was waiting patiently nearby, and Fergal announced, 'Here's what we will do . . .'

After hearing the plan, Dáithi said he had no objection and urged them to proceed and return in all haste. 'And now,' the druid told them, 'I must go help Eádoin prepare for the Coinemm. Farewell, both of you—until we meet again.'

'Do you know how to get home?' asked Conor as they watched the druid hurry away across the clóin.

'I'll find the way,' Fergal said.

'You'll have two horses. Take Ovate Galin with you. He can help if you should lose your way.'

The two warriors occupied the rest of the day making an árach to ease Donal's short journey to the cove. With a borrowed knife from Galin, they cut hazel and willow branches from the nearby wood and wove them into a long, narrow hurdle. Using strips of cloth torn from one of the druid's cloaks, they made it fast. The result was a light, but fairly strong support with which they could transport Donal to the ship. The women, meanwhile, changed the dressing on Donal's wound, fed him more broth, and prepared him to travel. Thus, the day was far spent when the travellers finally started down to the cove to await the boat sent by the faéry king.

They carried Donal on his makeshift bed down through the forest to a dry place high up on the beach and sat down with him in the shade of the rock stack to wait. Gráinne and Rhiannon moved a little apart where they sat head to head deep in conversation.

'They have not been out of sight of one another since the banfaíth's arrival,' Fergal mused, smoothing his moustache with his hand. 'I wonder what they talk about?'

'Do you have to ask?' Conor replied. 'You know how women are—faéry or banfaíth they will always make a chatter about something.'

'Men mostly, then.'

'Aye,' Conor agreed, 'that would be the way of it.' He looked at his friend. Who knew when he would see him again? 'Take care of Búrach while I'm gone.'

'That I will.' A wan smile appeared beneath Fergal's

moustache. 'And just see you don't embarrass yourself with all those faéry women, now. You know what you're like.'

'My heart belongs to Aoife, brother,' replied Conor. 'Will you greet her for me and tell her I am well?'

'Do you have to ask?'

They lapsed into silence then and Conor, growing restless, got up and walked down to the water's edge. There was still a great deal of ash and charcoal where Mádoc's funeral pyre had stood. The sea had been at work, washing the sand and pebbles, and soon all traces of the druid's sending would be cleansed away and that would be that. The thought brought all the sadness back and Conor stared glumly at the dead cinders, kicking them over with his toe. The waste of two lives and what had any of it accomplished?

And then he saw, amidst the spent embers and soggy grey ash, a gleaming white fragment: the small slender shaft of a finger bone. He stooped and picked it up and was instantly filled with a regret so strong it took his breath away. He closed his fist around the bone and squeezed his eyes shut lest the tears start anew. 'I am sorry, Mádoc,' he murmured. 'It has all been for nothing.'

'Then do something about it!'

Conor opened his eyes and looked around. He was still alone on the strand, but the voice was Mádoc's and he heard it as clearly as if the old ollamh had been standing behind him.

'Aye,' Conor muttered to himself, 'but what is to be done, eh?'

Though he half expected a reply to that, none came. Mádoc dead and Huw with him, and Donal stricken unto death . . . what was to be done?

Conor stood a long time, turning the finger bone over in his hand and thinking back on all that they done since leaving the Oenach—none of it meant anything . . . unless . . . he did something about it.

He heard footsteps crunching toward him over the pebbles and turned to see Gráinne approaching. 'The ship is coming,' she said, with a gesture toward the narrow opening in the cáel. 'It is time to prepare Donal to be put aboard.'

Conor looked where she had pointed and saw, as if out of nowhere, that the boat was already within hailing distance. Conor hurried back up the beach to where Fergal sat with Donal. 'They're here,' Conor told him.

'Are they?' Fergal looked around and then stood up. 'So they are.'

Together, the two men carried their wounded friend down to the water; Donal moaned softly when the árach swayed, but did not wake. They joined Gráinne and Rhiannon at the shore as the boat entered the cove. Larger than a fishing boat, but far smaller than the ship they had taken from the Scálda, it was a sleek and graceful craft, the lines clean and tight, the keel sharp, the stern low. The prow was high and topped by a carving of a wolf's head, painted grey and silver and set with polished green stones for eyes. The sails were the colour of grass and glinted slightly as if sprinkled with dew. In movement, the vessel seemed more like a leaf skittering across a pond than a ship ploughing the waves.

If the faéry craft was elegant and graceful, those on board were even more so. There were five—three men and two women—and each as beautiful as the next. Tall and handsome, slender, if a little long limbed, their features were nonetheless compelling: large, dark eyes set beneath high and noble brows; long straight hair that, for both the men and women, was gathered in an elaborate braid that hung from either the side or back of their heads; a straight nose above full lips and a mouth of perfect, even white teeth. For the beauty and symmetry of their bodies, Conor had never seen the like. 'Truly they are a magical race,' he murmured to Fergal beside him, but received no reply. His friend, for once at a loss for words, could but stand and stare.

'Close your mouth, brother,' Conor told him. 'Pretend you've seen a pretty face before.'

Fergal closed his mouth, speechless.

Lady Rhiannon, eager to be reunited with her people, did not wait for the boat to touch land, but waded out into the water, her gown trailing behind her. Upon reaching the boat, she held up her arms and was pulled from the water and set upon the deck in one smooth, seemingly effortless motion. She was taken up and so warmly embraced that Conor felt a pang of jealousy quiver through him—unmistakeable as it was inexplicable. *Why should this be?* he wondered, even as he turned his face away. *What is she to me?*

Greetings were exchanged and then Rhiannon, linking her arm through that of a solemn-faced man with hair so pale it shimmered like spun silver, gestured toward Conor and Fergal, and said, 'These are the men who saved me from the Scálda and released me from captivity.' She introduced them to the newcomers and said, 'I owe them my life.'

The faéry bowed regally and the solemn-faced one said, 'On behalf of myself and my people, I thank you. Your service is greater than you can know. Believe me when I say that you will be richly rewarded.'

Conor acknowledged the praise and, putting out a hand to Donal on the litter at his feet, said, 'Only heal our brother and send him back to us—that will be reward enough.'

Conor and Fergal picked up the hurdle bed and brought it to the side of the boat. They stood in the water and hoisted Donal into the hands of the waiting faéry, who said, 'All that skill and art can do for him shall be done. I am Gwydion, Lord of the Tylwth Teg, King of the House of Llŷr, and I make this vow. Yet, I would ask you to remember that each life has its times and seasons, and these remain in the Great Mother's hands to save or spend as she pleases.'

'I understand,' Conor told him. 'If not for your Rhiannon, our friend would be dead and in his grave already. Whatever you can do will be sufficient.'

In these words, Conor heard the echo of Mádoc's voice. *Whatever you can do . . .*

Turning to Fergal, he said, 'I'm not going.'

Fergal raised his eyebrows in surprise. 'One of us must accompany Donal—you yourself said so.'

'*You* are going,' Conor told him. As Fergal drew breath to object, Conor said, 'No—it should be you.'

'And what are you going to do?' Suspicion tinged his voice.

'Mádoc started all this, and I am going to see it through—finish it.'

Fergal hesitated, shaking his head. 'I am not liking this. What about taking word to your father?'

'Ovate Galin can do that. Druids are good at such things.'

'My friends!' called Gwydion from the boat. 'The tide is flowing. We must depart.'

Conor gestured to the waiting boat. 'Go, now,' Conor told him. 'For Donal's sake, the sooner you go the sooner he can be healed.'

Fergal hesitated only a moment longer and then, overcome by his own curiosity and fascination with the faéry, he turned abruptly and strode eagerly to the water. As he was clambering into the boat, Rhiannon slid over the side and splashed onto the strand once more. Conor hurried to meet her. 'As I see you are not to come with us, I would leave you with a parting gift,' she said as she came to stand before him. Taking her left hand, she placed the palm against his forehead. Her touch was cool against his skin. Her right hand she placed over his heart and, lifting her eyes to the sky, she intoned a few words in her own tongue, words that sounded to Conor's ears like water rippling over stones in a stream, or the liquid notes of a blackbird's song heard as a murmur on the wind.

When she finished, she said, 'Now I have only to speak your name to know where you can be found.' She smiled—a slight upward curve of her lips and a lightness in her ice-blue eyes—as she bent near and added, 'And you have only to whisper mine and I will be there.'

'Thank you, lady,' said Conor. 'I will remember you, too.'

'Rhiannon!' Gwydion called again, his voice insistent, urgent. 'The sea turns against us unless we leave at once.'

She hurried back to the boat and was taken up. The faéry set to their work, plying two long oars shaped like stalks of wheat. The boat rotated neatly and glided away. Conor joined Gráinne on the beach and the two watched until the graceful vessel had left the shelter of the bay and reached deep water.

'I thought you were going with them,' the banfaíth said, still watching the boat as it swiftly receded from view.

'There is something I must do,' Conor told her, already striding up the beach. 'And I am going to need your help to do it.'

'Whatever you require,' she replied, hurrying after him, 'if it is in my power, you shall have it.'

'I will need a spear and shield,' Conor called over his shoulder. 'I am a warrior, and I am going into battle.'

Rónán

I had but newly arrived in my new home at Clethar Ciall when disturbing news reached our Wise Head, a venerable old brehon named Talgobain. He called me to his modest dwelling at the edge of the Sacred Grove—the oak wood maintained by the Learned for more than twenty generations—and there he gave me a drink of watered mead, steeped in anise and heated in a copper bowl. 'How do you find your place here?' he asked, offering me the cup.

'Most agreeable,' I told him. 'I believe I will get on well.'

'Of that, I am certain,' said our chief. 'Morien has told me many good things about you. He was emphatic in his praise.'

'I have the greatest respect for him. He has guided me well and wisely. Whatever I have achieved I owe to him.'

Talgobain smiled and sipped from his steaming cup. We sat for a time in easy silence; as a druid of lower rank, I waited for my superior to speak first. He took another drink and then set aside the cup. 'Troubling news has reached me,' he said, smoothing his grey robe over his round stomach and folding his hands there. 'But I did not like to have you hear it from other lips than my own.'

'Oh?' I said. 'Am I to understand that this news is of special concern to me?'

'It is.' He arranged his kindly features in an expression of sympathy. 'Your brother has been cast out of the tribe and is exiled for three years, not to return to his home on pain of death.'

My heart sank inwardly, yes, but I was not shocked by this revelation. Although I had rarely visited Dúnaird since setting my feet on the druid path, scraps of news from my father and the many stray sources I had cultivated over the years fed my hunger for information about my tribe and kin. What I had heard confirmed the view I had of my father and brothers as I remembered them. Thus, I little doubted that my brother's gross ambition had caught him up at last.

'You are not surprised, I see.'

'Not at all,' I sighed. 'In truth, he has ever been mindful only of satisfying his own desires and placing his aims above the good of the tribe. A man who lives like that plaits a noose for his own neck.'

Our Wise Head nodded sagely. 'I am sorry to hear it.'

'Do not be sorry for Liam. He will look after himself, never fear.'

At this Talgobain's glance sharpened. His eyebrows raised. 'Liam?'

'Yes, my older brother—Liam is his name. Why?'

'That is not the name I was given.'

'No? Then who else—' I could not fathom what he meant. 'You cannot mean Conor!'

'Conor mac Ardan, yes,' he confirmed. 'That is the name of the ill-fated exile.' He regarded me for a moment, then said, '*This* name catches you unawares, I see.'

'I confess that it does, yes.'

'Why did you assume it was the other one?'

'Liam has a desire for power and renown that ever induces him to overreach himself—often to the cost of others,' I declared. 'I cannot but think that if it was Conor cast out, then the report must be in error.'

'Conor was the name given to me. I am sorry for the distress this causes you, but there is no mistake.'

'But how can this be?' I wondered. 'Do you know what happened?'

'Naturally, my information is limited. But, it seems he was caught in the theft of a gold bracelet belonging to one of the Learned Brotherhood—an ollamh of high rank and repute, long in service to King Cahir of the Coriondi—one called Mádoc.'

'Conor? Stealing? I cannot make myself believe it.' I shook my head in dismay. 'The report must be mistaken.'

Talgobain held his head to one side. 'You sound very certain.'

'I would sooner distrust myself than doubt Conor.' Indignation kindled within me and I could feel its warmth spreading to my hands and face. 'It makes no sense. Conor places little value on such trinkets—and even if he wanted a torc or bracelet, he would never have to steal to get it. King Ardan would give him anything he asked—and happily. A simple request and the thing, whatever he desired, would be his.'

'Conor is held in such high esteem, eh?'

'All that and more.'

The wise brehon nodded his head. 'If not for selfish gain, then the theft—or at least the accusation—must have served some other purpose.'

I slumped back in my chair. Had I so completely lost touch with my kinsmen that I no longer knew them? Still, I could not believe that Conor, the brother I loved and knew best, had become a despised thief.

Talgobain sat silently watching me. He took up his cup once more, blew on the hot liquor, and took a drink. 'I learned long ago that when a thing defies rational explanation then it is because I lack a complete understanding of the facts.'

'I am missing something—is that what you mean?'

'Either that, or there is some other motive yet to be disclosed, something hidden perhaps. Discover that hidden thing and what has happened will stand perfectly revealed.'

'That, at least, I can accept.' I raised my cup and swallowed down the sweet mead. 'Until I hear it from his own lips, I will not believe Conor would risk exile for anything so trivial—and certainly not for something he could get with a simple request.'

'So you say.'

He was right, and I told him so. Putting my cup aside, I rose. 'I must go to and speak to my father. I have been wanting to go for a very long time, and it may be that I can be of some service to him now.'

Our Wise Head regarded me a long time—no doubt weighing the implications of this action.

'By your leave, Brehon Talgobain, I will go at once. If I travel through the night, I can be at Dúnaird by morning.'

'No,' said Talgobain, his voice taking on a note of command. 'You asked for my permission, but it is denied. You will stay here.'

'But, I must—'

'Think, Rónán,' he said gently. 'Nothing good will come of your meddling in this affair. Your brother has been cast out of the tribe—owing, I expect, to some dire purpose devised by Mádoc, who, I remind you, will not be unmindful of the dreadful cost to your brother.'

'Yes, but—'

'That being the case, do you really wish to hinder, and perhaps ruin, what has been so carefully conceived and constructed?'

I swallowed down the lump in my throat. 'Then what am I to do?'

'Nothing,' Talgobain replied simply.

'Nothing at all?'

'Only let the affair run its course. When it is concluded, Conor, being the man of integrity that you believe him to be, will be exonerated and welcomed back into the tribe . . . but as hero, not as thief.'

'Forgive me, but it seems that my father may have acted on false information. Certainly, he would wish to know—'

'Your father,' our chief interrupted, 'would not welcome any intrusion just now. Judging from what I hear, he has enforced this exile to appease one whose support he is most desirous of preserving. Any interference, however well intentioned, would be rejected.'

'With all respect, how can you know this? I have had but little communication with my father for many years, and—'

'Have you not?' wondered Talgobain. 'Morien has not told you?'

'No,' I replied uncertainly. 'What should he have told me?'

'Morien said that your father has been in regular contact since the very first day of your arrival at Suídaur. He has ever been mindful of your progress and your care.' Talgobain gazed at me with an expression of mild puzzlement. 'Has Morien never told you?'

I shook my head. 'I never knew.'

'I am sorry for that,' said our Wise Head. 'I expect Morien had his reasons for keeping it to himself. Perhaps he thought it would impede your progress.'

He said some more, but I was no longer listening. All I could think was that my father had never forgotten, never given me up, but that I had ever been in his thoughts—even as he and my brothers had been in mine. The wonder of it astounded me.

I asked to be excused, then, and Talgobain released me. I

went into the oak grove and to the largest of the ancient trees. There I sank down upon those great, gnarled roots and let the tears fall. All I could think was, *I have never been forgotten.*

29

Conor lunged with the sword, crouching low and twisting his shoulders to finish with a vicious upward slash. He sprang back, blade upright, ready to parry the blow of his attacker—if the fellow happened to survive the initial thrust. No retaliation followed.

Conor smiled with satisfaction, then took a few steps backward and repeated the manoeuvre—this time with a double lunge and a sweeping sideways stroke. When his opponent did not renew hostilities, Conor lowered the blade, returned to his starting place, and proceeded to rehearse the motion three more times in quick succession. It was a move he had learned from Eamon, improved upon, and mastered to perfection. In all his battles, it had never let him down.

The leaving of the faéry boat—taking Donal to an uncertain future, and Fergal along with him—had freed Conor in a way he had not expected. From now on, he would pursue his own path to the end of his own devising, answering to no one. That alone put him in a better mood than he had enjoyed for a very long time, and he revelled in it—and when combined with the support of Gráinne and Eádoin, it created in Conor a sense of purpose, allowing him to see possibilities he had not seen before.

Whatever you can do . . . , he thought. *I am a warrior. This is what I can do.*

When Dáithi arrived at the clóin the next day with the weapons Conor had requested—along with a knife and a good sharp sword—Conor had lost himself in a long, tiring, and ultimately restoring routine of training—a thing he knew so well he no longer had to even think about it. With a sword or spear in his hand, Conor on the practice field faded to nothing and there was only the blade and its shimmering arcs, bright in the summer light.

And now, in the third day of his training, sweat ran in rivulets down his body. He wiped his face with his bare arm, closed his eyes, and breathed in the fresh meadow-sweet air of the druid glade. Weapons practice was always something Conor exulted in; he made it a point to be first on the practice field and last to leave. He liked the feel of spear shaft and sword hilt in his hand, and the solid heft of a shield on his arm. He enjoyed the burning warmth of tired muscles after a lengthy training session. And, after so many days away from the exacting disciplines of the warrior clan, it felt good to lose himself in the steady, studied precision of his craft; he luxuriated in the feeling of honing his skills to battle sharpness once more.

He did miss his own weapons; Bríg left behind when he had been exiled, and Gasta forgotten on the strand. But the weapons Dáithi had brought seemed serviceable enough; the shield, though somewhat smaller than Conor liked, was well made; the sword was a little lighter in heft than Gasta, but it was well balanced and had a keen edge—good enough until he found something better. Likewise, the spear would serve until he found another.

He finished his routine with a final burst of savage thrusts and parries, and then stretched himself in the grass to let the sun dry off the sweat. He had just closed his eyes for a short nap when he felt a shadow pass over his face. Conor opened one eye to see Tuán standing over him.

'Greetings, Tuán. Sit down and share the sun.'

'I have brought the provisions you requested,' said the short druid as he squatted on his haunches next to Conor.

'The soap and razor, too?'

'Yes, that and the dried peas, the oats, and salt. There is also a sparán filled with bósaill, and Eádoin said you can take some of the smoked fish with you, too, if you like it. Anything else?'

Conor thanked him and said, 'If I think of anything, I will tell you.'

'I see that you are leaving,' Tuán surmised. 'May I ask what you intend to do now?'

'Well, it seems to me that a good blade is always welcome in a warband. I am a warrior without a home. I intend to find one.'

'Whom, forgive the question, do you expect to take in an outcast?'

'The Brigantes.'

'You would go to Lord Brecan. . . .'

'Who better?' Conor then explained the plan he had conceived: he would go to the Brigantes fortress at Aintrén and he would gain entrance—not as a spy, but as an *amais*, a hired warrior. Once he had been accepted—*if* he were to be accepted—and taken into Brecan's warband, he would be in a prime position to learn both the shape and extent of the deceitful king's ambitions.

As he spoke, a slow smile spread across Tuán's broad face. 'I may have misjudged you, Conor mac Ardan.' He regarded Conor for a moment, then jumped up. 'But this mad plan of yours is going to need more than dried peas and a pouch full of cured beef if you hope to succeed.'

Tuán ambled off and Conor closed his eyes to doze in the sun. When he awoke, he went down to the stream to bathe, and then returned to the bothy to find Tuán and two ovates busily grooming Búrach. They had washed the grey stallion and scrubbed his coat until it gleamed, and were now braiding Búrach's mane and tail, attaching tiny silver bells to the braids. They had brought a fine blue horsecloth and a supple leather bag in which to carry Conor's provisions.

'You will spoil him with this pampering,' warned Conor, but looked on approvingly. 'He will expect the same from me.'

'If you hope to impress a king,' Tuán said, reaching into the bag at his feet to bring out a green apple, 'it will not hurt to look like a king yourself.' He offered the apple and the horse devoured it in two bites. 'As for the rider, so too for his horse.'

While they were talking, Gráinne appeared bearing a neat bundle wrapped in a fine blue-and-white-checked cloak and bound in a new leather belt adorned with silver sun disks. She greeted Conor with a friendly embrace and said, 'Tuán told me what you intend,' she said, offering the bundle. 'A bold plan and one that will succeed the better if you are arrayed like a man to be ranked among the nobility.'

Conor accepted the bundle from her hands, opened it, and withdrew a new siarc of brilliant scarlet, buff-coloured breecs, and new leather brócs adorned with blue spirals sewn over the instep. 'Banfaíth Gráinne, your generosity puts me at a loss,' said Conor, shaking out the siarc—it was stitched with a fine needle and embroidered at the hem and neck with silver knotwork; the lace ends were tipped with tiny silver caps. 'I have never worn anything half so grand.'

'Put it on,' she said, beaming her pleasure at his surprise. 'Let us see the fruit of our handiwork.'

Conor gathered up the clothes and took the bundle into the bothy. He stripped off his old things and dressed in the new, tied up his laces, and tightened the belt around his waist, emerging from the bothy a few moments later feeling every inch the Lord of the Glade.

Gráinne's smile widened when she saw him, and Tuán laughed out loud. 'Is this the Dagda I see before me?' the little druid cried. 'Behold—a man transformed!'

Stepping before him, Gráinne raised her hands and Conor saw she held out a thin bronze torc—the kind warriors often received for victories in battle. He bowed a little forward and she gently spread the ends and slipped it around his neck, then closed the ends again and stepped back.

'What do you think?' asked Conor, his birthmark tingling at this unaccustomed scrutiny. He spread his arms and turned around. 'Wait!'

He dived into the bothy again and, from his battered sparán, brought out the tiny bundle Fergal had given him. He gave it to Gráinne and said, 'Put this on as well.'

Unwrapping the bundle, she brought out Aoife's little silver leaf casán. The banfaíth smiled and pinned on the brooch just above his heart, then, her head held to one side, squinting her eyes in appraisal, she passed her gaze slowly over him from head to toe.

'Well?' said Conor, after a moment.

'Only one thing is lacking,' Gráinne said at last. She reached into the little pouch at her girdle and brought out a pair of scissors, gave his hair a few snips, and said, 'Now, where is that razor Dáithi sent you?'

* * * *

30

Conor stood at the edge of the field while Búrach cropped the grain heads from the ripening barley beside him. The lowering sun cast their shadows long over the golden heads of grain as Conor contemplated Lord Brecan's ráth atop the hill rising from among the fields and woodland around about. Aintrén, the principal stronghold of the Brigantes, was not only far larger than Conor imagined, it was also much better fortified.

With stout timber walls easily twice as high as his father's fortress at Dúnaird, and surrounded by not one or two, but four deep ditches—one filled with water and the rest crowded with brambles and stinging nettles—the stronghold occupied the top of a hill that commanded views of the two broad valleys flanking either side. Fields and grazing lands surrounded the hill, providing no cover for hiding. The location had been well chosen: no warhost could approach unseen, and would-be attackers would face a steep uphill slog just to reach the lowest ditch. Aintrén presented a formidable, if not menacing, aspect.

It had taken two days of steady riding to reach Brigantes territory. Fatigue lay on Conor's shoulders like a heavy cloak and, as he sat gazing upon the sprawling settlement of his sworn enemy, he contemplated the uncertainty of his reception. There was, after all, every possibility that he would be killed on arrival. And why not? Lord Brecan knew him as an adversary, a defiant challenger who had openly opposed him at the Oenach. Would the king even consider accepting him as an amais, a hired warrior, a member of his warband? That was, had always been, and remained the chief question.

Búrach whickered softly and jerked on the reins, lifting Conor's hand and stirring him from his reverie. He drew breath and blew it out. The time had come to put the question to the test. Climbing to his feet, he mounted his splendid grey stallion and proceeded to his destination and his uncertain fate.

He rode through the barley field, around the wide, spreading base of the hill to the long, sloping ramp in front of the fortress. The hard-packed incline crossed the first three ditches and the fourth was topped by a narrow wooden bridge that could be, Conor was certain, withdrawn or destroyed at the first sign of an enemy's attack. Beyond the bridge rose two stout, ironclad gates and, above them, the square box of a sentry tower.

Conor paused at the foot of the ramp for a moment—long enough to be seen—and then urged Búrach forward. As horse and rider neared the gates, two armed warriors appeared in the gap between the open doors. He raised his right hand to them and brought Búrach to a halt a few paces from where they stood. 'Greetings, friends,' he said. 'May you enjoy peace and plenty this night.' He indicated the open gate. 'Have you a bed and a meal for a weary wanderer?'

'We don't know you,' said one of the gatemen. 'Move on,' said the other.

'I have travelled far today to be here,' Conor told them. 'All I ask is the hospitality due any traveller. Would you deny me this?'

The two advanced a few paces toward him. 'We want no trouble. Move along,' said the first gateman, hefting his spear.

'And is it trouble now to treat a stranger with respect?' said Conor, keeping his tone light. 'Or, perhaps it is poverty that keeps your king's hand clenched tight against any demand—be it ever so small.'

The two gatekeepers glared at him, but did not yield.

Conor lifted the reins and prepared to leave. 'Far be it from me to take the food from your mouths. Tell your needy lord that Conor mac Ardan is heartily sorry to hear how low he has fallen in the world. But worry not. I will spread the word over the land that the Brigantes are suffering in their want. Trust that someone will take pity on you and your ill-fated king.'

'Stop, pig!' snarled the foremost of the gatemen. 'Come down off your high horse and say that again—if you dare.'

'What is this rough talk I am hearing?' said a voice behind the belligerent gatemen. A tall elegant woman of noble aspect and bearing moved through the gate behind them and both men instantly stepped aside to let her pass. 'Is something amiss here?'

'This stranger is trying to gain entrance, my lady,' answered one of the guards. 'We have kindly asked him to move on, but he refuses to go,' added the other.

'Why so?' asked the woman. She came to stand at the head of Conor's stallion and, reaching up, stroked the handsome creature's neck, giving Conor a chance to observe her closely. Youthful still, though past the first bloom of youth, she was a strikingly beautiful woman just entering her prime. Her hair was the deep, ruddy colour of rich copper; she wore it long, swept back and held in a clasp of red gold to fall about her back and shoulders. Her eyes were large and green and lively beneath even, dark brows; her skin was pale, untouched by the sun, and her fingers long and fine; her gown was finely woven linen, crisp, and cream-coloured and, like the wide girdle around her waist, it was heavily embroidered with knotwork bands in red and blue and gold, as was the short cloak fastened with a large gold casán in the shape of a harp.

'A beautiful animal you have here,' she said, flicking one of the tiny bells braided into its mane and listened to the tinkling sound. Looking up, she smiled as she took in the horse's richly arrayed rider: splendid in his red silver-trimmed siarc and belt of silver disks around his well-muscled torso, the fine leather brócs, and his clean-shaven face and neatly trimmed hair and moustache. 'I am Sceana, Queen of the Brigantes, and I give you good greeting, traveller. Have you come far?'

Conor pressed the back of his hand to his forehead in the sign of respect and said, 'I am Conor mac Ardan, a warrior of the Darini, and I place myself at your service, lady.'

'And is it a bed and meal you seek this night?' she asked. The question was innocent enough, but it was accompanied by a flirty lift of a smooth eyebrow and a knowing gleam in her green eyes.

'Shelter and a meal, to be sure—and perhaps more than that.'

'Then fortunate you are, Conor mac Ardan, warrior of the Darini, for a bed and meal are easily granted. As for the rest,' she said knowingly, 'well, that is best discussed over the welcome cúach.' She smiled again, and Conor found himself liking her in spite of the fact that she was his enemy's wife.

The queen turned to the gatemen, who were still glowering at Conor and brandishing their weapons; she instructed them to tell her ladies to ready the Guest Lodge at once and to deliver her visitor's belongings there. 'And,' she continued, 'take our visitor's horse to the king's stable and see that it is fed and watered and put up for the night. Tell the master groom not to forget to rub this fine creature's coat with dry straw and give him an extra portion.' She cast a backward smile at Conor. 'Meanwhile, I will do the same for his owner.'

Conor thanked her for her kindness and hospitality and dismounted, handing the reins of his princely stallion to the nearest of the gatekeepers, who fixed him with a malevolent stare. The queen beckoned him to follow. 'Tonight you are a guest under my roof. Worry for nothing.'

She led him through the great gate and into a wide yard well-paved with small flat slates from a northern shore. There were many people in the yard, working at various chores, and in amongst them children played, with dogs barking at their heels. Lord Brecan's vast hall stood at the far end of the yard with two large houses flanking either side: on the left-hand side, a large timber house with a high roof thatched with river reed, and a green door between red lintels; on the right-hand side a slightly smaller stone house with a lower roof covered in slate, blue lintels, and a door made from the hide of a pure white ox.

'The Women's House,' said Sceana, indicating the house on the left. Directing his attention to the dwelling on the right, and she said, 'The Bards' House.' Her gesture swept wide to include other outbuildings within the ráth. 'As you can see, there are houses for baking and brewing and cooking. And'— she pointed to a fair-sized house with a steep roof of thatch and blue-painted door—'and a lodge for esteemed visitors.' She gave him a prideful smile. 'My lord does not lack dwellings of quality and distinction for his people and his guests.' She gave Conor a quizzical look. 'Perhaps, after tonight you will amend your poor estimation of the king's poverty.'

'If all guests are treated with such care and attention by his queen, I will gladly ensure that the name Brecan mac Lergath is lauded for wealth and generosity,' said Conor. 'Where do the warriors sleep?'

'The king's ardféne sleep in the hall,' the lady told him. 'The rest of the warband is divided amongst three houses—each large enough for thirty men.' She gave Conor a sideways glance. 'There are other houses, of course, in other ráths nearby. But tonight you are my guest and you may sleep wherever your desires lead you.'

Conor was taken aback by the tone with which she spoke these last words—as much as by the slight, seductive smile that accompanied them. He dared not reply in kind, so merely bowed his head respectfully and said, 'Thank you, my lady. A more grateful guest you will not have had beneath your roof.'

Queen Sceana led Conor toward the hall. As they crossed the yard, people paused in their activities to watch the handsome stranger. Conor was aware that some of them noticed the crimson stain of his disfiguring birthmark; they nudged one another, and some of them made the sign against evil as he passed. Well accustomed to such treatment by strangers, he held himself erect and ignored them.

Two wide stone steps led up from the paved yard to a wooden platform in front of the door to the hall. Here, they paused to wait until they could be received into the hall. Two porters appeared, each dressed in a long siarc of red linen, with a wide woven belt of soft brown wool. Each carried a dagger tucked into the folds of the belt. They cast a hasty glance at the visitor, and their expressions of distaste for what they saw left Conor in little doubt that they were inclined to deal with him as with a fox caught in the dove cote. Nevertheless, he was accompanied by Queen Sceana, and that presented them with a special challenge.

While one porter stood aside to welcome the queen, the other opened the door and ushered them inside. The hall was dark; the only light came from the square hole in the roof above the large circular hearth in the centre of the room. A small tending fire sent thin tendrils of smoke up into the light. Surrounded by roof trees fashioned from the trunks of entire pines, stripped of their bark and painted red and green, it seemed to Conor as if he viewed the hearth through the hazy light of a dim forest retreat. Before the hearth, overlooking it, stood the king's throne on a high platform of logs and beams. The great chair itself was made from stag antlers intertwined and bound together with leather straps, and covered with wolf pelts. It was, Conor thought, the throne of one who styled himself as Cernunos, Lord of the Hunt. In any case it was a seat for a powerful ruler much given to the occupations of a more primitive royalty—not the chair of a man who, so far as Conor knew, had spent his life negotiating boundaries, raising tributes to pay for border defences, settling disputes between his client lords, and building his herds to pay for ever more lavish feasts to impress rivals and overawe the timid.

There were a few warriors idling on low couches set along the walls, and at gaming tables scattered here and there about the vast room; others were stropping swords and spear blades with sharpening stones. At the appearance of the queen, all talk ceased and the men set aside whatever they were doing, stood, and turned in her direction. Two of them hurried forth to greet their queen and her splendid visitor; both went down on one knee before her, and lowered their eyes. 'You honour us with your presence, my queen,' said one of them in a low voice.

'Rise and bid our guest welcome,' she said lightly, lifting her palm.

'Be pleased to rest and take your ease,' said the warrior as he rose. 'What we have, we gladly share.'

Conor thanked him and said, 'I am Conor mac Ardan. My father is Lord of the Darini, perhaps you have heard of him?'

At this admission, a hazy recollection flitted over the welcoming warrior's face—just a flicker and then it was gone. 'The Darini are not among the clients of our lord, I think,' offered the second warrior, a keen-eyed wiry youth who could not have seen more than eighteen summers. 'But that does not mean we are less friendly to a swordbrother such as yourself.' He smiled. 'I am Galart, and this is Médon, nephew of our king's champion and warleader.'

Both men gave their guest a slight bow of acknowledgement—more for the queen's benefit than for his own, Conor suspected. Seeing the sword strapped to Conor's side, the younger one said, 'Is your blade flame-tempered? Ours are, we find they hold an edge longer.'

'But it makes them more brittle, does it not?' countered Conor.

'You will have leisure to talk of blades and battles later,' the queen interrupted. 'But I have promised our guest a welcome cup, and as the king is not here at present, the duty falls to me. We will return when the meal is ready and, in honour of our guest, there will be songs and music for our pleasure tonight.'

She waved the two away and, taking Conor's elbow, led him from the hall. Conor was glad she had not forgotten the cup; a drink in convivial company was a thing he had not enjoyed since the Oenach, and Queen Sceana was a gracious and agreeable companion.

'The king is absent, then?' asked Conor as they started across the yard once more. The sun was setting now, casting the yard in shadow. Someone had started a fire outside the Bards' House in preparation for an evening meal. Several women were tending the fire and readying haunches of venison to be roasted.

'Indeed so,' she replied crisply. 'My husband is often away these days. The affairs of his client kings grow ever more demanding of his time and energies. He is rarely at home three days in a row.' She offered a slightly wistful smile, and touched his arm. 'Oh, but what am I saying? As a warrior, you must know this.'

'I am certain a ruler of his eminence is much in demand,' replied Conor, trying to sound sympathetic.

No more was said just then, and they continued to the Guest Lodge, where they stopped at the door. 'The lodge will be made ready for your stay. In the meantime, I hope you do not mind idling a while among my ladies?'

'I believe I can survive the ordeal,' said Conor.

The queen laughed. 'I am certain that you can.' They continued on to the Women's House, where the door was opened by a young girl in a long white tunic and brócs of soft deerskin. She bowed prettily to the queen and then stepped aside. 'Enter and take your ease,' invited the queen. To the girl she said, 'Bríd, bring the cúach for our guest, and fetch a mead jar from my bower.'

Conor stepped across the threshold and entered a large room lit by rushlight and beeswax candles. Much like the king's hall, the Women's House was a single main room with small cells or booths along each wall; each cell, from what Conor could see, was separated from the next by woven panels stretched on thin frames, and each contained a sleeping pallet covered in soft fleeces. In the main room, there were low tables with even lower couches for reclining at meals.

The queen led him to just such a couch in the centre of the room and took the one facing it. One of the queen's serving maids appeared, bowed, and moved a table between them. Bríd, the young céile, returned with a wide, two-handed silver bowl and a large silver jar on a wooden tray. She placed the tray on the table and filled the bowl with golden liquid from the jar. On the tray was a wooden plate with a small loaf of black bread and a little bowl of salt. The girl passed the cúach to the queen, then withdrew once more.

'In honour of your visit,' said the queen, lifting the bowl and passing it to Conor. He inclined his head and, accepting the cúach, took a long drink, letting the rich, sweet mead warm his throat all the way down. He returned the welcome cup to the queen and she drank, watching him over the rim of the bowl with an expression of amusement.

Sceana refilled the cup and, setting it aside, offered Conor the loaf and salt. He broke off a small chunk of the dark bread and dipped it in the salt. He popped the morsel into his mouth and chewed thoughtfully. The bread was soft and warm and seasoned with an herb he could not place.

'Drink, please,' the queen said, offering the cúach once more. 'Or they will say I stinted in my duties to a valued guest.'

Conor smiled and drank a little more, and they shared the cup, passing it back and forth between them. 'This is a very restful place,' Conor observed. 'But I cannot think the king welcomes many guests here.'

'To be sure,' she remarked. 'Lord Brecan would have preferred to receive you himself in the hall or the Bards' House. But our druid is away with my lord, and the hall is always so dark and noisy.' She drank again and passed the cup to Conor. 'Reclining here is much more comfortable—wouldn't you agree?'

'After a few days on horseback, even the cow byre would be more comfortable.'

The queen laughed and Conor realised again how much younger she was than Lord Brecan. 'You have only one druid?' he asked.

She looked at Conor in surprise. 'Your father has more?'

Conor laughed, and felt himself relax for the first time since entering the stronghold. 'Ach, nay,' he shook his head. 'We keep no druid—although, my brother is a filidh and soon, perhaps, to be an ollamh.'

'That, at least, is auspicious,' allowed the queen, pouring more mead into the double-handled bowl. She took a sip and passed the cúach to her guest. 'You have chosen a magnificent stallion to accompany you on your travels. You father must be a very generous ruler to let such an animal out of his sight. Does your tribe have many such?'

The question was well put, but Conor suspected the intention behind it. He decided the truth was the best course. 'Not at all. We own only what we take from the Scálda—and these we mostly give away. But the grey was allowed me because I won it in battle.'

'You must be a very skilled warrior to win such treasure,' mused the queen knowingly. 'Do you like to fight?'

The question was asked pointedly and Conor was put on his guard, but replied with what he hoped was good humour. 'I find a fight is sometimes necessary if I am to ply my craft.'

She smiled at him over the cup. 'Humility is a virtue, the bards tell us. But most warriors I know would never neglect an opportunity to boast.' She smiled seductively and Conor felt himself grow warm. 'Conor mac Ardan, I begin to suspect you have no need of boasting.'

She took a drink and passed the cup, saying, 'A man of your accomplishments must be welcome wherever he goes. In fact, it pleases me to welcome you to my hearth. I think,' she said, as if the idea had suddenly occurred to her, 'that we will dine here tonight—if that would be agreeable to you.'

Conor was considering whether now was a good time to reveal that he was an amais looking for a patron, but was saved having to explain by the appearance of a girl with a harp. Dressed in a simple rose-coloured mantle with a brown girdle, she seated herself on a stool beside the table and, with a nod to the queen, began to play. Conor watched her fingers dance over the strings as the music spilled from the harp like glittering water. He leaned back on his couch and listened. How long had it been since he had heard the sweet, plaintive voice of the harp?

Conor sipped the mead and listened, content to let the

company and drink and music carry him where it would. He caught himself thinking that if only Brecan were a better man, he might truly deserve to be high king of Eirlandia. To be sure, he had already secured the necessary trappings.

His next thought was that he was tiptoeing along a very dangerous precipice just then, and he had better keep his wits about him if he wanted to live to fight another day.

31

Conor feasted well that night and, despite the alluring charms of his royal hostess, went to his bed decorously—if not altogether gracefully. He ate his fill of venison, and stewed greens and vegetables, and plums soaked in mead, and then, when he was all but nodding in his bowl, the queen wished him a good and peaceful night, and retired with her ladies, leaving him to his rest. He was led to one of the little booths that lined the walls of the Guest Lodge.

The next morning, when the warband trooped noisily out to the yard to begin their weapons practice, Conor donned his old clothes from his saddle pack, replacing them with his new ones carefully folded, and then went out into the yard to join the warriors. He found the Brigantes pleased to have a visitor from another tribe in their midst—someone to impress and, if possible, humiliate for their amusement. Conor expected no less, and was happy to oblige. Humility, as he had been so recently reminded, was a virtue that might stand him in good stead in the days to come.

Like the others, he was given a sword with a blade made of ash and a small round, hide-covered shield; he was then paired up with another of the warriors for a session of good-natured sparring. Conor, feeling that as a guest it would be wise to give a decent account of himself but not to outshine his opponent, reserved his best skills for another time.

It was not difficult to hold back; the wooden sword felt awkward in his hand—the Darini always practiced with blunted iron weapons—and the weight was nothing at all like a real blade. Still, though he tried to rein in his proficiency, his practice opponent did not help matters; the fellow fought stiffly and was slow in his movements—and even the simplest moves were performed with studied deliberation. Conor could see each thrust and parry coming a long way off and was ready to meet it when it came. Twice he allowed a blow to land just to encourage his partner.

Sensing that they had got the measure of the newcomer, the onlookers drifted off and engaged in sparring bouts of their own. Soon the yard fairly resounded with the dull clacking of wooden swords and spear shafts. The warriors were fully immersed in their morning's training when Lord Brecan and his bodyguard of warriors came pounding through the gate and into the yard.

The practice session came to a halt as the clan came running to welcome their king and his retinue. As wives and children gathered to greet husbands and fathers, Conor stood aside with some of the younger Brigantes warriors. Among those returning was the king's druid, Mog Ruith. The baleful druid noticed Conor among the bystanders, and Conor saw the light of recognition come up in the man's hooded eyes. The druid said nothing, but reached out and touched the king on the arm and, with a single nod, directed Lord Brecan's attention to Conor's presence.

The king, still smiling, thanked his people for their welcome and, without dismounting, rode to where Conor stood watching. He sat for a moment astride his horse, gazing down at Conor, who now felt the eyes of every person in the yard upon him. As before, Brecan was richly arrayed; everything about him glittered and gleamed: his gold torc flashed at his throat; from the belt around his substantial waist a short, gold-hilted sword glimmered, and the silver knotwork sewn into his green siarc shimmered in the bright sunlight. His green-and-blue-checked cloak and brown breecs were slightly dusty from his ride and he seemed worn by his travels, but his dark eyes glinted with a lively menace. 'See now,' said Brecan, 'who have we here?'

'I am Conor mac Ardan, a warrior of the ranks.'

'Are you?' asked the king with a little chuckle. 'A warrior with a wooden sword, eh?' He looked around, expecting others to enjoy his jest, and some echoed his chuckle politely. 'Ardan, you say—your father might not be the same as him who is king of . . . the Darini, is it?' His lordship made a show of searching his memory for this obviously obscure monarch.

'None other.'

'But not one of my clients, I think.'

'He is not.'

'I am pleased to welcome a guest among us,' intoned the king grandly, 'even a Darini with a wooden sword.'

'Your hospitality is unequalled,' Conor replied. 'A traveller would have to travel far indeed to find better.'

The king sat on his horse, staring down at Conor, trying to work out why the man before him seemed so familiar. Meanwhile, Mog Ruith, having dismounted, came to stand beside his king. He motioned to Brecan, who leaned down and the two exchanged a whispered word, whereupon Brecan said, 'Your name is Conor mac Ardan, you say—'

'Yes, lord. So it is.'

'I am reminded that you were the one caught stealing a gold bracelet belonging to Lord Cahir's toothless old druid— what was his name?'

'Mádoc the Bald,' offered Mog Ruith. 'Isn't that true?' His tone was an accusation.

'It is true that his name was Mádoc,' replied Conor. This also drew a laugh from some of the warriors looking on, and gave Conor to suspect that the druid, for all his eminence, was not well liked by one and all.

'Did you steal the bracelet?' demanded the druid, irritated now. 'Tell the truth—and that quickly.'

'In truth, I did not steal anything.'

'Yet, it appears you were exiled from among your tribe,' said Mog Ruith as if catching Conor in an obvious lie. 'You are an outcast—is that not so?'

A murmur fluttered through the crowd at this revelation. Queen Sceana bit her lip and clasped nervous hands before her, a wrinkle of worry creasing her smooth brow at the thought that she had entertained a despised outcast and thief.

'I am exiled for three years,' admitted Conor in a clear loud voice. 'That is so. And that is the reason I have come to you.' This was addressed not to the druid, but to Lord Brecan. 'I was wrongly accused, and cast out from my tribe. Yet, it seems to me that a man who can wield a sword—even one of wood—might find service with a warband that values such skill. Naturally, I chose to start first with the most highly regarded of Eirlandia's many tribes.' He made a little bow of deference to the king.

'Ha!' cried the king. 'You want to be an amais in my warband?'

'That is my desire, lord.'

'You claim to know how to use a sword,' said Brecan with a slow, insinuating smile. 'If I am to consider taking you into my service, I would have to see proof of this alleged proficiency.'

Conor merely gave a nod of assent. Mog Ruith, his face creased in a disapproving frown, opened his mouth to protest, but the king waved aside his objection before it could be voiced, saying, 'I think a test of skill between you and my champion will serve our purposes nicely.' The king lifted his hand and one of the warriors who had arrived with him shoved through the crowd to stand beside the king. With a flush of loathing, Conor saw that it was the leader of the group that had attacked him at the Oenach. What is more, the champion remembered Conor as well.

'Let us see a demonstration of your skill,' said Lord Brecan, 'if skill you possess. What say you, Cethern—shall we test his mettle?'

Cethern, the champion, nodded his assent as his eyes moved over the warrior before him. 'At your command, my lord king. Nothing would give me greater pleasure than teaching this red-stained outcast a lesson in how the Brigantes do battle.' His thin smile became a leer. 'Unless, he finds fear has the better of him and he would rather slink off now and avoid a thrashing?'

Conor, angered at the mention of his disfigurement, forced a smile as he answered the taunt. 'Fear and I are old friends,' he said. 'He will wait for me until I have schooled myself here.'

The king clapped his hands and ordered everyone to form a ring in the centre of the yard and give the two combatants plenty of room to fight. He dismounted and ordered a wooden sword and shield to be given each man so there would be no advantage in weapons. He then instructed both combatants to quit the contest when the other surrendered, or when ordered to stop.

Conor took up his wooden blade and shield and stepped into the circle; Cethern did likewise and stood slashing the blade this way and that to loosen his arm.

'Go to it!' shouted Brecan.

The champion did not waste a moment trying to gauge the strength or prowess of his adversary, but launched himself at a run. The tactic took Conor by surprise—not because it was unexpected, but for the fact that it was such a clumsy, ill-advised move. It was, in Conor's mind, a device favoured only by young green toughs, arrogant in their strength and supposed superiority, but ignorant in the true ways of war.

Consequently, as Cethern bulled forward, Conor fell back, apparently giving ground until, when his attacker was committed to the clash, he simply stepped aside.

Cethern thrust his shield before him like a ram—connecting with nothing but air. He staggered forward, unbalanced, his shield arm flailing wide. Conor, mindful of his onlookers, did not take advantage of the blunder, but allowed his opponent to pass untouched.

The champion, cursing his error, righted himself, turned, and then commenced another attack, once again charging in, waving his ash-wood blade. This time, Conor made a pretence of meeting the charge head on. But, again, as his opponent closed on him, he took a blow on his shield and slid off to the side. Cethern lurched forward, twisting away to avoid being struck a blow. This time, however, Conor did not let him pass unscathed, but gave him a resounding smack on the leg with the flat of his sword.

To make the same blunder twice in quick succession told Conor much: his opponent was a man used to having contests go his own way and, perhaps, that he held Conor far beneath his regard as a worthy opponent. This, too, was an error—and Conor knew it. On a real field of battle, it was the kind of mistake a warrior only made once.

The whack on the leg seemed to bring the champion to his senses. He spun around, squared himself, and showed some restraint by feinting to his left, then to his right, yet without committing himself to an attack. Instead, he waited for Conor's reaction. When Conor did not challenge the feint, he spat in the dust and shouted, 'Are you afraid? Come! Let us see what you can do.'

Conor made no reply, but stood aside in a ready, yet relaxed, posture, spinning the wooden blade in his hand, first one way and then the other.

'Fight!' shouted Cethern, beating on his shield with his blunt weapon. When Conor made no move, the champion threw back his head and laughed. Flinging his arms wide, he turned around to address the crowd. 'See here! This is how the Brigantes defeat their enemies! The mere sight of a—'

He had not completed this exposition when he felt a sharp slap of Conor's blade on the back of both legs, for the moment his back was turned, Conor flitted in and delivered the blow—thereby reinforcing one of the first rules any warrior learns: never turn your back on an adversary.

The clout was sudden and sharp and executed with precision, causing one of Cethern's legs to buckle. The champion went down on one knee. He made an ineffectual backward swipe with his blade, but Conor had already skittered out of reach.

With a growl of frustration, Cethern leapt up and lunged at Conor. This time, Conor met him head on, taking the first blow on his shield and striking back with one of his own. The contest settled into a steady rhythm, each combatant trading blows with the other—until, as it seemed neither would gain an advantage this way, Conor parried a blow, loosed his grip, and let his wooden weapon fall from his hand.

As he expected, Cethern drove in close, sword raised high for a savage strike. Conor made a feint to the side, as if to avoid the stroke. His opponent swung the blade and Conor ducked low—but instead of reaching for his weapon, he grabbed the champion by the ankle and gave it a mighty tug. Instantly, Cethern was thrown onto his back. Conor scooped up his sword and while his opponent squirmed to regain his feet, Conor gave him a solid blow on the side of the head with the flat of his sword. The whack resounded across the yard; several onlookers winced, and some of the warriors laughed.

Again, Conor did not press his obvious advantage, but stood back and allowed Cethern to rise—which, he considered, was far more than the hulking thug had done for him when he lay half unconscious on the ground at the Oenach. Instead, he exercised cautious restraint; he would win neither thanks nor praise for embarrassing the king's battlechief before his tribe. He backed away.

Full angry now, Cethern rose, his face black with rage. 'You cheat!' he cried, spittle flying from his lips. 'Tricks! Is that all you know? Stand and fight like a man.'

'Oh?' replied Conor. 'You mean the man who fights three-against-one against an unarmed foe? *You* would be the one to teach me, I think.'

Cethern cast a hasty glance toward his lord, but Brecan stood expressionless, his arms crossed upon his chest. The warriors who had been training with Conor began beating their wooden swords against their shields—a signal for the combatants to join battle.

Cethern drew a breath and, loosing a great cry, rushed forward once more. Conor also ran forward to meet him. And, yet again, as the two closed on one another, Conor swung his shield low, smashing the champion's shins and sweeping his feet from under him. Cethern hit the ground hard and before he had even stopped bouncing, Conor drove the point of his sword into the champion's unprotected ribs. Cethern loosed a cry of pain and rage, and Conor, abandoning the sword and shield, flung himself upon his sprawled opponent and threw an arm around his throat.

Cethern thrashed beneath him, but Conor kept his grip and squeezed harder. The champion's face grew purple and his movements more erratic. Conor looked around to the king, who gazed back at him impassively.

'Have you seen enough, lord king?' he called in a loud voice.

Mog Ruith, standing beside his lord, started forward. 'Enough!'

Conor released his hold, letting the proud champion's head thump on the ground. He rose, dusted himself down, then walked to where the king stood and, making a little bow of deference, said, 'Perhaps your lordship might consider this some small demonstration of a true warrior's skill.'

'Do you imagine a few low tricks and feints will impress me?' said Brecan dryly.

'I was taught that in battle a warrior's chief duty is to stay alive while punishing his opponent by any means possible.'

'You took unfair advantage.'

'Unfair? How so? It seems to me that the Scálda make no such distinction.'

Brecan's eyes narrowed and his mouth pressed into a hard line. But before he could frame a suitable reply, one of the warriors in the close-gathered crowd shouted, 'Conor!'

The shout seemed to spur the silent onlookers. Another voice echoed, 'Conor!' And soon others took up the cry, making a chant of his name which was accompanied by the rhythmic beating of wooden swords on shield rims, creating a loud clatter—such that Conor did not hear Cethern creeping up behind him.

He felt the presence of the battlechief as a shadow fell across his back. He half turned and, in the same instant, saw the glint of a knife in Cethern's hand. Conor dodged to the side and managed to avoid the sweeping blade as Cethern, brows lowered, half blind with hate, lunged forward again, swinging the long blade in a wide, looping arc. Conor danced backward, out of the way. As he passed Mog Ruith, the druid put out a foot to trip him. Conor stumbled and fell on his rump.

Cethern leapt on him and, straddling him, raised the knife to plunge it into Conor's heart. Conor grabbed a fistful of dirt and as the champion's arm started down, he flung the dust and gravel into his assailant's face. Instinctively, Cethern's hands went to his eyes, and Conor seized the hand holding the knife and tried to wrest it away. The champion jerked his hand this way and that to free the blade, but Conor held on.

Some in the crowd began to protest that the contest was over. The cry rose louder until finally, the king called out, 'Enough!'

Several warriors rushed out and, taking Cethern by the shoulders and arms, bodily pulled him off his struggling victim and hauled him aside. Conor, sweating and panting heavily, rolled onto his side and lay for a moment catching his breath and gathering his wits.

Mog Ruith strode to where he lay and, gazing down at Conor with a vicious grin, said, 'Was that unfair? I doubt the Scálda would make such a fine distinction.'

Conor nodded. 'True enough. But then again, a Scálda would have killed your champion in the very first clash.'

'With a sword of hardened ash wood? Ha!'

Conor climbed to his feet and stood to face the false druid. 'It is twice your champion has attacked me when my back was turned and I had no weapon. Be assured it will not happen again.'

'And if it does?'

'Your king will be looking for a new champion.'

32

That night, Conor was taken to one of the Warriors' Houses; the smallest and least occupied of the three, it housed the younger warriors, and here the men seemed more accepting of his presence, and some—the same who had called out his name in acclaim following the contest—were even friendly. From this, Conor surmised that many of them had also suffered Cethern's taunts and mindless cruelties, and were glad to see the overbearing champion bested at last. At the very least, Conor had won a modicum of respect among his lordship's warband. What the king thought, however, remained to be seen.

This he discovered the next morning when, as the day before, the warriors trooped out into the yard for their training. This time, however, Conor was treated as a veritable battlechief and asked to demonstrate some more of his skills; he obliged, and had worked up a healthy sweat when a boy came running with a summons from the king. Conor followed the lad across the yard to the king's hall; the doors were open and one of the ardféne stood guard—needlessly, it seemed to Conor, because nothing would have induced him to enter that darksome abode unbidden. He halted at the foot of the steps leading up onto the platform fronting the hall.

While he was waiting, two warriors emerged—one of them was Cethern. Conor tensed for a renewal of their conflict but, to his credit, the battlechief let his glance slide over Conor without any hint of animosity, embarrassment, or even recognition. He did not deign to notice Conor at all and, in fact, did not break stride but went on his way without a word. As Conor turned to watch him walk away, he felt the tension release him from its grip.

'So!' came a voice from the platform. 'Here you are.'

Conor swung back to see Lord Brecan looming over him, hands on hips, a scowl on his disapproving face.

'I was told you wished to see me,' said Conor with a slight dip of the knee and bow of the head.

Brecan frowned, staring down at him with a sour expression. Conor supposed he was expected to speak, but decided to say no more lest he provide any excuse for confrontation. The king was first to break the silence, saying, 'You probably think yourself lucky—beating my champion.'

'I understood it was to be a test of skill,' Conor replied.

'You hold yourself so far above Cethern?' Brecan's scowl deepened. 'And him a trusted champion and warleader? You think yourself better than my best?'

'That is for others to say,' replied Conor evenly.

'What, then, do *you* say?'

'Only this—that if another blade would be useful to you, then take mine. If not, I will go my way and find another to serve.'

'You think another lord will be eager to hire you—a despised outcast?'

Conor felt the crimson blotch on his face tingle as anger flickered within him. But he covered the insult with a disinterested shrug. 'Able warriors are always welcome—somewhere, if not here.'

Brecan considered this for a moment. Finally, his glower lifted and he made up his mind. 'True enough, and it would be a shame to lose a blade such as yours. I will take you.'

'And the pay?'

Before Brecan could reply, his druid appeared behind him. Having heard what had passed, Mog Ruith stepped forward and, in a loud voice, declaimed, 'My lord king, I advise you to refuse this insolent thief and troublemaker. Have nothing more to do with him.'

'Your counsel comes too late,' the king told him. 'The matter is decided.' To Conor, he said, 'You will take your place in the ranks of the younger warriors. There will be no pay, but if you prove yourself worthy, you will receive an equal share of all spoils taken in battle.' He fixed Conor with a firm and steady gaze. 'Agreed?'

Conor made a little bow to show he accepted the terms. 'Agreed,' he said. The king dismissed Conor and, as he turned away, Mog Ruith took hold of Brecan's arm and whispered something in his lord's ear. The king recoiled at the touch and, brushing aside the druid's hand, retreated to the hall. Conor quickly averted his eyes and hurried to rejoin the warriors at their weapons practice.

That first day passed without further incident and, though Cethern apparently accepted the king's decision to allow Conor to join the warband, Conor remained cautious around the battlechief. He also maintained a wary distance from the king's druid; he knew Mog Ruith watched him, perhaps waiting for any excuse to punish him, or banish him from the ráth. Nor did he neglect the reason why he had come among the Brigantes in the first place, but stayed alert to any sign of suspicious behaviour on the part of the king. These precautions were fairly easily sustained, but one threat remained: the queen.

Once it was clear that Conor would become part of the king's warband, Queen Sceana's interest in him became more palpable, more obvious, more potent. She appeared outside the Women's House during weapons practice and training and, when she took her place at the king's table for the evening meal and music, she allowed her gaze to rest upon him from time to time, always with a ready smile and lift of an eyebrow when he caught her watching. Nor did she miss an opportunity to speak an intimate word whenever she happened to pass him in the yard, or in the hall. 'You do well, Conor,' she might say. 'A true master of your weapons. Are you as skilled in more gentle forms of combat as well?'

Each time, Conor tried to deflect such comments with a light word, a smile, or gesture. Though the king did not appear to notice any of this, Conor was only too aware, and found it increasingly difficult to pretend that she was not actively pursuing him. He told himself that the sooner he could discover the nature of Brecan's dark designs, the sooner he could be restored to his tribe and reunited with Aoife. That was, to Conor, a prize higher than any other he could name, and certainly far higher than any hasty dalliance with a beautiful woman. Conor took to avoiding her as much as possible—difficult to do without seeming to give offense. But, he kept his head down and made certain he always entered and left the hall surrounded by his special coterie of young admiring warriors, and sat as far away from the king's place at table as possible.

This simple tactic worked well enough—until Brecan departed on one of his frequent travels.

The first Conor heard that the king was leaving was the morning his lordship and druid, along with a small bodyguard drawn from among the ardféne, rode out of the ráth in a clatter of hooves and shouts of farewell. Conor had been with an early-morning band of warriors delegated to one of the hunting parties that, from time to time, helped to provide meat for the table, larder, and smokehouse. Summer was passing, and it was time to begin storing up for the winter ahead. The party had gone out into the wood before daybreak, completed their hunt, and were returning to the ráth with two fine young bucks. As they came in sight of the settlement, they saw a body of horsemen issue from the gates, thunder down the long slope of the ramp, and head off toward the east.

'Was that the king away?' asked Conor.

'Aye,' replied Galart, one of the young warriors in the same house as Conor. 'That's our lord off on another of his circuits. The duties of a king never cease.'

'I did not know he was leaving. Will he be gone very long, do you think?'

'Not long. A few days is usually all it is.'

'Do you ever go with them?'

'Nay, nay—only old Mog and Cethern, and some of the ardféne,' Galart told him. 'I wouldn't like to go myself, you know. All that palaver makes my head ache.'

Conor watched the riders until they disappeared over the hill. He would, he decided, try to get himself invited along the next time the king rode out and in that way see if he might learn more about where the king went, who he met, and what they talked about. The problem of how to do this occupied his thoughts through the day—so much so that he failed to notice the queen standing outside the Women's House as the warriors trooped to the hall for the evening meal. Conor, head down as usual, felt a light touch on his arm. He paused and turned to see one of the queen's ladies. 'A moment, *angclú*,' she said.

Conor wondered at her use of the old word for "champion." He paused and turned. 'You must have mistaken me,' he said. 'Cethern is away with the king.'

'No mistake, I think,' she replied, stepping close and, in a softer tone, said, 'It is *you* the queen wishes to see, not Cethern.' She gave a little shiver and added, 'Never Cethern.'

'I am on my way to eat in the hall,' he said, grasping for a way out of this predicament. 'Perhaps I might come another time.'

'My queen has laid a table especially for you, angclú.' She turned, expecting Conor to follow. 'She is waiting even now.'

Conor cast a quick glance around. The other warriors had entered the hall and the yard was empty save for a dog or two, and a group of older children playing a game with a sheep's bladder. 'Now, you say?'

'Even now.' She offered him a winsome smile. 'It is this way.'

She said this as if Conor might not know the way to the Women's House. How could he not? For all it was only across the yard. But, seeing as he had not found a way to decline the invitation, Conor made no further attempt to escape; he followed, glad that there was no one to see him enter the queen's lair.

He was met on the threshold by the céile, Bríd, who offered him a clean siarc and new breecs, and said, 'My lady the queen thought you might like to bathe before your meal.' She led him to the back of the house and a small chamber containing a large vat of hot water. 'She knows warriors do not often have heated water,' Bríd told him, gesturing toward the vat. 'There are cloths for drying and also soap. I will bring a razor and mirror if you like.'

'No need.' Conor looked at the steaming water and fingered his stubbled jaw. 'On second thought, I would like that very much.'

As soon as she was gone, Conor shed his clothes and climbed into the warm water. It was true that warriors seldom enjoyed hot water for washing; usually they bathed in a stream or lake, so hot water was a rare indulgence and Conor was determined to make the most of it. He quickly soaped up, washed, and rinsed off, then sank back to enjoy the extravagance. He was sitting half submerged, eyes closed, when Bríd returned with the razor and mirror. 'Just leave it beside the vat,' Conor told her.

'For a kind word, I could be persuaded to shave you as well,' came the reply.

Instantly, Conor's eyes flew open. 'Lady Sceana! Forgive me, I meant no disrespect. I thought you were the maidservant.'

The queen laughed. 'It is no less than I deserve for intruding on a man at his bath.' She moved closer and held out the mirror. 'Even so, it would please me to ply the razor.'

Conor did not know how to refuse without offending her, so replied, 'If so lowly a task would amuse you, then I would be honoured.'

Taking a small stool from the corner of the room, Sceana sat down next to the vat and gently lathered his face, and with deft, practiced strokes applied the razor. Her mastery was so sure and steady, he sat back and tried to enjoy the experience. But only one woman had ever shaved him before, and that was Aoife. He could not relax entirely for feeling that he was somehow betraying her.

'That is better,' said the queen, appraising her handiwork. She held up the disk of polished silver so he could see. 'What do you think?'

'Very well done,' replied Conor, rubbing his hands over his newly smooth cheeks. 'I thank you for your care.'

'A queen cannot have her angclú looking like one of the Scálda,' she told him with a wink. 'When you are finished, you will find me waiting for you at the table.'

Conor did not linger long. As soon as she was gone, he dried himself on the linen cloths and then dressed in his old clothes—to be seen in new things from the queen's hand would raise too many eyebrows among the residents of the Warriors' House. Bríd was waiting outside the door and, without a word, led him to back to the central room where the queen reclined on her couch beside a low table. Dressed in a thin linen robe belted with an embroidered red sash, a slender golden torc at her throat, Queen Sceana beckoned him to join her.

Rushlights and candles had been lit and a small fire burned on the round hearth in the centre of the room. From somewhere the sound of a harp spun silvery music into the air, reminding Conor of a crystal fountain splashing in a forest pool. A brazier had been set up nearby and was being tended by one of the queen's ladies who was turning spits on which cubes of meat sizzled over coals, filling the air with the smell of roasting meat flavoured with sage—and something else Conor could not name; but it titillated his nostrils and made him think of something dark and sweet and rare.

'Ah! Conor mac Ardan, my very own champion, it is so good of you to join me,' she said—as if they had not already shared a most intimate moment. This, Conor suspected, was for the benefit of any gossips within hearing. She rose slowly and stepped around the table to meet him. 'And have you come to cheer me in my abject loneliness now the king is away?'

She made it sound as if this little tryst were all Conor's idea. He heard himself reply, 'I believe you summoned me, my lady.'

'And here you are.' She put a hand on his arm and the skin warmed beneath her touch. 'Come and sit. You must be ferociously hungry—a strong and active man like you.'

'The warriors at the king's table eat very well. We rarely go away hungry.'

'Ach, well and good, I suppose,' she said, arching one graceful eyebrow, 'if you are not overly particular. But the queen's table is more lavish.' She clapped her hands and called for the cups to be brought. This time, the mead was poured from a silver jar into shallow silver bowls. The ordinarily golden liquid had been stained deepest blue from black currants used for flavour. Conor accepted the bowl from the serving maid's hand and the queen said, 'I drink to you, my angclú—if you will accept.'

She lifted the bowl to her lips and took a long, lingering draught. Conor drank and felt the sticky, sweet liquor slide down his throat, warming him all the way down. 'Angclú,' Conor repeated. 'It is an old word for 'champion,' or 'hero'—is it not?'

'I expect you are wondering why I chose it.'

'The question did occur to me.'

'The king has his champion,' she said. 'The queen should have one, too. Do you not think so?'

'Cethern would happily serve you both,' Conor ventured. 'Of that you may be certain.'

'Cethern is a brute.'

'Perhaps a brute is required—if a king and his family are to be best protected.'

'Perhaps,' she allowed with a lazy smile. She lifted the bowl to her lips and drank. 'But you bettered the king's brute. And if a queen is to be best protected, she would certainly require the better of the two. That is you, I think.'

'Lord Brecan might not look on such a turn with friendly eyes,' Conor countered. 'I am a member of his warband and his to command.'

'My husband views little enough with friendly eyes,' replied Sceana with some force. 'In any event, as my champion, it is *my* eyes you should be worried about.'

Conor raised his cup to her and took another drink, thinking furiously how he might extricate himself from this dangerous conversation. He was saved having to make a reply by the appearance of a serving maid bearing a large wooden tray laden with bread and salt, and tidbits of succulent pork, lamb, and duck. She placed the tray on the table between the diners, and then retreated—only to return with bowls of creamy sweet walnuts boiled in sheep's milk, greens, mashed beans, and stewed plums in honey. She refilled both bowls with spiced mead and then, with a bow to the queen, retreated.

Sceana offered her guest first helping of the choicest morsels and they began to eat. While they ate, the queen told him of her early life in the far south with the Luceni—a fishing people of the coastal waters. 'Everything smelled of fish,' she laughed, 'even our hair!'

'How did you find your way here?' asked Conor.

'You mean how did I find my way to the king's bedchamber?' The queen offered a sad smile. 'Like most tribes of the south, we were driven from our homes by the wicked invaders. They burned everything that could not move. All with wings or feet fled before them. My father was chieftain of the clan and when we came north, he sought alliance with the Brigantes. Old Lergath, Brecan's father, was king then—he and my father became good friends. Brecan was already the warleader—and years older—but he took me for his wife. When Lergath died, Brecan was acclaimed lord and king.' She raised an indifferent palm. 'I have been queen ever since.'

'Lord Brecan is a powerful chieftain,' Conor allowed, reaching for another cube of perfectly cooked lamb. He licked his fingers. 'You have been fortunate.'

'That is not a word that comes easily to my lips,' she replied.

'No?'

'All this fighting and warring—it never ends. Does it not make you tired? Do you not yearn for something better?'

'I do, my lady. In my heart, I know there must be a better way.'

She regarded him shrewdly. 'Those are not the words of a warrior.'

Conor did not know what to make of that comment, so he ignored it. 'The Scálda will not cease until they have rid this island of every tribe and clan. They mean to erase the memory of the Tuatha dé Danann from Eirlandia.'

'But they will not be defeated,' Sceana said bluntly. 'There are those among us who believe this endless war has already been lost and that we must make the best of it that we can.'

Conor hid his surprise at this reply by adopting a careless air. He tore off a bit of bread. 'Those are not the words of a queen,' he said, chewing thoughtfully.

Sceana sighed. 'Talk of war and fighting fatigues me,' she said. 'Brecan talks of nothing else, thinks of nothing else, believes. . . .'

Her voice trailed off and Conor wondered what she had prevented herself from saying. 'Is that why you live in the Women's House?'

The playful spark rekindled in her eyes. 'I choose to live among my ladies because, unlike my war-hungry husband, I prefer . . .' She paused and, picking out a honeyed plum, put it in her mouth and chewed, before adding, 'A gentler life.'

The queen filled their cups once more and then, rising, held out her hand to Conor. 'Come, my champion, let us finish our meal in more intimate surroundings.'

In Conor's opinion they were already intimate enough, but he knew that to refuse such an invitation would not advance his purpose, nor did he wish to create an enemy where he might secure an ally. All the same, he knew he could not risk the wrath of the king: If Brecan ever found out he had made love to his wife, it would be Conor's head on a spear over the fortress gate, not the queen's.

Accepting her hand, he rose and allowed himself to led to

one of the booths that lined the wall. Like the others, it was separated from its neighbours by cloth hangings that could be so arranged as to allow more or less privacy between bed places. Each booth contained a pallet heaped with rushes over which furs had been laid and the whole covered with linens to form a cozy nest. There were large cushions of goose feathers scattered around, and tall beeswax candles on iron stands in each corner, casting a dim and wavering light over all.

Queen Sceana pulled him into the bedchamber and down onto the cushions. 'Sit awhile,' she said invitingly. 'Take your ease.'

She reclined opposite him, invitingly close. Conor pulled a cushion between them, and balanced his cup on it.

'I do not think I should be here, my lady,' he said.

'Shall I tell you what I think?' she asked, sipping from his cup. 'I think it is the duty of the queen's champion to protect her in whatever way she deems appropriate.'

'Do you need protecting?'

'We live in perilous times,' she replied, setting aside the cup. 'We all need protecting—especially at night when we are . . . most . . . vulnerable.'

So saying she loosened her sash, pulled it away, and allowed her robe to fall open. Conor saw the flawless white flesh and the graceful curve of her breast, and the sight warmed him more than the mead he had drunk. She reached for the cup and, watching him over the rim, drained it, and then leaned toward him, opening the robe even more. Cradling the back of his head in her free hand, she drew him to her in a kiss. Conor felt warm mead fill his mouth.

His mind spun as he swallowed down the sticky sweet liquid. When she released him to catch his breath, he caught the playful gleam of reflected candlelight in her eyes. 'I feel safer already,' she said, her voice becoming husky and low with longing. She opened her robe a little more, as if to cool her body, exposing a smooth flank and hip to Conor's view.

Conor had seen enough. He took a last gulp from his cup and, setting it aside, made a lunge toward her. He seized her in a lover's embrace and drew her down beneath him, planting another kiss on her delicious lips. She made a soft mewing sound and gave herself up to his passion.

While she was thus occupied, Conor hooked his foot around one of the tall candles and pulled it down onto the bed. He kept Sceana busy with nuzzled kisses while willing the candle flame to take hold.

He gave her one kiss and another, and was diving in for a third when the queen whispered, 'Do you smell something?'

'I smell only the scent of your enticing perfume, my queen.'

She pulled back a little and sniffed. 'What is that?'

'Nothing that should disturb our pleasure.' Conor leaned in for another kiss. She turned her face, so he kissed her neck just beneath her jaw.

'I smell something burning. . . .'

'Only my desire for you—'

She pushed him forcefully aside. 'Something's burning!'

Conor leaned back and looked at her. 'Perhaps—' he began.

'The bed is on fire!'

He looked around, saw flames pooling at the bottom of the bed and licking at the cloth partition. The rushes and furs of the bed itself were beginning to smoulder. Conor leapt up and, seizing a cushion, batted at the flames—an effort that succeeded in fanning them to greater life.

'You're making it worse!' shouted the queen. 'Get water!'

He fled the bower and went in search of the water stoup, calling as he went, 'Fire! Fire! The queen's bower is on fire!'

Ladies came running to his cry. 'Bring water!' he shouted, pushing the first one to reach him away again. 'Hurry!'

He ran back to the queen. The flames were now racing up the cloth partition and had almost reached the top. He pulled the queen from the chamber and then leapt in, seized the hanging curtain, and pulled it down. He then stamped on the burning cloth. Clouds of smoke filled the chamber and spilled out into the house. More women came running to their aid. One of them carried a bucket of water.

Conor grabbed the bucket and rushed back into the chamber. He waited a moment or two, and then doused the flames, creating even more smoke. He shoved the bucket into the hands of one of the ladies and sent her for another. 'Get out! Everyone!' he called over his shoulder. 'Do not breathe the smoke.'

While her ladies led the queen away, Conor poured another bucket of water over the end of the bed, and then one more for good measure. In all, the damage was slight—but the bed would not be fit for sleeping that night. Nor, he imagined, would anyone care to stay in the house until the stink of smoke and burning fur could be cleansed away.

The flames extinguished, Conor stood by and thanked all the gods that he could name for his deliverance.

Fergal

Of the voyage to Tír nan Óg and the island of the faéry, I will say only that it was accomplished with a speed and ease that seemed a dream to me then, and a dream now as I think on it. Though Gwydion assures me there was no enchantment cast upon the sea to smooth our passage through the waves, the voyage was so swift it could not have been otherwise. One moment we were gliding out into the deep grey waters of the Narrow Sea, green sails full bellied and gulls keening and wheeling above us . . . and the next we were sailing into a sea mist rising from the water in a silvery fog so thick and dense as to form a very wall.

The faéry ship slowed as it approached this stronghold of silvery mist and passed into it. The wind died. The bright green sails emptied. I stood at the upswept bow and watched the clouds close in upon us. The fog crept along the deck and twined around the mast and slackened sails. I felt it cool and damp against my face and hands. I folded my arms across my chest for warmth and stood gazing into the haze.

'I am sorry to be leaving you alone,' said Rhiannon, coming up silently beside me. 'But I have been helping my father understand the nature of your friend Donal's ailment, and what Gráinne and I have done to keep him alive.'

'Your father . . . ?' I said, casting a glance back to where the other faéry were gathered at the stern.

'Lord Gwydion,' she said. 'He is my father.'

'Then you are not the queen? We thought—' I glanced at her face and it seemed even more lovely to me than before— her skin whiter, her eyes a deeper blue, her hair, if possible, even darker. Perhaps, knowing that she would soon be among her own people again so brightened her spirits that she fairly shone with an inner glow.

'I know,' she said lightly. 'It makes no difference—except, perhaps, to my mother.'

I nodded and turned back to the cloaking mist, wondering how we could make much headway in such obscure weather.

'It will not last long,' Rhiannon told me. She possessed the knack of knowing my thoughts before I could speak them out.

'The sea fog?'

She waved a hand to indicate the vapours flowing all around and over us. 'It will not last. We will soon leave it behind.'

'You know this?' I asked. Truly, nothing should have surprised me about the faéry race, for they are uncanny odd. Yet, the idea that she might know the whims of the weather did turn my head.

She laughed lightly and put her hand to my arm. 'No, I am not a phantarch to know such things. This mist and wrack—it is one of our island's many protections.'

'It is always here?'

'Most always, yes. Sometimes a storm will drive it away for a day or two—then Ynys Afallon can be seen by any ships that happen to be passing. We are most vulnerable then.'

She raised a long-fingered hand to the close encircling wall of soft, shifting cloud. 'Look! Even now it is coming to an end. We are almost through it.'

As she spoke, the sea-grey cloak began to wear thin, tearing away in shreds to reveal a calm and glassy sea, gleaming in the light of a late summer sun. Where the time had gone,

I cannot say. But there, in the near distance, rising from the water before us, were the green hills and steep crags of an island.

'Behold!' said Gwydion, coming to stand beside us, 'Ynys Afallon in the Region of the Summer Stars.'

He stood head and shoulders above me, and no one ever called Fergal mac Caen a small man. The lean and slender bodies of the faéry folk make them seem even taller still; however, it is not their only height, and grace of movement and face, but the depth and solemn wisdom in their every glance and manner that show they are no mortal race.

'I did not know this island was so close,' I said, for it seemed that we had crossed the sea in no time at all.

Gwydion looked at me with a curious expression.

'So near to Eirlandia, I mean.'

'It is neither near,' explained Gwydion, 'nor far away.'

Now it was my turn to be confused. 'A middle distance, then?'

'It is as far as the farthest reach of the ocean, and as close as your dearest thought,' he said.

'You sound like a druid, now. So you do.'

'I would like to meet a druid,' he said. 'Rhiannon assures me they are excellent men and women. Her praise for Talgobain and Gráinne are unstinting.' The faéry king glanced at his daughter, and then looked at me with his pale green eyes and said, 'Thank you for returning my Rhiannon to us.'

'Without her, none of us would have survived,' I told him. 'I am sorry that your lady Tanwen did not.'

At this, the light went from his eyes and he turned back to the island. 'She will be mourned.'

After a moment, the king of the faéry put his hand on my shoulder and said, 'That is for another time. Tonight, you will be my guest and you will sit at my right hand at the feast to be given in your honour.'

'It was Conor's doing mostly,' I told him. 'And I would be a false friend if I did not tell you it should be him standing before you and feasting at your table, not me.'

'And yet,' said Gwydion, 'you are here and he is not. Our Great Mother orders all things to her will—and this is how it is.'

They left me then to prepare for making landfall and soon our sleek boat slid into a wide, sandy bay. Guiding the vessel with sweeping strokes of the steering oar, the pilot brought us to berth in the shadow of a towering headland which sheltered a stone wharf; two other ships were harboured there, each larger than the one that carried us. Three faéry stood waiting on the quayside—two men and a woman; the men were dressed in long siarcs the colour of midnight, and the woman wore a scarlet gown that glimmered like water as she moved.

The moment the ship kissed the quay, the faéry woman ran forward and, without waiting for the vessel to be secured, came aboard and took Lady Rhiannon in a fervent embrace. With hair so dark it shone with blue glints, and braided with strands of silver to match the silver torc around her slender throat, she was, to be sure, as much like Rhiannon as could be—her sister, so I thought—a mistake soon corrected.

'Daughter, I cannot tell you how glad I am,' she said. 'I feared I should never see you again.'

'Nor I you, Mother,' replied Rhiannon.

'But here you are, home safe at last.'

'Home and safe—thanks to this man and his stalwart friends.' She turned and held out a hand to me. I stepped forward and Rhiannon took my arm and pulled me to her. My arm tingled at her touch. 'This is Fergal mac Caen of the Darini.' To me, she said, 'Fergal, I am pleased to present my mother, Arianrhod, Queen of the House of Llŷr.'

The queen stepped forth, seized both my hands in hers,

and, looking into my eyes, said, 'My gratitude is boundless, lord Fergal. As mother and queen, I thank you for returning my heart's treasure to me.'

Momentarily lost in the wonder of the fairest face under heaven—surpassing even the matchless beauty of her daughter—I could think of no suitable reply and instead, muttered, 'I am no lord—only a warrior.'

Seeing my embarrassment, Rhiannon quickly said, 'Mother, we have brought a wounded man for healing. He is fearfully ill and hovers even now at death's threshold. I have promised all the aid and skill of our physicians to heal him.'

Queen Arianrhod turned her eyes to me and said, 'What is your friend's name?'

'Donal,' I told her. 'Donal mac Donogh.'

She reached out and squeezed my hand. 'We will do for him what we would do for one of our own—that is to say, everything in our power. If healing can be achieved, and his wound overcome, it will be done.' She pressed my hand again and then, taking her daughter by the arm, led her away, their heads pressed together to speak more private thoughts.

Lord Gwydion had undertaken to move poor Donal onto the quayside; with the other men and Rhiannon's attendant maidens, they gently lifted him on his litter and carried him onto the island. We then started off; the queen and princess led the way, then came the men bearing Donal. I followed close behind. We walked inland from the sea and soon struck upon a well-trodden path through a wood that seemed somehow more than a wood—trees are trees, after all, and bushes and shrubs the same—similar and strange at the same time. Though, if anyone had asked me, I could not have explained any better than to say that I felt as one who has entered a forest for the first time and all that met my eye was new to me, and strange. Even the air was peculiar, for it seemed to chime with a bright music that tantalized the ear just on the edge of hearing.

I also had the distinct feeling that we were being watched. I glimpsed no watchers, but out of the corner of my eye, every now and then, I sensed a furtive movement, the flick of a shadow, or the shiver of a single leaf on a branch as when a startled animal has fled.

How long we walked, I do not know—not long, I think. Yet it was almost dark when we reached a wide clearing—a valley meadow in the heart of the wood. At the far end of the vale, a sheer wall of tumbled rock over which spilled a lively stream that pooled at the bottom of the waterfall to form a lough before gathering itself to run off into deeper forest. Around the pool and hard against the rock wall stood a number of graceful buildings with high peaked roofs thatched with river reeds and deep eaves sheltering wide platforms lined with benches and chairs and tables. Two of the larger houses stood on stone pillars sunk into the water so that they half stood out over the lough. Yet, for all their generous size, the dwellings did not seem enough to house an entire faéry tribe. Nor did they—as I soon discovered.

For, upon reaching the little lough and passing by the first of the dwellings, we proceeded around the water marge on a wooden walkway that followed the shoreline. The faéry carried Donal on his wattle bed to the foot of the rock wall where the waterfall splashed into the lake. Here we stopped before the largest of the houses and I thought we would enter there, but we did not.

Instead, Gwydion moved to the end of the walkway and, raising his hands, made a subtle motion in the air and the curtain of water parted and I saw an opening—the mouth of a cavern hidden behind the waterfall. There were steps concealed among the rocks leading up to the cave. We climbed the steps and entered the cave. At first glance, it seemed more or less like any other cave: a room with a low roof and bare rock walls. A few paces farther in, however, we came to another opening—this one closed by a large round stone carved with odd runes and swirls and marks like branches of a tree.

Queen Arianrhod stepped forward and, with a simple sweep of her hand, caused the stone to move aside with a low rumbling sound to reveal another chamber beyond—a chamber unlike any in all Eirlandia.

33

Queen Sceana and her maidens were still cleaning up the mess from the fire in the Guest Lodge when the king and his travelling party returned to Aintrén. Since the mishap was more inconvenience than disaster, Lord Brecan took little interest in the matter and instead busied himself with more pressing concerns—in fact, he had hardly brushed the dust from his cloak before he began arranging another journey.

Conor saw the furtive activity around the hall—warriors running in and out on hurried errands, supplies being readied, fresh horses groomed—and decided to find out what was happening. While he practiced in the yard with some of the other warriors, he kept his eyes open and, when he saw Galart emerge from the hall, he made a point to seek him out later when he could get him alone.

After supper, Conor loitered outside and when Galart appeared, he fell into step beside him as they returned to the Warriors' House. 'Will you be joining us at the ale tun tonight, brother?' he asked.

'Aye, to that—and about time. I have had nothing to drink since we rode out.'

'Ach, well, and it looks like you are leaving again for all you've just returned.'

The warrior rolled his eyes. 'Not if I had my way. All these journeys—and for what?'

'I suppose Lord Brecan needs protection when he meets with his client lords—all kings are like that as we know.'

'Ha! We are allowed nowhere near any of these meetings,' the young man huffed. 'Only Cethern and his druid go with him. We make camp and guard it while they ride off to the meeting place.'

'Kings are like that,' Conor replied again with a shrug.

'I don't know why we go at all.'

'Well, at least you have tonight in your own bed.'

'Only tonight, mind. We leave again in the morning.'

'Where do you go this time?' Conor yawned, trying to feign disinterest.

The fellow cast a quick sideways glance at Conor, and lowered his voice. 'I'm not allowed to say—even if I knew. The king never tells us where we are going until after we've left the ráth.'

'Ach, well,' replied Conor, 'kings will have their secrets.'

There was much more Conor wanted to ask, but felt he had pried enough, and the last thing he wanted was to make his best source of information wary of speaking to him. Instead, he was determined to remain alert for any other stray crumbs he might glean around the board later that evening when the ale had loosened a few tongues. In the meantime, he would consider what he had been told—and how he might use it to get himself included among the king's travelling companions. Only then would he find out where the king went, whom he saw, and what he did.

Unfortunately, there were but few crumbs to be gleaned over the cups that night. The talk was all of hunting and hounds. Yet, Conor did learn something that he thought might yet prove useful. According to Galart, the king was in negotiations with two of his client lords to acquire a number of dogs to be added to his kennel—a fact that caused Conor to say, 'I didn't know his lordship had a kennel.'

'Nor does he,' replied Médon, settling the bench next to him. He sucked foam from his moustache and returned to his cup.

'So then?' Conor prompted.

'Well, he is building one—see?'

'Ach, well then,' said Conor, raising his jar to his lips. 'I had not noticed. Still, I think I might have seen the carpenters at work.'

'You wouldn't,' offered Galart; he leaned across the table, cradling his cup between his hands. 'The kennel is not within the ráth at all.'

'Is it not?' said Conor. He drank again and wiped his mouth with the back of his hand. 'Strange that—such valuable animals, too—if I know anything about dogs. I should think he'd want them close to keep an eye on them.'

'Not beasts like these you wouldn't,' replied the half-drunk Médon. 'They're no peace-loving creatures.'

Conor thought for a moment. 'War dogs, then?'

'Aye,' agreed Médon, 'the fiercest fighting dogs you ever saw. Bred to blood and battle they are. Born to kill.'

'Well, this close to the borderlands and the Scálda always skulking about, having a dog or two around is a good thing.'

'It is, aye.' Médon emptied his jar. 'But it's not just a dog or two, mind.' The warrior leaned close. 'It is twenty at least—maybe more.'

Conor wanted to hear more, but did not wish to appear too inquisitive; so he said nothing and instead rose from the bench. Holding out his hand for Médon's jar, he said, 'I will go fetch us another. How about you, Galart?'

Galart took a last gulp and thrust out the cup to Conor. 'See you hurry back, now,' he called, slouching contentedly on the bench. 'A man could die of thirst for all this talking.' The two laughed as Conor stumped off.

He had to wait his turn at the vat, and by the time he returned, Médon was almost asleep and Galart was looking none too lively. Conor decided he'd pushed matters as far as he could for one night; he asked no more questions, and instead turned to talk of horses. Still, he went to bed thinking that he must find out more about these mysterious war dogs.

The next morning, the king and his bodyguard rode out once more. Later, as Conor was finishing weapons practice for the day, he noticed two visitors at the fortress gate: one older, one younger, both dressed in blue siarcs and green breecs and high-laced brócs—and both with the distinctive sharp-shaved crowns of the druid kind. After a brief word with the guards, they were admitted and proceeded directly to the Bards' House. Conor saw them crossing the yard and had the curious sensation that he had seen one of them before—but he could not say where. As they came nearer, so too the feeling of familiarity grew, hardening into a certainty—and more, for the younger one bore more than a passing resemblance to . . . himself!

The two moved to the door of the house and the young one turned to look across the yard. Conor almost dropped his spear. 'Rónán!' he gasped under his breath. 'Can it be . . . ?'

Glancing around quickly, he saw the last of his battle group leaving the yard and only a few women and children going about their chores. Lowering his head, he made directly to intercept the two visitors.

'Rónán!' he called as he drew nearer. The young druid did not so much as glance his way. 'Rónán! It is me, Conor. . . .'

The two visitors continued up the steps to the wooden platform fronting the house. Conor caught them just as they reached the door. 'Why so fast, brother?' he said, smiling. 'Did you not hear me call your name?'

'Do we know you?' asked the elder of the two.

Ignoring the question, Conor appealed to his brother. 'Rónán, it's me, Conor. What are you doing here?'

'Rónán, you say? I know no one of that name, warrior. My name is Ferdiad,' the young druid told him. 'You must have mistaken me for someone else.'

Conor, amazed, stared at the newcomer. Although it had been many years since he had last seen his brother, the man standing before him looked as much like himself as he looked like Ardan. The family resemblance only increased when he spoke. 'What game is this, friend?'

'It is no game,' Conor replied. 'You look like one of my blood kin—my younger brother. He is one of the Learned, too. His name is Rónán mac Ardan.'

'We know no such person,' the elder druid told him. 'We have come to see Mog Ruith, filidh of the Brigantes, on matters of our own—not that it is anything to you. You will kindly let us go about our business.'

Conor, blinking in disbelief, stepped back, and the two disappeared into the house. With some difficulty, Conor dismissed the incident, and went on his way. Then, late that night, Conor left the hall with some of the warband heading off to bed in the Warriors' House. The sky was overcast; no moon or stars were visible anywhere. The noisy group moved through the darkness and Conor kept one hand lightly touching the walls beside him—first the hall, then the brew house, and then the bake house. The scent of fresh bread from the day's production still lingered in the warm air drifting out from the wind hole above him. Arriving at the Warriors' House, the first of the group entered and, as Conor stepped to the door, a voice called out of the darkness behind him. 'Conor mac Ardan—a word, if you please.'

Conor halted; the others trooped into the house. As soon as they were gone, the voice said, 'Follow me.'

'Where?'

'Keep your voice down.' A face loomed out of the darkness and Conor recognised the older of the two visiting bards. 'This way.'

The druid led him back along the path to the bake house where, under the wide, overhanging eaves, another figure waited in the shadows. 'What goes here?' Conor asked, and was instantly folded into a firm embrace.

'Conor! You cannot believe how often I have longed to see you. And here you are at last. How I have missed you, brother.'

Conor pushed the other away, straining in the darkness to see his face. 'Rónán? It *is* you, after all.'

'None other.'

Conor, tears started to his eyes, grabbed his brother to him and both clung to one another, sobbing, speaking in choked-off words, the sentiments of longed-for reunion. Finally, when Conor regained control of his voice, he said, 'How are you? How is it you are here? Did you know I was here? Is that why you came?' He shook his head, still gripping his brother by the arm. 'What are you doing here?'

Rónán laughed, 'Which question am I to answer first?' He beamed at his brother, shaking his head in the wonder of the moment. 'After all these years, you are still just as I remembered. You have hardly changed at all.'

'I don't think I had a moustache then. But you, now—' Conor grinned, smearing away the tears with the back of his hand. 'You have grown up. But I *knew* it was you! I knew it was you—and then when you claimed to be Ferdiad and spurned me, I did begin to think I had made a mistake. . . . Yet, it *is* you after all. Have you been back to Dúnaird? Have you seen our da?'

'Not yet,' Rónán told him. 'I will go to him after this. I wanted to see how you were getting on. Are they treating you well here?'

'Exceedingly well . . . better than I could have hoped. The queen is a double handful and no mistake—' Rónán raised his eyebrows in concern. Conor hastened to reassure him, saying, 'But I think I have cooled her passion for a while. Why are you here?'

'To see *you*, brother. After all that has happened, I wanted to see for myself how you fared.'

'But how did you know I was here?' asked Conor; and before Rónán could answer, he guessed, 'Tuán.'

'Tuán,' echoed his brother. 'When he found out you were my brother, he came to me and told me all that had happened—about Mádoc and the exile and your escape from the Scálda.' Rónán grinned. 'Did you really steal one of the Black Ships? And wreck it?'

'We did.' Conor went on to explain Mádoc's elaborate scheme to uncover evidence of Brecan mac Lergath's treacherous ambition, the discovery and rescue of the faéry. 'Fergal and Donal were with me,' he said, 'Donal was wounded in the escape, but Fergal—do you remember Fergal?'

Rónán ran his hand over the top of his head, along the shaved edge of his tonsure. 'I remember only you and da and Liam—maybe one or two others.'

'Well, the Darini will remember you,' Conor told him. 'Go to Dúnaird. They will be glad to see you. I would go with you, but for the work I have set myself here. Still, I would give a golden torc to see the look on their faces when you walk through the gate—all grown up and a druid, now.'

'You think the Brigantes lord is a traitor?' asked Rónán, lowering his voice even further.

'That is what I am trying to discover.' Conor shook his head slowly from side to side. 'I still cannot believe you are here—and grown. Tuán said you were to be an ollamh.'

'One day, perhaps. We shall see.'

The other druid, who had been standing by keeping silent

watch as the two enjoyed their reunion, spoke up. 'Someone's coming!'

They paused. Voices sounded on the path yet some small distance away.

'We must go,' said Rónán. 'It will be better for you if we were not seen together. Is there anything you'd like me to tell Father?'

'Tell him that I thrive and that, if all goes well, I will return with evidence of the Brigantes treachery one day soon.'

'Only that and nothing else?'

'Tell Aoife that I miss her and long to be with her.'

'Aoife? I don't know her.'

'She is my betrothed. We are—or were—to be married at Lughnasadh.'

'I will find her,' replied Rónán, 'and when I do, I will tell her you are a mere scrap of a man pining away for the love of her.'

'Tell her that,' Conor replied, 'and she will believe you never saw me.'

Conor put his hand to his brother's shoulder and gave it a squeeze. 'I'm glad you came, Rónán. Will I see you again tomorrow? After weapons practice we could go—'

'Rónán!' whispered their sentry. 'They're coming!'

'We depart tomorrow at dawn. We're on our way to help cure a foundered cow and an Eblani man with a runny eye. It would not do to have Brecan or Mog Ruith find us here. But I will come again when I can.' Rónán gripped his brother's arm and said, 'Fare you well, Conor. Until we meet again.'

Conor gathered him in a brotherly embrace. 'Until then,' he said, and released him with a firm pat on the back.

Rónán stepped away, already fading into the darkness. 'Tread lightly, brother—you've set your feet on a dangerous path.'

34

Conor found it hard to sleep that night. Seeing Rónán again after all these years not only lifted his spirits, but filled him with an almost giddy delight. Rónán . . . all grown up . . . how well he looked, how he'd grown in stature and authority. No longer the skinny frightened little boy taken away by the druid, here he was a man—and one to be admired and obeyed at that. Conor could not quite believe the change he'd seen with his own eyes; with great pleasure he turned it over and over in his mind.

But, over the following days and weeks, as the joy of their glad reunion faded, Rónán's warning lingered.

King Brecan and his retinue returned to Aintrén two days after Rónán's visit, and Conor redoubled his efforts to worm his way into his lordship's ardféne, where he would be in a position to be chosen to accompany the king on his next foray. To this end, he threw himself into the life of the Brigantes settlement. At weapons practice, he undertook to lead some of the sessions, teaching the young warriors his skills and developing their confidence and proficiency. When they went hunting, he made certain to ride in the forefront so as to be in on any kill made. When they rode for sport, he helped out in the stables afterward, walking the horses to cool them; other times, he lent a hand at feeding and grooming the animals, working his way to becoming a favourite of the stable master. At meals, he picked out a younger warrior or two to join them at table with their higher-ranking elders; and when other warriors began telling stories, Conor fetched the ale for the table.

In this way, Conor rose steadily in the estimation of his fellows. He became an accepted, and valued, member of the warband and the clan as a whole and, as such, enjoyed the benefits. The Brigantes, under the rule of their lord, flourished.

Lughnasadh came and the festivities around him cast Conor into a melancholy mood for several days. He missed Aoife and made himself miserable lamenting the fact that it was to have been his wedding he was celebrating, not the harvest. Even so, his sulky humour went unremarked, if not unnoticed.

Autumn turned the land golden and Conor's spirits rose. As the days passed, the reaping progressed, and proved abundant—pleasing the farmers with ample reward for their labours, and gratifying the brewers with a wealth of grain with which to fill their vats and tuns and turn into sweet brown ale. The herdsmen began slaughtering beef, sheep, goats, and pigs for the winter larder, and success crowned the various hunting parties, keeping the cooks busy preserving and storing the beef and pork, as well as the venison, wild boar, hare, ducks, geese, and other fowl. The fishing camps on the coast brought in fish—smoked or salted or dried—by the wagonload. The abundance of the land was demonstrated by the bounty of the table; everyone in the ráth and others throughout the territory ate well.

The warriors worked hard at honing and perfecting their skills and, as summer dwindled down, there were games organised in the yard and gleaned fields for the whole ráth and others to enjoy: horse races, spear-throwing contests, and wrestling matches where two or more combatants drenched

IN THE REGION OF THE SUMMER STARS · 361

themselves in bear grease and went at it hand-to-hand. By far the favourite pastime was *cammán*—with its massed teams armed with stout, curved sticks, a little hard ball, and the inevitable melee—often involving not only the players but partisan spectators as well. The black bruises, bloody scrapes, and scratches earned in these games were worn like trophies gained in battle.

Conor took part in the games as mood and the urging of his fellow warriors moved him. He wrestled a few times—twice drawing Cethern as an opponent and, through this, earning the champion's grudging respect, and a nascent friendship formed. He entered the spear-throwing contests, and rode Búrach in some of the races—winning one of them, and earning himself a copper arm ring from the hand of the king himself.

Nights were filled with music and stories: musicians came to the settlement to gain places for the winter; harps, flutes, and pipes were heard at mealtimes and far into the night. Mog Ruith, or visiting bards, told the old hero tales and stories of love and death, of triumph and ruin.

Amidst such lavish excess, it was easy to forget that not every tribe throughout Eirlandia enjoyed the same luxury the Brigantes commanded with such ease. And Brecan showed himself to be a generous lord to his people. He gave liberally and happily. True, he plucked the best plums for himself, but that was a king's privilege—and in this he was no different than most other monarchs. Thus, as the weeks went by, and autumn ripened on the vine, Aintrén hummed with a satisfying industry and everyone looked forward to a snug and comfortable winter. Moreover, the king had curtailed his travels; he made no more clandestine circuits, no more hurried and unexplained departures. Instead, he remained in his stronghold, feasting in his hall, enjoying his own largesse. Queen Sceana curtailed her advances—with her husband in residence, she could not renew her pursuit beyond the occasional smile or seductive lift of a shapely eyebrow, which Conor easily ignored.

Yet, as contentment flourished in the tribe, so too did Conor's frustration. For all his effort, he was no closer to gaining membership in the king's ardféne, much less of discovering evidence of Brecan's treachery. Indeed, life with the Brigantes was so amiable, so pleasurable, it was easy to forget why he had come among them in the first place, easy to forget his suspicions. He even found himself beginning to doubt his own aims. Brecan mac Lergath, to every appearance, was not a tyrant. Might Conor have misjudged him?

Then, a few days before Samhain, a messenger appeared at the gate—a dirty, undernourished youth in tattered clothes, barefoot, and shaggy haired. Conor happened to see the lad standing in front of the Bards' House in the company of one of the guards—but only for as long as it took to deliver his message to Mog Ruith. The boy was given some bread and meat and a cup of ale, and then sent on his way.

Conor noted this, but thought nothing more about it until Cethern showed up in the practice yard a short time later and began pulling warriors away from their training. One of those chosen was Galart, Conor's sparring partner of the moment. 'What's this?' called Conor as the fellow quit the yard.

'Find another,' replied Galart. 'The king is called away. We have to go.'

Conor turned toward Cethern, who, having picked his men, was walking back to the hall. Clearly, Conor had been passed over to accompany the retinue.

The frustration he had felt and suppressed broke through Conor's fragile defences then and flooded over him. He stood watching the warriors chosen for the retinue, gripping his sword hilt so tightly, his knuckles went white. By the time the last man entered the hall, Conor had decided what to do.

He spent the rest of the day making his preparations. He ate and slept well that night and the next morning, after Brecan and his retinue left the stronghold, Conor picked up his bag of provisions—now stuffed with food and his fine clothes—and took a sword and knife from the wall of the Warriors' House. He stole around the back to the stables, and ordered one of the stable boys to prepare the grey stallion for a ride. When the horse was ready, he led Búrach across the yard and out through the gates, pausing to exchange a word with the gatemen. Then, he swung up onto the grey's back and, with a last backward glance at the ráth that had been his home for the last months, rode out. He picked up the king's trail as soon as he reached the bottom of the ramp—fresh and not difficult to follow—but maintained a fair distance at a leisurely pace, pausing often to rest and water Búrach—all the while taking care to remain well out of sight of the retinue.

When the king's company made camp for the night, he stopped, too—in a young birch grove beside a clear-running burn. Tethering the stallion to graze nearby, he ate a little from his bag, washing down the cured meat and new cheese with cool water from the stream. Then, wrapping himself in his cloak, he stretched out on the mossy bank and watched the stars come out as the sky darkened into night.

He slept well and rose to the sound of birdsong in the trees round about. He stripped off his clothes and bathed in the stream, then watered Búrach and moved the tether to better grass so the horse could graze a little before they started off again. He strolled to the edge of the birch grove and scanned the near horizon for the smoke signature of Brecan's camp— and found it right where he expected it to be: no more than half a league south and a little west of where he stood. The king and his travelling company would be breaking their fast and striking camp soon, but he would wait and allow them a fair head start before picking up the trail again.

He returned to his horse and offered him a few handfuls of oats from his bag; after Búrach had eaten, Conor pulled up the tether pegs, remounted, and continued on his way. By the time he reached the place where Brecan and his retinue had camped, the company had moved on leaving nothing behind but bent grass, horse dung, and warm ashes in the fire ring.

Conor kept a respectful distance through the morning, but nevertheless came upon them unexpectedly when he crested a low hill and found the company stopped at a stream at the bottom of the glen directly below. He wheeled the grey and ducked out of sight below the hilltop, dismounted quickly, and crawled back up to a place where he could overlook the camp without being seen.

Perched in a nook between two big rocks, he watched the activity below. The sun had only just passed midday, but it appeared that his lordship was already making camp for the night. Conor watched long enough to confirm this suspicion, and also to determine that his lordship, his champion, and his druid were no longer among the men in the valley. After a time, Conor grew restless and decided to see if he could find where the king and his two closest advisors had gone.

Remounted, he rode back down the hill and worked his way around to the woodland east of the camp where, hidden among the trees, he could pass by unseen. With the camp to the north now, he traversed the wood from east to west until he found the track Brecan and his retinue had used—actually, he smelled it before he saw it, for fresh horse dung alerted him to the fact that horses had very recently passed that way. He marked the fragrant green pile and paused to examine the trail where it soon became apparent that the little woodland path was a well-used track: there were many hoofprints, some quite old and washed out, as well as scatterings of dung, some of it well rotted and broken up. By this, Conor surmised, the king had passed this way before; perhaps it was a place he came to often on his clandestine travels.

With a click of his tongue, he nudged Búrach onto the trail and began to follow it, alert now to any sign of his quarry up ahead. To be seen now would ruin all his hard work so far—as well anything he hoped to gain in the future. He proceeded with slow stealth until he heard the murmur of voices on the trail ahead—not far away, but muted so that he could not make out what they were saying. He dismounted and led Búrach off the trail a little way, and hid him behind a stand of elder. Putting his mouth to the stallion's ear, he whispered, 'Shhh . . . quiet now, brother. Wait here and keep still.'

Returning to the trail, he moved cautiously through the heavy undergrowth, pausing now and then to listen. The voices had gone silent—either out of earshot, or the riders were no longer speaking. Sword in hand, he advanced with a hunter's stealth, placing each foot carefully lest he break a twig or snap a branch. He came to a hedge wall of berry-heavy brambles overcrowding the path on either side. As he made to pass, one spiny tendril of thorns snagged the shoulder of his siarc. He halted to work the barb free, trying not to become further entangled in the mass of spikes.

That was when they caught him.

35

Conor was still trying to work himself free of the thorny vines when he heard the rustle of leaves behind him. He cast a quick look over his shoulder and saw a dark shape on the path a short distance away. Reaching up, he tugged the cloth free and bolted ahead—ignoring the brambles snatching at his clothes and raking his skin. His pursuer gave chase. Conor quickened his pace, pushing through the undergrowth.

A little farther ahead, the brush thinned somewhat and he entered a stand of alder saplings—to be met by three members of a Scálda scouting party. Hard-eyed, wary, their long hair unbound and beards untrimmed, they stared in grim-mouthed earnest at their accidental captive, long iron spears levelled and ready for a fight. Conor fell back a step, preparing a swift retreat into the wood—and felt the spear point of the enemy scout behind him. His captor nudged him forward.

Clad in the hardened leather armour of their kind, the four circled around him and Conor, blade steady, searched their impassive faces for any trace of fear and, finding none, decided to go for the biggest of the four—a hulking, battle-scarred brute with knotted veins on his arms and a curved knife stuck in his sword belt. This one, Conor decided, must be the leader of the group. A swift, sudden attack might create a moment's hesitation on the part of the others, and a moment was all Conor would need. He tightened his grip on the hilt of his sword and rose onto the balls of his feet, ready to strike when a voice called out from the wood.

Without taking his eyes from Conor, the leader called a reply, his voice loud in the silence. A moment later, the group was joined by a fifth Scálda: a slender, beardless fellow, he wore no armour and carried no weapons. His hair was bound in a leather band and he had a Dé Danann cloak of yellow-and-blue-checked weave fastened at his shoulder by a Dé Danann brooch. The fellow pushed past the leader and stepped before Conor, regarding him curiously and, with an air of cool indifference, said, 'Who are you?'

The question caused Conor to jump. Though simple enough, the words in the mouth of a Scálda raised a cloud of confusion in Conor's mind. *What? What did I just hear?*

Conor stared, his mind scrambling for a suitable reply as the Scálda addressed him in his own tongue, and asked, 'You Brigantes?'

There was something in the fellow's tone that awakened hope in Conor and he snatched it with two greedy hands. 'Yes.' Conor tapped his chest with the hilt of his sword. 'Brigantes.'

'Why you here, Brigantes? What you wanting?' The tone was cautious, the words twisted almost out of recognition by the rough intonation, yet Conor understood, and replied, 'Lord Brecan—I have a message for the king.'

The words were out before Conor even knew what he had said. But the plan came with the words and he committed himself to it completely. Fixing the young interpreter with a firm expression, Conor summoned up an air of command and demanded, 'Take me to Lord Brecan.'

'You should not be here,' the youth told him. 'Go back.'

Conor lifted his chin and shook his head. 'Not until I have seen the king. Take me to him now.'

The leader growled something at the young interpreter, who replied, and the two conferred briefly. Turning back to Conor, the young Scálda said, 'He say you cannot see king. Go back now. Or we kill you.'

Conor shook his head slowly. 'I have a message for Brecan. Very important.'

One of the other scouts called to his chief, who answered in his own uncouth tongue. The chief addressed the young interpreter, who then asked, 'What is message?'

Conor shook his head again. 'Only for the king. Only for Brecan.'

The leader glared and tugged at his unruly beard. Though not the opening Conor had hoped, he seized it, saying, 'Tell him'—he pointed at the leader—'tell him the message is from the queen—Queen Sceana. There is trouble at home. I must see Lord Brecan. Now!'

This message was relayed and the Scálda chief hesitated and looked to his men, who were now looking to him. Conor was quick to increase the pressure. 'If I go back, *you* will pay. Brecan will tell Balor—and you will pay.'

'I will tell your king,' offered the youth. 'You tell me.'

'I will not tell anyone but the king.' Lowering his sword, Conor thrust a finger at the leader of the scouting party, and said, 'Blood is on *your* head.' Then, tucking his blade into his belt, he turned around and, shoving aside the spear levelled at his chest, started back along the trail as if he would return the way he had come.

The Scálda began shouting then—at him and at each other. But they made no move to stop him. Conor was six steps down the path when the young interpreter called, 'Stop!'

Conor turned around and crossed his arms. 'Well?'

'We take you to king. He will decide.' He gestured to the nearest scout, who rushed forward with his spear and took possession of the captive once more. Conor allowed himself to be led away, and the party proceeded through the wood a fair distance; after a while the tall trees gave way to scrub oak and brush, which in turn gave way to a boggy marsh. Beyond the marsh rose a rocky humpbacked hill and, crowning the hilltop, a small ráth. A timber causeway snaked out across the quagmire and up the base of the hill. The Scálda scouts led him onto the wooden walkway, and they proceeded toward the hill over the bog to the base of the hill and began the climb on a steep, switchback path to the settlement which, on closer examination, appeared to be a haphazard construction made of flimsy materials carelessly thrown together. The makeshift ráth had a low circular wall made of nothing more than wattles trussed together with strips of rawhide, and a crude gate made of cedar boards. Above the rickety walls rose a single, high-peaked round house; the lower half was constructed of rubble, and the upper of, again, crude wattles of hazel branches woven over frames made from elm saplings.

The group passed through the unguarded entrance and into an equally paltry yard of beaten earth studded with a few miserable weeds. A low, mean outbuilding, little more than a shepherd's hut, squatted in the shadow of the round house. With a flat roof made from rough planks and a ship's sail held down with a net of stones, the crude structure, like the rest of the ráth, gave every appearance of having just been bodged together in haste with whatever materials came to hand.

Along the wall next to the hut, several horses stood at a picket line, and five more Scálda warriors slouched in the shade nearby. They rose to watch the new arrivals, but made no move to join them.

As the scouting party approached the entrance to the round house, Conor's eye fell upon the door and his interest quickened: three bare oak planks bound with wide iron bands, simply constructed, and in no way unusual, but something about the door piqued his interest. He stopped and turned around, scanning the yard behind him. And then he saw it—a feature so subtle he had missed it in his initial survey of the place: iron hoops. The same iron hoops Conor had seen being made in the Scálda forges and stacked in the Scálda storehouse; the same, in fact, that formed the rims for the wheels of the Scálda war carts. The wattle wall of the ráth was reinforced by a circle of chariot rims, overlapping one another in such a way as to form an interlocking ring of iron.

Before Conor could wonder about this curious feature, one of his escorts gave Conor a prod with the butt of the spear and shoved him on. He moved to the door of the hall where, much to his disgust, loomed the grisly remains of a severed head. Stuck on a sharpened stake above the door, and burned black by the sun with patches of white skull showing through the rotting flesh, the hideous thing had obviously been on display for some time. Conor spat and averted his eyes as he stepped across the threshold.

The light was dim inside; there were no wind holes or openings, not even above the central hearth where Brecan, Cethern, and Mog Ruith sat in three crudely made, overlarge chairs. The three turned as Conor and the Scálda scouts and their interpreter entered.

'You!' cried Cethern, leaping to his feet.

'Greetings, Cethern,' said Conor as his eyes adjusted to the semidarkness of the room. 'I thought I might find you here.'

'What is this?' said Mog Ruith, rising slowly. He looked to the king. 'Why is *he* here?'

'But you, Mog Ruith—I would have expected you to caution your lord against conspiring with the Scálda.'

Lord Brecan, sighing heavily, heaved himself out of his

chair and came to where Conor stood just inside the door. 'Why did you bring him here?' demanded Brecan. He looked to the young interpreter. 'I told you no one was to come up here.'

'He has message from queen,' explained the young man. 'He would not go back to the others.'

'He was never *with* the others,' said Cethern.

'A message?' said the king, looking to Conor. 'Is that true?'

'That is what I told him.'

'I don't believe you,' said Cethern.

The king put out a hand to his champion. 'Step back. He's here now. The damage is done.' To Conor, he said, 'How did you find this place?'

Conor indicated the Scálda scouts crowding the door of the hall. 'They brought me.'

'You followed us?'

'Aye, and they did the rest.'

'Well then,' said Brecan, 'this message—what is it?'

Conor looked around at the Scálda scouts. 'You might want to hear it first in private—and then decide if you want it repeated in company.'

Lord Brecan considered this, then, with a nod to the interpreter, said, 'You have done well. Leave him, and tell the others to return to their duties.'

This command was relayed to the scouts, who, with much grumbling discussion, reluctantly obeyed. With a nod to Brecan, the interpreter departed and the scouts followed, closing the door behind them. As soon as they were gone, Brecan grabbed Conor by the arm and said, 'I grow weary of this fool's game, warrior. Tell me what you came to tell me, or I *will* let the Scálda have you.'

'Is that supposed to frighten me?' said Conor mildly.

Brecan seemed at last to understand that Conor would not

be bullied. 'Then tell me quickly, because you are not staying. What is this message of yours?'

Mog Ruith stepped up beside his king. 'Who else knows you are here?'

'Only a few druids just now,' replied Conor, stretching the truth beyond breaking point. 'Still, I imagine they could quickly spread the word to all Eirlandia if pressed to it.'

Brecan regarded him thoughtfully.

'Kill him and be done with it,' suggested Cethern. 'There is too much at stake here to have him flapping his tongue.'

Mog Ruith leaned forward to sneer in Conor's face. 'Do you imagine the Learned Brotherhood will bother themselves over the disappearance of a solitary, troublesome warrior of the ranks?'

'Perhaps not,' Conor allowed. 'But if *this* troublesome warrior disappears, then they will know that what I told them is true and they will have the evidence they require to unite the tribes against you.'

'Why?' demanded the druid. 'What did you tell them?'

'I told them that his lordship here has made an alliance with the Scálda to help him snatch the high king's torc.' He watched Brecan's face as he said this and, to Conor's surprise, the false king did not flinch—nor did he make the slightest attempt at a denial.

'Is that all?' Brecan said, a sly smile sliding over his lips.

'I would have thought it enough to see you bound hand and foot and cast into the sea—or roasted on a spit over hot coals.'

To his amazement, the king put back his head and laughed. Conor stared in disbelief as Brecan shook his head in mirth. 'You went to all this trouble? Soon all of Eirlandia will know about this alliance I have made. There will be no need to hide it any longer.'

He paced away a few steps, paused in thought, then returned to face Conor, his hands gripping his wide leather belt. 'I may not be the most intelligent creature on two legs, Conor, but I am smarter than you—a fact you seem not to have fully appreciated.' The king began pacing back and forth, then stopped and said, 'You came to me seeking refuge. I took you in. I made you an amais in my warband. Have I mistreated you in any way?'

Conor made no reply.

'Is this how you would repay my consideration and generosity?'

'It is how I repay a traitor—one who would sell Eirlandia and its people for his own gain.'

'Is that what you think? Is that as far as your paltry dreams can take you?' Brecan paused and regarded him shrewdly. 'If my desires extended only so far as a high king's torc and throne, you might be right. I might even agree with you. But, Conor,' he said, his voice falling to a whisper, 'I have far greater plans than that—plans to see Eirlandia prosperous and secure for generations to come—for all time. My reign will be known as the Kingdom of All Tomorrows.'

'All this by crawling into bed with Balor Berugderc?' Conor muttered.

'You are wrong to make an enemy of me when we could be allies,' his lordship continued placidly. 'We could be friends. We can still be friends. A man like you, Conor, can have a high place in my court.'

Cethern pressed forward, his hand on his sword. 'Be done with him, my lord,' he urged.

The king waved him aside. 'The time for that has passed.'

The king walked away a few paces, then walked back. 'How long have we been at war with the Scálda?' he asked.

'What difference does that make?' Conor asked, suspicion edging into his tone.

'You would have been but a boy when they came,' continued the king, 'if you remember it at all.'

'I remember.'

'Not a day goes by that I do not recall the arrival of the Black Ships. I was a warrior of the ranks then—much like yourself,' Brecan told him. 'But I remember the alarm and running up over the bluff and seeing all those ships filling the bay and I knew—even then I knew life would never be the same for me, for any of our race. Eirlandia would never be the same. And we have been at war with this evil horde ever since.' He gazed at Conor with a heaviness that bordered on grief. 'All these years . . . nothing but fighting and killing, burning and slaughter and waste . . . and what have we gained?' He spread his hands wide in a gesture of appeal. 'What has any of it ever brought us but more death and destruction?'

'That is the way of things,' Conor muttered. 'Until the dog-eaters are driven into the sea, nothing will change.'

'But that is my point exactly,' Brecan said. 'Nothing ever changes. Nothing *will* change until the Scálda are defeated. To our shame, we have yet to defeat them.' Lacing his fingers, he pressed his hands to his lips as if deep in thought. Then, brightening suddenly, he glanced up at Conor and said, 'Have you ever asked yourself why?'

Conor made no reply. He had his own opinions about why Dé Danann had never been able to conquer the Scálda invaders, but he was not going to tell Brecan what he thought.

'Why have we never defeated them?' continued the king. 'Is it for lack of courage? Or strength? Is it for lack of skill or intelligence perhaps?'

'Our warriors are as brave and strong as any in this worlds-realm,' Conor told him. 'And as smart. We are in every way a match for any enemy that dares raise hand against us—the filthy Scálda included.'

'And yet,' said Brecan, becoming adamant, 'here we are, all these years later, and the Scálda are still raiding and burning and looting—still blighting the soil of Eirlandia with their odious presence. Why?'

'Because the small kings of Eirlandia allow it!' Conor snapped. He had not intended to be drawn into any discussion with Brecan, but could not contain the outburst. 'The nobles of our fair island are more content to squabble among themselves than fight our common enemy.'

'There!' crowed Brecan. Turning to Mog Ruith, the king said, 'You see? I told you he was more than just a . . . what did you call him? A canny scrapper?'

Conor glanced at the druid, who gazed at him with suspicion. 'You may be right, my lord. But can he also be trusted?'

'Can he be trusted?' The king turned back to Conor as he asked this. 'We shall see. Come,' he said, 'sit with me and I will tell you how we will defeat the Scálda and free our lands from their hateful presence.'

Despite his visceral opposition to the would-be high king, Conor felt his hostility eroding under the man's bewildering candour. Never would he have imagined the scheming lord to be so bluntly forthcoming. Still suspecting a trick, he nevertheless agreed to sit—if only to hear what his lordship would say next.

As they seated themselves in chairs at the empty hearth, Brecan called to his champion. 'Balor will be here soon and I would rather not be disturbed just yet. Go outside and warn me when he arrives.'

Cethern's face darkened and he opened his mouth to object, but Mog Ruith intervened. 'Go, but stay near. We want fair warning.'

The champion obeyed, but left no lingering uncertainty about his feelings for Conor's unwanted presence. The druid claimed the third chair and, as Cethern took up his place outside, Brecan said, 'Time grows short. I will not waste words.

You think I aspire to the high king's throne, and you are right. I do. I admit it. Indeed, it is my consuming desire to bring all of Eirlandia under my rule.'

'With the Scálda's help,' muttered Conor.

'Enough!' cried the king, his voice sharp as a slap. 'We do not have time to argue. I will speak and you will listen.' He resumed in a softer tone. 'I will be high king, aye, and with the Scálda's help. But that is not the end of my ambition—it is only the beginning. For once I am on the throne and all the lords of Eirlandia acknowledge my reign, I will unite this island and all its tribes and, more importantly, all its warriors into one great warhost. Think, Conor, all Eirlandia's tribes united in defence of our land to drive our common enemy into the sea. United, we can do this—and ensure peace and prosperity for generations to come.'

As Brecan spoke these words, Conor felt his once-solid confidence begin to crumble. The king watched Conor's expression change as his meaning became clear. 'Yes,' Brecan said, nodding with satisfaction. 'You see it now.'

'All of Eirlandia's warbands,' Conor repeated. Indeed, he *could* see it now—both the breadth of Brecan's determination and its ultimate purpose. 'You would unite the tribes in order to drive the enemy from our lands?'

'Why else? The high kingship cannot be the plaything of one man—a mere trophy to adorn his achievements. It is bestowed for a purpose—and it can serve no greater purpose than to win a lasting peace for our beleaguered, long-suffering race.'

Conor leaned back in his chair. Beguiled, confused, he did not know what to think. Could Brecan be right? And if he was, could this insane scheme work? Could the cunning lord be trusted to deliver the enormous promise he was making?

'You doubt me,' said the king, reading the uncertainty and

hesitation in Conor's face. 'I understand. But ask yourself this—why have we enjoyed three seasons without any battles?'

'We've had battles,' Conor pointed out. 'Plenty of them.'

Brecan waved aside the comment. 'A few contests, border skirmishes, brawls only.'

'Tell that to the warriors who died in those brawls.'

'We've had no pitched battles, no massed confrontations,' the king insisted, 'and certainly none of these ruinous clashes we endured in the early years. Three summers of calm and quiet. Why do you think that is?'

'Because three years ago is when you made the alliance with the Scálda,' Conor surmised, and it was as if a veil had been lifted from his eyes.

Brecan nodded slowly. 'I did that. And I can do more. Balor is a heavy-handed brute and vicious as the day is long. But even a brute must maintain the goodwill of his people or he will be deposed and another raised up in his place. He rules now, but the Scálda tribes grow ever more contentious and even Balor cannot appease them forever.' Brecan sat back in his chair. 'Once I become high king, I will turn the discontent of the Scálda chieftains and tribes against Balor. I can do that—*we* can do that if the lords of Eirlandia allow it—and the moment the Scálda turn against Balor—the moment he is weakest . . . we will strike!'

Brecan all but leapt from his chair. 'The massed warhost of our tribes will strike, and we will drive the Scálda filth into the sea . . . for good . . . forever.'

Conor gazed at the king, his mind and spirit roiling with a welter of conflicting thoughts and feelings. He was far from convinced, but far less suspicious than he had been when he sat down. After all, this was his dream, too; he had often said as much: to drive the hated Scálda out, the kings of Eirlandia had to be united. But, the petty kings could never unite long enough to mount a meaningful challenge to the invaders. Too

caught up in their own prideful jostling and pointless quar-
rels, they wasted their substance and energy on each other
rather than combatting the common enemy. What is more,
the Scálda had taken endless advantage of this fact, exploit-
ing it for years. Brecan was right—as Ardan and Cahir and
others, and even Conor himself, understood only too well—if
the tribes were united the balance of power could change.
And, clearly, something had to be done to end Eirlandia's suffering.

The king saw Conor's confusion and doubt. 'This is not
what you were expecting to hear.'

'I'm not sure anymore what I expected,' replied Conor.
'Something else, not this.'

'So, I ask you, Conor mac Ardan, will you help me?'

To delay having to decide, Conor replied, 'You say we've
enjoyed calm these last three years, but Balor has not been
idle. He has used that time to make machines of war—
chariots, hundreds of them—to complete the invasion. And
that is not all. He has taken faéry captives to learn their magic
and use it against us.'

'You know this?' Brecan's gaze became sharp. 'How? How
do you know this?'

'I was there. I saw it.' Conor told briefly of his sojourn behind enemy borders—of seeing the forges, the wheels, the
completed war cart, and of finding and rescuing the faéry
Rhiannon of the Tylwyth Teg. Before he finished, Brecan was
seething with anger.

'I knew it!' cried Mog Ruith, pounding the arm of his chair
with his fist. 'I told you that black-hearted son of Cromm
could not be trusted.'

'So you told me,' replied Brecan. He paced back and forth
for a moment, then turning to Conor, said, 'This is why I need
you.'

'Need *me*?'

'I need men like you to stand with me—men who are clear thinkers as well as clever fighters, men who can see further than their own interests and appetites, men who can lead other men.' He reached out an imploring hand. 'Join me, Conor. Help me rid Eirlandia of the wicked Scálda blight.'

Conor, in defiance of every natural feeling he had ever had for the man, found himself reaching for Brecan's hand. 'I will,' he said, and surprised himself saying it. 'To this end, and this alone, I will help you any way I can.'

The deal was sealed then and there, and Conor felt a sudden release, mingled, to be sure, with a healthy dose of caution. Brecan might not be the most worthy lord to wear the high king's golden torc, but neither was he the worst. In the end it came down to the simple fact that Conor reckoned he could do more working with Brecan than he could likely accomplish in the hostage pit, or with his head on a spike over the door of a Scálda hall.

Mog Ruith rose from his chair and, taking the joined hands of the two men into his own, said, 'A bond is forged this day that will see the end of the Scálda dominion and the return of freedom of our people.'

Beneath the wily druid's approving gaze, Brecan pulled Conor from his chair and, gripping his arms in a warrior's greeting, welcomed him into his ardféne. 'We will do great things together,' he said. 'You will see.'

There came a shout from outside and a moment later, Cethern bulled into the room, announcing, 'Balor is here! He has brought some of his dogs and wants you to see them before they are taken away to be fed.'

The champion glanced at Conor sitting next to the king and seemed to understand what had passed in his absence; he gave a curt nod of acceptance, and went out again. Brecan and Mog Ruith followed, and Conor trailed after, stepping into the yard as the Scálda king rode through the gates on a superb piebald stallion—almost entirely brown, but with a ghostly white neck and head; one of its eyes was black and the other white. *Like horse, like rider,* thought Conor, for the man astride the back of this remarkable beast was none other than the baleful one-eyed chieftain he had met twice before: first on the battlefield with his faéry captive in tow and, lastly, driving the chariot in the fortress where they had freed Lady Rhiannon.

36

With the Scálda king rode three more heavily armed warriors. The enemy scouts Conor had encountered earlier came running behind, and all entered the yard behind their lord. Balor threw a leg over his mount and slid down as the Scálda idling in the shade ran to take the reins. Without a glance left or right, he marched across the yard in long, ground-eating strides, raising a hand to Lord Brecan, who smiled and, under his breath, muttered, 'Stinking barbarian whorespawn. I do believe he gets uglier every day.'

Lord Brecan glanced at Conor and warned him to stay out of the way, and then hurried forward to grip the Fomórai chieftain by the arms in a warrior's welcome. The young interpreter with the Dé Danann cloak hurried to join them and the two kings exchanged greetings.

So this is Balor Berugderc, mused Conor, *Lord of the Fomórai, King of the Scálda, he of the Evil Eye.* The big brute appeared much the same as Conor remembered him: long, matted hanks of black hair hanging in unruly ropes about his thick neck and heavily muscled arms, the permanent sneer caused by the red scar dividing his face from forehead to chin, cleaving his right eye, further distorting what was already a grotesque countenance well on its way to being hideous. The insignia of a coiled serpent was carved into the hardened leather of his breastplate; the same device adorned the pommel of the enormous knife he wore in his iron-studded belt and the iron-rimmed shields carried by his men. Clad in similar armour, with additional protection to their upper arms and legs—which were encased in hardened leather plaques studded with iron rings—the forearms of each man were gloved from wrist to the elbow with protection made of thin bands of iron over more supple leather, and each wore battle caps embellished with black horsetails.

As Balor and Brecan were talking, there came a creak and rattle from across the yard and a team of horses appeared in the gateway pulling a flatbed wagon with a square iron cage; inside the cage were three enormous creatures of vaguely canine appearance: long-legged beasts with massive forequarters and slender backsides; short-haired and sleek and uniformly black, save for a ridge of stiff reddish hair down their sloping backs. Thick, short necks supported flat, outsized heads that bulged at the sides to accommodate their prodigious jaws.

The three armoured men hastened to the wagon and, with ropes and chains, wrangled the growling animals out of the cage and brought them to stand in the middle of the yard. Conor, having never faced a dog on the field of battle, was both fascinated and dismayed; the very sight of these foul creatures made his skin crawl and sent a cold tendril of fear snaking through his bowels.

The snarling beasts were paraded before the kings, first one way and then the other, and brought to stand before them, and ordered to sit. With some coaxing and the liberal application of the whip, the animals complied. Brecan, having appraised the animals, gave his nod of approval, and the fighting dogs were led back to their cage in the wagon.

Having observed formalities, the kings moved toward

the round hall. 'Are they difficult to train, these dogs?' asked Brecan as they approached the entrance where Conor, Cethern, and Mog Ruith were standing to one side.

The bedraggled young interpreter repeated his lordship's question and Balor offered a lengthy reply, and the translator answered, 'My lord say these are dangerous creatures and require much, ah . . . control. And care—very much care.'

Brecan observed that he was eager to see this training for himself one day, and that the kennel he was building would soon be ready to receive the dogs. Then he turned to the hall and indicated that they should go inside. He nodded to his champion to open the door, and Cethern stepped to the entrance. As the kings passed, Balor glanced over at Conor and Mog Ruith, who were standing off to the side. Conor met the Fomórai lord's eye and saw the light of recognition flare instantly in that singular, dusky visage.

Balor stopped. With a low, guttural growl, he raised a massive hand and pointed directly at Conor. The interpreter came running up, his eyes wide and fearful.

'What is this?' said Mog Ruith.

Brecan looked to Balor's interpreter, who said, 'My king say he know this man. He is thief.'

Brecan glanced at Conor. 'A thief? I do not think—'

'Lú-ní-zuch!' roared Balor. Reaching out, he grabbed Conor's face. Conor resisted, but the Fomórai lord's grip was strong and, turning his head, Balor slapped the lurid birthmark on Conor's cheek. 'Na tsi kanú!'

'He see this man before. His skin betray him.'

Conor jerked his head from Balor's grip. Glaring balefully at the Fomórai lord, he rubbed his cheek. Balor loosed an angry burst, and Brecan demanded to know what was being said.

'My lord say this man is thief. Take a thing of great value. Thief must pay for crime. He must die.'

'He is *my* man,' Brecan said. 'I will deal with him. I will see that—'

The Fomórai king swung away and with a bark and a gesture brought five of his retinue on the run. He shouted again and two of the men drew their swords, two rushed in and seized Conor by the arms, and, as Conor struggled in their grasp, the fifth relieved him of his weapons and the contents of his sparán.

'E-re! E-re ugur,' Balor shouted, and pointed to the low building beside the wall of the ráth.

'Stop!' shouted Brecan, growing red in the face. 'What is this? What are you doing? You cannot—'

'Lord Balor say he is now captive. Wait for execution.'

'Release him!' shouted Brecan. 'We came here in peace to discuss our treaty. No fighting, no violence—that is what we agreed. This is my man—under my protection. There will be no execution. Tell him. Make him understand.'

The Scálda translator turned a stony face to the Brigantes king. 'He understand this. My lord has spoken.'

Over Brecan's outraged protests, Conor was hauled bodily away. He dug in his heels, but a sharp blow to the head gave him to know that any meaningful resistance was not only futile, but likely to end in injury. Far better to keep both wits and strength intact and await a better opportunity.

Across the yard to the low house, they marched him. The argument between Brecan and Balor continued, but Conor turned his attention to the ill-made hut, taking in every detail, searching for any chink of weakness he could use to escape. The door of the flimsy keep was secured by a simple hasp fastened with an iron spike; the door was a few wide scraps of untrimmed timber bound together. One of the guards pulled the spike and yanked open the door and gave Conor a shove that sent him sprawling onto the dirt floor. The door banged shut on the angry voices in the yard, but Conor was no longer listening. He was aware of only two things: the suffocating stench of excrement and urine, and the sight of a dozen or more faéry chained to the back wall of the hut.

Conor saw the faéry captives and was overcome with the sense of having seen this before—the only difference being that previously he had found only two of the faéry locked in a storeroom; this time there were fifteen or more—male and female together, some standing, some sitting on the dusty floor, but all staring with dull-eyed interest at him. Dressed in the shimmering jewel-coloured raiment favoured by their kind—now much abused by filth and hard wear, their hair limp and pale skin grey and ashen—they nonetheless retained much of their noble bearing and the extraordinary beauty of their race.

Thoughts collided in Conor's head, so many and so quickly that he could only gape at the tall, silent, regal beings huddled before him. One thought jostled its way to the fore, and it was this: free the faéry and his own deliverance was assured. Dismay and desperation fled, their encircling shadows driven back by the dazzling light of this bright hope. Save the faéry and he would save himself.

'Do not be afraid,' he said, pushing himself up off the floor. 'I am here to help you.'

This, he thought, was worthy of at least some small reaction, but produced not so much as a flutter of interest, much less a welcome.

'Tylwyth Teg?' asked Conor, moving a step closer. 'Who is leader here?'

The faéry looked at him impassively, or at each other, but none made bold to answer.

'Who can speak to me?' He looked from one to another.

'Does anyone understand me?' Conor searched their faces. 'Anyone?'

One of the females stretched out a hand and pointed to a male seated on the floor nearby. 'Can *you* understand me?'

The faéry unfolded himself slowly, stood, and shuffled forward as far as his chain would allow; towering head and shoulders over Conor, he stared down at him with filmy eyes and an expression of unspeakable sadness. 'Who are you?'

'I am Conor mac Ardan, a warrior of the Darini.'

'Why are you here?'

'Like you, I have been taken by the Scálda. They mean to kill me, but if we work together, we can save each other. We can escape.' He put out a hand to those who stood looking silently on. 'All of us. I can help you.'

The faéry shook his handsome head. 'No one can save us.'

Conor moved a step closer. 'What is your name?'

He gazed at Conor with sad eyes and just when Conor thought he would not reply, he said, 'I am Loucetios, Lord of the Kerionid.'

Conor tried the name, muddled it, and his attempt brought a frown of distaste to the lips of the faéry, who said, 'Call me Lenos—if that is easier in your mouth.' He spoke with elaborate condescension, as if to a slow-witted child for whom he was having to make enormous allowances. 'You can help us?'

'I can.'

The faéry lord thrust out his chin in defiance. 'For all I know it is a trick of the Vermin King.' He jerked his head toward the door, indicating Balor Berugderc beyond.

'On my life, you can trust me,' Conor told him, placing his hand on his chest. 'I am of the Dé Danann. I am not one of them.'

Lenos's face squirmed into an ugly sneer. 'On my life! So he says! What do you know of life and death? It is our lives that are stolen day by day—not yours. You know nothing.'

Confused by this response—so different from Rhiannon's—Conor was taken aback and more than a little annoyed by what seemed to him a veiled but unwarranted and unjust accusation. 'What do you mean?' he demanded. Lenos turned his face away. 'Tell me. I want to understand.'

The faéry lord rounded on him. 'Then look and see! How many?' He pointed to the other Kerionid who stood looking on, silent in their misery. 'You see how we are? Once, not long ago, there were thirty of us. Thirty! Now only sixteen remain. Why? Because each day the Vermin King comes and takes one of us out to be slaughtered at the hands of his butchers. When they brought you, we thought they had come to steal another life.'

Conor saw the problem at once. 'They would force you to trade your lives for the secret of your magic,' he surmised. Rhiannon had intimated as much during her captivity.

'Trade our lives for our *geasan*, yes—and like everything the vermin say, it is lies. When they gain what they want, they will kill us anyway.'

'Not if I can prevent it,' Conor said, his tone adamant. 'That will not happen. Trust me. I have done this before.' He quickly explained about finding other faéry captives in another Scálda stronghold, how he and his friends had freed them. Avoiding any mention of the unfortunate Tanwen's demise, he moved closer to examine the iron chains binding the faéry. The lengths were wrapped high and tight around the waist, biting into the flesh; individual links were as thick as a finger and so narrow Conor could not wedge so much as a finger into the spaces to pry them apart. 'I'll need a tool of some kind,' Conor told him. 'But as soon as I can find a way to break these chains, you will be able to use your magic again and we can escape.'

'Magic,' repeated Lenos in a tone of disgust. 'Are all Dé Danann as ignorant as you?'

That brought Conor up short. 'Why? What did I say?'

'Look around you, blind one.' He flung a hand at the surrounding walls. 'The entire ráth is iron!'

'The hoops!' Conor whirled around—like the encircling walls of the ráth outside, the hut was reinforced by an overlapping ring of iron chariot rims. Now, at last, he understood the curious construction of the stronghold: the frail wickerwork walls were never meant to keep anyone out, but to keep the captives in. He had indeed been blind. 'I am sorry,' he sighed. 'I should have known.'

Lenos gazed at Conor, his anger drained away—as if he had not the will or energy to fight anymore. 'The ráth is killing us—slowly. Every day the poison eats away at our hearts and every day we grow weaker. Even without the chains, our *geasan* can have no power here.'

In that simple declaration Conor heard hopeless resignation, a surrender to defeat.

But Conor was far from defeated. 'Then we will make good our escape without your magic.'

The faéry lord turned and spoke to the Kerionid gathered behind him. A brief discussion ensued. Meanwhile, Conor crossed to the door and pressed his face to the tiny gap between the door and frame. The Scálda guards had returned to their shady place across the yard; he could see no one else around. He pressed against the door with his shoulder and felt it give slightly; a strong kick would break it open. Getting out would pose little difficulty, the work of a moment; getting his hands on a weapon might pose more of a problem.

First, however, he had to find a way to free the faéry from the killing constraint of the iron chains. A quick inspection of the hut revealed that, other than the stinking cess hole off to one side, the hut contained nothing that might further his purpose. Next, he examined the chains; moving from one docile prisoner to another, he quickly learned that each captive was linked to the one on either side by short lengths of chain, and various sections secured to one or another of the chariot rims lining the walls of the hut; these in turn were each bound to every other rim. Crude, but effective, Conor concluded, with no obvious weakness.

'I will find a tool,' Conor told Lenos. 'Something to break the links.'

'If the Vermin King does not come for you first.'

'Well,' reasoned Conor, 'there is nothing I can do about that. But . . .' His eye fell upon the chains binding the faéry lord, and he brightened. 'Perhaps you can help me there.' He quickly explained the plan just then forming in his mind.

'It is dangerous. Likely, you will get killed in this deception of yours.'

'Then I will die,' Conor replied lightly, 'but I will have sold my life at a price and you will be no worse off than you are now.'

Lenos thought about this for a moment. 'You are a brave one—for a mortal. I will do as you say.'

They discussed this some more, refining the plan as they went along until both were satisfied that it was as good as it could be made under the circumstances. They were not long finished when there came the sound of footsteps outside the door of the hut. Conor and Lenos took their places, ready to play their parts. Conor lay down at the foot of the faéry lord and closed his eyes.

'Hisst!' whispered a voice from outside the door. 'Conor, can you hear me?'

Conor jumped up, ran to the door, and pressed his ear to the plank. 'Cethern?'

'We're working to get you out. Be patient. One way or another Brecan will gain your release.'

'Let me out now,' Conor countered. 'Before they come back.'

'I can't,' said Cethern, already backing away. 'The dog-eaters are watching. Two of them are coming this way now. Don't do anything to make them suspicious.' His voice trailed off. 'We'll get you out.'

A heated exchange followed; raised voices in the yard—slightly one-sided since neither the king's champion nor the Scálda guards could understand the speech of the other.

Conor returned to where an anxious Lenos stood watching, and explained what the king's champion had said. 'There is hope,' Conor concluded.

'For you, perhaps,' Lenos replied. He looked down at the chain tight around his waist and then raised sad eyes to Conor. 'But there is no hope for us.'

'I will not abandon you, Lenos.' Conor heard in his own words the echo of Rhiannon's vow to him, and there was a rightness to it that seemed more than simple conviction—inevitability, perhaps, or destiny.

An uneasy day faded to an anxious twilight, but still the Scálda guards did not return. As night deepened over the hills and around the ráth, there came raucous voices from inside the hall and echoing across the yard outside. Conor pressed his eye to the gap once again and saw that the guards had made an enormous fire in the centre of the yard and were cooking hanks of meat on spits as jars of ale made their way hand-to-hand among the guards. More or less the same seemed to be taking place inside the round house, for oily smoke seeped up through the thatch of the high-peaked roof. A celebration, no doubt, to mark the successful completion of another negotiation. Conor took this as a good sign, for it meant he would soon be released.

He could not have been more wrong.

＊ ＊ ＊
＊   ＊

37

The faéry, silent in their suffering, huddled together for the night and Conor stretched himself out on the ground nearby. Thirsty, hungry—the scent of the roasting meat brought the water to his mouth and reminded him that he had not eaten anything but a scrap or two of bósaill in the last day. He reached into his sparán for more, but the leather pouch, like his stomach, was empty. Turning his mind instead to thoughts of Aoife and how he missed her and whether he would ever see her again, he eventually drifted off to sleep listening to the hushed, willowy sound of faéry speech as they conversed softly with one another . . .

. . . and was awakened again sometime later by loud voices outside the hut. Rolling onto his knees, he crawled to the door. Through the crack, he could see that the fire in the yard had been built up again; against the ruddy glow of the embers, six or so of the Scálda guards: two or three of them armed with spears; another held a rope.

'Lenos!' said Conor. 'Wake up. They're coming.'

'I am awake. How many?'

'Five. Only two have weapons, I think.' Conor moved to take his place at the faéry lord's feet, as planned. When the guard came to rouse Conor, Lenos was to throw a loop of his chain around the Scálda's neck by way of distraction, allowing Conor to disarm him.

Conor quickly arranged himself and a moment later there came a scrape at the door as the spike was lifted from the hasp; two guards entered the hut and crossed to where Conor lay pretending to be asleep with Lenos standing over him. But, their plan was scuttled at the outset. Rather than seize Conor, which he expected, they first struck the faéry in the chest with the butt of a spear, driving him back. The second guard pressed the point of his spear blade into Conor's side. Lenos had no chance to distract either guard, and Conor, suffering a grazing cut to his ribs, was dragged by his feet from the hut. Once outside, the guard with the rope dropped a knotted coil around Conor's head and pulled the noose tight around his throat. A second spear was placed against Conor's spine and the captive was hauled to the fire ring in the centre of the yard where several more Scálda had gathered to watch.

Out of the darkness, another of Balor's bodyguard came forward, leading two horses—one of them Búrach; Conor's bag was still tied to the stallion's back. Fighting the icy dread that squeezed his heart like a fist, Conor gulped air and forced himself to remain calm as the first horse was led up and Conor's left wrist was lashed to its halter by a rawhide strap; he resisted with commendable strength—a struggle rewarded by the tightening of the noose around his neck. Clawing at the rope with his free hand, he fought to breathe. His sight grew dim and began to fade. He was on the point of slipping into unconsciousness when the pressure eased. Breath and vision returned, but he was now tied to the horse.

Then they grabbed his right wrist and began attaching the rawhide strap to Búrach's halter. Perhaps, as some kind of Scálda jest, they thought to torture him with his own horse. Conor drew breath and gave out a mighty shout. 'Help!' he cried, his voice ringing out in the quiet yard. 'Cethern! Help!'

As soon as his right hand was joined to Búrach's halter,

the Scálda began leading the animals in opposite directions, one slow step at a time. Conor's arms opened wide.

'Cethern! Brecan!' he shouted again. The tightening of the noose choked off any further attempt to rouse his friends.

Unable to breathe, he nevertheless fought against the ever-increasing pressure on his arms. The horses took another step and his ligaments began to stretch. Pain streaked through him in a blazing fireball. He threw back his head and uttered a strangled, half-garrotted scream—much to the amusement of his Scálda torturers.

Conor's field of vision narrowed, became a single point of light surrounded by darkness. But his hearing remained as keen as ever. He heard the laughter of the guards and their jeering voices as they urged the horses on another step—but one more and his arms would be ripped from his body. He felt the muscles in his shoulders stretch and the bones began to separate. His previously injured shoulder gave out a meaty pop as a weakened sinew gave way, sending a cascade of pain shimmering through him.

Conor summoned the little left of his breath and said, 'Búrach, here!'

The horse, hearing his master's voice, stopped, and made a half turn toward him. Conor felt the bonds loosen. The pressure eased instantly. One of the Scálda guards cried out and Conor, in his dazed state, imagined his arm had been pulled off. But then the noose slackened. Air rushed back into his lungs and he gulped it down in greedy draughts and scrabbled at the noose with unfeeling fingers of his suddenly free right hand.

His head cleared and the black veil lifted. He looked around. He was on his knees, his left hand still tied to Búrach's halter, and his horse stood over him. One of the guards lay dead on the ground a few paces away, his head all but severed from his shoulders.

In the light of the fire, he could see Scálda warriors running here and there, frantic, shouting. Their cries awakened Balor's fighting dogs. Scenting blood, the vicious creatures started howling and hurling themselves at the bars of their cage. The once-quiet yard was awash in confusion and, strangest of all, no one was paying any attention to Conor. With a colossal effort, he climbed to his feet and swung himself up onto Búrach's back.

Mounted now, he looked around for the gate. A face loomed up out of the darkness at him. Conor kicked at it and its owner grabbed his ankle, shouting, 'Conor! It's me!'

Conor ceased struggling. 'Cethern!'

'Here—take this!' he cried, shoving a sword hilt into Conor's hand.

Two Scálda rushed at them out of the darkness. Cethern turned and took them both, his sword a dull glimmer in the dancing firelight. Conor wheeled Búrach into the fight; the horse leapt forward and one of the Scálda broke off his assault on Cethern to meet him.

The spear swung around and the point came up but Conor, rather than striking at the weapon with his sword, simply allowed the blade to slide down the long iron shaft, neatly shearing three fingers from his attacker's hand. The Scálda yelped, dropped the spear, and fell back. Conor then sliced the rawhide strap binding his left hand to Búrach's halter. His scarlet birthmark began to tingle and burn as his blood warmed to the fight; he spun around, looking for the next place to strike.

More Scálda warriors burst from the round house, and with them, Lord Brecan and Mog Ruith—together with Balor Berugderc. The two kings took in the confusion of the clash and Mog Ruith, raising his hands, cried out in a great booming voice, employing the Dark Tongue to call down a imprecation of destruction upon the enemy.

Balor thrust out a restraining hand and roared at the old druid. When Mog Ruith persisted, the Scálda king seized the druid by the arm, dragging him back. Mog Ruith shook free of his grasp, all the while crying doom and confusion upon the foe. Infuriated now, Balor plucked the knife from his belt and drew back his arm to strike.

Two things happened at once: Lord Brecan darted forward to obstruct the thrust, and Conor reared back and let fly with the sword.

Balor lunged at the druid and Conor's sword shivered the door in the exact place the Fomórai's head had been an instant before. Balor's wild, sweeping slash with the knife caught the druid on the upper arm. Mog Ruith faltered. Clutching the wound, he turned and, in a voice to melt stones, loosed a tirade of black invective as Balor buried his blade in the druid's stomach. Blood surged through the druid's fingers and then erupted in a black torrent from his mouth; still trying contain the awful rupture, the old bard slumped back against the wall and slid down as his legs gave way.

Cethern, having fought free of the guards, raced to join his king. Conor slid off his mount, snatched up the spear abandoned by his newly fingerless opponent, and sprinted after Cethern.

Lord Brecan seized Conor's thrown blade and pulled it from the door. He swung the weapon hard and succeeded in driving the Scálda chieftain back against the round house wall. Balor's armour breastplate saved him. The sword point slid off to one side, grazing a furrow in the hard leather. Balor knocked the blade carelessly aside and, with a savage backhanded rip, buried his blood-streaked blade in Lord Brecan's chest.

The Brigantes king collapsed, tried once to rise, and then lay still.

Cethern, seeing his lord fall, loosed a cry of rage and charged. Balor, in an almost serene gesture, stooped and retrieved the sword from Brecan's slack grasp. As Cethern closed on him, sword raised high to strike, the Scálda lord levelled the weapon. Conor saw the champion jolt to an abrupt halt—so sudden that his head and arms snapped forward. The sword spun from his hand.

Balor lunged, ramming the sword home. The blade point appeared in the middle of Cethern's back amidst a spreading crimson bloom. The champion raised his face to the night-black sky and screamed. Balor gave the sword another brutal thrust and released it. Cethern slumped to his knees, jerked twice, and, still kneeling, toppled sideways to the ground.

Conor, in full flight, swerved off the charge and slipped away around the side of the hall. From there he surveyed the yard. Three Scálda warriors lay dead on the ground and another writhed moaning nearby. At least three more circled the fire ring and two others had joined Balor at the door.

The one-eyed king called a command to his warriors at the fire; they halted at once, turned, and began coursing through the yard. Conor dashed to the outer wall, thinking to climb over and take his chances in the woods outside the ráth. As he worked his way around the perimeter wall, however, he came to the hut and remembered his vow to the faéry who were still chained in the hut. For the briefest of instants, he stood rooted in indecision. And then the wind gusted cool and fresh out of the west, and it began to rain.

Within moments, the yard was awash. A curtain of rain swept across in a drenching sheet, dousing the fire in the centre of the yard. Smoke billowed up in a dense white fog and Conor awakened to a desperate idea. Retracing his steps, he proceeded the opposite way along the outer wall and soon came to the wagon containing the caged dogs. The odious creatures were snarling and frothing at the mouth, eager to join the fight—so, Conor let them have their way. With difficulty owing to his reinjured shoulder, he pulled himself onto the wagon and scrambled up the side of the enclosure, and then, lifting the simple latch, released the dogs.

The frenzied beasts burst from captivity and hurled themselves from the cage. All three streaked off, quickly disappearing into darkness.

Conor jumped down from the wagon and flitted to the side of the hall and looked out across the yard. Rain and smoke and darkness combined to make an impenetrable soup. He could no longer see the dogs, but he could hear their feral howls as they chose and chased down their prey. Soon the yard rang with the agonised screams of the Scálda bodyguards and the shouts of the dog's handlers as they tried to gain control of the blood-lusting beasts.

Flitting back to the outer wall, Conor resumed his circuit around the ráth and back to the hut—remaining out of the chaos now claiming the yard. Upon reaching the hut, he ducked around the side of the ramshackle structure and in through the still-open door. 'Lenos!' said Conor, stumbling into the darkness. 'Rouse your people. It is time to go.'

Then, employing the iron shaft of the spear, he prised open the first of the rings linking the chains to the hoops lining the walls of the hut. One by one, he freed the faéry from the iron hoops. 'What about these?' demanded Lenos, indicating the chain around his waist and those of the others.

'That will have to wait.' He moved to the door and peered out. Smoke and rain and the feeble embers of the fire formed a lurid confusion of shouts and flickering shadows. 'The dogs will not keep them busy for long. Stay near the wall and make for the gate.' As Lenos repeated his instructions, Conor stepped out into the rain-swept night. Disappearing into the soggy, smoke-filled yard, he called back, 'Go! I will join you.'

The faéry lord called after him, but received no reply, so he led his small band of survivors along the wall to the narrow front entrance to the stronghold and out into the night and freedom.

38

Light of foot and silent as shadows, the Kerionid fled into the night. The rain settled into a steady soaking drizzle and the faéry hurried along the muddy road until they came to a fording place. They paused at the water's edge and had scarcely caught their breath when they heard hoofbeats on the road behind them. Instantly, they scattered, fading into the trees like smoke.

A moment later, a horse and rider slid to a halt at the ford. 'Lenos!' called Conor. 'Where are you?'

He waited, and then called again. The faéry lord appeared—as if taking substance from the rain-wet leaves and branches.

'Good, you're here,' said Conor, sliding off his mount. He leaned on his spear and kneaded his injured shoulder to ease the pain. 'Did everyone make it out?' He glanced around, but could see almost nothing in the rain-streaked dark.

'All that are left.' Lenos gestured to the chain cinched tight around his waist. 'Can you remove the iron now?'

Conor shook his head. 'The links are too strong. We'll need a tool to break them. Truly, we might have to find a blacksmith. I'm sorry. I know what the iron is doing to you—

'Do you?' snarled Lenos, his voice biting. 'Do you know how the irons burn into our flesh . . . how it saps our strength, bleeds our vitality . . . every moment is torture. . . .'

'As soon as I find a tool to free you, it will be done!' Conor snapped. 'But we cannot rest now. The Scálda will soon discover your absence and they *will* give chase.'

'You brought a horse,' sneered Lenos. 'That will make it easier for them to find us.'

'I could not let them have Búrach.' Conor clambered onto the stallion's steaming back. 'If you want to be caught again, stay here. If not, we have to keep moving.'

'Where? Where can we go that they cannot find us?'

'Brecan left some warriors in a camp nearby. If we could find them . . .' Conor looked around and realised the futility of thrashing around in the forest hoping to stumble across the camp. 'Anyway, we cannot stay here,' Conor concluded, 'or they *will* find us.'

Conor picked up the reins, but the faéry lord just stood and stared.

'Lenos!' barked Conor. 'Do you understand what I'm saying? We must move on.'

'Why do you care?'

'We have to go—now!'

Still Lenos remained unmoved, the rain streaming down his face and dripping off the ends of his hair; he appeared at once defiant and pathetic in his defiance. Conor forced his voice to remain calm. 'This is not the time to argue. If you stay you will be no better off than you were up there.' He jerked his head in the direction of the ráth. 'No, it will be worse. This time they will kill you.'

'Why do you care what happens to us?'

Conor wiped the rain from his face and replied, 'I made a vow to Lady Rhiannon to help your people whenever and however I could. I always honour my vows.'

'Rhiannon?' muttered the faéry darkly.

'Aye, Rhiannon, daughter of Gwydion, Lord of the Tylwyth Teg,' Conor told him. 'Why?'

'We are *not* Tylwyth Teg!' Lenos all but spat the name. 'We are Kerionid of the Aes-sídhe. The Tylwyth are not *our people*, they are our enemies—as hateful to us as the Scálda are to you.'

Conor stared at the tall faéry and his heart dropped into his stomach. What had he blundered into? It had never occurred to him that there might be more than one faéry race—let alone that Rhiannon might not thank him for saving her enemies. But what could he do about that now? He drew a deep breath and lifted his face to the night-dark sky and let the rain splash over him. It had been a long journey to this place.

'We do not have time for this discussion,' he said after a moment. 'If you value your lives and care to preserve them, follow me.'

With a flick of the reins, the grey stallion walked on, splashing through the ford and into the wood on the other side. The faéry lord did not hesitate again, but summoned his people from the surrounding wood and they resumed their soggy march. Owing to the rain and darkness, Conor let the stallion have its head, and he turned his mind to the problem of eluding the Scálda pursuit. There were fewer now than when the fight began; how many remained he had no way of knowing, but assumed that if any had survived the dogs, Balor Berugderc was surely one of them. And Conor knew in his gut that the Fomórai lord would not rest until he had recovered his prisoners—or seen their heads displayed above the door to his hall.

At some point, Conor reckoned they would have to leave the road and take to the forest and head north, back toward the borderlands and safety of Dé Danann lands. He would watch for a chance to do just that, but in the meantime it was best to put some distance between themselves and Balor's men.

Cold, wet, his injured shoulder throbbing with every jolt and lurch of the trail, Conor pushed grimly on, pausing only now and then to draw breath and search out the path ahead. The Aes-sídhe followed on foot, their progress—hindered by the wind and the rain and the strength-sapping iron—slowed to a fitful, stumbling slog. Conor did what he could to keep his little band of faéry folk moving, but it was clear that they were at the end of their endurance and would have to rest soon.

Finally, as the sky began to lighten in the east, the rain stopped and the wind fell away. By the time the sun peeped above the horizon a short time later, the woodland had given way to a rocky stretch of rough moorland of gorse and broom and tough little thorny shrubs and, directly ahead in the near distance, the slate-blue expanse of the sea.

Conor stopped to get his bearings. He dismounted and left the shelter of the trees, walking out onto the moor. The new-risen sun caused the mist to rise and painted the moor in a pale buttery light. The air smelled of wet earth and leaves. Low clouds streamed in ragged tatters on a steady northerly breeze and the white flecks of seabirds filled the air, wheeling and diving in the distance. Lenos joined him a few moments later. 'Do you know where we are?'

Conor shook his head. 'Do you?'

Lenos gazed at the empty moorland with an expression of immense sadness. 'The Scálda caught us and brought us here from our home in Albion,' Lenos told him, his voice a thready whisper. 'The Aes-sídhe do not come to Eirlandia—once, perhaps, a long time ago. But not anymore.'

'Well,' Conor replied, 'the coast is just ahead. Down on the beach there are places to hide, and we might even find a boat.'

'A boat,' Lenos repeated dully. 'And if we find this boat— what then?'

'Our lands are north of here. If we can stay ahead of Balor's men, we might reach a Dé Danann stronghold.'

'My people are weak and tired. We need food and rest.' Lenos turned to regard the ragged ranks of the faéry straggling out of the woods to the edge of the moor. 'We have lost two already.'

'What!' Conor rounded on him. 'Two dead! Why didn't you say something?'

'Would it have made a difference? You said we had to keep moving.'

Conor stared at the faéry lord and a feeling of bleak, hopeless fatigue descended upon him. What kind of people were these? More to the point, what kind of trouble had he gotten himself into? And what, if anything, could he do about it? 'I am sorry,' he said at last, drawing his hand over his face as if to wipe away the pain and exhaustion. 'Tell your people to marshal whatever strength they have left—it is only a little further. Once we get down to the shore, we can find someplace to hide. We will rest then.'

Conor glanced back at the woodland behind them. All seemed quiet and still. Three faéry women had sunk down into the gorse nearby; grey faced, their hair in long, tangled ropes, they huddled together, shivering in their thin, wet clothes. Those around them were no better. Clearly, he had to find a way to get the binding chains off—and soon, if there were to be any faéry left to save.

Conor went to the women and, with gestures and gentle words, offered them his place on Búrach's back. Once they were mounted, he then led the company out across the moor. Closer to the sea, the land stepped down in steep declines— the remains of shattered promontories. Nearer the edge of the low cliffs, a few finger-thin streams braided themselves together to form a deeper runnel. Conor stepped into it and made the faéry do likewise, hoping that walking in the water might serve to muddle their tracks and throw the Scálda off their trail.

The runnel became a ravine, carving a deep path through the stone of the crumpled headland. Here, Conor paused. The decline was steep and rocky, and bounded on two sides by high rock walls; at the bottom was a small, sandy cove and the only way down was through the streambed.

'This is as good a place as any,' Conor told Lenos, 'and better than most. Let's get out of sight before anyone sees us.'

Down they went, picking their way over the loose scree of broken rock and stones that covered the narrow floor of the deep-carved passage. Upon reaching the bottom, the faéry dropped onto the sand and Conor had to convince them to at least drag themselves into the shade of the towering bluffs so they would not be seen from the cliff tops above. There they fell asleep. And that was where the Scálda caught up with them.

39

While the faéry slept, Conor climbed back to the gap at the top of the promontory to keep watch. He scanned the gorsy moorland, watching the line of trees in the near distance—and struggling to keep his eyes open. Any Scálda pursuit would have to leave the shelter of the wood and cross the barrens to reach the coast and he would see them in plenty of time to rouse the faéry and escape along the strand.

A little after midday, the first of the pursuers appeared.

Conor was hunkered down among the rocks at the mouth of the defile—drowsing with his spear in his lap, his head nodding on his chest—when the high piping call of a curlew reached him from across the moor. He shook himself awake and looked up. A flicker of movement at a particularly dark patch of woodland caught his eye and, suddenly, he was not looking at a shady spot, but at a lone Scálda warrior, armed but on foot.

The searcher paused at the edge of the wood and stood gazing out across the moor. He must have seen something he found worth further investigation, Conor guessed, because he quickly disappeared back into the trees and a moment later two Scálda emerged on horseback. These were quickly followed by two on foot, and then three more mounted warriors—one of them Balor of the Evil Eye himself.

Conor backed away from his post and raced down to the

beach to rouse the sleeping Kerionid. He ran to where the faéry lay curled in the shade at the base of a black boulder, shouting, 'Lenos! Get up! They're coming.' He jostled the faéry lord by the shoulder. 'Get up! Wake the others.'

The faéry came awake with a start. 'They're here.' Conor told him. 'Awaken your people and fly.'

'How many?' Lenos rose slowly, shaking off his slumber with difficulty.

'Eight so far. Balor is with them. Take my horse and go.' Conor pointed up the shingled strand to where the stony stubs of a tumbled outcrop washed in the waves. 'Get yourselves in amongst the rocks. Hurry!'

Lenos stood looking at him. 'Where are you going?'

'Back up the ravine,' Conor replied, already racing away. 'I will hold the gap as long as I can to give you time to get away.'

'You alone?' said Lenos. 'I will stay with you.'

'There is only one spear,' Conor called back. 'Go!'

Conor scrambled back up the steep incline of the gully to the place where the stream had forced its way between two sheer slabs of broken rock, creating a natural breach—a space wide enough to admit two or three, but no wider. The Scálda would have to abandon their horses and attack on foot and here, at this narrow place, Conor might sell his life at a respectable price.

Having chosen the place to make his stand, he continued on to the top to have a last look and was dismayed to see how close they were. The lead scout was almost at the entrance to the ravine, and two others were close on his heels. Conor pulled himself up the rest of the way and, standing at the top of the defile, lofted his spear in defiance of the enemy, shouting, 'Balor! Lord of the Vermin Host! Come and fight a true warrior!'

The sudden appearance of their quarry brought the Scálda advance party up short. They halted, suspecting a trick.

'Here!' cried Conor. 'Death awaits you, Balor Berugderc. Come die like the dog you are!'

The Scálda lord gave out a low snarl of contempt. Though he and his men did not understand what Conor was saying, the intent was clear enough. Balor growled a command and the three warriors nearest him dismounted and ran to join their comrades. Conor scuttled back to his redoubt. As he descended into the gap, Conor realised that this would likely be his last battle. In that instant, he was assailed by regret—not that he would die, but that he would never see Aoife again, never feel her warm hand slip into his, never tell her how much he loved her, and would go to his grave loving her.

That he might somehow survive did not enter his mind. Eight against one . . . hopeless odds. The only question was how to make the best account of himself. He held a slight advantage in the choice of defence, and unless he was unlucky he could hold out for a considerable time—perhaps long enough to allow the faéry to get away. But, whether luck was with him or not, he would face the enemy and he would fight until he could no longer hold a spear. Still, he missed Fergal and fighting by his side. It would have been a great honour to enter the Otherworld with his friends beside him.

What a fine thing, he thought, to stand with Fergal and Donal and Eamon—and Liam, too, and the rest of the Darini warband—on a windswept plain surrounded by his swordbrothers, and to go down fighting for the survival of Eirlandia and its people. That was how he had always imagined it would be, and how it was meant to be. Not like this—not dying in a ditch, unmourned, unknown . . . alone. . . .

'Well, brothers, you will miss a good fight,' he sighed, turning to face the oncoming enemy. 'If you were here beside me, I would not fear this end so much.'

He put the thought firmly aside. It was not worthy of a warrior entering battle for the last time.

The first enemy to reach the gap realised the inherent danger and hesitated; he called to the two behind him and the three formed a hasty plan: two charged into the breach and one hung back to offer support and keep their prey from escaping.

Conor had no thought of escape.

The first two bulled ahead with reckless speed. Conor allowed them to come within striking distance, and then, ducking low, met the nearside warrior with a low, darting jab at his feet. This odd move was unexpected and caused the fellow to leap; in his attempt to avoid the blade, he crowded his comrade into the rocks, throwing him off balance. Conor was ready for that blunder. He swung the spear blade around and delivered a solid thump on the upper part of the shield, thereby driving the rim into the warrior's face.

The shield-struck Scálda staggered sideways, colliding with his partner, who put out his hand to keep himself from stumbling over the rocky path. Conor stabbed out with a sharp downward slash of his blade, striking the outflung arm just above the wrist. The cut was deep to the bone and, though it did not sever the hand, the blade did slice sinews and veins. Blood spurted from the wound and the warrior cried out in surprise and pain, dropping his sword. Clutching his arm, he fled, leaving his battered comrade momentarily alone.

Conor went to work on him, shortening his grip on the spearshaft and charging in close. The Scálda, bloody nosed and somewhat dazed from the wallop to his shield, lashed out with his spear. Conor, without a shield to encumber him in the tight space, easily parried the thrust, and struck the upper rim of the shield again—driving the shield rim into the warrior's face for a second time and breaking his nose, which began a cascade of blood. The dog-eater staggered back a step, steadied himself and advanced more slowly this time. Conor backed away, retreating deeper into the ravine. There was a cry from above and the third enemy warrior appeared; with a shout and a flash of his sword, he clattered down into the channel.

Crimson birthmark burning now with the blood heat of battle, Conor took up his place in the narrowest part of the gully. His two adversaries drove down on him. As the bloodied Scálda closed in, Conor made as if to strike the shield a third time and the fellow, wise to this ploy, lowered the shield slightly, thereby exposing his throat. That was all the opening Conor needed; he lunged forward, driving the spear tip into the unprotected spot. The warrior gave out a half-strangled cry and fell back into his comrade, who shoved him aside and came on, screaming and swinging his sword back and forth to keep Conor from getting in a quick thrust.

Conor let him come on a few more steps and then, rather than exchange blows, drew back the spear and let fly. The Scálda tried to dodge out of the way, but the rock walls on either side offered little room to evade the manoeuvre. The cast blade caught him on the upper arm and opened a nasty crease. The weapon clattered away and, seeing that Conor was unarmed, the warrior loosed a victory shout and charged in for a swift and easy kill.

Conor snatched up a stone from the ravine floor and launched it at the Scálda's head, causing him to duck behind his shield; the stone struck the rim and bounced off, and the warrior came on. But even as he drew back his sword to strike, a second stone was already in Conor's hand and on its way.

The missile smacked the warrior on the brow directly over his right eye; he lurched forward two more steps before sprawling at Conor's feet. Conor dived forward, snatched the sword from the warrior's hand, and, with a quick downward chop, dispatched him to the next world.

Breathing hard and sweating now, Conor looked around

for the dying warrior, and saw him: he had managed to drag himself to the gully entrance, only to collapse there.

'One dead, one dying, and one out of the fight,' Conor reckoned, tallying up the results of the first foray. He wiped the sweat from his face with his arm and readied himself for the next onslaught. 'Only five more to go.'

Five more, aye, and one of them was Balor Berugderc himself. At this thought, Conor began to think that, should he be fortunate enough to meet the Fomórai lord and war leader, he might yet achieve a result worth the cost.

Gazing back up the sheer rock walls of the little gorge, he waited for the next assault. When, after a fair stretch of time, no one appeared, Conor cautiously made his way up to the top once more. Crouching low, he peered out to see the six remaining Scálda gathered on the moor some little distance away. The wounded warrior sat beside a bush with his arm bound in a rag, ignored by the others who stood around Balor; the Fomórai king was still mounted, but looking off across the moor—giving every appearance of waiting for something.

So, Conor waited, too.

The sun quartered the sky, and still they did not initiate another attack. This, Conor considered a good thing—the longer Balor delayed, the more time the faéry had to escape. Twice the Scálda had captured the faéry, and twice Conor had found and freed them, thus preventing Balor from discovering and employing their mystical skills. He remembered the first time, seeing Rhiannon, regal and defiant—even as a captive on the back of Balor's horse—and his heart moved within him at the memory. 'Fairest Rhiannon,' he murmured. How pleasant it would have been to join her on the ship that bore Donal and Fergal away to safety. Then again, if he had gone that day he would not have uncovered Lord Brecan's deceit, nor discovered King Lenos and the Kerionid. *Conor*

Faéry-freer, that's what they'll call me. The thought made him smile.

Conor watched and waited a while longer, and it occurred to him to go down to the beach to join the retreat, but he hesitated. If the Scálda caught him out in the open, he would be easy prey. Here, at least, he could hold the breach; and if he could hold out until nightfall he might still have a chance to slip away unseen.

That hope wilted as quickly as it bloomed. Out from the woods appeared a company of mounted Scálda warriors. Conor made a swift count and felt himself go numb: there were twenty or more at least, and others emerged from the treeline to the north even as he counted. He watched with dull dread as the first riders reached the place where Balor sat waiting. They dismounted and, at Balor's command, quickly formed into three groups of six each. The remaining warriors dismounted and assembled a second wave of attack with the riders just then arriving.

As the first battle group of six started toward the ravine on the run, Conor turned and bounded down the steep incline to take up his position once more, pausing only to retrieve the two spears—the one he had thrown, and the one dropped by the dying warrior. He also collected the sword abandoned by the wounded warrior. The shield he let lie; Scálda shields were too heavy and unwieldy, more hindrance than protection, in his view; better to let it, like the body on the path, be one more obstacle for the enemy to overcome. Two swords and two spears—not much against so many. Then again, he could only use one weapon at a time anyway and, with one in his hand and three in reserve, at least he was better armed than before. Not for the first time, however, he wished the spear in his hand were Bríg, and the sword at his side were Gasta. To enter the Otherworld with his trusted weapons was a thing every warrior esteemed, and to be cheated of it in the end seemed a gross injustice. With this unhappy thought in mind, Conor stashed the retrieved weapons close to hand and once again took up his position as the enemy appeared at the top of the defile.

Emboldened by the sight of a lone warrior standing in the breach, the first battle group attack entered the ravine at a run, whooping and shouting as they came, their voices ringing off the close rock walls. While still at a fair distance, the two in the forerank launched their spears, which Conor easily avoided. They rushed on, drawing their swords—an awkward manoeuvre with a shield on one arm. Conor took his chance and hurled his first spear, impaling the leader before his blade had cleared his sword belt.

As the warrior fell, Conor snatched up his second spear and levelled it at the next attacker, who plunged headlong toward him over the body of his writhing comrade. He met Conor's spear thrust with the edge of his shield and Conor let the spear shaft fall—neatly entangling itself in the warrior's legs and tripping him; he stumbled and was overrun by the two behind him—and one of these also went down. These three effectively blocked the narrow passage, slowing the attack. Conor seized the moment, darted forward, picked up his thrown spear and, reaching out, yanked down the heavy shield. He shoved the spear blade home as his foe drew back his sword to strike. With three swift strokes, Conor sent the three fallen Scálda to Queen Badb's bleak hall. Before he could do more, the two remaining warriors at the rear of the assault turned and scuttled back up the gully, leaving Conor to collect a few more weapons for his stock.

The Scálda paused to regroup. Conor could hear the voices and shouting echoing down the from the moor. A moment later, he glimpsed a few heads straining for a sight of him in the shadowed defile below. As their comrades had discovered to their cost, the passage was narrower than it appeared from above, and they were forced to slow their descent, lest they trip over the bodies and broken ground. It was, Conor considered, very like the shipwreck in the cove. In both cases, narrowing the approach effectively tilted the scales in his favour.

He felt strong and his confidence remained high. After all, he had weathered the first assault with little difficulty. For all their ferocity, the Scálda were not as skilled combatants as Dé Danann warriors—something Conor had noticed on the battlefield before. The enemy relied on superior numbers to overwhelm their victims rather than the prowess of individual warriors; taken one on one, however, their shortcomings were exposed.

The second wave of attackers did their best to overcome this drawback: they drew together in a cluster and, crouching low behind their shields, advanced down the rock-strewn gully with utmost caution. The moment they came within striking distance, Conor set his feet, expecting a sudden rush. When it did not come, he looked at their faces, watching their eyes. A spear bearer in the front rank glanced at Conor and dropped his gaze—as if looking at something at the bottom of the gully. Conor saw the man's lips twitch with the hint of a smile beneath the beard, and risked a swift glance behind him.

Two Scálda warriors were creeping up from the beach. They had climbed down by another way and were coming up to take him from the rear. He was trapped. To meet the two sneaking up from behind meant granting the six advancing foemen his singular advantage of the gorge; to stand his ground and engage the six before him exposed his unprotected back to the two below.

Conor drew breath deep into his lungs and released it. Then, in an effort to speed the end to its foregone conclusion, he hailed the slowly advancing Scálda. 'The feast halls of the dead are vast,' he shouted, 'and Queen Badb is eager for new blood to fill the empty cups at her table. Come! Lady Death awaits. . . .' Conor slid a second sword into his belt and tightened his grip on the iron spear shaft, adding to himself, 'Aye, and it is that rude to keep a lady waiting.'

He had no expectation that the Scálda would understand what he said, but the words were not for the enemy: they were for the dignity of Eirlandia and its beleaguered tribes. By adding his voice to those of all the warriors who had fallen before him, Conor would acquit himself with honour in his final battle; he could enter the Otherworld as a man of courage and valour. He could die a champion.

Conor did not wait for the enemy to reach him. He took the fight to them. The downward advance had reached the bodies of their dead comrades and, with a shout, Conor lowered his shoulders and charged. At his sudden rush, the Scálda in the foreranks raised their shields. Conor bulled into them and the force of his assault rocked the enemy back a step and opened a hole in their shield defence. Conor jammed the point of his spear into the crack and felt it strike something solid; but, before he could withdraw the spear, one of the enemy grabbed the shaft and held on. Conor tried to yank it from his grasp, failed, and released the weapon. He scurried back to his cache of weapons, snatched up another spear, and turned to face the onslaught.

The Scálda levelled their spears and advanced over the fresh corpses of their dead. Cautious still, but relentless and determined, they edged forward. Conor heard the ring of iron behind him and shouts as the two coming up from the cove below readied their attack.

One of the Scálda in the forerank heaved a spear. The throw in such a tight space was awkward: just over Conor's head and wide. Conor heard it clatter down the gully, but did not turn to see where it landed. His eyes remained on the blades levelled before him.

The enemy did not waste another throw. With a cry, they pushed forward all at once and Conor was overwhelmed. Time and again, he struck with his blade, once or twice finding a chink or crevice in their defences; but the Scálda kept their shield wall tight and did not break ranks, and Conor was forced to give up ground. Step by step, and blow by blow, they drove him from his secure position and down the defile toward the blades of their comrades.

Walking backward over the rocky ground, Conor's foot struck a loose stone; it rolled under him and he went down on one knee. He struggled to rise, fending off the jabs of the spears. One blade flicked out and caught him a nick on the upper chest; another grazed his side as Conor struggled onto his knees. He fought to stand, but could not get his feet under him as the blows rained down thick and fast from every angle. He parried one jab and evaded two others, but one errant thrust slashed his arm, opening an ugly, ragged gash. Blood splashed out in a scarlet rush.

Conor roared out in pain. 'That will cost you!' he shouted, and, as he made a last effort to push himself upright once more, was startled to feel strong hands grasp him from behind and hoist him onto his feet. He made a desperate backward stab with the shaft of the spear.

'Easy there, brother,' came the voice of the warrior who had caught him. 'You have few enough friends in this place, I think.'

Conor glanced over his shoulder. 'Fergal!'

'Aye,' he said, setting Conor on his feet. 'I should have known you would get yourself into trouble.'

'It is true I could use a little help just now.' He shook away the blood pouring down his arm.

The sudden appearance of a second Dé Danann warrior had caused the attack to falter. They drew back to regroup and Fergal, his long spear lowered, dived into the midst of the tightly bunched group. He lunged once, and again, and two Scálda fell screaming; one of these threw down his weapons and scrambled away on hands and knees. The three remaining foemen abandoned the assault and fled back through the gap and up the gully.

Fergal glanced back at Conor. 'Should I give chase?'

'Not unless you wish to become crow food,' replied Conor. 'There are at least twenty Scálda up there—probably more, by now. They will be climbing down to the beach as well.'

'How bad is your arm?' Fergal lifted the injured limb and inspected the damage. Conor winced as he pressed it lightly. 'This will need binding. I suggest we leave while we can. Follow me.' He turned and led the way down the ravine to the beach, passing the bodies of the two he had met on his way up.

'Do you have a horse?' asked Conor as they stepped out onto the strand.

'Ach, nay, brother,' he said. Pointing across the cove with his spear, he said, 'It was easier to bring a boat.'

Conor turned to see Rhiannon standing at the prow of a faéry ship. Below her on the strand stood Gwydion, holding Búrach's bridle. Five more faéry, long swords in hand, stood guard nearby. Lenos was there with them, helping the Kerionid survivors up the boarding plank and into the ship. When the last had boarded, Lenos ascended the plank and took his place with the other faéry already gathered on deck. As Fergal and Conor hurried across the sand, Lenos caught sight of them and raised his hand in solemn salute; several of his people did the same.

'Friends of yours?' said Fergal.

Conor felt a sudden flood of relief course through him. 'How?' was all he managed to say.

Fergal smiled. 'Ask Rhiannon. It was all her doing—one of her spells, I think.'

'The charm . . . ,' breathed Conor, remembering . . . *You have only to whisper my name,* she had promised. The implications of that vow broke upon him then, and that, combined with the loss of blood from his wounds, staggered him. He rocked back on his heels and pressed a hand to his head.

'I can't be always saving you,' Fergal told him, taking Conor's elbow to steady him. 'One of these days you must learn to fight. You might find it a useful occupation.'

'I'm heartily sick of fighting, brother. I am thinking of becoming a druid.'

Fergal laughed and shook his head. 'They won't be having you. Ach, now, a shepherd, maybe.' Indicating the ship where Rhiannon stood waiting, he said, 'Come on, let's get you safe aboard and bind up that arm. Then we can discuss your future prospects.'

Fergal helped Conor up the boarding plank and onto the deck, and delivered him to Rhiannon's care. Gwydion and his men followed them on board and quickly made ready to sail. By the time Balor Berugderc and his men reached the cove, the faéry ship was gliding into deep water and on its way to the Land of the Everliving.

Donal

Some things I remember, many things I don't. I remember we were in the Scálda ráth with the faéry women—Rhiannon and her maid, Tanwen. A bard might be able to put words to the way I felt when I saw the two of them standing in that dirty hut—so miserable, so afraid, so helpless, and so very beautiful. It did fair cleave the heart of me in half to see them that way, so it did.

There was no question in my mind but that we must rescue them. Though I had to gnaw through the chains with my teeth, I would have done it. Rhiannon said she could do no magic because of the iron, so we had to find a way to break the chains and set them free. That is what we did—and none too soon, for the Scálda were prowling all round us in that foul place. Two of the devils even came into the hut, but by that time we were clinging to the good lady's robe for the charm she used to hide us. And, Badb take me, the dog-eaters never saw us.

We got ourselves out of there sharp, and it was all smooth and fine until the charm started to go thin. We got our horses and made for the gate. I was unlucky last, and took a Scálda blade in the back up under the ribs on my side. At first I didn't know what happened. I felt something slam into me sure enough, and the Lady Tanwen sucked in her breath and gripped me so tight I could hardly breathe. But she never let on, said not a word.

I got us down from the ráth and then the pain hit and I thought someone had set fire to my siarc. Water came to my eyes and I almost bit off my tongue it hurt so bad. I looked around and saw the end of the spear still sticking out of Tanwen's back. Poor Tanwen. The Scálda blade went through her and into me. It cut me bad, but not so bad I couldn't ride, so we flew off toward the coast, and Conor went the other way to draw off the pursuit. And it worked. At least, none of the Scálda followed us.

We rode until we couldn't ride anymore. The pain hurt so bad until it didn't hurt anymore, either. It just got very cold—first a spot on my side and then more and more, spreading out, spreading all through me like ice forming on a lough. The next thing I knew we were just standing still in the moonlight. Everything was quiet, peaceful even, so it was. I remember looking up at the moon and thinking it was almost so close I could reach out and touch it.

But it wasn't the moon—or maybe it was at first—because I was on the ground looking up and Conor was there and he was calling to me. He gave me something to drink and it tasted foul, but I drank it and the next thing was that I smelled sour smoke. I looked around and saw that I was in the cave down on the beach. I could hear the waves outside, and Mádoc was there, and Lady Rhiannon, and they were giving me that foul stuff to drink and all I wanted to do was sleep.

When I woke up again, I was high up in the roof of the cave. I don't know how I got up there, but I looked down and saw some sad fella lying on the floor and covered with a cloak. Lady Rhiannon was beside him, holding his hand, and old Mádoc asleep and snoring, and little Huw, the Cymry boy, nearby. The strange thing was, I didn't hurt anymore. I felt

good, but the wretch on the ground below me didn't look fit
for much. At first, I thought he was dead, but Rhiannon raised
up his head and gave him some water to drink, and he opened
his eyes. I almost swallowed my tongue—for that poor broken fella was me!

As soon as I saw that, I wasn't up in the roof anymore, but
right down there under that cloak, and it was Rhiannon holding my head and talking to me. I don't know what she said—
for the faéry folk speech is stranger than strange—but just
the sound of it made me feel warm and easy in my mind. The
pain in my back was hurting again, but I didn't care anymore.
I just drifted along on the sound of her voice—sometimes
awake, sometimes not. I don't remember much about being
on the ship except once when I opened my eyes and looked
around I found that I was way up on top of the mast with the
sail bellied out big and full.

The sea spread out wide all around and down below and I
saw Conor and Fergal on the deck and Huw with the horses.
And they were sailing the ship. Warriors! Sailing a ship! This
made me laugh—until I realised they were afraid. I could
sense their fear—almost like the smell, like rotten eggs, so it
was. I looked around and saw the red sails of Scálda ships in
chase, and then I knew why my brothers were so terrible uneasy and I felt bad for them.

And then Rhiannon put her hands on me and I was somewhere dark and she was beside me. I think Mádoc was there,
or maybe not. She spoke soft faéry words to me and I went
farther into the dark place and it was very dark indeed. I
couldn't see anything, but I felt as if I were moving, walking
maybe, and then far ahead, I saw a light—blue like the sky it
was, and I walked toward it and then I was in the light, like
when you move out from under the shade of a big tree and
into the bright sun. But it wasn't the sun, it was a person—a

lady. Or maybe the light hid the lady and that was the way of it. She spoke to me and in the gentlest voice I ever heard said, 'Welcome, Donal. Would you like to stay here with me?'

'Where am I?' I asked, because all I could see was the light shining everywhere.

'Look around and tell me what you see.'

As soon as she said this, the bright light faded and I saw that I stood at the edge of a great meadow—bigger and more fair than any in all Eirlandia, even Mag Brega. We walked out onto the greenest field I ever saw, greener even than Tara's hill, and full of white and yellow flowers. The air was soft and smelled of sweet grass and roses; there were birds with feathers so bright it hurt my eyes to look at them, and everything sparkled like gems. Three rivers divided the plain and I came to one of them and stood on the high bank above the deep-flowing water. I looked down and saw that the river was full of fat silver-speckled salmon, and otters played in the shallows, and swans and ducks paddled among the reeds. A tall oak tree grew in the centre of the plain—so big it could shelter a hundred head of cattle under its boughs—and other trees lined the borders of the plain. And sweet-sounding music filled the air, so it did—the music of harps and pipes and bodhran drums and singing. Everything breathed an air of peace and calm like early morning before the troubles of the day begin.

'Lady, what is this place?'

'Do you not know it?'

'If I had seen it before, I would know it. How could anyone forget a place like this?'

She smiled and my heart soared. 'Think and the answer will come to you,' she said, and her voice was like a kiss to my ears.

'Is it Mag Mell?' I said.

'So it is,' she said, and laughed—and I could have lived

on that sound alone. 'The old tales have not been wasted on you, I see.'

I gazed at her in awe, and saw before me a woman of such beauty as to cause the sky to blush and the stars to hide their faces and burn with bitter envy. She was clothed in a gleaming blue gown with a cloak and girdle of golden light—like cloth made from the rays of afternoon light, perhaps—and her hair hung in thick braids and was white as virgin snow, though she was not old in years. I stared at her in a daze of wonder and said, 'Fair lady, forgive an ignorant warrior's asking, but who are you?'

'I have so many names,' she said. 'But if you look to your heart, I think you will see you already know the answer.'

'And are you Queen Danu?' The name came to me as I spoke it out, and I knew her. Indeed, it seemed that I had always known her.

She smiled the smile of love and my heart filled to bursting with longing for her. I went down on my knees before her and said, 'Tell me what I must do to stay here always and serve you. Speak the word and whatever task you place before me—that I will do.'

'That is easily said, and just as easily done.' Lifting a hand to the wonderful plain, she said, 'Do you see that river? All you need do is cross it. At the water's edge you will find a boat down amongst the rushes and if you row to the other side, you will stay here in this place and live in my hall forever.'

I would have leapt to my feet and run to find that boat, but something prevented me—I don't know what, but something heavy for I did so want to stay. Queen Danu nodded and looked at me with eyes the colour of the sea after the rain. She seemed to see into my heart and said, 'You are not ready yet, I see.'

'I *am* ready,' I insisted. 'I have never been more ready for anything in all my life.'

'No.' She shook her head gently. 'It is not your time. You must go back.'

'My lady, please!' I cried, and tears came to my eyes at the thought of leaving that glorious place. 'Please, show mercy.'

'It is for mercy that I send you away now,' she replied. 'You have work to finish, and you must return to take up your life again. But, never fear, one day you will come and join me and when you do there will be no going back.'

All at once, the light faded and darkness took me. I felt hands on me—many hands, different hands, some gentle, some not so much—pinching and probing, doing things I know not what. Ach, I was wrapped and unwrapped, draped and swathed in coverings hot and cold, wet and dry, and given strange cups to drink, bitter and burning, some of them—one I spat out, I know, for it was foul—but others sweet on the tongue. All the while, I continued walking on that unseen path, not knowing where I was going, but putting one foot in front of the other, after a time I felt the world grow lighter around me. When I opened my eyes again, I was in a bed of goose feathers in a room I had never seen before—it was big with a high roof and candles all around and Fergal was there, sitting in a chair beside me.

'What is this?' he cried, leaping to his feet. 'Donal! Are you awake?'

'Fergal, is it you, brother?' I looked around the room and it was very grand. 'Where are we?'

'They've done it!' he said, and seized my hand and squeezed until the bones ground together. 'They've saved you!'

This made no sense to me. 'Who has saved me?'

'Gwydion's physicians—they have healed you.'

'Are you insane now, brother, that you speak only in riddles? I cannot understand a word you say.'

He sat down again and told me all that had happened and

how we had come to be there in that room together. 'Where are we?' I asked again.

'We are with the Tylwyth Teg in Tír nan Óg.'

'And Conor?' I asked, looking around the room as if I might find him. 'Where is Conor?'

'Conor has stayed in Eirlandia,' he said, and I remembered how we had searched for proof of Lord Brecan's wicked scheme to make himself high king. And I knew then why I had been sent back from the Land of Promise—it was to help Conor. I threw aside the soft covering and made to get up, but my legs were weak and my head swam, the room tilted away from me, and I fell back into bed instead. 'Ach, now, I may need a little more time yet.'

We talked some more and then Rhiannon came with two of her ladies and when she saw me awake, she kissed me and made much of me so that my face grew hot to hear it. Then she said that glad as she was to see me awake, she had come to find Fergal. 'Conor is in need,' she told him. 'He has summoned me. A boat is being prepared even now. I must leave at once.'

'I'm going, too,' said Fergal.

'And I as well,' I said.

But both of them looked at me and shook their heads. 'Soon, perhaps. But not this time,' Rhiannon said. 'You stay and gather your strength. I will have one of my ladies attend you.'

They left a short time later, and two days after that I was strong enough to get up and walk around a little. Alwen, the maiden Rhiannon sent, was a young woman—but, then they *all* looked young to me—slim as a willow wand with hair pale as flax and great dark eyes. She brought a razor and a bowl of warm water and, using the charm of tongues, offered to shave me. Many of the men among them have beards, from the little I had seen, while others shaved or trimmed their hair. Ach, now, I am not accustomed to having any hand other than my own come near my throat with a knife or razor, so I thanked her and asked for a mirror instead.

One look in that polished silver disk and I almost dropped the razor in the bowl, for the face gazing back at me was not one I recognised. The eyes were dull, red-rimmed, and sunk deep in their sockets; the flesh was pale and waxy; and the hair was limp and matted. And the poor fella was terrible thin, with hollow cheeks, cracked lips, and a nasty beard. I saw that wasted stranger and a tear came to my eye for the shock of it.

Alwen, who was holding the disk, saw my undoing and gently took the razor from my trembling hand, sat me down, and then proceeded to wash my hair and shave me. I cannot say which troubled me more—that I was so much diminished in my own eyes, or that I was being shaved by a woman, and a faéry woman at that!

I endured the trial with as much manful dignity as I could scrape together, and emerged feeling the better for the ordeal. At her command, one of the lads brought me some clean clothes—I had been given such at some time I don't remember, for the clothes I was wearing were not my own. But the new ones were more befitting a fella to be seen among decent folk—a new siarc of fine wool combed soft and woven in checks of red and green, and long breecs of the same stuff, but dyed blue, and high-topped brócs that laced to the knee. There was no cloak, but I needed none, for the weather there was fine.

In this way, I walked out into a fair sunlit day for my first look at the place they called Tír nan Óg. I saw much that would have amazed me in a former time—but, mind now, I had greeted Queen Danu in the true Region of the Summer Stars—a realm that lies both above and through our own—a place of such wonder that it made even the faéry isle seem a little drab. All that day, I found myself returning to the Plain of Promise and my talk with the goddess queen. The wonder of it was renewed and I remembered all that had happened there and all that she had said to me.

The next day, thanks to the care of my good physicians, I was stronger still. I walked down to the harbour and was standing on the stone wharf when the ship came gliding into the bay. Conor was there and he gave out a loud shout when he saw me—but then collapsed, and I saw that he was wounded. Because of his injuries, he had to be carried from the boat—but there were many to help him for he had brought with him more than half a score of faéry folk—and, Badb take me, didn't he have that horse of his, Búrach, as well? Aye, so he did.

They brought him to where I stood and I embraced him, and he squeezed my arm. 'It is good to see you standing up for a change, Donal,' he said, his voice a dull croak. 'I wish I could say the same for myself here.'

'Worry for nothing, brother, the healers here will soon have you back on your feet and dancing,' I told him.

'Ach, I'll be fighting fit in no time,' he boasted. But his voice was a whisper and his face was grey as death.

'Aye, see that you are, brother, for we have a chore of work to do.'

Read on for a preview of

* * *
* *

IN THE
LAND
OF THE
EVERLIVING

Stephen R. Lawhead

Available from Tom Doherty Associates

Eamon

Like many another fella, I remember where I was when word of Lord Brecan's death came my way. I was about joining the younger lads at their weapons on the field below the ráth. I like to keep my arm strong and help with the training whenever I can. Seghan is a spruce hand with the spear, and a shrewdy with feints and backhand thrusts and such. Everybody likes the pretty flowers, so they say—but sometimes I think a warrior should tend to the roots of our craft as well. I know I do.

Ach, well, I had collected my sword from the hall and was heading across the yard when visitors came clopping through the gates. I knew them on sight—a party of seven Coriondi warriors with their lord, King Cahir, at the head. Cahir is a good friend to us and our king's closest ally. Still, he had not been seen at Dúnaird since the shameful incident at that disastrous Oenach when our Conor went and got himself mixed up with that mad druid, Cadoc, or Mádoc, or whatever was his name.

By the sword in my strong right hand, I never believed Conor a thief. Neither thief nor liar is our Conor. If a fella ever wanted to see what honour on two legs looked like, all he had to do was catch a glimpse of Conor mac Ardan and he'd know it right enough.

I still ent got to the end of it all, but the long and short was the trouble got Conor exiled from the tribe and made outlaw, so he did.

We lost Conor, sad enough, but we also lost Fergal and Donal, and that is a bitter blow, I can tell you. Those two would not be separated from him and so they followed him into exile. Nor have they been heard from since—any of them.

And now, here was Cahir, come nosing around. I stood aside as they rode into the yard and watched them dismount, but I did not go to see what had brought them here. Truth, I begrudged Cahir for his part in Conor's exile. He could have stopped it and he stood aside and said not a word.

I went on to join the lads at practice, but could not keep my mind on the task. Like a nervous sparrow, my attention kept flitting back to Lord Cahir and that lot and wondering why they had come and what news had brought them.

Ach! What news it was. . . .

King Brecan mac Lergath, Lord of the Brigantes, was dead. Murdered!

That was the word from the wider world and it was on everyone's lips the moment we strolled back into the yard. 'Is it true?' I shouted up at Braida, the young lad on guard duty that morning. 'Brecan dead?'

'That's what they're saying,' he called back from his place on the walkway above the gate. 'Slaughtered like a pig by the Scálda.' Wiping the sweat from my face, I thought, *Aye, and there's a fox put among the geese for sure.*

Braida was talking to me. I glanced up, squinting in the sunlight. 'Say again?'

'If you go to the hall, will you send word back?' He gestured to the gate. 'I'm here the whole day long.'

'I expect you've heard the best of it,' I told him. 'If there's anything more to be said, you'll find it out soon enough.'

I hurried to the hall then and entered to find the lords already on their second or third welcome cup. A few of Ardan's advisors, including Liam, our battlechief, occupied one end of the long board, with my lord Ardan, and Cahir and Dara, the Coriondi king's battlechief, at the other end. Dara I knew from previous meetings at gatherings and such, and reckoned him a good man with a blade.

Hanging my sword and spear on the wall, I started toward the table. My lord Ardan saw me and hailed me, saying, 'Here, now! Eamon, to me. Friend Cahir has news for us.'

'Sit with us,' said Cahir. 'Have a drink to wet your tongue.' He shoved the cup across the board to me as I lowered myself to the bench across from him. Ardan, jar in hand, sat in his chair at the end of the table. He poured more mead into the silver welcome cup.

'Brecan Brigantes is dead,' Cahir announced. I noticed he could not keep the smile long from his face. He was enjoying the chance to tell us something we did not know.

'Scálda killed him?' I raised the cup to my lips and took a long draught of the cool, sweet liquor. 'What was it—a raid on Aintrén?' I took another drink, handed the cup back, and wiped my mouth on the back of my hand.

'Nay, nay,' replied Cahir. 'I'm hearing it was Balor Evil Eye himself did the deed.'

My eyes must have grown wide to hear this, for both Cahir and Ardan shared a chuckle at my expense, and my lord said, 'It appears that Brecan was on his way to a secret meeting some little way beyond the southern border.'

'A meeting with Balor Berugderc?' This did not make sense to me. I shook my head, trying to think what that could mean. 'How do you know this?'

'Ach, well, the dog-eaters sent his poor dead carcass back home on his horse.' He gave me a knowing look. 'And that brute of a battlechief of his—'

'Cethern,' I said. 'His name was Cethern.'

'Aye, that's the fella,' confirmed Cahir. 'Him they killed, too, and him they sent back in little pieces scattered along the road.'

'Bastards,' huffed Ardan. 'Puffed-up gloating bastards.'

'The Brigantes are outraged, as you might expect. Demanding an honour price and all.'

'How much?' wondered Ardan, lifting the cup to his lips.

'Twenty pounds of gold, forty pounds of silver, a hundred horses, and fifty hounds,' Cahir said, shaking his head at the audacious amount.

'You might as well ask for the moon and the stars and all the fish in the sea,' concluded Ardan, swirling the mead in the cup, 'for you will never see so much as a shrivelled bean from the black-hearted Scálda scum.'

'Too right,' agreed Cahir, taking the cup Ardan offered.

'I suppose,' I ventured, 'fixing the honour price at such a ridiculous sum is just to show how grieved and angry they are.'

'A hundred horses . . . ,' muttered my lord, shaking his head; he poured more of the sweet golden nectar into the cup before passing it back to me. 'Or,' he suggested, 'they mean to impress everyone with how great a king was Brecan Big Brócs.'

'Big Brócs!' hooted Cahir. 'I like that.' He leaned his sturdy bulk forward and put his arms on the table. 'More likely that fluffy little chit of a queen set that absurd high amount in order to disguise the simple fact that their top-lofty lord, for all his grand ways, was not well loved.'

'Either by his wife *or* his people. They say even his dogs avoided him!' added Ardan, and lofted the cup in mock salute.

We drank in silence for a moment, passing the cup hand to hand, listening to the low murmur of voices from the other end of the board and sounds from the yard outside: women talking, laughing, shouts of children running around. Occasionally, a horse would whinny, or a dog would bark.

'Mark me,' said Cahir, growing sly, 'there is a stink to this that festers in the nostrils.' He wrinkled up his face as if that stench got up his nose just then.

'Have you ever known Scálda raiders to return our dead to their tribes?' I said, feeling the liquor spreading its warm, soft fingers through me. 'They have never done that before. You are right, lord'—I lifted the cup to Cahir—'there is more to this than we know.'

'Aye, I'm right. I know it,' said Cahir, taking a long pull at his cup, then wiping his moustache on his sleeve. 'I'm thinking there's legs to this rumour that Brecan and Balor had a secret meeting of some sort and a fight broke out. That's what I'm thinking.'

'Now we'll never know,' concluded Ardan, gazing into his cup. Then, glancing up, he said, 'Will you stay the night? I will have Aoife sing and play for us. We can talk some more.'

'Ach, well, that is tempting,' replied Cahir. 'But I will move along down the road. I just came to tell you the news and see if you had any word from your Conor.'

'Neither peep nor cheep,' I said. 'Though there are those among us who wish otherwise.'

'Ach, don't tell me,' said Cahir ruefully. He gazed into the depths of his cup. 'Accusing your Conor of the crime—that was all part of old Mádoc's cockeyed plan, I am embarrassed to say.' He looked to Ardan. 'I'm sorry I had any part of it. Believe me, it was a mistake I regret. I only hope to make it right one day.'

'What's done is done,' replied Ardan. 'Are you sure you won't stay—have something to eat at least?'

'Ach, nay,' said Cahir, rising. 'I thank you for the drink, my friend. But I have one more stop to make. Lord Sechtan will want to hear the news.' He paused, rubbing his chin as he reconsidered his plan, then said, 'I don't suppose you would care to send a messenger to him?'

'Stop here tonight and we will go together in the morning,' suggested Ardan. 'I have not seen Sechtan since the Oenach, and the Robogdi were that close to joining Brecan. It would be good to sit down together and see where their loyalties lie now.'

Cahir smiled and accepted the offer. 'Maybe I am getting old,' he said, 'but a dry bed and a tight roof are too appealing to resist. Very well then, I will stay and we will ride out together tomorrow.'

The Coriondi lord went out to inform his men, and I took up my sword and begged leave to return to my weapon's practice. Lord Ardan walked with me from the hall and called a boy to go fetch his stable master to prepare a place for his visitors' horses. As the lad raced away, my lord murmured, 'How I wish Conor was here.' He turned to me. 'Where do you suppose he is now?'

I shook my head. 'By my shield, if I knew I would go and bring him back.'

1

Conor stood at the water's edge with waves lapping at his feet. The late sun threw his shadow across the glistening slate shingle. A solitary seagull soared effortlessly in the clear blue sky, dipping and gliding high overhead, and a light landward breeze lifted stray wisps of his light brown hair—grown longer now in the months of his slow and painful recovery— long enough to wear it in a tight braid gathered at the side of his head like one of the ancient kings whose exploits the bards turned into song.

Indeed, dressed in his splendid new clothes he appeared the very image of a prince of Eirlandia's noble line. Thanks to his host's generosity, he now possessed a siarc of gleaming scarlet edged in heavy gold thread; brown breecs the colour of oak leaves on the turn; fine brócs of soft deer leather that laced halfway to the knee; and a wide black belt studded with tiny gold rivets in the pattern of sea waves, and a cloak of tiny blue-and-black checks. This magnificent attire, like the healing care given him in the last many weeks, was a gift from a grateful benefactor: Gwydion, King of the Tylwyth Teg and Lord of the House of Llŷr, whose daughter Conor and his friends had rescued from the Scálda.

Just now, Conor paused in his stroll along the water's edge and gazed out across the green-grey water of the Narrow Sea, suddenly overcome by the realisation that time was passing in the wider world. How much time, he could not say. Here, in the Region of the Summer Stars, time behaved differently. He did not know why and understanding, much less any explanation, remained just beyond his grasp. Tír nan Óg, and the island realm the faéry folk called Ynys Afallon, was part of, and yet somehow separate from, the wider world beyond its shores.

Conor stood on the strand, his dark eyes searching the shimmering horizon, in the hopes of catching a glimpse of Eirlandia lying out on the rim of the sea. All the while, he massaged his arm and shoulder with his free hand. The wounds that had laid him low for such a long time were almost healed; he could move his arm freely and strength was fast returning. His side no longer ached every time he moved, nor sent a pain stabbing through him when he stooped or ran. According to Eurig, chief of the faéry physicians, his feet were on the path to health restored and he would soon be able to travel freely once more.

He felt more than ready. Although, curiously, as strength returned, the homeward pull diminished. Each day that passed, it seemed to Conor that he forgot a little more the cares and concerns of his homeland: the war with the Scálda, its ever-present urgency, its towering importance, receded a little more; even his memories seemed to grow more distant—as if they belonged to another Conor in another time and place. Lately, he had begun to fear that if he and his friends did not go soon, they would never leave.

As he looked out across the gleaming silver sea, he reminded himself once again that, as pleasant as life among the faéry was for him and Fergal and Donal, they could not stay. He told himself that the Land of the Everliving was not their home and they were needed in Eirlandia. *He* was needed in Eirlandia. The thought conjured an image of Aoife, long hair streaming in the wind as she, like him, stood on the strand gazing out to sea. She was waiting for him; his beloved, his betrothed was waiting, willing his return. If not for Lord Brecan, that devious and deceitful schemer, the two of them would be married by now.

But the fatal intrigues of the arrogant and ambitious Brigantes king had set Conor's feet on a different path. Perhaps, Clíona, that fickle and flighty daughter of destiny, had decreed they would forever remain apart. Conor cringed from the thought, and felt a pang of longing pierce him to the marrow. *Aoife, dearest heart of my heart, how cruelly you have been treated. I* will *come back for you.*

Hearing a crunch of footsteps approaching over the strand, he tensed. No doubt it was his physician come to fetch him and chide him for his errant ways. A moment later, a voice called out, 'Here you are, brother—and me looking for you half the day.'

'Aye,' agreed Conor without turning around. 'Here I am.'

'Did Eurig say you could come out?'

Conor gave vent to a resigned sigh as Donal came to stand beside him. 'Ach, well, good Eurig did not say I *couldn't* go out.'

'They are wonder workers, these faéry healers,' Donal observed.

'They are that,' agreed Conor. 'If they could mend *you,* I suppose they could put anyone back together.' He turned to his friend. 'It is that good to see *you* up on your two hind legs—a sight I never thought I would see again.'

'Was I that bad, then?' wondered Donal in a matter-of-fact tone.

'Worse—at least, worse than me.' Conor put out a hand to grip Donal by the shoulder. Despite his friend's recent ordeal, he seemed much his old self: his broad good-natured face glowed with good health; his long, thick moustache was neatly trimmed, his jaw clean shaven. Certainly, his solid, well-muscled frame—clothed now in the fine brown breecs and splendid siarc, and a cloak of faéry weave that combined blue and brown and violet in a check pattern—had never looked better. But his pensive black eyes hinted at new depths of knowledge or understanding that Conor had never noticed before. The observation prompted Conor to say, 'I am sorry you had to suffer so. If only—'

Donal shook his head. 'It was not *your* spear that caught me. You brought me here and that was the saving of me. You have nothing to feel sorry about.'

Conor accepted this without comment. Bending down, he selected a small, flat bit of slate, hefted it, and gave it a quick flip that sent it flying out into the bay. The stone skipped four times before sinking.

'Not bad,' observed Donal. 'But is that the throw of the fella who used to win all the contests when we were sprouts?'

'I did not throw with my left hand then,' Conor told him, lifting his injured right arm slightly. He rolled his shoulder and swung the arm to loosen it.

'A good warrior would be able to throw with either hand,' Donal reminded him. 'A *good* warrior can skip a stone seven times at least.'

'Seven times?' Conor challenged. 'Go on then, let's see how a good warrior skips a stone.'

Grinning, Donal picked up a round, flat sliver of slate from among the countless small stones at his feet. He stood, hefting it in his hands for a moment, squinted his eyes and said, 'Six.'

With that, he drew back his arm and, with a whipping motion, released the stone. It flew low over the water before dipping and skipping six times over the surface.

'Six, is it?' said Conor, searching for a stone. 'Six is fair, but it is not seven.' He bent and chose another stone, then prepared to let fly.

'Three,' said Donal, squinting his eyes and looking out into the bay.

'Seven,' Conor insisted. He threw again, awkwardly, and the stone sank after the third skip. 'Ach, well, you distracted me.'

'Then by all means, try again. Find a better stone this time.'

Conor did and, as before, just as he was about to let fly, Donal said, 'Five.'

The stone made five equal skips before plunking into the water some little way out in the calm water of the bay. This process was repeated six more times: with each throw Conor announced a number, Donal countered it with another—sometimes higher, sometimes lower—and each time the stone skipped the number of times Donal predicted.

After the seventh throw, Conor regarded his friend sharply, and was about to comment on this uncanny run of predictive luck when the expression on his friend's face stopped the words in his mouth.

Donal stood with eyes squeezed shut, his features clenched tight. After a moment, Donal's features relaxed, and Conor said, 'Is it your injury? Are you in pain?'

'Ach, nay,' he said, averting his eyes and lowering his head. 'Well, maybe—maybe we've both been a little too brisk just now.' He gave Conor a fishy, hesitant smile—which did nothing to allay Conor's concern.

'We should go before they come to drag us back.' Conor turned and started back up the strand toward the path leading to their house at the little lake the faéry called Llyn Rhaedr. Donal, however, remained gazing out to sea. 'Coming?' called Conor and, with a shake of his shoulders, as if he had been doused with cold water, Donal turned and quickly followed.

The two walked easy in one another's company as they

crossed the strand; they had just reached the greensward when there came a shout from the linden-lined path directly ahead. 'Conor! Donal!'

Both men glanced up to see Fergal standing in the middle of the trail, hands on hips, waiting for them. Conor raised a hand in greeting. 'Fergal!' he called. 'How goes the battle?'

Fergal hurried to meet them. 'Does it never occur to either of you to tell anyone where you're going? What were you doing out here?' This last was directed at Conor.

'Well, you know me and the sea,' Conor replied. 'Try as I might, I cannot stay away from it. I have the ocean in my veins now.'

'Seawater for brains, more like.' The tall fair-haired man arranged his long face in an unsuccessful frown of disapproval.

Like the other two, his sojourn among the faéry-kind had made a new man of him. He seemed both taller and broader, Conor thought, his hair longer, and neatly braided into a thick hank that, like his own, hung at the side of his head, making his face and bearing seem more regal. In his splendid new rust-coloured siarc and breecs he looked every inch a lord of wealth and stature. Adjusting the flawless cloak of yellow and green checks across his well-muscled shoulders, Fergal rested his hand on the pommel of the gold-hilted knife the faéry king had given him and shook his head. 'You should be in bed resting, you know. You look terrible, Conor.'

'Ach, well, that is a matter of opinion.'

'Nay,' said Donal. 'It is a plain fact. You *do* look terrible.'

'But better than before.'

'*That* is a matter of opinion,' replied Fergal, falling into step beside Conor. 'Lord Gwydion is asking for you. He says he has news.'

'Has he now?' said Conor. 'As it happens, I would like to speak to him, too.'

Donal raised a questioning brow.

'Brothers, it is time to go home. I mean to ask our gracious host to take us back to Eirlandia.'

'Soon, aye,' agreed Fergal, 'but you are nowise ready to travel. For all you're only just up from your sickbed—and you probably shouldn't even be out here at all.'

'Ach, Eurig says I have exhausted his art. I am full ready to travel.'

Fergal gave him a long, scornful look to show what he thought of that idea and pulled on the corner of his moustache. 'Exhausted his patience, more like.'

'As pleasant as it would be to stay on this most favoured isle and while away our days among the faéry folk,' said Conor, 'we are needed elsewhere. King Brecan's death is bound to create problems for everyone. We are needed at home.'

'To do what?' demanded Fergal testily. 'What do you think we can do that would make any difference to anyone at all?'

'For a start, we can tell them what we know.'

'Who will listen?' said Fergal. 'I will tell you, shall I? No one. No one is going to listen to us—three exiles, cast out of our tribe for our crimes. Will anyone even deign to receive us? I think not. And if they do, it will be only to hold us to blame for Huw and Mádoc's deaths—maybe that swine Brecan's, too, for all I know.'

Donal saw the dangerous look in Conor's eye, and said, 'Enough, Fergal. You've said enough.'

'Too much,' muttered Conor.

Fergal sighed. 'I am sorry, brother. I meant no disrespect to Mádoc or Huw, or anyone else. But we must try to see how things stand now. You are injured and Donal is still recovering, and whatever you imagine is happening across the water in Eirlandia has most likely happened already and without us.'

'For once, Fergal is right,' offered Donal. 'You should rest and fully recover the strength of that arm of yours. Let Eurig and his helpers take care of you so that when we *do* go back, you will be fighting fit again.'

'I am fighting fit already,' Conor insisted. He looked at his two friends and a slow smile spread across his pale features. 'Thank you for your wise counsel. I know you intend it for my good.'

Fergal threw a cautious glance at Donal. 'Does that mean you will abide?' he asked.

'Nay,' replied Conor. 'I am still going to ask Gwydion to take me back to Eirlandia as soon as possible.'

2

Lord Gwydion sat with his long hands beneath his chin, his large dark eyes glinting in the bright golden flame burning silently in the expansive hearth of the great hall of Caer Raedr, his palace carved from the living stone of their island home. The enchanted fire splashed dancing shadows across the rough-hewn walls of the great cavern. In a far corner, sunlight from a fissure in the ceiling showered down upon a silver cage; tiny birds of yellow, blue, and green twittered pleasantly, mingling their song with the tinkling sound of water burbling up from a perpetual fountain in the centre of the enormous room. Few of the faéry remained in the hall; the day was bright and with the season on the change, most wanted to enjoy the last of the sun before winter wrapped their island in blankets of mist and snow for months on end.

Conor stood before the king and though he itched for an answer to his question, he held his tongue and waited for his reluctant patron to make up his mind without further urging or argument from him. Finally the faéry king raised his head and, offering a kindly smile, replied, 'I can well understand your eagerness to return home. I myself was in a similar position not so very long ago—and it is thanks to your skill and courage as a warrior that I was able to make my return at all. For that, I am grateful and forever in your debt.'

Conor accepted the praise, but said, 'There can be no debt between friends.'

Gwydion spread his hands as if to indicate that Conor's response only confirmed his own high opinion. 'Be that as it may, I have a charge to lay upon you and I hope you will honour it.'

'Ask what you will, lord king, and if it is in my power to fulfil, then trust it will be done.'

'It is, I think, well within your command,' the king replied. 'For I ask only that you remain in Ynys Afallon a little longer. Allow your healing to be completed so that you will be well equipped to meet the demands of your return. I have no doubt those demands will be many.' Gwydion saw or sensed the objection rising within Conor and quickly added, 'I am confidently informed by Eurig that you are well on the path to full recovery of both strength and health, but that destination is still some way distant. It is my understanding that taking on too much too soon will undo all his good work—and that, you will agree, is not the best outcome either of us would care to see.' Gwydion smiled again, rose, and came to stand before Conor. He put his hand on Conor's shoulder and said, 'Abide but a small while, my friend. The world will wait a little longer.'

At this, Conor's heart sank; nevertheless, he had to admit that the king made a fair point and that it would be ill mannered to refuse. 'You are most gracious, lord king. I will allow your wisdom and that of your physician to be my guide. But please know that I will welcome his release as soon as possible.'

Gwydion raised an eyebrow. 'You are that anxious to return to battle?'

'So long as my people suffer the cruel ravages of a wicked and relentless enemy, my duty is clear. I have no other choice.'

The faéry king released his hold, signalling the end of the

audience, but said, gently, 'Spoken not like a warrior,' he said, 'but like a king.'

Conor left the cavern and returned to the lake house he and Fergal and Donal had made their home, and where the next days were spent much as the days before. Conor dutifully followed the care and direction of Eurig, the chief physician: he rested, slept, and ate well; he took walks along the strand, or in the surrounding woodland, or swam in the lake and bathed in the sweet-water stream below the waterfall. Taken this way, each day was a simple delight. Yet, each day also brought its own torment because, beguiling as the Isle of the Everliving was, there was someplace else he wanted to be. And, as enchanting as the faéry could be in all their grandeur, there was someone else he wanted to see.

He missed Aoife, ached for her. She was his first thought every morning and his last thought every night. Through the day he would find himself wondering what she might be doing at that moment, or wondering whether she thought of him. Did she miss him as much as he missed her? In his most abject moments he wondered if she even knew he was still alive.

The thought that Aoife might think him dead tortured him. He yearned to send word to her, to reassure her, to let her know he was alive and thought of her daily, that he had not forgotten her, that one day they would be together, that their long betrothal would be over and they would be married and never parted again. All this, and more, he burned to tell her. But each day ended the same: Aoife away in Eirlandia over the sea, and he in the Region of the Summer Stars.

Fergal and Donal also missed their homeland, but Conor sensed that longing diminishing, weakening as time went by. Like him, they enjoyed the easy splendour and luxury of Gwydion's court, and the fine company of the elegant and graceful inhabitants of the House of Llŷr; unlike him, they enjoyed it a little too much—or so it seemed to Conor. Together with their guide, Nodons, they explored the length and breadth of Tír nan Óg and returned, sometimes days later, with reports of the various wonders they had seen in the faéry strongholds and dwellings they visited: a magical vat that served up mead, or ale, or wine, or sweet water according to the desire of whoever dipped a cup . . . or a harp that played of its own accord whenever music was requested . . . or a cauldron that would quickly boil the meat of a champion, but would cast out the meat of a coward . . . a tree that produced both blossoms and ripe fruit at any time of the year . . . of a grain hamper that could not be emptied so that whatever grain was placed in it, however much was taken out, that much more remained . . . of a knife with a blade that could never be dulled . . . a small green plant, the leaves of which, when applied to any cut or bruise, instantly healed the injury . . . of a sparán made from the feathers of three hundred larks that multiplied by three any gem or coin placed in it . . . and many other weird and wondrous objects and artefacts besides.

They visited dúns located inside mounds and caverns, and strongholds on crannogs in the middle of lakes, and ráths so high up on the hilltops they seemed to float in the clouds; and in each of these settlements they were received like noble kinsmen and royalty. They visited Caer Ban where Cynan Eiddin, a kinsman of Gwydion, kept a palace to rival the king's: an enormous dwelling that contained sixty rooms and seven halls—rooms for sleeping, for working, for storing food and drink; and halls for eating, for dancing, for gathering in solemn assembly. Twenty pillars held up its walls, each one cut from an elder oak of the Great Forest of Orobris that once covered all of Albion. The walls themselves were covered in tiles that shone like polished gems. The roof was high-pitched, and covered with slates of seven different colours. There were nine doors, each wide enough and tall enough to admit a warrior on a horse, and each carved with runes of enchantment so that no one who entered could disturb the peace of anyone dwelling within.

The two mortals spent their nights in chambers sleeping on beds lined with cushions and pallets stuffed with goose down and soft feathers, and woke to music that drifted in from open wind holes set high up in the wall. Wherever they looked, they saw the intricate, sweeping lines of faéry design that adorned the brooches and torcs, buckles, bracelets, and rings. And it was everywhere: woven into clothing and engraved on cups of silver and platters of gold; enticing patterns were carved into doorposts and lintels, on beams and roof-trees, chiselled on pediments and columns and arches; it adorned the walls of their halls and was set into the paving stones on the floors of homes and courtyards. The cunning interwoven lines, at once so lithe and flowing, dazzled the eye and lifted the heart of the beholder, lending an air of grace and refinement to all of faéry life.

Everywhere they cast their eyes, they glimpsed something of the beauty that was part of the nature and character of the faéry race—so much so that travelling through the Region of the Summer Stars became a continual delight. The sights they saw and later described were the objects of stories and songs long familiar to druid bards, tales told and sung at festivals and gatherings of every kind in Eirlandia; the very things the Dé Danann marvelled at as children and dreamt about at night were commonplace to the faéry. Even the humblest items of everyday use—a chair, a bowl, a lampstand, a spoon, a stool, a cooking pot—would be treasures anywhere in the world of mortals; but here, in this otherworldly realm, the objects of daily life were not the stuff of dreams or the fancies of singers and storytellers. Here, in Tír nan Óg, in the Region of the Summer Stars, those dreamt-of things were real.

Conor listened to his friends recount their travels and marvelled—just as he had when he was a boy sitting with his brothers at the Lughnasadh fire. He admitted it would be a fine thing to remain in a place where such wonders of splendour and magnificence were not only possible, but common occurrences. Even so, the greater part of him knew that could not be; they could not remain in Tír nan Óg while the evil Scálda infested his homeland. He was needed elsewhere.

When the day finally came that Eurig declared himself satisfied that Conor's healing was complete, Conor embraced his physician and thanked him for his unstinting care, and then ran off to find Fergal and Donal to tell them the good news: they were going home!